Texas Cattleman's Club

BACHELOR AUCTION

MAUREEN CHILD   **JULES BENNETT**   **JANICE MAYNARD**

MILLS & BOON

CONTENTS

Runaway Temptaion

Maureen Child

Maureen Child writes for the Harlequin Desire line and can't imagine a better job. A seven-time finalist for a prestigious Romance Writers of America RITA® Award, Maureen is an author of more than one hundred romance novels. Her books regularly appear on bestseller lists and have won several awards, including a Prism Award, a National Readers' Choice Award, a Colorado Romance Writers Award of Excellence and a Golden Quill Award. She is a native Californian but has recently moved to the mountains of Utah.

Books by Maureen Child

The Baby Inheritance
Maid Under the Mistletoe
The Tycoon's Secret Child
A Texas-Sized Secret
Little Secrets: His Unexpected Heir
Rich Rancher's Redemption
Billionaire's Bargain

Texas Cattleman's Club: Bachelor Auction

Runaway Temptation

Visit her Author Profile page at
millsandboon.com.au,
or maureenchild.com, for more titles.

Dear Readers,

I'm back in Royal, Texas, for another visit with the Texas Cattleman's Club. I love being in Royal. It's a chance for me to spend time with old friends—characters I've written about in the past—and to have the joy of writing about new people coming into my life.

In *Runaway Temptation*, you'll meet Caleb Mackenzie and Shelby Arthur. Caleb's a rancher in Royal with deep roots in the community and a tendency to not trust many people. Shelby's a professional organizer from Chicago. She comes to Royal to get married—and minutes before her wedding, she runs away and crashes right into Caleb.

While the sparks fly, they each try to hold out against the other. Between Caleb's determination to get Shelby out of his life and Shelby's stubborn refusal to go, these two people have to find a way to get beyond the past and find a path to the future.

I really had a great time with these two and I hope you all enjoy their story as much as I did.

Make time for yourself. Curl up on the couch. Have a cup of tea. Then relax, enjoy your trip to Royal and visit me on Facebook. Let me know what you think of the book. I love to hear from my readers!

Until next time, happy reading!

Maureen

To Carter and Cade. For the hugs.
For the laughs. For the love. For the future.

One

"I hate weddings." Caleb Mackenzie ran his index finger around the inside of his collar. But that didn't do a thing to loosen the tie he wore, or to rid himself of the "wish I were anywhere but here" thoughts racing through his mind. "I feel like I'm overdressed for my own hanging."

Caleb wasn't real fond of suits. Sure, he had a wide selection of them since he needed them for meetings and business deals. But he was much more comfortable in jeans, a work shirt and his favorite boots, running his ranch, the Double M. Still, as the ranch grew, he found himself in the dreaded suits more and more often because expansion called for meeting bankers and investors on their turf.

Right now, though, he'd give plenty to be on a horse riding out across the open range. Caleb knew his ranch hands were getting the work done, but there were stock ponds to check on, a pregnant mare he was keeping an eye on and a hay field still to harvest and store.

Yet instead, here he stood, in the hot Texas sun, in an elegant suit and shining black boots. He tugged the brim of his gray

Stetson down lower over his eyes and slanted a look at the mob of people slowly streaming into the Texas Cattleman's Club for the ceremony and reception.

If he could, he'd slip out of town. But it was too late now.

"You're preaching to the choir, man."

Caleb nodded at his friend Nathan Battle. If he had to be there, at least he had company.

Nathan settled his cowboy hat more firmly on his head and sent a frown toward his pretty, very pregnant wife standing with a group of her friends. "I swear, I think Amanda really enjoys it when I have to wear a suit."

"Women'll kill you." Caleb sighed and leaned back against his truck. As hot as he was, he was in no hurry to go inside and take a seat for the ceremony. Given a choice, he'd always choose to be outside under the sky. Even a hot and humid August day was preferable to being trapped inside.

"Maybe, but it's not a bad way to go—" Nathan broke off and asked, "Why're you here, anyway? Not like you've got a wife to make you do what you don't want to do." As soon as the words left his mouth, Nathan winced and said, "Sorry, man. Wasn't thinking."

"No problem." Caleb gritted his teeth and swallowed the knot of humiliation that could still rise up and choke him from time to time. The thing about small towns was, not only did everyone know what everybody else was doing—nobody ever forgot a damn thing. Four years since the day his wedding hadn't happened and everyone in Royal remembered.

But then, it wasn't like he'd forgotten, either.

Amazing, really. In the last few years, this town had seen tornadoes, killer storms, blackmailers and even a man coming back from the dead. But somehow, the memory of Caleb's botched wedding day hadn't been lost in the tidal wave of events.

Nathan shifted position, his discomfort apparent. Caleb couldn't help him with that. Hell, he was uncomfortable, too.

But to dispel the tension, Caleb said lightly, "You should have worn your uniform."

As town sheriff, Nathan was rarely dressed in civilian clothes. The man was most comfortable in his khaki uniform, complete with badge, walking the town, talking to everyone and keeping an eye on things. He snorted. "Yeah, that wouldn't fly with Amanda."

A soft smile curved his friend's mouth and just for a second or two, Caleb envied the other man. "When's the new baby due again?"

"Next month."

And, though he knew the answer already, Caleb asked, "How many will that make now?"

Nathan grinned and shot him a wink. "This one makes four."

A set of four-year-old twin boys, a two-year-old girl and now another one. "How many are you planning, anyway?"

Nathan shrugged. "Who says there's a plan? Mandy loves babies, and I have to say I do enjoy making them."

Marriage. Family. All of that slipped by him four years ago. And now that Nathan had reminded him, Caleb idly wondered how many kids he and Meg might have had by now if things had gone the way he'd expected. But the night before their wedding, Meg had run off with Caleb's brother, Mitch. Now the two of them lived on the family ranch with their set of twins. Three years old, the boy and girl ran wild around the ranch and Caleb put whatever he might have felt for kids of his own into those two.

There might still be tension between him and his brother, Mitch, not to mention Meg. But he loved those kids more than he would have thought possible.

"Mitch and Meg still out of town?" Nathan asked, glancing around as if half expecting to see them walking up.

"Yeah. Visiting Meg's family." And Caleb had been enjoying the respite.

"That's one way to get out of going to a summer wedding."

"Amen." Caleb loosened his tie a little. Felt like he was beginning to melt out here in the sun. He spared a glance at the sky and watched a few lazy white clouds drifting along. "Who plans a wedding in August, anyway? Hotter than the halls of hell out here."

"You know how the Goodmans are," Nathan answered. "The old man figures he knows everything and the rest of them—except Brooke—just fall in line. Probably his idea to hold it in high summer. No doubt he was aiming for it to be the talk of the town."

That sounded like Simon Goodman. Though the man was Caleb's lawyer, that was more from inertia than anything else. Goodman had been Caleb's father's lawyer and when the elder Mackenzie died, Caleb just never bothered to change the situation. So his own inaction had brought him here. Truth be told, Caleb usually avoided attending *any* weddings since it inevitably brought up old memories that he'd just as soon bury.

"Anyway," Nathan said, pushing past the uncomfortable pause in the conversation, "I'm the town sheriff. I'm sort of *forced* to be at these society things. Why the hell did you come?"

Caleb snorted. "Normally, I wouldn't have. But Simon Goodman's still the ranch attorney. So it's business to be at his son Jared's wedding." And he made a mental note to do something about that real soon. He shrugged. "If Mitch and Meg had been in town I'd have forced my brother to go instead of me. But since they're gone, I'm stuck."

Served him right, Caleb told himself, for letting things slide. He never should have kept Simon on. He and Caleb's father had been great friends so that didn't speak well of the man.

He'd let the lawyer relationship stand mainly because it was easier than taking time away from work to find someone new. Between running the ranch and expanding the oil-rich field discovered only twenty years before, Caleb had been too damn busy to worry about a lawyer he only had to deal with a few times a year.

Looking for a change of subject, Caleb said, "Since you're here, that means the new deputy's in charge, right?"

Nathan winced. "Yeah. Jeff's doing fine."

Caleb laughed. "Sure, I can hear the confidence in your voice."

Sighing, Nathan pushed one hand through his hair and shook his head. "With Jack retired, I needed a deputy and Jeff Baker's working out. But he's from Houston so it's taking him some time to get used to small town living."

Caleb had heard about it. Jeff was about thirty and a little too strict on the law and order thing for Royal. The new deputy had handed out more speeding tickets in the last six months than Nathan had in years. Folks in Royal hit an empty road and they just naturally picked up speed. Jeff Baker wasn't making many friends.

"Hell," Caleb said, "I've lived here my whole life and I'm still not used to it."

"I hear that," Nathan replied, shifting his gaze to where his wife stood with a group of friends. "But I've been getting a lot of complaints about the tickets Jeff's handing out."

Caleb laughed. "He's not going to slow anybody down."

"Maybe not," Nathan agreed with a nod. "But he's going to keep trying."

"I expect so," Caleb mused, then glanced over at Nathan's wife who was smiling and waving one hand. "I think Amanda wants you."

Straightening up, Nathan gave a heartfelt sigh. "That's it, then. I'll see you after. At the reception?"

"I don't think so. Soon as I'm clear, I'm headed back to the ranch."

Another sigh. "Lucky bastard."

Caleb grinned and watched his friend head toward the Texas Cattleman's Club building. The place was a one-story, rambling sort, made of dark wood and stone, boasting a tall slate roof. It was a part of Royal and had been for generations. Celebrations of all kinds had been held there and today, it was a wedding. One he'd have to attend in just a few minutes.

Shelby Arthur stared at her own reflection and hardly recognized herself. She supposed all brides felt like that on their wedding day, but for her, the effect was terrifying.

Her long, dark auburn curls were pulled back from her face to hang down to the center of her back. Her veil poofed out around her head and her green eyes narrowed at the gown she hated. A ridiculous number of yards of white tulle made Shelby look like a giant marshmallow caught in netting. The dress was her about-to-be-mother-in-law's doing. She'd insisted that the Goodmans had a reputation to maintain in Royal and the simple off-the-shoulder gown Shelby had chosen wouldn't do the trick.

So instead, she was looking at a stranger wearing an old-fashioned gown with long, lacy sleeves, a cinched waist and full skirt, and a neckline that was so high she felt as if she were choking.

"Thank God for air-conditioning," she muttered, otherwise in the sweltering Texas heat, she'd be little more than a tulle-covered puddle on the floor. She half turned to get a look at the back of the dress and finally sighed. She looked like one of those crocheted dolls her grandmother used to make to cover up spare toilet paper rolls.

Shelby was about to get married in a dress she hated, a veil she didn't want, to a man she wasn't sure she *liked*, much less loved. How did she get to this point?

"Oh, God. What am I doing?" The whisper was strained but heartfelt.

She'd left her home in Chicago to marry Jared Goodman. But now that he was home in Texas, under his awful father's thumb, Jared was someone she didn't even know. Her whirlwind romance had morphed into a nightmare and now she was trapped.

She took a breath, blew it out and asked her reflection, "What are you doing?"

"Good question."

Shelby jumped, startled by the sudden appearance of Jared's mother. The woman was there, behind her in the mirror, bustling into the room. Margaret Goodman was tall and painfully thin. Her face was all sharp angles and her blue eyes were small and judgmental. Her graying blond hair was scraped back from her face into a bun that incongruously sported a circlet of yellow rosebuds. The beige suit she wore was elegant if boring and was so close to the color of her hair and skin the woman simply disappeared into her clothes.

If only, Shelby thought.

"Your veil should be down over your face," Margaret chastised, hurrying over to do just that.

As the veil fell across her vision, Shelby had a momentary panic attack and felt as though she couldn't breathe through that all-encompassing tulle curtain, so she whipped it back again. Taking a deep breath, she said, "I'm sorry, I can't—"

"You will." Margaret stepped back, took a look, then moved to tug at the skirt of the wedding gown. "We're going for a very traditional, chaste look here. It's unseemly that this wedding is happening so quickly. The town will be gossiping for months, watching for a swollen belly."

Shelby sucked in a gulp of air. "I've told you already, I'm not pregnant."

"We'll soon see, won't we?" One blond eyebrow lifted over pale blue eyes. "The Goodman family has a reputation in this town and I expect you to do nothing to besmirch it."

"Besmirch?" Who even talked like that, Shelby thought wildly. It was as if she'd dropped into a completely different universe. Suddenly, she missed Chicago—her friends, her *life*, so much she ached with it.

Moving to Texas with a handsome, well-connected cowboy who had swept her off her feet had seemed like an adventure at the time. Now she was caught up in a web that seemed inescapable. Her fiancé was a stranger, his mother a blatant enemy and his brother had a way of looking at Shelby that had her wishing she'd paid more attention in self-defense class.

Jared's father, Simon, was no better, making innuendoes that he probably thought were clever but gave Shelby the outright creeps. The only bright spot in the Goodman family was Jared's sister, Brooke, and she couldn't help Shelby with what was about to happen.

Somehow, she had completely lost control of her own life and now she stood there in a mountain of tulle trying to find enough scraps of who she was to cling to.

"Once the ceremony is finished, we'll all go straightaway to the reception," Margaret was saying.

Oh, God.

"You and Jared will, of course, be in the receiving line until every guest has been welcomed personally. The photographer can then indulge in the necessary photos for precisely fifteen minutes, after which you and Jared will reenter the reception for the ceremonial first toast." Margaret paused long enough to glance into the mirror herself and smooth hair that wouldn't dare fall out of place. "Mr. Goodman is an important man and as his family *we* will do all we can to support him. Is that understood?" Her gaze, hard and cold, shot to Shelby's. "When you've returned from your honeymoon..."

Her stomach sank even further. She wouldn't have been surprised to see it simply drop out of her body and fall *splat* onto the floor. Her day was scheduled. Her honeymoon was scheduled and she had no doubt at all that her *life* would be carefully laid out for her, complete with bullet points.

How had it all come to this?

For their honeymoon, Shelby had wanted to see Paris. Instead, Jared's mother had insisted they go to Philadelphia so Shelby could be introduced to the eastern branch of the Goodman family. And much to her dismay, Jared was simply doing as he was told with no regard at all for Shelby. He'd changed so much since coming back to Texas that she hardly recognized the man anymore.

Margaret was still talking. Fixing a steely gaze on the mirror, she met Shelby's eyes. "When you return to Texas, you will of course give up your ridiculous business and be the kind of wife to Jared that will enable him to further his own law career."

"Oh, I don't think—"

"You'll be a Goodman," Margaret snapped, brooking no argument.

Shelby swallowed hard. When they'd met in Chicago, Jared had talked about his ranch in Texas. He'd let her believe that he was a cowboy who happened to also have a law degree. And yes, she could admit that the fantasy of being with a cowboy had really appealed to her. But mostly, he'd talked about their having a family and that had sealed the deal for Shelby.

She'd told herself then that she could move her professional organizer business anywhere. But from the moment Jared had introduced her to his family, Margaret had made it clear that her "little business" was hardly appropriate.

Shelby met her own eyes in the mirror and read the desperation there. Maybe all of this would be easier to take if she was madly in love with Jared. But the truth was, she'd fooled herself from the beginning. This wasn't love. It couldn't be. The romance, the excitement, had all worn off, like the luster of sterling silver as soon as it was tarnished. Rather than standing up for himself, Jared was completely cowed by his family and that really didn't bode well for Shelby's future.

Margaret checked the slim gold watch on her wrist, clucked her tongue and headed for the door. "The music will begin in exactly five minutes." She stopped, glanced over her shoulder and added, "My husband will be here to escort you down the aisle since you don't have a father of your own."

Shelby's mouth dropped open as the other woman left the room. Stunned, she realized Margaret had tossed that last bit with venom, as if Shelby had arranged for her father to die ten years ago just so he could disrupt Margaret Goodman's wedding scenario.

She shivered at the thought of Simon Goodman. She didn't want him anywhere near her, let alone escorting her, touching her. And even worse, she was about to promise to be in Simon's family for the rest of her life.

"Nope, can't do it." She glanced at her own reflection and in a burst of fury ripped her veil off her face. Then, blowing a stray auburn lock from her forehead, she gathered up the skirt of the voluminous gown in both arms.

"Have to hurry," she muttered, giving herself the impetus she needed to make a break for it before it was too late. If she didn't leave now, she'd be *married* into the most awful family she'd ever known.

"Not going to happen," she reassured herself as she tentatively opened the door and peered out.

Thankfully, there was no one in this section of the TCC. They were all in the main room, waiting for the ceremony to start. In the distance, she heard the soft thrum of harp music playing as an underscore to the rise and fall of conversations. She could only guess what they'd all be talking about soon.

That wasn't her problem, though. Clutching her wedding gown high enough to keep it out of her way, she hurried down the hall and toward the nearest exit.

She thought she heard someone calling her name, but Shelby didn't let that stop her. She hit the front door and started running. It was blind panic that kept her moving. After all, she had nowhere to go. She didn't know hardly anyone in Royal besides the Goodman family. But she kept moving because the unknown was wildly better than the alternative.

Her veil caught on one of the porch posts and yanked her back briefly. But Shelby ripped the stupid thing off her head, tiara and all, and tossed it to the ground. Then she was off again, tearing around a corner and running smack into a brick wall.

Well, that's what it felt like.

A tall, gorgeous brick wall who grabbed her upper arms to steady her, then smiled down at her with humor in his eyes. He had enough sex appeal to light up the city of Houston and the heat from his hands, sliding down her body, made everything inside her jolt into life.

"Aren't you headed the wrong way?" he asked, and the soft drawl in his deep voice awakened a single thought in her mind. *Oh, boy.*

Two

A *real* cowboy.

Shelby tipped her head back to look up at him and caught the flash of surprise in his gaze as he reached out to steady her. Ridiculously enough, considering the situation—running away from her own wedding—she felt a hot blast of something...*amazing*.

The cowboy had shaggy light brown hair, icy-blue eyes, a strong jaw and a gray cowboy hat tipped down low on his forehead. He wore a black suit, crisp white shirt with a dove-gray tie and oh, sweet mama Lou, shining black cowboy boots. His hands were strong and warm on her upper arms and a slow smile curved his mouth as he took in what she was wearing.

And the soft drawl in his deep voice really worked for her. He was everything Jared wasn't. Although, even as she thought it, Shelby reminded herself that her judgment had been so crappy about Jared that she could be just as wrong about Mr. Tall, Dark and Yummy.

"Hey now," he said, that deep voice rolling along her spine again. "Are you all right?"

"Absolutely not," she said firmly. The humor in his eyes was gone, replaced by concern and she responded to it. "I have to get out of here. Now. Can you help me?"

His eyes narrowed on her and his delectable mouth moved into a grim slash. "You're running out on your wedding?"

Disapproval practically radiated from him and Shelby's spine went stiff as a board in reaction. "Just as fast as I can," she said. "Can you help me?"

Before he could say yes or no, another voice erupted behind her.

"Shelby! What the devil do you think you're doing?"

Spinning around until the cowboy was at her back, Shelby watched as Margaret Goodman stalked toward her, fire in her eyes. "Your guests are waiting."

"They're not my guests," Shelby said. Heck, the only people she knew in Royal was the family she was supposed to marry into and frankly, if they were the best this town had to offer, she was ready to *run* back to Chicago.

"Of course they are." Margaret waved her hand impatiently, dismissing Shelby's argument. "Don't be foolish."

Shelby moved back until she felt the cowboy's tall, strong body press up against hers. Cowardly? Maybe, but she'd live with it. Right now, this tall, exceptionally well-built man was the safest spot she could find.

Margaret's gaze snapped to the cowboy. "Caleb, bring her along inside right this minute."

Caleb. His name was Caleb. For a second, Shelby worried that he might do just that. After all, he didn't know her and the Goodman family, as they kept telling her, were a big deal here in Royal. Maybe he wasn't the safe harbor she'd thought he was.

Then the cowboy stepped out from behind her and moved to partially block Shelby from the woman glaring at her. While Shelby watched, he tipped his hat and said, "I don't take orders from you, Mrs. Goodman."

Margaret inhaled through her nose and if she could have set

the cowboy on fire, she clearly would have. "Fine. *Please* bring her along inside. The wedding is about to start."

"Well now," Caleb said slowly, that deep drawl caressing every word, "I don't believe the lady wants to go back inside."

"No," Shelby said, exhaling in a rush. "I do not."

"There you go. She sounds pretty sure," Caleb said, shrugging as if he couldn't have cared less which way this confrontation turned out.

"Well, I'm sure, too." Margaret took a menacing step forward. "This woman is engaged to my son, God help me."

Insulted, Shelby frowned, but the older woman kept going.

"We have a club full of people waiting for the ceremony to begin and the Goodman family has a reputation to uphold in Royal. I refuse to allow some city tramp to ruin it."

"Tramp?" Okay, now she was more sure than ever that running had been the right thing to do. The very idea of having to deal with this woman as a *relative* for the rest of her life gave her cold chills.

Shelby took a step toward the woman with the plan to tell Margaret exactly what she thought of her. But the cowboy alongside her grabbed her arm to hold her in place.

"That's enough, Margaret," he said quietly.

"It's not nearly enough." Margaret fired a hard look at the cowboy before shifting her gaze back to Shelby. "You stay out of this, Caleb Mackenzie. This has nothing to do with you."

Though the urge to stand here and have it out with this appalling woman was so strong Shelby was almost quivering, she knew it would be a waste of time. And, since the most important thing was to escape before any more Goodmans showed up, she turned her head to stare up at the man beside her.

"Can you get me out of here?" Shelby asked, staring up into those cool, blue eyes.

"What?" Ignoring Margaret, the man looked at her as if he hadn't heard her right.

"Take me somewhere," she blurted, and didn't even think

about the fact that she didn't know this man. Right now it was enough that Margaret clearly couldn't stand him. The enemy of my enemy, and all that.

"You want me to help you run out on the man waiting for you at the altar?"

"Well, when you put it like that, it sounds terrible," Shelby admitted, shifting uneasily from foot to foot.

"What other way is there to put it?"

"Okay fine. I'm a terrible human being," she whispered frantically as Margaret heaped curses on her head. "And I'll apologize to Jared later. But right now..."

Caleb stared down at her as if trying to see inside her. And Shelby was grateful that he couldn't. Because right now, her insides were tangled up into so many knots she'd probably look like a crazy person. Heck, she *felt* like a crazy person. One that had just made a break from the asylum and was now looking for a ride back to sanity.

Hitching the yards of tulle higher in her arms, Shelby murmured, "Margaret said your name's Caleb, right?"

"That's right."

God, his voice was so deep it seemed to echo out around her. His blue eyes were focused on her and Shelby felt a flutter of something she'd never felt for the man she'd almost married. Probably not a good thing. "Look, I don't have much time. If you can't help me, I need to find someone else. Fast." She took a breath and blew it out again. "So. Are you going to help me, Caleb?"

One corner of his mouth lifted briefly. "What's your name?"

"Shelby," she said, mesmerized by the motion of that mouth. "Shelby Arthur."

"I'm Caleb Mackenzie," he said. "My truck's over there."

He jerked his head toward a big, top-of-the-line black pickup that shone like midnight, its chrome bumpers glittering in the sun. At that moment, the huge black truck looked like a magical carriage there to transport her away from a nightmare. Shelby sighed in relief and practically sprinted for it.

"Where are you going?" Margaret's voice, loud, desperate, followed her. "You can't leave! What will people think?"

"Whatever the hell they want to," Caleb tossed over his shoulder. "Just like always."

He opened the passenger door and helped Shelby to climb in. "We have to hurry," she said, throwing frantic looks at the building behind them.

"It'd be easier if you didn't have so damn much dress," he muttered, grabbing a fistful of the material and stuffing it into the truck.

"Never mind the dress," she said, staring down at him. She was doing it. Getting away. But she wasn't gone yet. Grabbing at the dress, she shoved it between her knees and then ignored the rest of the hot mess gown still hanging down the side of the truck. "Just get in and *drive.*"

He looked up at her and again, Shelby felt that rush of something hot and unexpected. That was just too weird. A few minutes ago, she'd been set to marry another man and now she was getting all warm and shivery for a cowboy in shining armor? What was *wrong* with her?

"Yes, ma'am," he said. "You're the boss." Then he slammed the truck door, leaving a couple of feet of dress hanging out beneath the bottom.

Shelby didn't care. All she wanted was to get away. To feel free. She pushed her hair out of her face as it slipped from the intricate knots it had been wound into. While Caleb walked around the front of the truck, she stared out the window at the woman still cursing her. Shelby had the oddest desire to wave goodbye and smile. But she didn't. Instead, she looked away from her would-be mother-in-law and when Caleb climbed into the truck and fired it up, she took her first easy breath. When he threw it into gear and drove from the parking lot, Shelby laughed at the wild release pumping through her.

He glanced at her. "Are you crazy?"

She shook her head and grinned. "Not anymore. I think I'm cured."

Caleb told himself that if she wasn't crazy herself, she was probably a carrier. How else did he explain why he was driving down the long, nearly empty road toward his ranch with a runaway bride sitting beside him?

Two words repeated in his brain. *Runaway bride.* Hell, he was helping do to Jared what Mitch and Meg had done to *him* four years ago. Was this some kind of backward Karma?

Caleb shot a sideways look at his passenger. The dress was god-awful, but it was fitted to her body like a damn glove. Her high, full breasts were outlined behind yet another layer of lace. The high neck only made a man wonder what was being hidden. Long sleeves caressed her arms and a damn mountain of white net poofed out around her body even while she fought it down.

Her face was pale, making the handful of freckles across her nose stand out like firelight in a snowstorm. While he watched, she rolled down the window and her hair was suddenly a wild tangle of dark red curls flying in the wind.

She closed her eyes, smiled into the wind, then turned to look at him and smiled even wider. "Thanks for the rescue."

Yeah. He'd rescued her and helped to humiliate Jared, just as he himself had once been. Caleb didn't much care for Jared Goodman, but that didn't make what he'd done any easier to take.

"Why'd you wait to run?" he asked.

"What?"

"Why wait until the last damn minute to change your mind?"

"Good question." She sighed, pushed her hair back, then propped her elbow on the door. "I kept thinking it would get better, I guess. Instead, it just got worse."

He could understand that. It was the Goodmans, after all.

"And you couldn't leave before today?"

She looked at him and frowned. "I could have. But I gave my word. I said I'd marry Jared—"

"But you didn't."

"Couldn't," she corrected, shaking her head. "Staring at myself in the mirror, wearing this hideous dress, listening to Margaret tell me about the honeymoon plans *she* made..." Her voice died off and it was a few seconds before she spoke again. "It finally hit me that I just couldn't go through with it. So I ran. I suppose you think that's cowardly."

"Well..."

She shifted in her seat, hiking all of that white fabric higher until it was above her knees, displaying a pair of long, tanned legs. When she stopped just past her knees, Caleb was more than a little disappointed.

He looked back at the road. Way safer than looking at her.

"You're wrong," she said. "It took more strength to run than it would have to stay."

Frowning to himself, Caleb thought about that for a minute. Was it possible she had a point?

She threw both hands up, the fabric spilled off her lap to the floor and she muttered a curse as she gathered it all up again to hold on her lap. Caleb spared another quick look at her long, tanned legs, then told himself to keep his eyes on the road.

"Honestly," she said, "I could have gone through with it and not been called a 'tramp.' I could have stayed, knowing that I didn't really love Jared after all, but going through with the wedding to avoid the embarrassment. But it wasn't right for me or fair to Jared for me to marry him knowing I didn't want to be married, especially to him, you know what I mean?"

Before he could say anything, she rolled right on.

Waving one hand, then grabbing up fabric again with another curse, she said, "I know he'll be angry and probably hurt today but sooner or later, he's going to see that I did the right thing and who knows, maybe he'll even *thank* me for it at some point."

"Don't hold your breath," Caleb muttered.

"What? Never mind." Shaking her head, she took a deep breath, looked out over the open road and said, "Even if he doesn't thank me out loud, he'll be glad. Eventually. This is better. I mean, I don't know what to do *now*, but this is definitely better. For both of us."

"You sound sure."

She looked at him again until he felt compelled to meet those forest green eyes of hers however briefly. "I am," she said. "So thank you. Again."

"You're welcome." Caleb didn't know what the hell he was supposed to do with her, so he was headed home. Back at the ranch, she could call her own family. Or a cab. And then she could be on her way and he could get out of this damn suit.

With that thought firmly in mind, Caleb focused on the familiar road stretching out ahead of him and did his best to ignore the beautiful woman sitting way too close to him.

There were wide sweeps of open land dotted with the scrub oaks that grew like weeds in East Texas. Here and there were homes and barns, with horses in paddocks and cattle grazing in the fields. The sky was the kind of clear, deep blue he'd only ever seen in Texas and those few gusting clouds he'd glimpsed earlier had gathered up a few friends.

Everything was absolutely normal. Except for the bride in his truck.

"Weird day," he muttered.

"It is, isn't it?" She whipped her hair out of her eyes to look at him. "I never thought I'd be a fugitive from my own wedding. And I know I've said this already, but thank you. I kind of threw myself at you and didn't give you much room to back off, so I really appreciate you riding to the rescue."

"I could have said no," he reminded her.

She tilted her head to one side and studied him. "No, I don't think you could have."

He snorted. "Is that right?"

"Yeah. I think so." She shook her head. "You've got the whole 'responsible' vibe going on. Anyway, I didn't know how I was going to get away. Didn't even think about it. I just ran."

"Right into me." And he had gotten a real good feel of the body beneath that ugly-ass gown. High, firm breasts, narrow waist, nicely rounded hips. He frowned and shifted as his own body suddenly went tight and uncomfortable. Hell. Just what he needed.

"Yeah, I'm sorry you got dragged into this."

He glanced at her. "No, you're not."

She grinned. "No, I guess I'm really not. Hard to be sorry about finding a white knight."

He let that one go because he was nobody's hero.

"So now what?" he asked. "What are you going to do from here?"

She sat back and stared at him. "I have no idea."

"Well, what was the plan?"

"Like I said, there wasn't a plan. I just had to get away." Shaking her head, she stared out the windshield. "I didn't even know I was going to run until just before I did."

She'd torn down her hair and now it was a tangled mess of dark red curls that flew around her face in the wind whipping through the opened windows. He'd had the AC on, but she'd shut it off and rolled down her window, insisting she needed to feel the wind on her face. Caleb didn't know what it said about him that he preferred that hair of hers wild and free to the carefully pinned-up style she'd had when she ran from the club.

She still had the skirt of her wedding dress hiked up to her knees and Caleb took another admiring look at her long slim legs. Then he fixed his gaze on the road again. "Look, I'll take you out to my ranch—"

"Your ranch."

"That's right."

"Jared said he had a ranch."

Caleb snorted. "The Goodmans used to run a ranch, generations ago. Now they rent the land out to other ranchers so they can live in town."

"So I discovered." She held her hair back, narrowed her eyes on him and asked, "Anyway, we know I'm not crazy."

"Do we?"

She ignored that. "Now I have to ask. Are you a crazy person?"

Both eyebrows lifted and he snorted a laugh. "What kind of question is that?"

"One I probably should have asked *before* I hopped into your truck."

"Good point." A reluctant smile tugged at his mouth.

"Well, I thought I should ask before we go much further down this pretty empty road."

Amused in spite of everything, he asked, "What happened to me being a damn hero rescuing you?"

"Oh, you're still a hero," she assured him, "but you could be crazy, too. You aren't, though, are you?"

"Would I admit it if I was?"

"You might." She shrugged. "There's no telling with crazy people."

"Know a lot of nut jobs, do you?" Caleb shook his head, he couldn't believe he was having this conversation.

"A few, but you don't seem like you're one of them." A wide swath of lace lifted into the wind and she snatched it and held it down on her lap. "Have you ever seen so much tulle?"

"What's tulle?"

"This." She lifted the swath of netting again. "It's awful."

"If you don't like it, Why'd you buy it?"

"I didn't." She sighed. "Jared's mother picked it out."

Caleb laughed. "Sounds like her."

"Okay, you're not crazy." She nodded and gave a sigh of satisfaction. "If you don't like my almost mother-in-law you're obviously stable."

"Thanks." Still shaking his head, he said, "Like I was saying, I'll take you to the ranch. You can figure out where to go from there."

"I don't know where I can go," she said quietly turning her head to stare out the window at the scenery flying past. "I don't have my purse, my wallet. God, I don't even have clothes."

Caleb didn't like the sound of the rising hysteria in her voice.

"I don't know what I was thinking," she said, and her words tumbled over each other in their rush to get out. "My God, I don't have anything with me."

"I can take you to an ATM—"

"No purse," she interrupted. "No wallet, remember? No clothes except for this giant marshmallow of a dress." She slapped one hand to her chest as if trying to hold her heart inside her body.

"You're starting to panic," he pointed out.

"Of course I am." Her eyes were wild. "Now that I got away, I can think about other things and what I'm thinking is that I'm alone. In a strange place. Don't know anyone but the people I'm escaping from."

He watched from the corner of his eye as she shook her head frantically.

"I can't exactly go over to the Goodmans' house and say please can I have my things? My clothes. My purse. My ID. My *phone*." She dropped her head into her hands and now her face was covered by what looked like an acre of tulle. "This is a nightmare," she muttered.

"Remember, you wake up from nightmares."

She lifted her head to glare at him. "Easy for you to say since I'm assuming you actually *have* a change of clothing."

"Good point." He nodded. "Yeah, you're about the same size as my sister-in-law. You can wear some of her stuff."

"Great. And what if she doesn't feel like being generous?"

"She's out of town."

A short laugh shot from Shelby's throat. "So I've been on my own about fifteen minutes and already I'm stealing clothes."

"Not stealing. Borrowing." He paused. "Are you always this dramatic?"

"Only when my world implodes," she said and looked at him again. "So basically, I'm homeless and destitute. Well, hasn't this day turned out all sparkly?"

He laughed.

She narrowed her eyes on him, then reluctantly, laughed herself. "This is not how I pictured my life going."

"Yeah, not how I saw my day going, either," he replied, grateful that she seemed to be coming down from that momentary panic.

"Honestly," she said with another shake of her head, "I didn't think beyond moving to Texas to marry Prince Charming who turned out to be a frog."

"And you didn't notice that right off?"

"No." She huffed out a breath and turned her face into the wind. "Usually I'm a terrific judge of character."

When he didn't agree, she reminded him, "I picked *you* to rescue me, didn't I?"

Amused again, Caleb laughed. "Yeah, but your choices were limited."

"I could have just run screaming down the street," she pointed out. "Which was first on my to-do list until I saw you." She paused for breath. "Did you ever notice how appropriate the name Grimm was for an author of fairy tales?"

"Can't say I ever thought about it."

"Well, I've had the time lately. And the motivation. I mean, seriously. Look at this mess. It's got it all. The feckless fiancé who'd gone from hero to wimp. His vicious mother and creepy father, not to mention his grabby brother."

"Grabby?" Caleb scowled at the road ahead and admitted silently that he was really starting to sympathize with his runaway passenger. The Goodman family wasn't exactly the best Royal had to offer and Shelby Arthur had discovered that the hard way.

She shuddered. "Justin is not someone a woman should be alone with. The only bright spot in that family was Jared's sister, Brooke. She must be adopted," Shelby added under her breath, then continued, "but by now, even *she's* probably furious with me."

"Do you need me to respond or are you good to talk all on your own?"

"God this is a mess."

"Seems to be."

She turned to look at him. "Not going to try to console me?"

"Would it do any good?"

"No."

"Then it'd be a waste of time, wouldn't it?"

"Are you always so chatty?" she asked.

"Yep."

Shelby laughed, and the sound was soft and rich and touched something in Caleb he didn't want to acknowledge. Still, her laughter was better than the anxiety he'd just been listening to.

"Look," he said. "You come out to the house and you can stay there a day or two. Figure out what you want to do."

"Stay there. With you."

He shot her a look. "Don't look so damn suspicious. I'm not offering you a spot in my bed." Damn shame about that, he admitted to himself, since just looking at her made him want to reach out and cover her mouth with his. And a few other things besides. But not the point.

"You can stay on the other side of the house," he said. "My mother died a couple years ago. You can have her wing. We won't even see each other."

"Her *wing*?" Shelby frowned. "How big is this house?"

"Big enough."

At the Texas Cattleman's Club, the reception for the wedding that didn't happen was in full swing. A band played dance music as a Goodman wedding would never have accepted something so pedestrian as a DJ. The tables were decorated with snowy white cloths and a bud vase on each table held a single pink rose. The soft clink of china and crystal was an undercurrent to the music and, while the crowd gathered in knots to exchange gossip about the runaway bride, Rose Clayton sat alone at a table watching it all.

At sixty-seven, Rose was an attractive woman with a figure she took care of, stylishly cut dark brown hair with just a hint of gray—thanks to a talented stylist—that swung in a loose fall at her jawline, and her sharp, smoke-colored eyes never missed a thing.

Conversations rose and fell around her like a continuous wave. She was only half listening, and even at that, she caught plenty of people talking about the upcoming TCC board elections. There had been a time when she wouldn't have given them a thought. But, now that women were also full-fledged members in the Texas Cattleman's Club, she was more than a little interested.

As far as Rose was concerned, their current president, James Harris, was doing a wonderful job and she saw no reason to make a change. It was nice to eavesdrop and hear that most of the other members felt the same way.

As people passed her table, they nodded or smiled, but kept moving. Rose's reputation as the uncrowned queen of Royal society kept people at bay even as they treated her with the respect she'd earned through years of a stubborn refusal to surrender to the unhappiness in her own life.

Rose knew everyone at the reception. She'd watched many of them grow up. Including Margaret Fraser Goodman. The woman, Rose thought, had been *born* an old stick. She had always been more concerned with appearances than with what really mattered. But even as she mentally chastised Margaret, Rose had to admit that she had done the same. The difference was, she assured herself, that Rose found enjoyment within the parameters that had been forced on her so long ago.

Her gaze fixed on Margaret Goodman briefly and noted the crazed look in her eyes and the grim slash of a mouth she kept forcing into a hard smile. Rose had already heard bits and pieces of chatter, no doubt started by Margaret, that had turned the situation around. Now, the story went, it was *Jared* who had changed his mind at the last moment. Told his unfortunate bride to leave.

And a part of Margaret might even believe it. Rose had never met the now missing bride, but damn if she didn't admire the woman. She'd taken charge of her own life and done what she'd had to do. Who knew how Rose's life might have turned out if she'd had the same gumption?

But times had been different fifty years ago and Rose's father, Jed, had been a man no one crossed. Her gaze swept the room until she spotted her grandson Daniel. Daniel Clayton was her reward for all of the misery she'd managed to survive over the decades.

A grown man now, he was handsome, intelligent and damned funny when he wanted to be. He was the light of her life and there wasn't a thing she wouldn't do to see him happy. Within reason.

"Oh, that is simply unacceptable," Rose murmured to herself as she saw Daniel bend down and gently kiss a pretty woman who looked dazzled by his attention.

Alexis Slade.

The granddaughter of Gus Slade.

Just thinking the man's name gave Rose's heart a jolt. Once upon a time, she'd been crazy in love with that old goat and risked her father's wrath to be with him. Until the night her father made the threat that had ended everything between her and Gus forever.

She squared her shoulders and lifted her chin. Nodding to people who addressed her, she was a part of the crowd and yet separate from it as her mind raced back through the years.

For decades now, the Claytons and the Slades had been if

not enemies, then at least at odds. They didn't socialize. Didn't trust each other. And they surely didn't look at each other as Daniel and Alexis were right that minute. She wouldn't have it. And what's more, Rose was quite sure that on this subject at least, Gus would agree with her.

Their grandchildren had been sweet on each other years ago, but Rose and Gus had put a stop to it. Gus sent Alexis off to an out-of-state college, while Rose kept Daniel so busy with ranch work, he didn't have time to miss the girl he couldn't have.

"Unacceptable," she whispered again, tapping her manicured nails against the tablecloth in a muffled staccato. Again, she scanned the room, but this time, she was looking for someone in particular.

When she found him, Rose stood, crossed the room and stopped at his table. "Gus. We have to talk."

Three

Gus Slade wore a steel-gray suit with a white shirt and a bold red tie. His black cowboy hat rested on the table alongside his arm. His thick hair, once black as midnight, was silver now, and his skin was tanned and leathered from years of working out in the Texas sun. He was leaning back in his chair, one booted foot resting on a knee. At sixty-nine, he was still a powerful, magnetic man.

Damn it.

His piercing blue eyes fixed on Rose with neither welcome nor warning. "Talk about what?"

Ignoring his rudeness, she took a seat near him, glanced over her shoulder toward their grandchildren and said pointedly, *"That."*

He took a look, then frowned. "Nothing to talk about. Keep your boy away from my girl and we have no problem."

"Take another look, you old goat," Rose said in a whispered hush. "It's Alexis doing the flirting. And she's got the look of a woman who's been thoroughly—recently—kissed."

Gus's frown deepened and his gaze shifted to Rose. "A

woman flirting doesn't mean a damn thing. And kisses are fleeting, aren't they, Rose?"

She took a gulp of air at the implied insult. Rose had been sixteen years old when she fell head over heels in love with Gus. And if she had to be honest—the man could still give her insides a jump start. But damned if she'd sit there and be insulted.

"I didn't come over here to talk about the past."

"Then why are you sitting at my table?" he snapped.

Rose swallowed back her annoyance. Since the death of his wife, Sarah, from cancer a few years before, Gus had become even more unsociable than usual. And another piece of her heart ached. Sarah Slade had once been Rose's best friend, but Rose had lost them both when she'd rejected Gus. He had turned to Sarah for comfort and soon the two of them had been together, shutting Rose out completely.

But old hurts couldn't matter at the moment. It was the present they had to worry about, not the past. "Gus, unless we're prepared to have the two of them getting together—*again*—we have to come up with something."

He scrubbed one hand across his jaw in a gesture Rose remembered. Deliberately, she shut down a surge of memories and waited impatiently for the man to speak. Gus always had taken his time choosing just the right words. And even back when she had loved him, that particular trait had driven Rose crazy.

"Fine," he said at long last, keeping his voice low as he glanced around to make sure no one could listen in. "But not here. Don't need a damn audience of gossips trying to figure out why we're suddenly being friendly."

Rose winced. She hadn't really considered that. Her one thought had been to enlist Gus's help in breaking up any attachment between her grandson and his granddaughter. "You're right."

He flashed a grin. "Well, this is a banner day. Rose Clayton admitting Gus Slade is right about something."

She was unamused. "Write it on your calendar in big red letters. Meanwhile—"

"Fine, then. We'll meet tomorrow. Two o'clock at the oak."

Rose inhaled sharply at the jab. *The oak* could have been anywhere in the state of Texas. But Rose knew exactly what meeting spot Gus was talking about. She was almost surprised that he remembered. Then, as his gaze focused on her, she realized that he was testing her. Seeing if *she* remembered.

How could she not?

"Agreed. Two o'clock." She turned to walk away, unwilling to give him the satisfaction of seeing that he'd gotten to her. Then she stopped, looked back and said, "Try not to be late this time."

Smiling to herself at the accuracy of her own little barb, Rose walked back to her table.

Shelby stared up at the main house and gave a sigh.

She'd been impressed when Caleb drove through the gates with the scrolled ironwork *M*. Then the oak-lined drive had taken her breath away. But the house itself was amazing.

It was big, sprawling across the ground, like a lazy dog claiming its territory. The house jutted out at different angles that told Shelby people had been adding on to the house for generations. There was a long, wide front porch running the length of the house, with stone pillars holding up the overhang roof.

There were chairs and swings along the length of the porch, crowded with pillows and huge pots filled with flowers spilling down in rivers of bright colors. The effect was a silent welcome to sit and enjoy the view for a while. And the view was pretty spectacular. It was exactly the kind of ranch you would find in a *House Beautiful* article called "The Lifestyles of Rich Ranchers."

She turned in a slow circle, still holding her wedding dress up around her knees. There was a barn, a stable, a corral where three horses were gathered in a knot as if whispering to each other. There was another house, a two-story cottage style just across the yard and in the distance, there were other long, low buildings.

"Wow." She half turned to look up at Caleb. "This is all yours?"

"Mine and my brother's, yeah." He frowned. "Part of your dress is in the dirt."

She looked over her shoulder and muttered a curse. Then she huffed out a breath. "I don't care. Not like I'm going to wear it again. Ever."

He shrugged. "Your call." He pointed to the two-story house. "My brother and his family live there. I'll go get you some of Meg's things."

"I don't know…" It felt weird. She was already so much in his debt, how much deeper could she go? He'd rescued her, offered her a place to stay and now he was going to give her clothes.

"Hey, okay with me if you want to stay in that dress."

Biting her lip, she looked down at the white nightmare she was wearing. "Okay, yes. I'd like to borrow some clothes." *Please don't let him be crazy.*

"Be right back. Oh," he added, "when you go inside, just… watch yourself."

What kind of warning was that? She turned to glance at the wide oak front door and wondered what she was going to find behind it. A torture chamber? Rat-infested rooms? A collection of wedding dresses from the brides he'd rescued before her?

Shelby groaned at that last ridiculous thought. How many brides could one man run across, anyway? After what she'd already been through that day, what in that house could possibly affect her?

So, bracing herself for everything from explosives to bears, Shelby walked across the porch and opened the door.

A blast of icy, air-conditioned air greeted her and she nearly whimpered. She'd thought Chicago summers were killer. But Texas was a brand-new ball game. The humidity here was high enough to fill a swimming pool. Eager to get into the cool, she pushed the door wider but it hit something and stopped.

Curious, Shelby peeked inside and gasped.

Stuff.

Wall-to-wall *stuff.*

The door wouldn't open all the way because there was an antique dresser right in front of it. She didn't need to ask why, either. One step into the main room told Shelby everything she needed to know about Caleb's late mother.

The furniture was lovely, but jammed into what should have been a large, generous room. And on every table, every dresser, every curio cabinet, was stuff. Not old newspapers or magazines, but statues and crystals and rings and bracelets and candlesticks and crystal bowls and baskets and trays.

If Caleb had thought this room would send her screaming, he couldn't have been more wrong. Shelby's organized soul was instantly energized. Her business, Simple Solutions, depended on people like Caleb's mother. Back in Chicago, she'd built her reputation on being able to go into a mess, straighten it out and teach the homeowner how to keep it tidy. Her client list had been built on word of mouth and she was thinking of expanding, hiring more employees, when she'd met Jared Goodman.

Frowning a little, Shelby realized it was hard to believe that she'd given up everything she knew for a man who had ended up being nothing but a facade. She'd trusted him. Believed him. Thought she was in love.

But as it turned out, she'd been in love with the idea of being in love and the reality of actually *marrying* Jared had been enough to jolt her out of the illusion.

Shelby walked farther into the room, lifting one of the crystal bud vases for a closer look, then carefully setting it down again. In her business, she'd learned early about maker's marks on crystal and glass. She knew antiques when she saw them and had a pretty good idea of the value of different pieces.

She did a slow turn, admiring the bones of the room and she

wondered why Caleb's mother had felt that emotional need to surround herself with things. The ranch itself was elegant and even in its current state, Shelby could see that the home would be, once cleared out, amazing.

"Yeah, it's pretty bad," Caleb said from behind her.

She turned to look at him. "I've seen worse."

He laughed shortly. "Hard to believe."

"Oh, this is nothing, really." She lifted a porcelain tray and ran her fingertips across the library table it rested on. "No dust. I've been in places where the dust was so thick the furniture looked like ghost pieces. The wood was white with neglect."

"My foreman's wife, Camilla, takes care of things around here."

"Well, she does a good job of it." Shelby looked around again. "It can't be easy to keep all of this dusted."

He sighed and gave a look around. "I keep telling her that we'll get people in here to haul all of this stuff away, but—"

"But you get busy," Shelby said.

"Yeah."

"And that's where I come in."

He turned a wary look on her. "What's that mean?"

"I'm a professional organizer," Shelby said, smiling up at him. "This is what I do. I go into people's homes and help bring order to chaos. I had my own business in Chicago. A successful one."

"And you gave it up to marry Jared," he mused.

"Yes, well." She stopped, frowned. "Bad judgment aside, I'm excellent at what I do." She turned to look at the room again before staring up at him. "I can take care of this for you."

"Is that right?" He was holding a pair of jeans and a T-shirt. She supposed shoes were too much to hope for.

"Sure. It's great, really." Shelby's mind was racing, figuring, planning and when she had most of it all set, she started talking again. "I need a place to stay for a while."

"Now, wait a second…"

"Just hear me out." She took a breath and released it in a rush. "You've been fabulous. Really. So thanks again for the whole rescue and bringing me here and not being a serial killer."

One corner of his delectable mouth quirked briefly. "You're welcome."

She grinned at him. Really, he was ridiculously good-looking, but when his mouth hinted at a smile, his looks went off-the-chart hot. Still, not the point at the moment.

"But the truth is," she said, "until I can get all of my stuff from Jared's parents' house—not to mention get into my money, I'm stuck."

"What about family?" he asked. "Isn't there someone you could call?"

"No." Sorrow briefly landed on her, gave her a fleeting kiss, then moved on again. "My mother died last year, so I'm all that's left."

"Sorry." He looked uncomfortable.

Shelby understood that, since she'd seen it often back home. So she spoke up quickly to even things out between them again. "Like I said, I'm a professional organizer.

"The plan was to open a business here in Texas…" She frowned, unsure now just what she would do about that. "Back in Chicago, I had hundreds of satisfied clients."

"Uh-huh."

He didn't sound interested, but he hadn't walked away, either. Which meant she hadn't lost him completely. And seeing this house had given her the first shot of good news she'd experienced in days. Before, she'd felt like a beggar, asking for help, borrowing clothes. But if he let her do this, she could feel as though she were paying her way. And that, more than anything, was important to her. She liked being her own boss. In charge of her own life. And right now, she could use a jolt of that in her system.

"My point is," she said eagerly, "I can straighten all of this out for you. I can organize everything of your mother's. All you'll have to do is decide what you want to do with everything."

He glanced around the room again and looked back to Shelby. "It's a big job."

"I'm up to it."

He studied her for a long minute, long enough that she shifted position uncomfortably. What was he seeing when he looked at her? He was seriously gorgeous, so Shelby had to wonder if he was feeling the slightest bit of attraction that was humming through her blood. And the minute she thought it, she pushed it away. *Really? Run away from your wedding and have some completely indecent thoughts about your rescuer? God, Shelby, get a grip.*

"My brother and his wife have already taken what they want, and as for me, keep what works in the room and we could donate the rest of it, I guess," he said.

Concession, her mind shouted and she jumped on it. "Absolutely, and that would be very generous. The crystal alone is probably very valuable. I could contact an antiques store and see about selling some of it if you want me to. I can check all of it for you. Make lists of what you have and where it is and—"

"Do you *ever* stop talking?"

She frowned at him. "Not often. And this is important. I really need to get you to agree with this or I'll be sleeping in a park or something. So I'll do all the work here in exchange for room and board until I can get my life back on track."

"And how long do you figure that will take?"

She winced. "Depends on how cooperative the Goodmans are."

"So forever," he said.

She sighed and felt a momentary dip in her enthusiasm. "I know it's an intrusion on you and I'll try not to bug you much…"

He was watching her and she wished she could read whatever thoughts were digging furrows between his eyebrows. The man was unreadable, though. He was the embodiment of the iconic cowboy. Tall, rugged, gorgeous, stoic. So she was forced to wait. Thankfully, it didn't take long.

"I suppose we could try it."

She sighed, grinned and slapped one hand to her chest. "Thanks. Wow. I feel better already. This is great. You won't be sorry. I'll have this taken care of so fast you won't even recognize the place."

"Uh-huh." He started walking toward the wide hall. "Anyway. You can stay over here in the east wing."

Shelby was looking around the house as she followed him. From what she could see in the hallway, there were plenty of places for her to organize there, too.

"I've never lived in a house with wings."

He glanced down at her as she hurried up to walk at his side. "Yeah, this one's got all kinds of wings spreading out from here, the center. Every generation has added to it for nearly a hundred and fifty years."

"Wow." Shelby was impressed. She and her mother had been constantly on the move, from apartment to condo, to rental house. They'd never stayed anywhere longer than three years. So hearing about a family who had been in the same spot for more than a century filled her with a kind of envy she hadn't expected. That was roots, she told herself. Digging in, planting yourself and building your own world. One for your children and your children's children.

And that hunger for family, for roots, was what had prompted her to allow herself to be swept off her feet by Jared. Lesson to be learned there, Shelby told herself.

The walls in the house changed from log to stone and back again as they walked. The hardwood floor was shining, letting her know that the house was well cared for in spite of the clutter in the main room that had dribbled into the hallway. She imagined that Camilla had to work like a Trojan to keep everything as clean and beautiful as it was.

Caleb opened a door on the right and stepped inside. Shelby

was right behind him, but she stopped on the threshold to simply stare. She gasped because she couldn't help herself. The room was beautiful. Big, with a four-poster cherrywood bed covered by a dark blue-and-white star quilt. There were two end tables, a chest at the foot of the bed and a dresser on the far wall. Two bay windows offered a view of the front yard and the oaks lining the drive.

"This was my mom's room."

Shelby looked at him. "She didn't clutter this one."

"No," he said with a slow shake of his head. "She only did that in the main room and the kitchen. Anyway—" he pointed to a door "—there's a bathroom through there."

"Okay, thanks." Shelby walked farther into the room, laid one hand on the footboard and looked back at Caleb again.

How quickly things turned around, she thought. Only that morning, she'd been in the Goodman family home, dressing for her wedding. She'd felt trapped. Dreading the future she'd set for herself. Boxed into a corner and hadn't been able to see a way out.

Now, hours later, she was in a *real* ranch house with a gorgeous cowboy who'd rescued her from Jared's dragon of a mother. Yeah. Life could turn on you in an instant, so you'd better keep your seat belt on at all times.

"I've got work," he said, dragging her up and out of her thoughts. He tossed his sister-in-law's clothes onto the foot of the bed. "I'll be at the stable or in the first barn."

"Okay." He was so close she could smell the aftershave still clinging to his skin. It was like the woods, she thought. At night. With a full moon. Maybe skinny-dipping in a lake— Okay. She shut her brain off, then blurted, "Just where do *you* sleep?"

"In the west wing," he said. "On the other side of the great room we were in before."

"Oh. Okay." Probably not far enough for her peace of mind, but there wasn't much she could do about it.

One eyebrow lifted. "Problem?"

"No," she said, and then went on because she couldn't tell him that the problem was she was really attracted to him and wanted to see what it would be like to kiss him. Especially since just a couple hours ago, she was supposed to be marrying somebody else. For heaven's sake. It was like she was two people—and one of them was in serious trouble. "You already said you're not crazy and I don't suppose you'll be sneaking over here during the night."

His gaze swept her up and down, then locked on her eyes. "I'll try to control myself."

Frowning, she said, "Well that's flattering, thank you again."

"Do you really need me to tell you that you're beautiful?"

A flush of pleasure snaked through her even as she said, "Of course not."

"Good, because I won't be."

"Is that an insult?"

"Nope. It's a promise." Caleb nodded. "I try not to seduce women wearing wedding gowns. Sends the wrong message." He turned around and headed down the hall. He stopped halfway, looked back over his shoulder and said, "My housekeeper, Camilla, and my foreman, Mike, live in a house behind this one. Out the kitchen door and across the yard. To find the kitchen, just take the main hall straight back."

"Right." She wasn't hungry. Her stomach was still in knots of desperation mingled with relief. But she might go in search of a coffeepot later. And if she was staying—at least temporarily—she would have to meet Camilla and enlist her help. "And, um, thanks. Really."

He nodded and his gaze moved over her again. This time, his inspection was so slow, so thorough, Shelby felt heat flicker to life in her bloodstream.

Seriously, what was wrong with her? She had just run from one man and now she was getting all fizzy over another one? Maybe this was a breakdown. Some emotional outburst to relieve the tension she'd been living with for weeks.

He shrugged out of his suit jacket and slung it over one broad shoulder, hanging it from the tip of one finger. He tipped his hat back farther on his head and gave her one last, long look. Then he turned and walked away.

His long legs moved slow and easy and Shelby's gaze dropped to his butt. A world-class behind, she thought and swallowed hard. Whatever was happening to her, it hadn't hurt her eyesight any. Dragging in a deep breath, she fought to steady herself and hadn't quite succeeded by the time he disappeared around a corner.

Leaning back against the wall, Shelby sighed a little. *What was it about a cowboy?*

Rose was waiting at the oak the next day when Gus arrived. True to his nature, he was a good fifteen minutes late. Back in another life, when she was young and in love, his tardiness had always irked the hell out of her. But then he'd smile and kiss her and every thought in her head would just melt away.

But that was then.

"You're late."

"And you still like to point out the obvious," Gus said, taking a seat beside her on the bench he had built for the two of them nearly fifty years ago. He slapped one work-worn hand onto the wood, rough from surviving years of wind and rain and sun. "Nice to see this held up."

"You were always good with your hands," Rose agreed.

He glanced at her and one graying black eyebrow lifted. "You used to think so."

She flushed and was surprised by it. Who would have guessed a woman her age was even capable of blushing? Taking a breath, she smoothed her hands across the knees of her khaki slacks and found herself wondering when her hands had aged. How was it the years flew past so quickly?

A lifetime ago, she and Gus would meet here beneath this oak tree. On summer nights, the wind whispered through the leaves, the stars shone down on them like points of flame and it had been as if the two of them were alone in the universe. The present had been exciting and the future looked bright and shiny.

Then it all ended.

Frowning to herself, she looked out over the land. This part of her family ranch hadn't changed much in the last fifty years. There were still cattle grazing in the distance beneath a steely blue sky and the thick canopy of leaves overhead muted the sun's power and lowered the temperature a good ten degrees. And here she was again. With Gus.

"Why did you pick here to meet?"

"Because I knew it would bother you," he admitted with a shrug.

That stung. "At least you're honest about it."

"I put a great value on honesty," Gus said, his voice deep and meaningful as he stared into her eyes. "Always did."

And Rose knew what he was talking about. Once upon a time, she'd promised to love him forever. Then she'd later turned him away and told him she would never marry him. That she didn't love him and never had. And the lies had cost her, slicing at Rose's soul even as they tore Gus's heart apart while she was forced to watch.

"We're not here to talk about the past," she said, dragging air into tight lungs.

"No, we're damn sure not," he retorted. "So let's get to the point. You tell your grandson to keep his hands off my girl or there's going to be trouble."

Rose laughed shortly. "Don't use that 'lord of all you survey' voice on me. It won't work. And it won't work on Daniel, either." She lifted her chin and met her old lover glare for glare. "My grandson is made of tougher stuff than that. You won't scare him off, Gus, so don't bother trying."

"Well, what the hell do you want me to do, then?" He pushed up from the bench, walked a few feet through the dry brush, then spun about and came back to stand in front of her. "I assume you've got a plan. You always did have more ideas than you knew what to do with."

She sniffed a little, but stood up to meet him on her own two feet. He was still taller than her, but thanks to her Italian-made boots with a two-inch heel, she didn't have to crane her neck to meet his eyes.

"As it happens," she said, "I have been thinking about this."

"And?"

He was irritated and impatient, and she couldn't help but remember that he hadn't always been so anxious to get away from her.

"What we have to do is find each of them someone else."

"Oh," he said, laughing, "is that all?"

Rose scowled at him. "You might hear me out before you start mocking the whole idea."

"Fine." He folded his arms across his wide chest. "Tell me."

"I was thinking we could do something in Royal. An event. Something big. Something that would attract attention not just here, but in Houston, too."

"Uh-huh." Frowning, Gus said, "And what've you got in mind?"

"Well, nothing. Not yet. But you could throw out a few ideas you know." She tapped the toe of her boot against the ground. "This affects both of us, remember?"

"Wouldn't if you could just control your grandson," he muttered.

"Or if you could get your granddaughter to stop looking at Daniel with stars in her eyes," Rose countered.

His scowl deepened, but he gave her a grudging nod. "All right. So something that would involve the two of them, but throw them at other people."

"Exactly."

He scrubbed one hand across his jaw and Rose watched him,

seeing not just the powerful man he was now, but the man he had once been. The man who'd stolen her heart when she was only sixteen years old. The man she had thought she'd be with forever.

The man her father had stolen from her.

The irony of this situation wasn't lost on her. Her own father had kept her from the man she loved and now she was scheming to do the same thing to her grandson. But she didn't have a choice. Claytons and Slades were just not meant to be together.

"All right," Gus said, his voice low and deep and somehow intimate. "I'll do some thinking on this, too. We can meet up again in a few days. See what we come up with."

"Fine." She nodded, refusing to acknowledge, even to herself, that she was glad she'd be seeing Gus again.

They stood only a few feet apart, separated by fifty years of mistrust and pain. A soft wind rattled the leaves overhead and pushed through Rose's hair like a touch.

"Well, I've got to be getting back," Gus said abruptly, and Rose jolted as if coming up out of a trance.

"Of course. Me, too."

Nodding, Gus said, "So we meet here again in three days? Same time?"

"That works," she agreed and watched as he turned to walk to his truck. Rose felt a sting of regret, of sorrow and spoke up before she could rethink it. "Gus."

He stopped, turned and asked, "What is it?"

Looking into those eyes that were at once so familiar and so foreign, Rose said something she should have told him two years ago. "I'm sorry about Sarah."

His features went tight, his eyes cool at the reminder of his wife's death. Sarah had once been Rose's best friend, closer than a sister, but Rose had lost her, too, when she had broken things off with Gus. Then lost any chance of reaching out to her at all when she died two years ago.

"Thank you."

Rose took a step closer because she couldn't stand that shut-down look in his gaze. "I should have said something before, but I thought you wouldn't want to hear it from me."

He studied her for several heartbeats before saying softly, "Then you were wrong, Rose."

When he walked away again, she let him go.

Four

Four

For the next couple of days, Caleb did his best to avoid Shelby Arthur. It wasn't easy though because every time he turned around, there she was. She came out to the stables or the barn every so often with a question about one of his mother's "treasures."

He'd been ignoring the problem of his mom's collections since her death a couple of years ago. Hell, with the ranch to run, cattle to see to and the new oil leases to oversee, who had time to clear out furniture? Besides, Caleb didn't know anything about antiques and had no interest in learning.

But now, Shelby was determined to, as she put it, "earn her keep," so he was bombarded with questions daily. She had even enlisted the help of his housekeeper, Camilla, with the job of hauling furniture out to the front porch and covering everything with tarps.

Raina Patterson, the owner of Priceless, the antiques store at the Courtyard shops in Royal, had already been out to the ranch once. She'd looked everything over and bought a few pieces right away. Soon, there'd be a truck rolling up to take most of it away. But Shelby wasn't half-finished. She was working with Raina to catalog the smaller things Caleb's mother had been hoarding for years.

Caleb already knew his brother, Mitch, wasn't interested in their mother's things, and Meg had taken the few pieces she wanted to remember her mother-in-law by. So the road was clear to clean out the house—and Shelby seemed determined to get it done fast.

Leaning on the rail fence surrounding the corral, Caleb watched the woman working on the front porch of the house. Even from across the yard, Caleb felt that hot zip of something tantalizing shoot through his blood and settle in his groin. Shelby was still wearing Meg's jeans, and they were a little tight on her, which worked fine for him. She'd also asked Caleb for a couple of his T-shirts, and she was wearing one of them now.

The shirt was way too big, but she'd fixed that by tying it off under her breasts so that her midriff was bare and he could admire that swath of tanned skin and daydream about seeing more of her. Her curly auburn hair was pulled up into a ponytail that danced across her shoulders, and the wedding sandals she wore looked both out of place and enticing on her long, narrow feet.

Caleb gritted his teeth as Shelby bent in half to tug a table out the front door. Her butt looked good in those faded jeans and he'd give a lot to see it naked. To touch it. To stroke down the curves of her body and then to—

"She's a hard worker, you gotta give her that."

Squeezing his eyes shut briefly, Caleb willed away the tightness in his jeans and turned his head to watch his foreman, Mike Taylor, walk up to join him.

"Yeah, she's busy enough. Driving me nuts with all the questions, though."

"I can see that," Mike allowed, bracing both arms on the top fence rail. "But gotta tell you, Cam's happy as hell that Shelby's getting all that extra furniture out of the house. She's been grumbling about keeping it all dusted and clean."

Caleb nodded and turned his eyes back to Shelby. She'd moved on from tugging the furniture outside and now she was stretching to cover it all with yet another tarp. Of course, stretching like she was bared more of her midriff and had her extending one leg out like a ballet dancer.

Clearing his mind of every wicked thought currently gleefully tormenting him, he said only, "Will be nice to be able to walk through that room again."

"Uh-huh." Mike glanced at him, then grinned when he followed Caleb's gaze. "She's a good-looking woman."

"And you're a married man."

"Don't make me blind," Mike said, grinning. "Couldn't help but notice you noticing her."

"Is that right?" Caleb pushed off the fence and stuffed both hands into his jeans pockets. "If you've got so much extra time to spend 'noticing' things, maybe we should find you more work."

"You could do that," Mike said, teasing tone still in his voice, letting Caleb know he wasn't the least bit intimidated. "Or you could admit that woman's got you thinking."

"What I'm thinking is, we need to call the vet back out to check on the mare again."

"Yeah. You know, Cam tells me Shelby's not only beautiful, but she's smart, too. Hell, she has to be. Got herself out of marrying Jared Goodman."

"Got herself *into* it, too," Caleb reminded him. And in spite of the attraction he felt for her, that was the one thing that kept nibbling at his mind. Yeah, she was gorgeous and had a body that haunted him day and night. God knew she could talk the ears off a statue. And she wasn't afraid of work, so that was another point for her.

But bottom line was, she'd run out on her own wedding and left her groom—even if it was Jared Goodman—standing at the altar looking like a fool.

And that hit way too close to home for Caleb. He'd been in

Jared's position and he knew firsthand just how hard it was. Yes, Meg had run off the night before their wedding, so Caleb hadn't actually been caught standing in front of a roomful of people looking like a jackass. But close enough. How in the hell could he be with a woman who had done to a man what had been done to *him*?

Caleb had been keeping his finger on what was going on in Royal over the failed wedding. The Goodmans were handling all of this a lot differently than he had, of course. They'd spun the story around until Jared was a damn hero who'd cut a gold digger loose before she could marry him.

Shelby hadn't heard any of that yet and he had a feeling she'd be furious when she inevitably did. Most people in Royal weren't buying the story, but enough folks were that he'd heard all kinds of ugly rumors about Shelby when he'd gone into town the day before.

And though a part of him wanted to defend her, he'd kept quiet because hell, he didn't even *know* the woman who'd taken up residence in his house. All he knew for sure was that he wanted her more than he'd ever wanted anyone and he couldn't have her.

"True enough," Mike concurred. "She did agree to marry him. But the important part is, she was smart enough to see the mistake before she made it permanent."

Caleb turned his head to look at his friend. "And that makes it okay?"

Mike frowned, squinted into the afternoon sun and shook his head. "Didn't say that, Boss. But you've got to admit this situation isn't like yours was."

He hated it. Hated that everyone knew what had happened and could drag it up and toss it at him when he least expected it. But memories were long in Royal.

"This isn't about me."

"Isn't it?" Mike smiled now. "I've seen the way you watch

her." He laughed a little. "Hell, like you were watching her a minute ago—until she went back in the house."

Caleb shot his friend a hard look. "Since when is looking at a pretty woman a crime?"

"Since never. Yet, anyway," he added. "I'm just saying, she's single, you're single—what the hell, Boss?"

"It's complicated and you know it."

"I know you can untangle any knot if you want to bad enough."

Caleb ground his teeth together, took a long, deep breath and said, "Don't you have somewhere to be? Something to do?"

"Sure do. Just came over to tell you Scarlett's coming over later to give the mare another checkup."

Scarlett McKittrick was the town vet and there was nobody better with every animal—from puppies to cows to stallions. "Fine. Let me know when she gets here."

"You got it. Hey…" Mike jerked his head toward the long, oak-lined drive. "What's the sheriff doing here?"

Caleb turned his head and watched Nathan Battle's black Suburban approach the house. "Guess I'd better find out."

Rather than walk around and go through the gate, Caleb hopped the fence and was waiting when Nate brought his car to a stop and parked opposite the ranch house front door. The sun was hot, the air was still and dripping with humidity. And the look on Nate's face promised trouble.

"Hey, Caleb," he said as he climbed out of the car. "Shelby around?"

"Yeah. She's in the house. What's this about, Nate?"

Nathan tugged his hat off, swept one hand through his hair and grimaced. "The Goodman family's making some noise about suing Shelby."

"What?" Behind him, the front door opened, slammed shut and Shelby's quick footsteps sounded out in the stillness.

She moved up to stand beside Caleb and he could have sworn

he felt heat pumping from her body into his. Probably just the Texas sun—or at least that's what he was going to tell himself.

"They're going to sue me?" she asked, dumbfounded.

"Didn't say that, miss," Nate told her, turning his hat in his hands. "Said they're making noises about it."

"Sue me for what?"

Caleb was interested in hearing that, too.

"Well, miss," Nate winced and looked as though he wished he were anywhere but there. "They say defamation of character. That you've made Jared look bad in his hometown."

Caleb snorted. "Jared's looked bad since he was in grade school."

Giving Caleb a wry smile, Nathan nodded. "I know that, but his mother sure doesn't seem to."

"They can't sue me," Shelby whispered and turned her gaze up to Caleb. "Can they?"

Why in the hell he would feel like protecting her, he couldn't say. But there it was. In the couple of days he'd known her, he'd seen fight and spirit and joy and relief in her eyes. He didn't much care for the worry he saw there now.

"They can," he said firmly, "but they won't."

"I wish I could believe that," she said softly.

Nate and Caleb exchanged a long look that Shelby saw. "What? What is it you two know that I don't?"

Giving a sigh, Caleb turned to her. "To Margaret Goodman, the only thing that matters is how something *looks* to someone else. It's all about appearances with her. Margaret's not going to drag Jared into a court battle where every woman in town would testify on your behalf that he's a weasel and you were smart to back out."

"Oh, God. I'm sort of relieved and a little horrified." Taking a step backward, Shelby kept moving until the backs of her knees hit a rocking chair, then she dropped into it. "How could I have been so stupid?"

Caleb almost answered, then he realized she was talking to herself, complete with wild hand gestures and shakes of her head that sent her ponytail swinging like a pendulum in a tornado. All he could do was stand there and listen.

"I never saw it," she muttered. "But truthfully, I didn't want to see it, either. I wanted the fantasy. He said he was a cowboy. Who could turn down a cowboy?"

"Is she all right?" Nate asked, a worried frown etched into his forehead.

"Damned if I know," Caleb admitted, watching the woman as she continued her private rant. He thought maybe he should say something, but then she might not even hear him. She wasn't really paying any attention to him and Nate at all. It was as if she were all alone and she was having a good argument. With herself.

"He said he had a ranch, but he doesn't have a ranch. He's a *lawyer.* And he's afraid of his *mother.* But then, everyone's afraid of her. I was, wasn't I?"

"Shelby…" Caleb wasn't sure she could hear him.

She shook her head even harder and that dark red ponytail went swinging again. "Was I really that stupid? Or just lonely? He was cute, sure, but I think I just wanted to be in love so badly that I purposely didn't see what I should have seen if I'd been really looking, you know?"

"Uh…" Nate was still watching her as if she might explode. "Is she actually talking to us?"

"I don't think so," Caleb mused.

"Texas is so different from home, but I thought that would be a good thing, but is it? Oh, no. So now I don't even have any extra *underwear* and they want to sue me? How is that fair?"

Talking to Caleb, even while he kept a wary eye on Shelby, Nate said, "I did manage to get her purse back from Mrs. Goodman—"

"My *purse*?" Shelby shot from the chair and snatched it from

Nate's hand as soon as he pulled it out of his truck. She clutched the big, brown leather bag to her chest like a beloved child. Then she glanced inside. "Oh, my wallet. And my phone and lip gloss and my knife..."

"You have a knife?" Caleb asked.

"Doesn't everyone?" Shelby retorted, pulling a small Swiss Army knife out to hold up and show them. Then she looked past Nate toward his car as if she could find what she was looking for. "But what about the rest of my stuff? My suitcases? My clothes? Shoes?"

Nate grimaced. "Margaret says she's holding on to them for now."

"What?" She looked up at him. "Why?"

"Pure cussedness, I'd guess," Caleb muttered. Nate caught his comment and nodded.

"That's what it looks like to me, too."

"I have *one* pair of underwear," she snapped. "I can't live like that. Nobody could."

Nate's expression went from concerned to embarrassed and back again. But Caleb wasn't thinking about Nate. It was Shelby who had his full attention.

The disappointment on her face tore at Caleb. In the last couple of days, she'd been hanging on, doing what she had to, to cling to whatever part of her world was left. She'd been working hard the last few days, making sense of his late mother's collections and trying to bring some order to the house. It hadn't been easy.

And hell, Caleb could admit, at least to himself, that he hadn't helped any. He'd avoided her, ignored her presence as best he could, since the mere thought of her was enough to tighten his body to painful levels.

Hell, he was no fan of Jared Goodman, but he felt for the man. Caleb had been in Jared's position and it was hard to let go of that. But at the same time, he had to admit that Shelby had done what she thought was right. Had made a decision that couldn't have been an easy one and now she was still paying for it.

"Give Margaret a couple days to cool off some. I'll get your things back for you," Nate said in a soothing tone that seemed to ease some of the tightness from Shelby's features.

She smiled at Nate, then looked up at Caleb. He saw the shine in her eyes and hoped to God she wasn't going to cry. He hated it when women cried. Always left him feeling helpless, something he wasn't accustomed to.

She blinked the tears back, forced a smile he knew she wasn't feeling and said, "Well, at least I have my purse. I can go shopping for clothes and—"

"Yeah." Nate sighed and said, "About that. You'll have to use a credit card. Apparently Jared took you off the joint bank account, so your ATM card won't work."

"He can't do that," she argued, and all hints of tears evaporated in a rush of fury. "All of the money I got from the sale of my house is in that account. It's *my* money."

Caleb dropped one hand onto her shoulder and he felt her tremble. But he had the distinct impression that tremor was caused by pure rage. He couldn't blame her for it.

"Nate," Caleb said, "they can't do that. It's the same as stealing."

"You think I don't know that?" Shaking his head, the sheriff looked at Shelby. "I've already spoken to the judge and she says if you have proof of the deposit you made, she'll release the money to you."

"Do you?" Caleb asked. "Have proof, I mean."

"I do, but the problem is, it's in my suitcase." Her shoulders slumped in defeat. "And the suitcase is at the Goodmans' house."

"I'll go over there," Caleb said. "Get her things."

"You'll stay out of it," Nate warned, aiming a steely look at Caleb. "Margaret's already half-convinced that *you're* the reason Shelby ran out on Jared."

"Me?" He was honestly stunned.

"Him?" Shelby echoed.

Caleb scowled at Nathan. "How the hell did Margaret come to that?"

"Shelby ran from the wedding straight to you." Nate shrugged helplessly. "You drove off with her. Now she's living here in your house."

Caleb bit back a curse. Damn it, he'd spent the last four years trying to live down a rich gossip vein and now he'd opened himself up to a brand-new one. Royal would be buzzing and though it was irritating as hell, it didn't really bother him as much as he would have expected it to.

Maybe it was because Shelby was standing there beside him looking outraged. Her eyes were flashing and there were twin spots of color in her cheeks. A hot Texas wind kicked up out of nowhere and sent those dark red curls of hers flying and all in all she made a picture designed to bring a man to his knees.

"But that's ridiculous," Shelby argued. "All he did was *help* me."

"Doesn't matter to Margaret," Nate said, then turned his attention back to Caleb.

"Yeah, I don't care what Margaret Goodman has to say and most people in Royal feel the same." Not completely true. He did hate the thought of being the subject of speculation and more gossip. But he didn't give a good damn what Margaret Goodman thought of him. Caleb looked at Shelby. "Whatever gossip springs up around this won't last long." He hoped. "The town's wagging tongues will move on to something more interesting."

"Just keep your distance from the Goodmans," Nathan said. "I'll go talk to Simon. See what I can do about getting your things, Shelby. If I have trouble with it, we can always email your bank and have them send you a copy of everything."

"Right. Okay. Yes. Good idea. Thanks I can do that. I'll do

it tomorrow. Just in case." She kept nodding and Caleb figured it was just reaction. A hell of a lot of information dumped on her in just a couple of minutes. And not much of it was good.

He couldn't help but wonder what she was thinking. Her eyes gave nothing away, but thankfully they weren't filled with unshed tears anymore, either. And he had to admit it was worrying how quiet she'd gotten all of a sudden. He'd become used to her just talking his ears off.

He glanced at his friend. "Thanks, Nate."

"Sure. I'll be in touch. Shelby," he added, "we'll get this all straightened out."

She only nodded at him, making Caleb wonder again. He never would have believed he'd actually *miss* her rambling conversations and monologues.

The sheriff got back in his car and drove away, leaving the two of them alone on the porch.

Shelby was still petting that brown leather bag lovingly and holding it as if it were a life vest keeping her afloat in a churning sea. She didn't say anything, but Caleb could guess what she was thinking. Her world was a damn mess and for a woman with an organized soul like Shelby, that had to be hard to take.

"Well," she finally said with a shrug, "I guess I should get back to work."

No complaints. No cussing. No kicking the porch railing in sheer frustration. Just acceptance and moving on. Damned if Caleb didn't admire her. Shelby Arthur was an impressive woman. She'd had the world tipped on her again and she wasn't letting it drag her down. He'd never known anyone who bounced back from bad news as quickly and completely as she did. Maybe that was why he heard himself make an offer he hadn't planned on. "The work can wait."

"What? Why?" She looked up at him, so he was staring into her eyes when he spoke again.

"How about I take you shopping?"

The flash of pleasure in those green eyes of hers stirred simmering embers inside him into blistering hot coals that threatened to immolate him.

It would be a hell of a burn.

Five

Caleb didn't take her to Royal and Shelby was grateful. She knew the small town was still gossiping about her and that catastrophe of a wedding. If they'd been in Royal, everyone would have been staring. Whispering. There was already talk and if people had seen the two of them together, that would have only fueled the fire. Not to mention there would have been a chance of running into some of the Goodman family.

But in Houston, no one knew her. No one cared that she and Caleb were walking together down a busy street. The only people looking at them were women, taking quick, approving glances at Caleb. He didn't seem to notice, but Shelby did. And if truth be told, she'd been sending him quite a few of those glances herself.

He was wearing black jeans and boots, a white shirt with a black blazer tossed over it. That gray hat he always wore was pulled down low on his forehead, shadowing his eyes and making him look...fantastic. The man was so sexy, her imagination was constantly fueled just by the thought of him.

There. She'd admitted it to herself. Caleb Mackenzie was like a walking sex dream. That slow drawl of his rumbled along a woman's skin like a touch and when his eyes fixed and held on her, Shelby felt as though he was looking right down into her soul. It was a little unsettling and at the same time thrilling in a way she'd never known before. Then there were the boots. And his long legs and the way jeans clung to them. His chest was broad and his hands were big and calloused from years of hard work and she really wanted to know what those hands felt like on her skin.

Then, as if he wasn't already droolworthy, there was the shopping. He could have gone to a bar or something to wait for her, but he'd walked with her. Kept her company and offered opinions—whether she wanted them or not—on the clothes she'd purchased. The only time he'd left her alone was in the lingerie department and she wished he had stayed. Having him watch while she picked out bras and underwear would have been…exciting. Which was just ridiculous, she lectured herself. She had no business fantasizing about *another* cowboy so soon after turning her whole world inside out for a would-be cowboy.

Shelby slapped her forehead. She must be losing her mind. Had to be the strength of the Texas sun broiling down and baking her brain.

"Is there a reason you're hitting yourself in the head?"

She glanced up at him and instantly, her stomach did a flip-flop and her heartbeat skittered a little. Not that she could tell him that. Heatstroke. That had to be it.

"Um, no," she said. "Just wishing I'd picked up a pair of sandals at the last store."

Oh, good one.

He shook his head. "The ones you bought aren't enough?"

"Right. Right." Idiot. Really. She *had* bought a pair of sandals. God, she was a terrible liar.

The sidewalk was bustling. Businessmen, teenagers, women out with friends to do some window-shopping or just hurrying to work. The city was loud and crowded and the sizzling sun ricocheted off the cement and slammed back into you just for the hell of it. And Shelby was loving every minute.

In the month or so she'd been in Texas, she'd gotten used to the small town feel of Royal, and she loved it, really. But there was an excitement and a buzz about being in a big city and a part of her had missed it. Especially right this minute.

She was wearing a brand-new dress that was sky blue, summer weight with spaghetti straps and a full skirt that fell to just above her knees. The three-inch taupe heels she wore with it were perfect and it was good to feel...pretty, again. She was so tired of borrowed jeans and T-shirts.

"Most big cities are pretty much alike you know," she said, pitching her voice to be heard over a blasting car horn.

"That right?"

"Well, that's what I've heard people say. And I actually believed it until today. I thought, how different can Houston be from Chicago?" She grinned. "Turns out, *very* different."

"The hats?" he asked, showing off the half smile that turned her insides into jelly all too briefly.

"Oh, absolutely," she said, "but it's more than that, too. Houston's busy and loud and people are racing around to get somewhere else. But even with all that, it's more...relaxed. More, casual somehow."

Caleb stepped out of the way of a businessman in a hurry and steered Shelby to one side with his hand at the small of her back.

She took a breath and held it. It didn't mean anything, she knew. It had been just a simple, polite gesture. Yet, the touch of his hand sent arrows of heat dipping and diving through her body. Her physical reactions to him were getting stronger, harder to ignore.

Every time they were anywhere near each other, it felt like a fuse had been lit and sparks were flying. She couldn't be sure if he felt it, too, but she was guessing he did because he was actively ignoring her. And she'd let him, figuring it was best all the way around.

After all, she was just out of one relationship and she wasn't looking for another. But no matter how much she ignored Caleb during the day, her dreams were full of him. Every time she closed her eyes, there he was. It seemed her subconscious was all too eager to explore possibilities.

"I want to say thank you again, for everything, but it feels like I'm always thanking you," she said abruptly in an attempt to drag her mind out of the bedroom.

"Yeah, you don't have to." He took her arm and steered her around yet another businessman—this one in an ill-fitting suit yelling into his cell phone, oblivious to anyone else on the sidewalk.

"Thanks," she said, then added, "oops."

His mouth quirked and Shelby silently congratulated herself. Honestly, when she coaxed that half smile out of the man she felt as if she'd been awarded a prize.

"This is great," she said, clutching two bags from local shops. "And oh, boy, am I looking forward to wearing fresh underwear. It's really a pain washing my one pair out every night and hanging them on a towel bar to dry. I was afraid I was going to wear out the fabric."

Okay, probably shouldn't be talking about her underwear.

"And shoes. I love my shoes. Especially those boots we found. I feel very Texan," she said, rattling the bag containing the boots.

"I don't think you can call hot-pink cowboy boots *Texan*."

"I bought them here, so… Texas."

"You bought *everything* here," he mused, holding up the three bags he was carrying.

She thought about everything in the shopping bags and smiled to herself, though she knew that when her credit card showed up, she'd probably have a heart attack. But that was a worry for another day. At least she didn't feel homeless *and* clothesless anymore. Her world was still up in the air. Her ex-about-to-be-mother-in-law was still making trouble for her.

She couldn't touch any of her own money, but damn it, she had new underwear.

"I really love this," she said, looking around the busy street and the high-rises surrounding them. "It's nice, getting away from Royal for a while."

"The city's all right, once in a while," he agreed, frowning when a bus stopped at the sidewalk and belched out a cloud of dark smoke. "But Royal's better, even if small towns are hard to take sometimes."

"Oh, I like the town and most of the people I've met but I hate knowing they're talking about me. I mean, back in Chicago, I was just a face in the crowd." She looked around at the city and the thousands of people. "Like I am here. I wanted the small town life, you know? Roots. Home. Family. That's mostly why I agreed to marry Jared, I think. I wanted it so badly, I didn't notice that the man offering it to me wasn't real. Wasn't worth it."

A woman pushed past them, shoving Shelby into Caleb and he took her arm to steady her before letting her go again. "Was it really so important to you?"

"Spoken like a man who's always had a home. A place." They stopped at the corner and she laid one hand on his forearm. "My mother raised me on her own after my father died. We were happy, but we never stayed. Anywhere."

Caleb's eyes met hers and she kept talking, wanting him to understand why she'd done what she had. "I always wanted a real home, you know? A place where people would know me, where I'd belong." Her hand dropped away and she looked past him, at the busy street. "When Jared came along, I think I convinced myself I loved him because I *did* love what he represented."

A sea of people walked past them, and neither of them moved—or even noticed.

"Why'd you wait till the last minute to walk out?" Caleb watched her, waiting for her reply. "You were in Royal a month before the wedding."

"I know." She sighed and started walking again. In her heels, they were nearly eye to eye when she glanced at him. Caleb moved up alongside her. The sun was hot on her back and she was squinting against the glare. In the bustle and noise of the city, she kept talking. "I felt...trapped. I'd said yes already and so I let Jared's mother steamroll me. It was easier to go along than to try to stop what I had put into motion, you know?"

"Not really," he said.

She gave him a wry smile. "Yeah, I don't really understand it now, either. But the day of the wedding, I just suddenly *knew* I couldn't go through with it. Couldn't let one lie become a lifetime lie. So I ran."

She glanced at him and was relieved to see him nod as if he got it, though his mouth was a grim line. Shelby didn't know why she cared what Caleb Mackenzie thought of her, but she did. Talking about the wedding, the Goodman family, all brought back what the sheriff had said to her earlier and as his words replayed in her mind, she worriedly chewed at her bottom lip. Shelby hadn't wanted to make a big deal about it at the time, but the more she thought about it, the more nervous she felt. "What if the Goodmans do sue me?"

"They won't."

She wished she felt as sure as he sounded. "We don't know that."

"Yes, we do." He stopped at an intersection along with what seemed like half the city as they waited for the light to change. Caleb glanced down at her and though his eyes were shadowed by the brim of his hat, she could read the reassurance there. "Simon Goodman's a lawyer—and honestly, not all that good a one. He's not going to start up a court case he's not sure he can win."

Sounded reasonable. And yet... "But like you said. Small town, people know him and don't know me, why wouldn't he win?" Shelby smiled at a baby in a stroller.

"Mainly because people *do* know him," Caleb told her as the light changed and they moved with the herd. "Know him and don't much like him."

"Isn't he *your* lawyer?" Shelby hurried her steps to keep up with his much longer stride. Even on a crowded sidewalk, Caleb walked like a man with a purpose. Determined. Unstoppable. Was there anything sexier? *Back on track, Shelby.* "I mean, Cam told me that's why you were at the wedding in the first place."

"Yeah," he admitted. "He is and that's my fault. He was my father's lawyer. I just never changed. Should have. Just got busy."

"Wow. Five sentences in a row."

"What?"

"The stoic cowboy spoke—almost at length," she said, tipping her head up to look into his eyes. It was weird, but now that she'd told him why she'd come to marry Jared and why she hadn't, she felt...free. Shelby had never been good with secrets. They always came back to bite her in the butt. So having the truth out there and Caleb's seeming understanding, lifted a weight off her shoulders.

He looked down at her and his mouth quirked again. Score.

"I must be a good influence on you," she said, giving him a wide smile. "I bet until I came around, nobody at the ranch talked much."

"Nobody comes close to you, that's for damn sure," he muttered.

"Isn't that nice?" He didn't mean it as a compliment but she was taking it as one. When he smiled again, as if they were sharing the joke, Shelby's heart gave a quick flutter.

"Caleb!" A feminine voice called his name and beside her, Shelby sensed him flinch in reaction.

They stopped, let the pedestrian crowd flow past, and then Shelby watched what was left of the crowd part, like a scene from a movie, to allow a drop-dead-gorgeous woman rush forward.

Her hair was long and blond, her eyes were blue and she

wore a sleek, black dress that hugged every voluptuous curve. Black heels completed the outfit and Shelby, despite her pretty new dress and shoes, suddenly felt like a country bumpkin. Whatever that was.

"Caleb, you look fantastic!" The blonde hurled herself into Caleb's arms and even Shelby caught the cloud of floral scent that clung to her.

"Marta," Caleb said, extricating himself as gently as possible. "Good to see you."

To Shelby, it looked as though he was trying to get away from an octopus and he didn't look very happy about it. Which really made her feel better. Although why this little scene should bother her at all was beyond her. She and Caleb weren't a thing. She'd only known him a short time. And yet…logic didn't seem to have a lot to do with what she was feeling at the moment.

"God, it's been forever," Marta exclaimed, stepping back, but keeping a tight grip on one of Caleb's hands as if afraid he might try to escape.

"Yeah," he said, "I've been busy."

She playfully slapped at his chest. "You and those cows of yours."

"Cattle," he corrected, but Marta obviously didn't care.

"How long are you in the city for?" She gave her hair a playful toss and pouted prettily. All the while continuing to ignore Shelby's presence completely. "We've got to have dinner, Caleb, do some catching up. You can come to my place and—"

"Sorry can't do it," Caleb said, interrupting the flow of words and startling Marta into temporary silence.

Caleb looked down at Shelby. "We've got to be getting back, isn't that right, darlin'?"

Stunned, Shelby could only stare into those icy-blue eyes of his. His gaze was fixed on hers and she could see that he wanted her to play along with him. For his own reasons, he wanted to get rid of Marta and that worked for Shelby. She smiled, letting him know that she was on board, ready for whatever he had in mind. Briefly, he let his forehead rest against hers as if in solidarity.

"That's right, honey," she said softly.

Smiling then, Caleb draped his free arm around her shoulders, pulled her in tight to his side and dropped a kiss on top of her head. "Shelby, honey, this is Marta. An old friend."

"Really. How old?" she asked innocently, and watched Marta's eyes flash and narrow.

"Marta, this is Shelby and we're together now, so…"

The blonde gave Shelby a quick inspection and judging by the look in her eyes, wasn't impressed. Then Shelby wrapped her arm around Caleb's waist and rested her head against his chest in a clearly proprietary gesture. A few seconds later, the blonde surrendered.

"Well, all right, then, if that's how it is."

"Good to see you, though," Caleb said.

"And I just love meeting my honey's old friends," Shelby added, snuggling in even closer to Caleb.

"Yes, I can see that," Marta said, amused now. "Well, you two enjoy your day in the city. Caleb, you've got my number if things change."

"They won't be changing," Shelby assured her. A part of her really wished that were true.

"Right. Well, I'll be getting along to my lunch appointment. Still, it was good to see you, Caleb."

"Yeah. You, too."

Marta walked away and they watched her go. Caleb's arm was still around Shelby's shoulders as she tipped her face up to look into his eyes. "You know those boobs are fake, right?"

He laughed and gave her a hard squeeze before letting her go. "You can trust me on this. They're real."

"Hmm." People streamed past them like a creek rushing past rocks in its way. "You know what? After all this shopping, the least I can do is buy you a late lunch. Or an early dinner." She glanced around. "Is there a diner or a burger place around here?"

Caleb shook his head. "I think we can do better than that."

"Mr. Mackenzie," the hostess at the Houston Grille said, giving him a wide smile. She had jet-black hair cut into a wedge that hugged her cheekbones. "Good to see you again."

"Thanks, Stella," Caleb replied, looking into the main dining room. Windows fronting on the busy street boasted dark red awnings over them, giving the diners a nice view without being blinded by the sun. The atmosphere was muted, with weeping violins at a whispered volume pumped through speakers mounted discreetly on the walls. Tables were covered with white linen and the waitstaff moved across the floor like ballet dancers, with grace and efficiency. "Is my regular booth available?"

"It sure is." She picked up two menus, smiled at Shelby and then stopped when Caleb asked her to keep their shopping bags for them. Once they were stowed, Stella preceded them to a booth with a wide view of downtown Houston.

Shelby slid across the maroon leather bench seat and Caleb followed right after. "Can we get a couple of iced teas as soon as possible?"

Stella said, "Right away," and moved off.

Shelby's eyes were wide as she took in the restaurant before turning to him. "This place is beautiful."

"Why are you whispering?"

She laughed and he wondered why the sound of it should affect him as much as it did.

"It feels like I should. Everything is so dignified and well, quiet."

"You'll have to come back on a Saturday night. It's a lot louder then." He nodded to the waiter who brought them their drinks, then looked at Shelby again. She really was beautiful. That new dress of hers hugged her figure and highlighted everything he wanted to touch.

"This has been a really terrific day, Caleb. Thanks for bringing me."

"Stop saying thank you."

She shrugged, took a sip of her tea and set it back down again. "If you want me to stop saying it, then you need to stop doing nice things for me."

A waiter came to the table then. "Are you ready, Mr. Mackenzie?"

Turning to Shelby, he asked, "How hungry are you?"

"Very."

"Okay. Trust me with the order?"

She looked at him and those grass-green eyes fascinated him as they always did. "Sure."

Nodding, he looked at the waiter. "We'll each have the strip steak, rare. Cheese potatoes and the bacon asparagus."

"Right away." The waiter hurried off and Caleb looked back to Shelby.

"Is there anything else you want to buy while we're in the city?"

"No," she said, her fingers delicately tracing the prongs of the sterling silver fork in front of her. "This will do me until I get my own clothes back from the Goodmans." She looked at him. "How much longer do you think?"

Irritation spiked. Caleb had been raised to do the right thing. Always. To have the Goodmans treating Shelby this way, holding back her property from her, just for spite, annoyed the hell out of him. Especially since Nate was convinced that if Caleb did anything, he'd only make the situation worse.

Caleb didn't much care for *waiting*.

"No telling, really," he finally answered. "But Nate's a good man and an even better sheriff. He'll take care of this and get it all sorted out as soon as he can."

"That's good," she said.

"I hear a *but* in there," Caleb pointed out, his gaze fixed on her. The woman held his attention no matter what she was doing.

And now her eyes looked anxious and the way she was chewing at her bottom lip sent tugs of heat to his groin even while he wondered what the hell she was worried about.

She smiled. "*But*, I can't just stay at your ranch forever. That's not right. I'm nearly finished clearing out your mother's collection and when that's done…"

He didn't want her to leave. What the hell? Caleb told himself it was because he was used to having her around. But the truth was more unsettling. He simply *wanted* her. There. In his house. In his bed. Under him. Over him.

He wanted Shelby Arthur like nothing else ever in his life.

But he could hardly admit to that. "Don't worry about it," he said dismissively. "Stay as long as you need to. There's plenty more in the house that could use organizing. Talk to Cam about it. In fact, have her show you the attic when you're finished with the kitchen and great room."

"The attic?"

"There are things up there dating back more than a hundred years." This was, at least, the truth. "It'd be good to get it sorted out, with the family papers and such filed properly."

Her eyes gleamed and he smiled to himself. The woman was hell on wheels when it came to straightening things out. Heck, if it kept her in his house, he'd create new chaos somewhere.

"Hey, Caleb."

He turned and smiled, holding out one hand to the man greeting him. Reese Curran, best horse trainer Caleb had ever seen and now married to Lucy Navarro Bradshaw. Just a few months ago, Reese had come home to Royal and it hadn't taken long for he and Lucy to find each other again. It was good to see Lucy happy again. "Reese. Nice to see you. Lucy," he added, with a nod to the woman standing beside the tall, lanky cowboy.

"I'm so glad to see you," Lucy said, then turned her gaze to Shelby and held out one hand. "You must be Shelby. Good to finally meet you."

"Thanks."

"Shelby, this is Reese and Lucy Curran. They run a horse rescue operation at Paradise Farms, on the McKittrick ranch. Not far outside of town." Caleb looked at his friend. "So what're you two doing in the city?"

"Shopping," Lucy crowed, with a grin as she wrapped an arm around her husband's waist to give him a squeeze.

"Lot of that going around," Caleb mused with a sly smile at Shelby. She grinned back at him and a fork of heat sliced right through him.

"Yes, but we're shopping for maternity clothes," Lucy said with a delighted smile.

"Well, congratulations." Caleb shook Reese's hand again, then pushed out of the booth to give Lucy a quick hug. He'd known Lucy's family his whole life, so Lucy was like a little sister to him. He'd watched her suffer when she'd lost her first husband, the father of her boy, Brody. He'd seen her worry over her brother Jesse and her step-brother Will when they'd recently tackled some hard family issues. And he'd celebrated with her when she and Reese had found each other not too long after Jesse and Will had both found loves of their own.

"That's wonderful," Shelby said as Caleb settled back into the booth.

"It really is," Lucy agreed. "And it's one more reason I'm glad to meet you. Cam told me what a whiz you are at organizing things. I'd really like you to come out to the ranch and take a look at our plans for the new house Reese is building. Brody needs a big-boy space all his own and I'd love to get your opinions on what to do for the baby's room."

Eyes sparkling at the idea of a new challenge, Shelby said, "I'd love to."

"Great." Lucy grinned at her husband again. "As soon as you get some time, come on over to the ranch. I'm always there."

"Because she doesn't trust anyone but herself to take care of the horses," Reese said wryly.

"Wrong, I trust you." When he quirked an eyebrow at her, she added, *"Now."*

Their food arrived, and Reese and Lucy said their goodbyes. Once the waiter was gone, too, Caleb looked at Shelby. "See? No reason for you to think about leaving. Reese and Lucy's place is close to mine. So looks like you'll be busy for a while, yet."

"It does, doesn't it?" Satisfied, she turned to her meal and was unaware that Caleb watched her silently for a long minute, lost in his own thoughts.

Later that night, Caleb was restless. Maybe it was seeing Marta again. He hadn't seen her in more than six months and truth be told he hadn't given her another thought since the last time he'd walked out of her apartment. All they'd shared was sex. Great sex, but nothing more than that. So if he hadn't thought about her in all this time, why would seeing her today make him feel like he was about to jump out of his skin?

"Because it's not Marta," he muttered. "And it's not seeing Reese and Lucy so damn happy and now pregnant on top of it."

No, it was the memory of holding Shelby. The feel of her. The smell of her. The touch of her hand at his waist and the feel of her head against his chest. They'd left Houston soon after a late lunch and the minute they got back to the ranch, Caleb had dived into work to keep his body so busy his mind wouldn't have time to dredge up images to torture him with.

That hadn't worked.

Hell, nothing had. He hadn't been able to stop thinking about Shelby all evening. Caleb had even skipped dinner because he hadn't trusted himself to sit across a table from her and not make a move. So now he was restless *and* hungry.

He walked through the silent house without making a sound. Caleb didn't bother to hit the light switches. He could have found his way around blindfolded. The kitchen was dark, as always, once Cam had cleared up and gone home. There was just moonlight sliding through the windows, casting a pale glow over everything. He noticed as he walked into the huge room that Shelby had made some headway in the kitchen, too.

His mother had collected kitchen appliances. Antiques, new, didn't matter. She had teapots, kettles, coffeepots, mixers and so many bowls she could have opened her own pottery shop. His mom had been like a magpie—if something shiny caught her eye, she had wanted it.

But Caleb didn't want to think about his mother—or Shelby. He just wanted to grab some cold fried chicken and then try to get some sleep before morning.

He was halfway to the fridge when he heard a voice from the eating nook by the bay window. "I think I should tell you, you are not alone."

"Shelby." Caleb stopped dead, glanced over his shoulder and spotted her in a slant of moonlight.

"Good guess," she said. Her head tipped to one side, spilling that beautiful hair of hers across one shoulder. "Got it in one."

"Why are you sitting here in the dark?" *Why are you in the kitchen*, he asked silently.

"The moonlight's pretty and light enough." She shrugged. "What're you doing sneaking around in the dark?"

"I don't sneak," he corrected and suddenly felt like an idiot for having done just that. What had it come to when he slipped through a quiet house in the dark to avoid seeing the woman driving him crazy? "Besides, this is my house and—" He sniffed the air. "Do you have the chicken?"

"Yes and it's great." She pushed a plate of chicken into the middle of the table. "Cam is a fantastic cook. Did you know she went to a culinary school in Park City, Utah, when she was a teenager? She told me stories about some of the chefs she met there and you wouldn't believe—"

"Stop." He held up one hand. "Just stop talking. I beg you. I came down here for some damn chicken before I sleep."

"No problem. Get a plate."

"Don't need a plate."

"Yeah, you do." She scooted off the bright blue bench seat and hurried past him to a cupboard.

He watched her go and swallowed the groan that rose up to choke him. She was wearing a tiny tank top and a pair of low-slung cotton shorts that just barely managed to cover her crotch. He couldn't tell what color they were. The moonlight disguised that. Could have been white or gray or yellow. And it didn't matter.

Her long legs looked silky and all too tempting. Her curly red hair fell loose around her shoulders, sliding back and forth with her every movement and he couldn't seem to look away.

"Here. Now sit down." She passed him again and he caught her scent. Unlike Marta's heavy floral perfume, Shelby smelled like summer. Fresh and clean and cool. She set the plate and a fork and napkin down opposite where she was seated. "I've got Cam's potato salad out, too. I wasn't hungry at dinner but a little while ago, I realized I could probably eat one of your cows, hooves and all, so...here we are."

"Yeah." He sat down and tried not to think of just how lovely she looked in moonlight. How close she was. All he had to do was stretch one arm across the table and he could take her hand, smooth his thumb across her palm, feel her pulse race.

She leaned forward and her thin tank top dipped slightly, allowing him an all too brief glimpse of her breasts. Somewhere there was a god of lust with a nasty sense of humor. He'd spent most of the afternoon and evening avoiding her and now she was here and he was more than tempted.

"Thanks again for taking me to Houston today."

Burying another groan, Caleb took a bite of chicken and scooped up some of Cam's famous potato salad. "Stop thanking me."

"I tried, but I can't seem to," Shelby said, taking a sip from the water bottle in front of her. "So you'll just have to get used to it."

Caleb sighed, filled his plate and then stood to open the fridge and grab a bottle of water. In the slash of bright light that lit up the room, Shelby looked far more delicious than the chicken he'd come in here for. Her nipples were outlined against the thin fabric of her tank top and that wonderful hair of hers fell in tumbled curls across her shoulders. Her green eyes were clear and bright and locked on him.

He let the door swing shut, cutting off the light, slamming the room into darkness again.

"I was avoiding you tonight." His eyes adjusted quickly to the dim glow of the moonlight sliding through the window she sat beside.

"Yeah," she said softly. "I picked up on that when you didn't come in until after dark. Why do you think I'm here now?"

"You set a trap?"

"Oh, *trap* is a hard word."

Maybe, but he had the distinct impression it was accurate, too. "What was the plan?"

"Do I need one?"

No. All she had to do was sit there, staring at him, looking like a promise. Something stirred inside him, and Caleb did his best to smother it. Hell, he was the one who needed a damn plan.

She was talking again. Of course.

"I knew you had to get hungry at some point. We ate a long time ago."

"Oh, I am." He stared directly into her eyes so she could see he wasn't talking about the damn chicken now.

"Me, too," she whispered.

Everything in Caleb twisted into painful knots. "This is a bad idea."

"Oh, no doubt," she agreed, but she didn't look away.

Caleb had the opening there. The chance to back the hell off. This was the Godzilla of bad ideas. And that still wasn't enough to sway him from taking what he wanted.

"Damn it, Shelby," he ground out.

"Oh," she said softly, "you're talking too much."

He choked out a harsh laugh, took two long steps, pulled her to her feet and kissed her like he'd wanted to for days.

Since the moment she'd run into his arms while escaping her wedding.

Six

She felt even better against him *now*, Caleb thought.

Her arms snaked around his neck, she leaned into him and opened her mouth under his. Their tongues twisted and tangled together. Breath came fast and hard. Hearts pounded, blood boiled and need rose up, quickening with each passing second.

Caleb's hands moved up and down her back, tracing her spine with his fingertips. Then he swooped down again, his hands settled on her butt and squeezed, pressing her to his aching groin in a futile effort to ease the throbbing within. She sighed in response and that soft sound of surrender crashed down on him.

Caleb groaned, lifted her off her feet and spun her around until her back was against the wall. Breaking their kiss, he looked into her eyes and saw passion glittering in the moonlight.

"Don't stop," she said, her voice a whispered plea.

"Won't," he promised and slid one hand down the front of her shorts.

She gasped and tipped her head back against the wall as he

touched her. Damp heat welcomed him and she hooked her legs around his hips, and arched into him. He stroked her center, driving them both a little crazy. She rocked her hips into his hand and let her breath pant from her lungs. When he pushed one finger, then two, deep inside her, she gasped and shuddered in his grasp.

"Caleb!" Her body trembled and her eyes closed briefly as she savored what he was doing to her.

He caressed her, inside and out, his thumb brushing over the heart of her, and as he watched her react, his body tightened to the point of agony. He hadn't wanted this to happen. Hadn't wanted to start something between them that would lead them both exactly nowhere. And now he couldn't imagine *not* touching her. She was driving him wild with desire. Had been from the moment he first saw her.

Caleb wanted her so much he could hardly breathe. He wanted—*needed*—to slide his body into hers, to feel her surround him and take him in. Darkness filled the room but between them there was light and heat and a bone-searing desire.

Touching her was filling him up and tearing a hole in him at the same time. It was good, but it wasn't enough. He needed more. Wanted more. She was a craving like nothing he'd ever known before and he poured his own desire into touching her more deeply, thoroughly, until her breath came short, fast. Until her body coiled in expectation. Until release slammed into her and she shook with the force of it. Until he held her in the darkness and felt her heart race against his.

At last, she took a long, deep breath, looked up into his eyes and grinned. "Wow."

Caleb stared at her for a second or two, then choked out a laugh. "You surprise me."

Tipping her head to one side, she asked, "Why? Did you expect regret? No. How could I be sorry *that* happened?"

He eased her onto her feet, letting her body slide against his, just because he was apparently a masochist and needed a bit more torture. Now that the initial frenzy of hunger had faded and he didn't have his hands full of her, Caleb could think clearly again. Beyond what he wanted to what he knew, so he took a long step backward and shook his head.

"This isn't going to happen."

"It already did," she said. "And at least from my point of view, it was really good."

He smiled briefly and wondered what it was about this woman that she could drive him nuts one second and make him laugh the next. She was honest and strong and funny and so damn hot, she was keeping him twisted into knots. Knots that couldn't be undone because there was nothing here for him. Nothing more than giving her a place to stay until she got her life back. Then it was done. He didn't need another woman in his life. Especially one who, like Meg, had made the choice to run from a situation rather than face it.

"Yeah, well," he muttered thickly, because each word cost him, "good time's over."

"What's going on, Caleb?" she asked, reaching out to him.

He grabbed her hand, squeezed it, then let her go. "Nothing, Shelby. That's the point."

Because he didn't trust himself to leave if he stayed even one more second, Caleb grabbed the damn plate of chicken and left her there in the dark.

Rose took extra care with her hair and makeup before her next meeting with Gus. Not for his benefit, of course. It was a small vanity to know that she'd kept her looks but for a few stubborn wrinkles she tried to ignore and the subtle gray streaks in her hair.

Her cream-colored slacks were matched with a butter-yellow shirt and a pair of light brown boots. The summer heat was at a blistering level, which made her grateful for the shade of the old oak she sat beneath. While she waited for Gus—who was late again—she checked her email. When she saw one from her grandson, Daniel, she frowned.

Gran,
Meeting a friend for dinner. Will be out late.
See you tomorrow,
Daniel

"A friend," she mused and tapped her well-manicured finger against the now darkened screen. She knew very well whom he was meeting. Alexis Slade. Did he think she was blind? Or too old to recognize the signs a man gave off when he'd found a woman he was interested in? She remembered all too well how Gus had once looked at *her*.

Her husband, Ed, never had, but then why would he? He'd been handpicked by her father to be her husband because Ed had been willing to take the Clayton surname and keep the family line going. Romance had had nothing to do with it.

Sliding her phone back into her purse, Rose looked up when she heard Gus approaching. He was still tall, built tough and strong, and just watching him walk stirred things inside her better left unstirred. Standing, she said, "You're late. Again."

"Good to see you, too, Rosie."

The familiar name took her breath away for a second. No one but Gus had ever called her *Rosie* and he hadn't done it in close to fifty years. His expression let her know that he was as surprised as she was that he'd said it now.

He scrubbed one hand across his jaw, cleared his throat and said, "This thing with Alexis and Daniel is getting serious. You've got to keep your boy away from my girl. Alex is telling me she's meeting her girlfriend for dinner tonight, but she's never bought a new dress to go out with her friends. It's *him* she's meeting."

"I know it," she said, "and I think I've come up with a solution."

"Glad to hear it." He braced his feet wide apart, crossed his arms over his chest and waited.

"A charity bachelor auction," Rose said. The idea had come to her while she was watching some silly TV reality show. "It's perfect. Daniel will enter and meet other women—hopefully finding one more suitable than your Alexis."

"Suitable? There's nothing wrong with my girl," he said in a near growl.

Rose waved one hand at him. "You know very well what I mean. Alexis is a perfectly nice woman, but neither of us wants those two together. Do we?"

His jaw worked as if he were chewing on words he didn't like the taste of. "No. We don't."

"Well, then." Rose picked up her purse again and rummaged inside. Pulling out a piece of paper, she handed it to him. "I've jotted down a few ideas. I thought Alexis could be a part of this, as well. Meet some new eligible bachelors to distract her from Daniel. She wouldn't bid on him so publicly."

He scanned her list, nodding as he read. "It's not bad. If we make it a fund-raiser—say for pancreatic cancer—Alexis will jump on board."

Rose's heart sank a little. Gus's wife, Sarah, had died of the disease two years ago and she knew how hard her passing had hit both Gus and Alexis. Royal was a small town and people were always willing to talk about other people's business. So even though Rose and Gus hadn't spoken in decades, she had been able to keep up with what was happening in his life.

"That's a wonderful idea, Gus."

He looked at her and seemed to study her forever before he spoke again. "Sarah missed having you in her life, Rose."

"I missed her, too." They'd been inseparable once, when they were girls. But then life happened and things had gotten so twisted around.

His voice was gruff, accusatory when he said, "You didn't have to cut her off just because you didn't want me."

Old pain echoed inside Rose. She'd never told anyone why she'd acted as she had so long ago and it was too late now to dredge it all up again.

"You don't know what happened, Gus."

"Then tell me."

"What purpose would it serve now?" she asked, "After all these years?"

"Purpose? Truth is its own purpose."

"Truth isn't always kind."

"What the hell does *kind* have to do with anything?" Gus scowled at her and his tanned features twisted with it. "Damn it, Rose, you owe me the explanation I never got."

"We're here to talk about the kids."

"We're finally talking after too many damn years. So while we're at it, let's get to the bottom of all this." He tucked the paper into his shirt pocket, balled his fists on his hips and gave her a cool stare. "What the hell changed while I was off making enough money for us to get married? Why'd you cut me loose?"

It seemed they were going to do this, after all. And maybe he was right. Maybe he was owed that long-held explanation. "My father wanted me to marry Ed. To make sure that happened, he threatened me. Told me that he'd take away my mother's doctor. Her medicine, if I didn't break it off with you."

Gus snorted. "He wouldn't have done it."

"Yes, he would." Rose thought back to her life under Jedediah Clayton's thumb. Her father had ruled his slice of Texas through fear and intimidation and no one had been spared. Rose's mother had always been delicate and Jedediah used that to keep Rose in line.

"Papa didn't like you. Didn't like me wanting something of my own, so he stopped it." She swallowed hard as she met Gus's eyes. "He *made me* stop it."

"That's it?" Gus was astonished. And furious. "You sent me away because you were afraid of your father?"

"Not for myself," she argued. "If it was just me, I'd have defied him. But I couldn't risk my mother. I was a kid, Gus," she reminded him. "I had no power. I couldn't stand up to him."

Gus turned away, then spun back around to face her. "*We* could have, Rose."

"You weren't there," she said. "I had no way of contacting you. Finding you. I had to do what I did to save my mother."

"You didn't give me a chance. Didn't give *us* a chance."

She shook her head, unwilling to even consider the possibility now that she could have done something different all those years ago. "You didn't know him."

"Damn it, Rosie, you should have trusted *me*!"

His shout thundered in the air.

"It wasn't about *you*, Gus. It was about my mother. When you went away to make enough money for us to get married, I was alone with him. He was in charge and he never let me forget it." Damned if she'd apologize for doing what she had to, to protect her mother. "I kept hoping you'd come back, but you didn't. You were gone four years, Gus."

"For us, Rose."

"But in those years, my father ate away at my mother, at me, until there was nothing left. I was alone," she repeated for both their sakes. "I did what I had to."

Shaking his head, he looked at her. "You cut me off, fine. But you cut Sarah off, too."

Heart twisting, Rose said, "Sarah was my best friend. Do you think I didn't miss her? Didn't *need* her, especially with you gone?"

"Then why?" he asked, voice tight and low.

"My father. He wouldn't allow it. Wouldn't allow me to have anything he didn't give me."

"I hope that old bastard's burning in hell," Gus muttered.

"You are not alone," she assured him.

Shaking his head, Gus asked, "Were you happy at least?"

She gave him a wry smile. For more than forty years, Rose had kept the secret of her hellish marriage. To outsiders, the Claytons were town royalty. Happy. Successful. But in reality, "Ed drank too much. When he did, he—"

"Did he hit you?"

Rose met his gaze and saw flashes of fire there. "Just once."

"Just *once*?" Gus's eyes nearly popped out of his head. "Damn it, Rose. Why the hell would you stay with him?"

"Where was I supposed to go?" she demanded. "He was drunk when he hit me and I hit him back. Let him know I wouldn't stand for that. You were already married. To Sarah. I'd lost my love and my best friend. I had no one else. I had my children. So I stayed. And I kept out of Ed's way."

"I can't believe what I'm hearing," Gus muttered and shot her another hard look.

"Oh, stop it, Gus. I'm not a battered woman. I'm not a victim."

"He hit you."

"Once."

"And that's okay?" His voice was thunderous again.

"Of course not." God, how had this gone so wrong? She hadn't meant to paint herself as a pitiable figure. "I survived my marriage. I kept my children safe. And now I've got Daniel and he is the light in my eye."

Gus's jaw worked furiously and Rose knew that he wanted to curse a blue streak. But she also knew he would never swear like he wanted to in front of a woman, so he was stuck.

"I'm not looking for sympathy," she said. "The past is past. Ed's gone now and I live my life the way I like it."

"You always did have spine," Gus mused. "It's why I always wondered why you didn't stand up to your daddy."

"For myself, I would have," Rose reiterated. "I couldn't risk my mother."

"Guess I understand that." He took off his hat and scrubbed his hand across his shaggy, silver hair. "But you should have told me. Told Sarah. You didn't have to cut yourself off from everydamnbody."

"Yes, I did." Rose smiled and shook her head sadly. "How could I watch you and Sarah being happy together when I—" She stopped, held up one hand and fought for control. Blast it, she hadn't meant to open up any of this mess and now that she had, she needed a way out.

Rose strove for dignity. Lifting her chin, she said simply, "I'm happy you and Sarah had so many good years together."

As if he understood that she had said all she was going to say about the past, Gus nodded. "We did. And now you and I are going to make sure our grandchildren have the futures they should have. Right?"

"Right." Grateful to be back on solid ground, Rose took a seat on the bench and patted it. "Have a seat, Gus, and let's talk about the bachelor auction."

"A man auction," Gus said with a shake of his head. "Who would have thought it?"

"Earth to Shelby," Camilla said with a laugh.

"Huh? What?" Shelby gave herself a mental shake and looked at the other woman. "I'm sorry. Zoned out there for a second."

"Again," Cam pointed out.

Shelby sighed as she gave Caleb's housekeeper her full attention. Cam was short, curvy and had a long, blond braid that hung across one shoulder, and her blue eyes were shining with amusement.

"You're right." Returning to the task at hand, Shelby looked into the trunk of Caleb's big Suburban and let her gaze slide across all of the crystal packed in there carefully. "Now I'm back, though. This is everything?"

Cam nodded. "Everything we set aside for the first trip, anyway. Mrs. Mackenzie really did hold on to a lot of stuff."

"She did, but I've seen worse," Shelby told her.

"I'm glad I haven't." Cam shook her head. "And I can't even tell you how happy I am that you're clearing this stuff out. I know Caleb is, too."

"He hasn't said much one way or the other," Shelby said. Her gaze slid across the yard to the stable, then to the barn. There was no sign of Caleb, but that was hardly surprising. Since their little interlude in the kitchen two nights ago, he'd been darn near invisible.

"Well, take it from me, he's happy," Cam said. "Before you showed up the man couldn't even sit down in the great room. Now it's more like a home than a warehouse."

A home that Caleb was avoiding. Because of *her*. A spurt of irritation spiked inside her and Shelby let it fester and grow. She'd tried to be understanding. But honestly, the man was acting like she'd laid out an ambush for him and then thrown herself at him.

Well, okay, she had set him up, sitting in the dark, waiting for him. But what happened after that was on both of them. For heaven's sake, why was he acting as if they'd done something *wrong*? And why was he making her feel as though it was all her fault?

"Shelby?"

"I'm sorry, Cam." Shelby glanced at all of the crystal she was supposed to be taking into the Priceless antiques store, then looked at the woman beside her. "Can you do me a huge favor? Could you drive this stuff into town? I have to find Caleb."

Cam frowned a little, but nodded. "Sure. No problem. But you know Caleb's out on the range somewhere. You'll have to get a horse."

"I can ride," she said, with more certainty than she felt. Shelby hadn't ridden a horse in years. But it had to be like riding a bike, right? Some things you didn't forget.

"Okay, then. Ask my husband where Caleb went. He'll point you in the right direction."

An hour later, Shelby spotted Caleb in the distance. It shouldn't have taken so long, but since she hadn't ridden a horse in forever, Mike had insisted on giving her a mare with all the energy of a snail. But the sky was a blue so pure and deep, it almost hurt to look at it. The sun shone down like fire from heaven and the surrounding pastureland was varying shades of dusty green and brown. There were cattle grazing and she was glad to note they were on the other side of a fence that seemed to stretch on forever.

As Shelby rode closer, she enjoyed the look of pure surprise etched into Caleb's handsome features. She'd enjoy it a lot more if she wasn't already starting to ache all over.

"What the hell are you doing out here?"

"Well, that was charming."

"I'm not trying to be charming," he ground out, "I'm trying to *work*."

"Good to see you, too," Shelby said and took a good, long look at him. Caleb was tightening a strand of barbed wire around a fence post. He'd taken his shirt off and the sight of that tanned, muscular chest made Shelby's mouth go dry. If he weren't scowling at her, she'd have melted a little.

"How'd you find me? And since when do you ride horses?"

"Mike told me where you'd be and I took lessons for years as a kid." She looked down at him while her horse nuzzled his.

Still scowling, he bent his head to his work. "Fine. You found me. Go away."

Both eyebrows arched high on her forehead. "This must be that Southern hospitality I've heard so much about."

"Damn it, Shelby, I'm busy."

"Me, too. I'm supposed to be taking a load of your mother's crystal into town right now."

"Why aren't you, then?"

"Cam's taking it for me because I told her I had to talk to *you*. Who knew it would be this difficult?" She swung her leg over the horse's back and jumped down from the stirrups. Taking a step toward him, she stopped, said, "Ow," and rubbed her behind.

"Serves you right," he muttered. "Haven't ridden in years, then hop on a horse and ride for miles? Be lucky if you can walk tomorrow."

"If you'd quit avoiding me," she said, "I wouldn't have had to resort to this."

"I'm not avoiding you." He turned his back on her and her gaze instinctively dropped to his butt. Yeah, the view from this angle was pretty spectacular, too.

"Me being out here has nothing to do with you. I'm working," he reminded her.

"Right." She didn't believe it for a minute and was surprised that he thought she might. "And you don't go to the kitchen for food anymore, so what? You're dieting?"

He sent her a glare, tied off the wire and clipped the excess. Tucking that bit of wire into a worn, cowhide belt he wore draped around his hips, he yanked off his gloves, tipped his hat back and fired a long, hard look at her. "What do you want? An apology? Fine. I'm sorry."

"You never listen, do you? I already told you I don't regret what happened."

He snorted. "You should."

"Why?"

He ignored her, tucking his work gloves into the saddle-bags. Shelby laid one hand on his forearm and demanded again, "Why?"

Caleb looked from her hand to her eyes. "Because, damn it," he ground out, "there's nothing here for you, Shelby. Not with me."

Her hand dropped away. "I never asked you for anything."

"Not yet."

She swayed back a little, almost as if his words had delivered a physical shot. "Are you under the impression I'm trying to trick you into a relationship or something?"

"You said yourself you waited in the dark for me the other night."

"Yes, because I was attracted to you," she snapped. "Though right now I don't remember why."

He took off the belt, hooked it on his saddle horn, then turned back around to face her. His jaw was tight, mouth grim and those icy eyes of his looked steely and dangerous. "I gave you a place to stay…"

"And I'm grateful—"

"Not the point." He held up one hand for quiet. "I don't go around using women just because they're handy."

Shelby just stared at him. "I don't let myself be used, either, so we're on the same page there."

"All I'm saying is that you're not the one-night kind of woman and that's all I've got to offer you—" He broke off, turned to snatch his shirt out of a saddlebag and then shrugged into it, leaving it unbuttoned. "So I'm staying clear of you."

"I don't know what to feel here," Shelby admitted, watching him, sorry to see him cover most of that really great chest. "Should I be flattered you think I'm worth more than one night? Or offended that you think I'm waiting for you to get down on one knee and promise me forever?"

"I didn't say—"

"No, you already said what you had to," Shelby said, and this time held up *her* hand for quiet. His mouth quirked at the gesture. "Now it's my turn. I'm grateful that you gave me a place to stay—but I don't need you to take care of me. To protect me. I'm a big girl—"

"I noticed."

Her mouth twitched briefly. "We're two adults, Caleb. If we want to be together, why shouldn't we? I don't expect anything from you—no wait. That's wrong. I do have one expectation."

"Yeah?" Wary now, he watched her.

Irritated, she said, "Oh, for heaven's sake. You really don't listen at all, do you? Stop getting that trapped look in your eyes."

He frowned at her, folded his arms across his chest and huffed out a breath. "Fine. What's your expectation?"

"That you'll stop avoiding me." She moved in on him, closing the distance between them. A soft, hot wind blew across the land, lifting her hair and blowing the edges of Caleb's shirt back. "That you'll kiss me again. Often."

As if thinking about what she'd said, he took a deep breath and released it slowly as he shifted his gaze to the wide pasture stretching out behind her. Several long seconds passed before he met her gaze again and when he did, Shelby saw storm clouds in his eyes.

"Damn it, woman." He set his hands at her hips and Shelby sighed as the accompanying rush of heat swept through her. "You should be careful what you wish for."

"I'm not wishing, Caleb. I'm *saying*." She reached up and tugged the brim of his hat lower over his eyes. Smiling at him, she said, "Stop pretending there's nothing between us."

"And if I do?" His voice was a low growl that hummed across her skin. His hands at her hips tightened, and Shelby sighed a little.

"If you do, then we're good." She stepped out of his grasp, took a step toward her horse and said, "And now that we both know where we stand, I'll go back to the house."

In a blink, he grabbed her hand, tugged her to him and then fisted one hand in her hair. Pulling her head back, he kissed her like a dying man looking for salvation. His tongue demanded, his breath pumped into her and when he finally let her go, Shelby's knees wobbled.

Looking deeply into her eyes, he said softly, "*Now* we're good."

Seven

When Caleb rode back into the ranch yard a couple hours later, his mind was on Shelby. As it had been since she'd left him and ridden back to the house. He'd thought it through and come to the conclusion that she was right. They were adults. They clearly wanted each other. So what the hell was he waiting for? Kissing her had fed the fires inside until it felt as if the Texas summer sun couldn't even compete with what was happening within.

The yard was busy. A couple of the men working with horses in the corral, two more putting a fresh coat of white paint on the stable fence. It was hot and miserable and Caleb wasn't thinking about work. All he wanted now was to find Shelby and ease the ache that had been torturing him for days.

Then he noticed the shining silver Porsche parked near the front door. Scowling at the thought of unexpected company, Caleb swung down from his horse, tossed the reins to Mike and jerked his head at the car. "Who's here?"

Mike frowned. "Jared Goodman."

"Hell." Caleb swiped one hand across his face and gritted

his teeth. He supposed it made sense that Jared would show up eventually. But why *now*? "What did Shelby say?"

Mike shrugged. "When I saw him drive up, I went to the house, offered to stay with her while Jared was here but she insisted she was okay."

That sounded like her. Stubborn and strong and independent as hell. "Is Cam in there?"

"Nope." Mike shook his head and stared at the house as if he could see through the walls to what was happening inside. "She went into town a couple hours ago. Not back yet."

So Shelby was alone. With a man who had to be furious at the humiliation she'd served him. Caleb remembered all too well how he'd felt when Meg had dumped him in favor of his brother. It hadn't been pretty. The thought of Shelby facing Jared down alone was something he didn't care for. Though why it bothered him, he wasn't willing to explore. "I'll see about it."

Caleb trotted across the ranch yard, opened the front door and the first thing he heard was Shelby's voice. She was talking fast. Not a surprise.

"I'm really sorry, Jared, but I did the right thing. You'll see that, eventually."

"Right." Jared's voice came across in a sneer. "I'm sure I'll be real happy that my bride ran out on me in front of the whole damn town."

They were in the great room and Caleb moved quietly across the hall, so he could see what was going on. If she was handling things all right, he could always slip out again. She wouldn't even have to know that he'd checked in on her.

But he was distracted almost instantly. His first impression was, he hardly recognized the damn place. Since Shelby had been at the house, he'd been coming and going through the doors in his wing. Hell, he'd been using those doors since his mother started her "collection." Caleb hadn't seen the great room since Shelby went to work on it.

And in a matter of just a few days, she'd cleared the place of all the extra cabinets and dressers and the mountain of crystal and glassware. This was a room people could sit in. There were couches and chairs he barely remembered and a couple of tables that belonged there, but the room was once again a huge space with a wide, unobstructed view of the ranch yard. Of course, at the moment, the custom wooden shutters were closed over the glass, keeping this little scene private.

But his interest in the room faded as he focused on the man standing way too close to Shelby. Jared Goodman, like his father, stood a few inches shorter than Caleb. His black hair was slicked back and his gray suit looked out of place on a ranch. His features were twisted with anger and his eyes flashed sparks of heat as he loomed over Shelby.

Beyond the slash of fury that surprised the hell out of him, Caleb felt a quick jolt of admiration to see Shelby holding her own. She faced the man down and didn't look the least bit worried.

"I've heard the stories your mother's put out," Shelby said calmly. "The word is that you're the one who called things off."

"But *we* know the truth, don't we, Shelby?" His voice was low and hard.

Impatient, she huffed out a breath. "Jared, it's over. We never should have tried this and you know that, too. I let myself believe that I was in love, but the truth is, I wasn't. I was just really flattered at how you swept me off my feet and that's not enough to build anything on, Jared—and you know it, too." She sighed a little, then added, "Honestly, you wouldn't be happy with me anyway. I talk too much and I'm a little bossy and I like to organize things all the time and you hate that. I mean, look at your office, it's just a mess, with files everywhere. We would never work out."

Jared tried to get a word in and failed. Caleb almost felt sorry for him.

"It's just that I'm sure you'll find the right person for you, but that's not me and it won't change, so we should just shake hands and part friends. I can do that, Jared," she said, "can you?"

"Friends?"

She gave him a sympathetic smile that was completely wasted on him. "Oh, Jared. This was never going to work. Really, it never should have *started*. So I'm sorry for that. But I'm not sorry for leaving."

"We're not friends," Jared snapped when Shelby finally wound down. He moved in closer and Caleb didn't like the look on the man's face. "You don't get to just walk away from me."

Okay, that was enough.

"She already did." Both people turned to look at him as Caleb walked across the room to stand beside Shelby. "You should go, Jared."

Shelby was clearly startled to see him, but Jared's features went tight and even harder.

"What the hell do you have to say about any of this, Mackenzie?"

"Caleb—" Shelby started talking, but Caleb cut her off.

He kept his gaze fixed on Goodman. "For one thing, this is my house. My land. You've got no business here, Goodman, and no right to stand here trying to intimidate Shelby. You're not welcome and it's time for you to go."

"I'll go when I'm ready," Jared said. "You don't worry me, Mackenzie."

"I should, though." Caleb wrapped one arm around Shelby's shoulders and pulled her in to his side. "I work hard for a living, Goodman. You push papers. So don't try to throw your weight around in my place."

Jared's gaze fixed on the way Caleb was holding her.

"That's right. Shelby's with me, now, Jared." She stiffened against him and Caleb hoped to hell that she for once, didn't start talking. "She ended your relationship when she ran out on the wedding. So I don't want to see you back here again. You had some things to say and you said them. So now you can go."

"That's why you walked out?" Jared demanded hotly, ignoring Caleb to focus on Shelby. "You expect me to believe you left me for *him*?"

"You can believe whatever you want," Caleb said before Shelby could speak.

"This is ridiculous."

Caleb dismissed him, bent to Shelby and gave her a fast, hard kiss to prove to Jared that he was telling the truth. And with the taste of her in his mouth, he turned to glare at the other man. "Now get out before I toss you out."

Jared looked at Shelby. "You bitch."

Caleb took a step forward and was pleased to see Jared skitter backward. "That's it. Go."

He did, storming across the room and out the door, slamming it behind him just to continue the child-having-a-tantrum attitude. Before the echo of that loud slam had faded, Shelby pushed away from Caleb and stared up at him.

"Why did you do that?" She lifted both hands to her temples and squeezed. "It just makes everything harder. I was handling him. I didn't need help."

Caleb remembered the look on Jared's face as he towered over Shelby and he wasn't so sure about that. Even the most timid dog finally bit if it was pushed too far.

"Not how it looked to me," Caleb said, gazing down into worried green eyes. "Jared was just getting madder by the second and with a man like him, you can't trust his reactions."

"He wouldn't have hurt me!" She seemed astonished at the thought.

"He won't now, anyway," Caleb agreed.

Frowning, Shelby seemed to think about that for a second or two. Then something else occurred to her. "The Goodmans still have my clothes. My money. Do you think he's going to be helpful now?" Letting her hands drop, she sighed. "Now he thinks we're a couple and that's just going to make this an even bigger mess."

"Maybe." Caleb pulled his hat off and tossed it onto the nearest table. He hadn't really been thinking about what Jared might believe or what he might do down the road. Hadn't been thinking much at all. It was pure instinct that had driven him across the room to stand between Shelby and potential danger.

He'd acted on impulse and Caleb couldn't even say he was sorry about it. He dropped both hands on her shoulders and held on tight. "I don't give a damn what he thinks. No one comes into my house and bullies you. Nobody."

She slumped a little and gave him a smile that was part pleased and part impatience. "That's really sweet, but didn't I tell you I don't need you to protect me?"

"Yeah, but turns out, *I* needed to protect you."

"Oh, Caleb. You realize this is only going to make the Goodmans even more furious with me." She chewed at her bottom lip. "Jared will tell his parents what you said and his mother will be spreading even more gossip. And now, you've told her she was right all along and that I'm with you."

"She already thought it. Remember?"

"Now she has your word on it. And then you just had to kiss me in front of Jared."

"He's not real bright," Caleb mused. "Thought he could use a visual aid."

"It's not funny, Caleb," she said, though her mouth curved briefly. Shaking her head, she said, "They'll never give me back my things now. And Jared's still got my money. I can't find a place to live or start a business or even move back to Chicago without that money."

Caleb frowned when she mentioned moving away. He hadn't really thought about it, but there was nothing holding her in Royal—or Texas, for that matter. She'd come to get married and now that she wasn't…well, hell.

"That what you're planning?" he asked. "To move back to Chicago?"

She looked up at him. "Honestly, I haven't thought that far

ahead yet. What's the point? I can't plan anything until I have access to my money."

Not an answer, but it wasn't important, was it? Hadn't he been trying to avoid her for days? So why should he care if she moved out of state? Wouldn't that be the perfect ending to this situation? Shaking his head, he shoved those thoughts aside and got back to the matter at hand.

"The bank emailed you the receipt for the sale of your house, for the deposit," Caleb reminded her. "If Nate doesn't get the money for you, the judge will have the Goodmans turn it over."

She blew out a breath and nodded. "That's true. I have proof that the money is mine. They can't keep it. And I know I shouldn't get so worked up over Jared, but this is all my fault. I never should have said yes when he proposed but it seemed right at the time, you know?"

She wasn't looking for a conversation, Caleb knew. This was another rant and damned if he wasn't starting to enjoy them.

"I never meant to pull you into the middle of all this, Caleb," she said, pushing one hand through her hair. "You were just being nice and I told you I didn't need to be defended, but it was really sexy when you came in and kissed me and told Jared to get out, and it shouldn't have been, but I can't help how I feel about it, can I?

"I mean, it's so old-world cowboy movie for you to come striding in with your hat and your stoic expression and be all—" she scrunched up her face and deepened her voice "—'That's my woman, so back off,' and for some reason, it made my stomach do a dip and spin that took my breath away—"

That's my woman. He hadn't meant it like that. Not really. He was pretty sure. But Caleb could admit that seeing Jared looming over Shelby, bullying her just by being bigger and taller than her had really pissed him off, so that all he could think to do was stand in front of her. To get rid of Jared so her face wouldn't look so damn pale.

And now, all he wanted was for her to quiet down and the best way to do that, he'd already discovered, was...

He kissed her.

Like he had out on the range, one hand in her dark auburn curls, holding her head still so he could take his time and indulge in the taste of her. And in less than a second, she was kissing him back, hooking one leg around his, snaking her arms around his waist and holding on. His tongue caressed hers. He took her breath as his and gave her back his own. Then held her so tightly, he could feel the soft, full mounds of her breasts against his chest. Her hips ground into his, spiking the ache in his groin to epic proportions. He'd never known the kind of want she inspired in him. Never experienced the kind of desperation pushing at him.

He lifted his head, looked down into those grass-green eyes of hers and saw them shining with the same kind of pulsing desire hammering at him. "I want you, Shelby. Right the hell now."

"What took you so long?" She grinned, then kissed him, opening her mouth to him, tasting him as he had her. Her hands went to his belt. He felt her unhook the damn thing and undo the top button of his jeans. Then she tugged the hem of his shirt free and slid her hands up beneath the fabric to stroke her palms across his chest.

He sucked in a gulp of air, lifted his head and smiled. "Glad you cleared out this room so nicely. Because that couch is a hell of a lot handier than a bedroom."

"Yes," she said on a breathy sigh and flicked her thumbs across his flat nipples.

He gritted his teeth and felt every drop of blood in his body rush to his groin. He was hard and aching and if he didn't have her in the next few minutes, Caleb was sure he'd die.

In two steps they were at the couch and he tipped her back onto it in one smooth motion. She landed with a thump and laughed up at him.

Her eyes were shining, her delectable mouth curved in a

smile that promised all sorts of wicked things. When she tore off her tank top to reveal a skimpy piece of sky blue lace covering her breasts, he couldn't look away. Then she unhooked the front of the bra and let the delicate cups slide away, baring her breasts to him. In the cool, air-conditioned room, her dark pink nipples peaked instantly and Caleb didn't waste a second. He came down on top of her and took first one of those nipples, then the other, into his mouth. His lips, tongue and teeth tormented her while she writhed and panted beneath him.

She tugged at his shirt so furiously that he finally paused long enough in his enjoyment of her body to rise up and let her pull the shirt off. Then her hands were on him. Small, smooth, strong. She stroked, caressed and scored his skin with her short nails while he again suckled at her breasts.

"God you smell good," he whispered, lingering to give one nipple another licking kiss.

She shivered. "So do you."

Caleb laughed. "No I don't." He half pushed up from her. "Just wait. Give me five minutes in a shower and I'll be back—"

"No, you're not going anywhere," she said, shaking her head against the brown leather couch. She licked her lips, let her fingers trail down his chest, across his flat abdomen to the button fly of his jeans.

Caleb went perfectly still. He felt every skimming touch of her hands as she worked the buttons free, one by one. And with each inch of freedom gathered, his dick hardened further. Finally, she reached down and curled her small, strong hand around him and squeezed, while stroking up and down his length.

Caleb dropped his forehead to hers and took deep, deliberate breaths. If he didn't maintain control, he'd explode before he'd done what he'd been dreaming of doing to her. Reaching down, he grabbed her hand and held it pinned to the couch above her head.

"Don't. You'll push me over the edge and I want to stay there for a while."

His free hand dropped to the waistband of the knee-length white shorts she wore and quickly undid the snap and zipper. One glance told him her skimpy panties matched the blue lace bra and everything inside him twisted in response. One time, he wanted to see her dressed only in those wisps of lace. But now, he wanted her in *nothing*.

He slid down the length of her body, trailing kisses and long, slow licks as he went. She shivered again and he loved it. His hands tugged her shorts and panties free and when she was naked, he took a long moment to simply enjoy the view.

"Slide that bra all the way off," he ordered.

She ran her tongue slowly across her bottom lip, then lifted off the couch high enough to pull the bra off and drop it to the floor. When she stretched out on the couch again, she crooked a finger.

"You're wearing too many clothes."

"Yeah, I am." He kept his gaze fixed with hers while he quickly stripped, so he saw the flash of pleasure dart across her eyes when she saw him, long and hard and ready.

Her hips rose off the couch in eager anticipation. She planted her feet, parted her legs more widely and whispered, "Be inside me, Caleb."

Four little words that tore him to pieces. There was simply nothing he wanted more. But first… He took hold of her thighs, held them wide and looked at the core of her, hot and pink and wet. She was as ready as he was and that pushed him over that dangerous edge he'd been clinging to.

He bent his head to her, covering her center with his mouth, tasting her, licking at her, nibbling until she was whimpering, rocking her hips and softly begging him for what he wouldn't give her. Not yet.

Again and again, he teased her, tormented her, relishing

every sigh and groan she made. She reached down and threaded her fingers through his hair as she cried his name brokenly.

He rode the power of her passion until he was nearly blind with the need choking him and only then did Caleb rise up, cover her body with his and slide into her heat.

He pushed deep and she wrapped her legs around his hips, giving him a better angle, allowing her to take all of him in. Locked together, they stared into each other's eyes as he moved inside her. He watched her eyes flash. Watched her lips part on a sigh that welled up from deep within her.

Caleb pushed deeper, higher, groaning as he filled her, as she surrounded him with a kind of heat that burst into an inferno within. Friction bristled between them as he set a rhythm that she raced to match. She was with him, every step of the way and he'd never known anything like this before. There was a connection here, linking them in ways that were more than physical. Everything she felt was stamped on her features. Every touch she bestowed on him left streaks of flame burning down into his bones. His blood.

Again and again, he moved, claiming her, taking them both well past that slippery edge until they were left, staggering wildly, fighting for balance, for release.

"Come now," he ordered, voice thick, strained with the effort to hold himself back when all he wanted to do was empty himself inside her.

She shook her head, gasping, panting. "We go together. Both of us."

Reaching down, she cupped him and rubbed, stroked him until he was beyond pleasure, beyond the boundaries of everything that had come before. And so he slid one hand between their bodies and stroked her core as he continued to pump into her.

And finally, together, they jumped off the edge and fell crashing into lights brighter than he'd ever seen before.

* * *

When her heart stopped racing, Shelby took a deep breath and closed her eyes in complete satisfaction. Her body was still buzzing, the echoes of a world-class orgasm still shuddering inside her. Sex had never been like that before. Until this moment, she'd always thought of it as a pleasant enough time that ended with a delicious little pop of release.

Caleb Mackenzie had changed all of that.

He knew things that all men should know. His hands were magic and his mouth should be bronzed. In fact, Shelby felt a bit sorry for every woman who had never been with him. While at the same time, she wanted to keep him all for herself and never let another woman near him.

A frown settled between her brows. Where had that thought come from? Caleb wasn't hers. There was nothing between them but convenience and blistering sex.

Well. That was nearly enough to take the shine off her feelings.

With his big, strong body pressing into hers, Shelby felt a stirring of a warmth that was slower and steadier than the heat she had just survived. That realization should have worried her. Instead, she took a second to revel in it. To enjoy this one perfect moment.

Then Caleb lifted his head, looked down at her and solemnly said, "This is a really bad time to be asking, but—are you on the Pill?"

There went the rest of the shine.

"Yes," she said and saw relief flicker in his eyes. "I've been on the Pill for a few years now so—" She broke off and thought about that for a second.

"What?" Caleb watched her warily. "What is it?"

"Probably nothing," Shelby assured him, though she wasn't as confident in that as she was trying to sound. Forcing a smile, she added, "I'm sure it's fine..."

"But?" he asked.

"*But*, remember I didn't have my purse for three days…"

"Yeah?" One word drawn out into five or six syllables.

"Well, my pills were in my purse, so…"

"So you didn't take any for a couple of days."

"No." He was literally right on top of her and she still felt him take a mental step backward. "I'm sure it's fine, though. I took the Pill yesterday and today and I'm sure I've got all kinds of those wonderful little hormones all stored up in my system."

"Uh-huh." Caleb pulled away, sat up and grabbed his jeans off the floor. "Damn it."

"No reason to panic," she said.

"Is that right?" He snorted a laugh and shook his head as he stood up to yank his jeans on.

It was a shame, she thought idly, to cover up that really amazing body.

"I don't know what I was thinking," Caleb said tightly, more to himself than to her. Then he looked at her. "I have *never* failed to use a damn condom."

"Until today." She shrugged, reached down for her blue bra and pulled it on.

"Yeah." He pushed one hand through his hair in sheer frustration. "Until today. Until *you*."

Shelby smiled. "The words sound like a compliment. The tone really doesn't."

"I should apologize, I guess, and if I can find a way to say it and sound like I mean it, I will."

Well, clearly their postcoital conversation was coming to an end with a whimper. Reaching down for her shirt, Shelby tugged it on, then grabbed her panties. Standing up, she wriggled into them and enjoyed the flash of interest in Caleb's eyes.

"No apology necessary," she said and stepped into her white shorts. Once they were snapped and zipped, she tossed her hair out of her eyes and said, "I didn't think of it, either. All I could think about was you. Having you inside me."

His eyes burned like a fire in ice. "Hell, that's all I can think of right now."

She gave him a slow smile and felt her body stirring. "Me, too. And I'm not going to regret that, no matter what else happens. Honestly, Caleb, I'm sure it's fine."

"Yeah." He sent her another long look. "You be sure and tell me if it's not."

"I will. But I'm not worried." Not quite true, so she added, "Well, maybe a little."

Grabbing his shirt off the floor, he tugged it on. "Not much slows you down, does it?"

"Well, what would be the point of being all…" She mocked tearing her hair out, throwing her head back to shriek, then looked at him and grinned. "Would it help to gnash my teeth and howl at the moon?"

His lips twitched and her heart gave a hard jolt.

Moving in closer to him, Shelby laid both hands on his chest and relished the heat when his hands cupped her shoulders. "My grandmother was Irish," she said softly, staring up into those beautiful eyes of his. "She always told me, 'If you worry, you die. If you don't worry, you die. So why worry?'"

Caleb just stared at her and, slowly, another smile curved his mouth. "You always throw me for a loop, Shelby. Never sure just what you're going to say next."

"Well, then," she said, sliding her arms around his waist, "brace yourself. What do you say we both go and take a shower?"

He cupped her face between his palms, bent his head and kissed her softly, gently. Everything inside Shelby fluttered back into life again and now that she knew just what he was capable of, she trembled with it.

"I think," he said, "that's a great idea. Plus, there're condoms in the bathroom."

She looked up at him and grinned. "How many?"

"Let's find out." Caleb picked her up and tossed her over his shoulder. Shelby's laughter trailed behind them.

Eight

Mitch and Meg returned home the following morning and everything between Shelby and Caleb changed in a blink of time.

In the rush and noise of the family arriving, and the kids shrieking with joy to be home again, Shelby felt Caleb pull away from her. He distanced himself so easily it was almost scary to watch. It was as if, for him, the night they'd just shared had never happened.

Only that morning, she and Caleb had been wrapped together in his bed, after a long night of incredible sex and putting quite a dent in Caleb's condom supply. They'd laughed and kissed and had a picnic in that bed in the middle of the night and yet, the minute Mitch and Meg had arrived, Caleb had shut down. He'd become cold. Distant.

With his family around, he was a different man. Except with the twins, she reminded herself. The two children had thrown themselves at Caleb and he'd held nothing back with them, smiling, laughing, swinging them around.

It was when he faced Mitch and Meg and Shelby that his features turned to stone. He'd introduced her to them and briefly explained why she was there, but beyond that, he'd hardly spoken to her since his family arrived. She had to wonder why. Was it her? Was he pulling back to remind her that there was nothing but sex between them? Was he making sure his family understood that Shelby was only there temporarily?

And if he was trying to shut her out, why was he being so cold to his brother and sister-in-law, too?

To be fair, though, she had to admit that Meg and Mitch weren't exactly being warm and friendly toward Caleb, either. Families were complicated, she knew that, but there was more here than simple sibling issues. And she really wished she knew what exactly it was bubbling beneath the surface of the Mackenzie family. Maybe then she could find a way to reach Caleb.

She probably should have gone into the house and busied herself with the organizational job that wasn't finished yet. But for two hours, she sat on the porch instead, watching the family she didn't belong to. It was fascinating to watch the play of relationships and as she studied them all from the shade of the front porch, she tried to spot signs that might explain what was going on.

Mitch Mackenzie was a younger, shorter version of Caleb, but to her mind, Caleb was much better looking and she couldn't help but notice that the brothers were *cautious* around each other. They kept a safe distance between them as they stood at the corral watching a few of the men work the horses. If body language could actually speak, theirs would be shouting. The two men couldn't have been more ill at ease with each other.

Meg Mackenzie was tiny, just five feet or so, with short blond hair and big blue eyes. Her husband appeared to adore her, but Caleb barely acknowledged her existence. Caleb treated her with a cool detachment, hardly glancing her way. And Shelby wondered again just what was happening here. The Mackenzie family was simmering with tension.

Except when it came to the twins. At three years old, they looked like miniature Mackenzies. Jack and Julie were loud, adorable and seemed to have an infinite amount of energy. For a couple of hours, it was crazy while the kids ran around and Caleb and Mitch talked business. Meg was in and out of their house across the yard, settling in.

Shelby tried to stay out of the way because she could see there was friction between Caleb and his brother—not to mention Meg. She didn't want to add to the problems, so she kept to herself in a rocking chair on the porch.

She'd brought out a pitcher of iced tea, four glasses and a plate of homemade cookies. But so far, she was snacking all by herself. Still, she was in the shade and had a bird's-eye view of the Mackenzie family. But for the first time since coming to the ranch, she felt exactly what she was—an outsider.

With her gaze locked on Caleb, Shelby wished she could see what he was thinking. Feeling.

"Sometimes," she murmured, "stoic is just annoying."

Still, she couldn't look away from him. He and his brother both stood, one booted foot on the bottom rung of the corral fence, their arms resting on the top rung. Did they even realize how alike they were? Or was that lost in whatever it was that was keeping them divided? She'd like to talk to Caleb, see what was driving the coolness that had dropped onto him like a shroud. But that wouldn't happen until he stopped shutting her out.

She took a sip of her tea then set her glass down on the table beside her. A hot wind bustled across the ranch, lifting her hair from the back of her neck and stirring the dust in the yard into a mini cyclone that dissipated as quickly as it rose up. The steady, pounding clop from the horses running in circles around the corral was like the heartbeat of the ranch. Shelby took a deep breath and let it slide from her lungs again.

Strange how much she'd come to love this place. The wide sky, the openness of the land, the horses… Caleb. And now she was forced to acknowledge that as much as she liked being there, she didn't *belong*. That admission hurt more than she would have expected and she wondered when this place, and this man, had become more than a port in the storm.

Then the twins spotted her and bulleted across the yard, headed right for her. Shelby smiled, watching their shining faces and those eyes, as bright a blue as the sky.

The little girl beat her brother by a couple of steps, climbed up onto Shelby's lap and grinned. Her soft brown hair was pulled into two impossibly short pigtails and she had a dimple in her right cheek. "Daddy says you live here. You do? Can I have a cookie?"

Hmm. Problem. How did she give them cookies without asking their mother first? Then Jack scrambled over, shouted "I like cookies!" and grabbed one, stuffing half of it into his mouth.

Not to be outdone, Julie squirmed on Shelby's lap until she could grab one, too. With crumbs on her cheek, Julie said, "Uncle Caleb lives here."

"Yes, he does."

"You like Uncle Caleb?" Jack demanded.

Danger zone, she thought and then dismissed it. The children were too young to read anything into her answers, so she kept it simple. "Yes, I do. Do you?"

"Uh-huh," Jack said. "He's funny."

"Uncle Caleb is crabby sometimes," Julie told her thoughtfully. "Can you make him not crabby?"

Out of the mouths of babes. Laughing, Shelby dusted the crumbs off the girl's face. "Well, I don't know, but I can try."

"I ride horsies," Jack announced.

"Ponies," Julie corrected, with a sisterly sneer.

"He's a *big* pony," her brother argued back.

"Okay, you two, take a hike."

Shelby hadn't even seen their mother arriving; she'd been too busy fielding questions and being entertained. Now Meg climbed the steps, sat down in the chair beside Shelby and sent both kids off with a cheerful, "Go bug your daddy for a while."

Both of them took off at a dead run toward the spot where

Mitch and Caleb still stood side by side, yet separate, at the corral fence. Little Jack's small cowboy hat flew off and he circled back to snatch it out of the dirt. When Julie came up on her father, he swung her up to his shoulders. Then Caleb did the same for Jack when the boy tugged at his jeans.

The summer sun was blazing out of a bright blue sky with only a few meager white clouds to mar the perfection of it. Shelby watched Caleb with the kids and everything inside her melted.

"Sorry," Meg said, "the kids are so glad to be out of the car, they're a little more excitable than usual."

"Oh, they're wonderful. And adorable, too."

"Well, you do know how to make points with mothers," Meg said with a grin.

"I wasn't—" Shelby stopped herself and smiled. "Sorry about the cookies. I should have asked you, but they just—"

"Swarmed you?" Meg nodded in understanding. "They double-team you and you don't stand a chance. Trust me. I know."

"They're so cute."

"And busy." She patted her flat belly. "Hopefully this next one will be a single."

"You're pregnant?" Her voice sounded a little wistful even to herself. "Congratulations."

"Thanks." Meg tipped her head to one side and studied Shelby for a couple of seconds. "You're staring."

Shelby jumped, startled away from looking at Caleb. "Yeah. I guess I was."

Meg mused, "Handsome, aren't they?"

"Hard to argue with that."

"Of course," Meg said, "I'm partial to Mitch, but Caleb's not bad…" She slid a glance at Shelby and seemed to like what she saw because her smile widened. Then she poured a glass of tea, took a long drink and went on to say, "Bless you for this. Honestly, visiting my folks in Oregon, I forgot just how hot it was going to be when we got home."

"It really is awful, isn't it?"

"Summer in Texas," Meg said on a sigh, "the devil's vacation spot. And, now that we've talked about the weather, why don't you tell me how you're doing after escaping your wedding and all?"

She blinked and swallowed hard. Just how much did Meg know? "What?"

"I heard about what happened."

"Caleb told you?"

"Oh, no." Meg shrugged and waved one hand at her. "You must have heard about the gossip chain in Royal."

"Yes, but you weren't here."

"Doesn't seem to matter," the other woman said and grabbed a cookie. "I love chocolate chip. Anyway, I called my friend Amanda—the sheriff's wife—to tell her she wasn't the only one pregnant, and she told me what happened at the wedding."

"Oh, God." Shelby covered her eyes with one hand as if she could simply hide from everyone with that one gesture. "This is so embarrassing."

Meg reached out and patted her hand. "Believe me when I say you don't have to be embarrassed."

"Well, I am," Shelby muttered, smoothing her palms across her khaki shorts.

"Why? Because you were strong enough to walk out of a marriage you knew would be a disaster?" Meg shook her head firmly. "As hard as it was, it was the right thing to do. Jared Goodman? No."

"That's embarrassing, too." Shelby looked at the woman next to her. It seemed weird to be talking about such private things with someone she'd only just met, but Meg had an open, friendly air that was hard to resist. "Why I didn't see what clearly everyone in Royal already knew."

Meg sighed and turned her gaze back to her husband and his brother. "I don't know. Sometimes I think we're deliberately blind to things we'd rather not admit."

Shelby wondered what Meg was thinking, but then, all of the Mackenzies seemed to have secrets and no outsider would breach the walls containing them.

Several hours later, Caleb told himself that this was the first time in memory he'd been glad to have a TCC meeting to attend. But he'd never needed to get away from the ranch more than he had today. With Mitch and Meg and Shelby all there, he felt like he had one foot caught in a damn bear trap.

He was glad his brother was back home, if only to share the burden of running the ranch. But things had been strained between them since Meg had walked out on Caleb to marry Mitch. He'd tried to get past it, but damn it, he was faced with the reality of what had happened every day.

It wasn't that he was still in love with Meg. Hell, that had faded faster than he'd thought possible and maybe every now and then he'd admitted to himself that it was possible his ex-fiancée had done the right thing—though she'd gone about it the wrong way.

Then there was Shelby. He'd gotten too close to her last night. Sex was one thing, but laughing and talking during and after that sex was another. Sure, being with her had been spectacular, better than anything he'd ever known before. But it wasn't the great sex that worried him.

It was sleeping with her in his bed. Waking up with her legs tangled with his. Staring down at her, waiting for her to open those beautiful green eyes and smile up at him.

Came too damn close to caring and he wasn't going to risk that again. Especially with a woman who'd done to another man exactly what Meg had done to him.

Well, hell, he told himself as his thoughts circled crazily, he hadn't gotten away from a damn thing. He'd dragged them all here to town with him. He forced thoughts of his family and the woman to the back of his mind and concentrated on the meeting.

Caleb sat in the back of the room, listening to everyone talking about the upcoming elections. Hell, he didn't have time to serve on the board, so he had to admire those who were willing to not only put in the time, but put *up* with the constant stream of complaints from the members.

The meeting was in the main dining room, mostly because it was big enough for everyone to be comfortable. And, you could get something to eat or drink if you felt like it. The TCC was a legend in Royal. The building itself had taken a beating over the years, but the club had been undergoing some renovations recently.

The dining room was big, with dozens of tables covered in white linen. There was a fireplace, empty now, since even a summer night in Texas was hotter than hell. The walls were dotted with framed photos of members through the years. There were historical documents—including a signed letter from Sam Houston himself and even the original plans for the club, drawn up more than a hundred years ago.

Tradition ruled the TCC and every member there had a long history with the place, through family or marriage. Caleb's father had been a member, and so were the Goodmans. Simon was at the meeting tonight, too, shooting glares at Caleb from across the room. He really had to fire that man.

"So, thinking about running for president?"

Laughing, Caleb slid a look at Nathan Battle sitting beside him. They both had a beer in front of them but they'd been nursing the drinks all night since they both had to drive home.

"Yeah," Caleb said, "right after I run naked down Main Street."

Nathan grinned, leaned back in his chair and shook his head. "Feel the same. Man, you couldn't pay me to be on the board and put up with all the politics and the fights."

Caleb shook his head and watched James Harris break up a heated argument that probably would have become a fight in a few more minutes. A rancher and horse breeder, James was tall, African American and gravitated toward calm, which served him well as president of the TCC. Caleb was pretty sure the man actually *enjoyed* being in charge of the club.

"Look at that, how he can calm folks down without breaking a sweat. I swear, if James wasn't glued to his ranch, I'd hire him as a deputy." Nathan sighed. "My new deputy could learn a few things."

"Well," Caleb said, "now that James has got his nephew to raise, I think he's stepped up his patience game."

True. James had been named guardian of his eighteen-month-old nephew and Caleb admired how he'd stepped up to the new challenge. Couldn't be easy, ranching and being a single father to a baby.

"Simon Goodman's giving you looks that could kill," Nathan pointed out.

"Yeah, I know," Caleb said. "I'm ignoring him."

"Good luck with that." Nathan leaned closer to whisper, "Tell Shelby I'll be going to see Simon tomorrow about getting her money back. I wanted to give him some time to cool off."

"Yeah, I don't think that's happening." Caleb told his friend about Jared's visit to the ranch the day before.

"Damn it, Caleb." Nathan took a swig of his beer and winced as if it tasted bad. "You realize you just made this worse by lying about you and Shelby…"

Caleb thought about yesterday with Shelby. And last night. And this morning. He scrubbed one hand across his face, but it didn't do much to wipe away the mental images that were burned into his brain. Shelby naked in his bed. Shelby crying his name as an orgasm rocked her. Shelby rising up over him as she took him into her body, bowing her back, her long, thick hair falling across pale, smooth skin.

"You *were* lying, right?"

"What?" He looked at his friend and saw suspicion on Nate's features. "Sure. Of course."

His eyebrows lifted.

"All right, I don't know," Caleb said. He took a sip of his own beer. "There's something there. I just don't know what it is."

"I hate complications," Nate muttered.

"You're telling me," Caleb agreed.

Then James called the meeting to order. "All right everybody," he said, "if you'll settle down, we've got a few things to discuss tonight, but first, Gus Slade wants the floor. He's come up with a fund-raising idea that I think is interesting. I hope you all agree to take part—I sure as hell am."

Gus stepped up and laid out his plans for a bachelor auction to benefit pancreatic cancer research. And while he talked, Caleb glanced around the room. A few of the men his age looked intrigued by the idea, which Caleb did *not* understand. Damned if he'd put himself on the auction block for a night out on the town.

James's expression didn't give away what he was thinking—but of course as president, he'd be in the auction, too. Just another reason to not be on the board. Daniel Clayton appeared to hate the idea, yet in the next second, he was announcing that his grandmother was insisting he take part and so should everyone else.

Caleb couldn't be persuaded to enter, but after a back-and-forth discussion, it was decided to go ahead with the auction. Gus looked happy about it, James looked resigned and most of the younger members were downright eager. Took all kinds, Caleb thought.

A few hours later, Shelby was wide-awake. Her bedroom was dark and outside the night was quiet and still. She saw headlights spear through the blackness and knew that Caleb had gotten home from his meeting. She was tempted to go and find him, tell him to talk to her. Find out what exactly was going on with him.

But the truth was, she didn't want to know. How could he have gone from the world's greatest lover to a distant, cool stranger in the blink of an eye? Was it possible that the fire between them had already burned out?

Or was he deliberately pouring water on it?

"You're being ridiculous," she told herself, her whisper lost in the empty room. There was no relationship here. She'd only known the man for a *week*. But a voice in her head argued, *Yes, but what a week it's been.* True, they'd been through a lot in just a short amount of time. But the moment his family showed up, he tossed her aside. He couldn't have made himself any more clear.

She heard the click of the doorknob turning and her breath caught as her bedroom door swung slowly open. Shelby's heart gave a hard thump in her chest as Caleb walked into the room.

Moonlight drifted through the window, illuminating everything in a soft glow. He was wearing black slacks, a white shirt, open at the neck, and his hair looked as though he'd been shoving his fingers through it.

"Sorry," she said wryly. "I didn't hear you knock."

He walked to the foot of her bed and stared down at her. "Yeah. That's because I didn't."

He stared at her for a long minute—long enough for Shelby to shift position uneasily. It seemed he was finally ready to talk. Whether she wanted to or not.

"How was your meeting?" She didn't care about the meeting, but she couldn't stand the strained silence another moment.

"What?" He shook his head. "Oh, that. Fine. How was your night?"

"Aren't we polite?" she murmured and had the satisfaction of seeing one of his eyebrows wing up. "My night was fine. Quiet. I organized the pantry in your kitchen."

"The pantry?" He frowned.

"Where the food is?" The longer this went on, the more impatient Shelby became. "Did you really come in here to talk about nothing?"

"No," he said abruptly and shoved both hands into his pockets.

"Then why are you here, Caleb?" Shelby threw the duvet off and climbed off the bed. Foolish or not, she felt better, more sure of herself, standing on her own two feet. "You ignored me all day. Left tonight without a word and then walk into my bedroom unannounced. What's going on with you?"

The moonlight accentuated the grim slash of his mouth and the frown etching itself between his brows. Ridiculous that what Shelby most wanted to do was *soothe* him. She should want to kick him.

"It's you," he said abruptly. "Damn it, this is all about you, Shelby."

There went the softer instincts.

"No," she said, firmly shaking her head. "You don't get to blame this on me." She walked around the side of the bed to stand right in front of him. "You're the one who changed, Caleb. The minute your family showed up, you turned into the Iceman."

His scowl deepened and she wouldn't have thought that possible.

"So you just don't want them to know that we—"

"We what, exactly?" he interrupted. "Slept together? Nobody's business but ours."

"Then *what* is it?"

He looked down at her, staring into her eyes with such concentration, it felt as if he were looking all the way into her soul. "I can't get my mind off of you," he admitted finally.

"And that's a bad thing?" she asked.

"It is," he said flatly, and his eyes flashed with temper she knew was directed internally. "I don't want to want you, Shelby."

She huffed out a breath to disguise the hard lump that had settled in her throat. Honesty might be the best policy but it was a bitch to hear it.

"That's very flattering, thanks." She folded her arms across her chest in a defensive posture. After the night they'd spent together, to hear him dismiss her like that was more than hurtful. It was devastating. And it shouldn't have been.

She never should have let herself care. Let herself be pulled into a situation that she had *known* wouldn't last. But it had happened anyway. Shelby couldn't even pinpoint exactly when she had fallen for him. Maybe it had all started that first day, when she'd raced into his arms and he'd helped her when he hadn't had to. Maybe it was when he'd trusted her with his late mother's treasures. Or when he'd kissed her out on the range. Or when he stood between her and Jared even when she hadn't wanted him to be some shining knight in armor.

Whenever it had happened, Shelby now had to deal with the fallout. She'd come to Texas to marry a man she hadn't really loved. Now she was in love with a man who didn't want her. She was really batting a thousand in the romance department.

What she felt for Caleb dwarfed what she'd thought was love for Jared. Shelby hadn't wanted to admit even to herself that she was falling in love with Caleb, because that would only make it more real. But now, staring into icy-blue eyes, she knew it was true.

"I'm not trying to flatter you," he snapped. Pulling his hands from his pockets, he grabbed her shoulders and held on, pulling her close while still, somehow, keeping her at a distance. "I'm trying to be honest, here. There can't be anything between us, Shelby."

"Oh, you're making that clear," she said tightly and squirmed to get out of his grasp.

He held on more tightly. "I don't want to want you, but I have to have you."

She went absolutely still. His eyes were fire now, ice melted away in a passion she recognized and shared. It was so stupid, she told herself, even as her body hummed into life. Why should she sleep with him when he'd made it plain he didn't want to care? But how could she love him and *not*?

"You're making me crazy, Shelby," he ground out, his gaze

moving over her, his hands sliding from her shoulders to cup her face in his palms. "Can't stop thinking about you."

She covered his hands with hers and took a deep breath. "Why do you want to?"

He bent his head, kissed her, then stared into her eyes again. "Because it's better for both of us."

"You're wrong," she said. "And I can prove it to you." Shelby went up on her toes, wrapped her arms around his neck and kissed him as she'd been wanting to all day. Her lips parted over his and her tongue swept in to claim his. He reacted instantly, jerking her close, holding her so tightly to him she could feel his heartbeat pounding against her. Breathing was fast and hard.

His mouth devoured hers and she took everything he offered and returned it to him. His hands snaked up under her tank top and cupped her breasts, his thumbs and fingers tweaking and tugging at her nipples until everything in her melted into a puddle of need. Her fingers stabbed through his hair, holding his head to hers, his mouth to hers.

Shelby's entire body was throbbing, her heart was racing and her blood felt thick and hot as it pumped through her veins. When he stripped her top off and bent his head to take one nipple then the other into his mouth, she swayed unsteadily and kept a tight grip on his shoulders to balance herself.

Caleb tipped her back onto the bed and she went willingly, eagerly. Shelby tore at his shirt, sending tiny white buttons skittering across the floor. She didn't care. She wanted to hold him, feel him.

"I missed you today," she admitted, kissing his shoulder, trailing her lips and tongue along his heated skin until she found the spot at the base of his throat that she knew drove him wild.

He groaned, tipped his head to one side and gave her free access. Shelby lavished attention on him, licking, nibbling until he stabbed his fingers through her hair and pulled her head back. "I missed you, too."

His mouth covered hers as she shoved his shirt off his shoulders and down his arms. Her fingers went to his belt and undid it, then unhooked the waistband of his slacks and slid the zipper down. She reached for him and sighed when her hand closed around the hard, solid length of him.

His hips rocked into her hand and he threw his head back and hissed in a breath. She half expected him to howl and everything in her fisted into tight knots of expectation. Anticipation. She stroked him, rubbed him, caressed the tip of him with the base of her thumb until he trembled and Shelby thought there was nothing so sexy as a strong man being vulnerable.

"Wait, wait," he ground out and pulled away from her.

"Come back," she said, coming up onto her knees to crook one finger at him.

He sighed. "Oh, yeah." Then he stripped, pausing only long enough to grab a condom from the pocket of his slacks. "Stopped at my room before I came here."

"I like a man who thinks ahead," she said and slowly shimmied out of her tank top. Moonlight pearled on her skin and she loved the flash in his eyes as he stared at her.

Then he was back on the bed with her and he was pulling her sleep shorts down and off, running his hands over her behind, stroking the hot, damp core of her. Shelby was writhing, twisting in his grasp and as the promise of another earth-shattering climax hovered closer, she reached for him. "Inside me, Caleb. Be inside me again. I need to feel you."

"What you do to me," he said, shaking his head as he watched her. "All I can think about is being with you. In you."

"Then *do it*," she demanded.

Nodding, he flipped her over onto her stomach and before Shelby could even manage a response, he was lifting her hips until she was kneeling. She looked over her shoulder at him and felt fresh need grab her by the throat. He looked dark, dangerous and deadly sexy. His skin was tanned, his body rock hard and as he smoothed on the condom, her heart leaped into a gallop.

Then he was behind her, sliding into her and Shelby cried out his name. He held her hips in his big, strong hands and rocked in and out of her in a fast, breath-stealing rhythm. She had no choice but to follow his lead. She curled her fingers into the sheet beneath her and held on.

She pushed back against him, moving with him, taking him higher and deeper than she would have thought possible. He became a part of her. Shelby didn't know where she ended and he began and she didn't care. All that mattered was what he was doing to her, making her feel. Her body erupted and she turned her face into the mattress to muffle the scream torn from her throat.

Shelby was still trembling, still shaken when Caleb shouted out her name and his body slammed into hers, giving her everything he was and promising nothing.

Nine

The Courtyard shops were a few miles west of downtown Royal. It used to be a ranch, but when the owners sold off, the property became an eclectic mix of shops. The latest was a bridal shop and Shelby had taken a moment to look through the window. In just ten seconds she'd seen five prettier gowns than the one she'd been forced to wear to her disastrous almost wedding.

A large, freshly painted red barn housed Priceless, the antiques shop, plus a crafts studio where people could come in and try their hands at everything from painting to ceramics and more.

Several other buildings on the property showcased local craftsmen such as artists, glassblowers and soap and candle makers. Local farmers rented booths to sell their fresh produce and canned goods and there was even a local cheese maker who always had a long line of customers.

Shelby loved it all. Actually she pretty much loved everything about Royal. Small town life really agreed with her. She wasn't looking forward to moving back to Chicago once she got her money from the Goodman family.

Which should be soon, since the sheriff had told Caleb that he was going out there today to take care of things.

And that left her exactly where?

Shelby sat at a small, round table outside the tiny coffee shop and sipped at a tall glass of iced tea. August hadn't cooled off any and she couldn't help but wonder what winter in Texas would be like.

But she didn't think she'd be finding out.

Watching people stroll past her, some hand in hand, Shelby sighed a little. Last night, she and Caleb had come to a détente of sorts. He didn't want to care for her and she couldn't care for him. It didn't matter how she felt because he wouldn't want to hear it.

"What a mess."

"Excuse me. You're Shelby Arthur, right?"

The woman was blonde, with big blue eyes and a wide smile. She wore a pale green summer dress that showed off tanned, toned arms and legs.

"Hi, yes."

"Do you mind if I sit down and talk to you for a second?" Without waiting for consent, she pulled out a chair and sighed as she sat. "I'm Alexis Slade and thanks for sharing the shade under your umbrella."

"No problem." Shelby smiled at her. "Didn't I just see you at Priceless?" She had been at the antiques store, to talk to Raina Patterson about the last load of crystal and glass they'd taken in. Raina already had buyers for most of the items and the others she would sell in her shop and pay Caleb when they sold.

She should have felt a lot of satisfaction for how Caleb's house was turning out with a little organization. Instead, she was sad because it seemed that her time in Royal was quickly coming to an end. But she shook off those feelings and concentrated on Alexis.

"Yes. I was there to talk to Raina about a fund-raiser the TCC is going to be putting on."

"Oh." Shelby nodded. "Sure, the bachelor auction. Everyone here is talking about it."

Alexis rolled her eyes, set her cream-colored bag on the table and dug out a notebook. When she flipped it open to an empty page she sent Shelby a wince of embarrassment. "I know. Paper and pen. I'm practically a cave person. But it's so much easier for me to just write things down."

"I do the same thing," Shelby assured her as a hot wind blew through the courtyard, tossing her hair across her eyes. She plucked it free, then asked, "But what did you want to talk to me about?"

"I'm not ashamed to admit that I need help," Alexis said, smiling. "You know, I run our family ranch, the Lone Wolf, with no problems at all. But running this auction and getting things like invitations and sponsors for prizes and the bachelors all lined up is giving me a headache."

"I can imagine." She tried to sound sympathetic, but Shelby couldn't help but feel a quick zip of excitement. There was nothing she liked better than taking over a confused mess and bringing order to it.

"Raina was telling me what a great job you did out at Caleb's ranch, organizing his mother's collection…"

"It's been challenging," she admitted, "but yes, it's all coming together."

"Well," Alexis said with another smile, "I figured if that didn't scare you off, then maybe I could find a way to coerce you into helping me get this auction off the ground?"

A little boy careened past the table, trailing a helium balloon in his wake. His giggles floated like soap bubbles on the air. A waitress came out with a fresh glass of tea for Shelby and one for Alexis, though it hadn't been ordered.

"Thanks, Ella," Alexis said on a sigh. "You're a lifesaver."

The young woman grinned. "You want your usual salad, too? Or something else?"

Alexis looked at the brownie on the table in front of Shelby and winced. "I'll have one of those, please, and screw the calories."

Shelby laughed and Ella said, "In this heat, you'll burn them right off as soon as you eat them."

Once they were alone again, Shelby said, "I'm happy to help, but I don't know how long I'll be in town."

Alexis sipped at her tea. "So you've decided to move back to Chicago when you get your money back from Jared?"

Shelby's jaw dropped and her eyes went wide. "Wow. Small town grapevines are really impressive."

"Yeah, sorry." She smiled and shrugged. "But I was at the wedding that didn't happen."

"Oh, God."

"Hey, don't worry about it," Alexis said and reached out to give Shelby's hand a reassuring pat. "I totally understand. I mean, I know you and Caleb are together and how could you marry Jared when you loved someone else?"

"Oh, Alexis, we're not—" God, she had to clear this up. People were talking and that wasn't fair to Caleb, even though he was the one who'd said it, feeding Margaret's gossip until it had become a huge blob of innuendo with a life all its own.

"I felt the same way, you know?" The friendly woman leaned back in her chair, crossed her legs and said, "Back in high school, Jared asked me out constantly, but I didn't go out with him because I was crazy about someone else..." Her words trailed off and a thoughtful frown etched itself briefly on her features.

She knew how Alexis had felt. Shelby was crazy about Caleb. And crazy for letting her emotions get so deeply involved. It was one thing to make a mistake unknowingly. But when you walked right into one with your eyes wide-open, that had to be nuts.

"Anyway," Alexis said and thanked Ella when her brownie arrived, "will you help me get this started? I'd be so grateful."

Shelby thought about it and realized that even if her time in Royal was short, she had to keep busy. Otherwise, she would torture herself with wishing things could be different with Caleb.

"I'd be happy to."

"Great!" Alexis pulled a pen out of her purse and looked at Shelby in expectation. "So. Where do we start?"

Shelby laughed and proceeded to do what she did best.

"Time we talked."

Caleb glanced over his shoulder and watched his younger brother walk into the shadowy barn. "Not now."

"Yeah," Mitch countered, still walking toward him in a determined stride. "You've been saying that for four years now."

"Then I probably mean it." Caleb turned back to the stall door and stroked the nose of the mare poking her pretty head out for some attention. Just last night, she'd had her foal and done it all on her own, with no supervision from the local vet.

He had a million things to do and not one of them included talking to his brother about ancient history. Caleb took a deep breath, letting the familiar scents—straw, horses, leather and wood—soothe him. But that didn't last because it seemed his brother was determined to finally have his say.

"Damn it, Caleb," Mitch said, stopping right beside him. "What the hell did you expect Meg and me to do?"

"You don't want to do this, Mitch. Just let it lie."

"You mean let's just go on like we have been?" Mitch asked, throwing his hands high then letting them slap back down against his thighs. "With you acting like you've still got a knife in your back?"

Caleb shot him a hard look and turned away, headed for the wide double doors. Mitch stayed with him, finally reaching out and grabbing his brother's arm to stop him in his tracks.

"Nobody wanted to hurt you," Mitch said quietly.

"Didn't stop you, though, did it?"

Mitch yanked his hat off and rubbed his hand back and forth over his nearly shaved head. "No. It didn't. Nothing would have stopped me from having Meg."

Caleb winced. That's how he'd felt about having Shelby. Instantly, images from the night before filled his mind and his body went tight and hard. The woman had touched something inside him that he hadn't even known was there. But as much as he wanted her, as much as being inside her burned him to a cinder, how could he trust her? How could he trust any woman enough again to risk the kind of humiliation he'd already lived through once?

Mitch drew his head back and stared at him. "You're not still in love with Meg, are you?"

"What?" Caleb exclaimed. "No."

Just the thought of it shocked him. He hadn't been bothered by Mitch and Meg being happy together on the ranch. Not jealous or even bitter about what they'd found together. It was the betrayal that had hit him harder than anything else. And wasn't that enlightening? If he'd really loved Meg in the first place, it would have driven him crazy watching his brother with her.

What did that say? Hell, looking back now, he wasn't even sure he'd loved her *then*. He'd wanted to be married. To have a family. And Meg was the one he'd chosen to fulfill the role of wife and mother. God, had he been that big an ass?

"That's good to know. I always admired you, Caleb. You know that. But Meg." Mitch shook his head and gave a wistful smile. "Hell, we'd all known each other for years and then that summer it was like I was seeing Meg for the first time. Love just slammed into us both. Neither of us was expecting it or looking for it. It was just *there*. And when you find something like that, you can't just turn from it."

He could see that now, with four years of clarity behind him. And, maybe, Shelby dropping into his life gave Caleb a little

more insight into how it must have been for his brother. Still...
"Running away the night before the wedding wasn't the way
to handle it."

"Yeah, I know that. And you should know, Meg didn't want
to do it. I talked her into making a run for it. Cowardly? Okay,
yeah it was." Mitch nodded thoughtfully. "But damn it, Caleb,
you were always so damn self-righteous. So sure of yourself
and how the world ought to run. If we had come to you, would
you have listened?"

He hated to admit it, but the answer was most likely *no*. He'd
had his plan and he wouldn't have listened to anything that
would disrupt that plan.

"Maybe not," he allowed.

Mitch blew out a breath. "Thanks for that. And you should
know we're both damn sorry for what we put you through. Hell,
Caleb. I'm sorry."

Caleb nodded and looked at his brother. It had been four
years since they'd really had a conversation that didn't revolve
around the ranch. And it felt *good* to get this out in the open.
To hopefully get past it.

"You and Meg are good together," he said finally and watched
his younger brother's smile broaden.

"I love her like crazy," Mitch said. "More even than when
I married her."

"Yeah. I can see that." Caleb slapped one hand against
Mitch's shoulder and took a step that would end the enmity
between them. "I guess things worked out just how they should
in the end."

"You mean that?"

"Yeah," Caleb said, a little surprised himself, "I do."

"Good. That's good." Mitch nodded and blew out a breath
again. "You know, you're gonna be an uncle again."

"Is that right?" Caleb grinned at the thought and realized
that the hurt of four years ago was well and truly gone now. He

could enjoy his brother. And his sister-in-law. He could put the past where it belonged and reclaim his family.

So, a voice in his mind whispered, *does that mean you can put what Shelby did aside and take a leap of faith?*

He shook his head to dislodge that thought, because he just didn't have an answer for it. Caleb could understand what Meg and Mitch had done, but the bottom line was, Shelby was a different matter altogether. How could he trust her to stay when she'd run out on Jared? She hadn't done it for love. She'd simply bolted when she couldn't handle the thought of going through with the wedding. If he took a chance with her, would she run again when things didn't go her way?

Shaking his head, he pushed those thoughts aside for now. He had no answers anyway. So he looked at his brother and said, "Let's go up to the big house and have a beer. We should talk about the new ranch land we're buying and the oil leases are coming due again in six months. We need to decide if we want to renew or start drilling ourselves."

Mitch settled his hat on his head and grinned. "Sounds good to me."

As they walked, Caleb was glad to finally be more at ease with his brother. But thoughts of Shelby made sure he wasn't at ease with anything else.

Cam had left a big bowl of pasta salad in the fridge and roast beef sandwiches on a covered plate for their dinner. After a long hot day, it sounded perfect. But for right now, Shelby sat at the kitchen table, making a list of things for Alexis to look into for the auction.

First, of course, had to be advertising. If they really wanted to make the most of this auction, then they needed as many single women as possible to take part.

"Houston papers as well as Royal," she murmured, making notes as she talked. "A website would be good, too. Maybe they could have a link on Royal's town site, but one of its own would be even better."

"Talking to yourself?" Caleb asked as he came into the room.

She looked up and smiled. Memories flooded her mind, how he'd been last night, how *they'd* been, together. Maybe she should have been embarrassed but instead all she could think was that she wanted to do it all again. And again.

Squirming a little on the bench seat as her body warmed, she forced cheer into her voice. "No, I actually told Alexis Slade I'd help her with the bachelor auction."

Caleb went to the fridge for a bottle of beer. Once he had it open, he took a long drink and shook his head. "Can't believe they're going to do it."

"Are you going to be one of the bachelors?"

"Oh, that's a big hell no," Caleb said, firmly shaking his head for emphasis.

Foolishly, relief washed over Shelby. Heck, she might not even be in Royal when the auction happened, but she was glad to hear he wouldn't be bought by some woman who wasn't *her*.

"I think it sounds fun," she said, deliberately making herself smile. "We're thinking of a Christmas theme."

"Christmas? It's *August*," Caleb pointed out.

"Well, it's not going to be held tomorrow. The auction is set for November, so a Christmas theme will really work. There's a lot to be done in not very much time." She looked back to her list and started a new column for decorations. "Plenty of mistletoe, and wreaths and ribbon. Probably a hundred yards or so of ribbon, since Alexis says they're holding the auction at the TCC in the gazebo. To make it look like a winter wonderland it will take a few miles of pine garland and red ribbon—"

"Ribbon."

"And snow." She looked up at him. "Does it snow in Texas? Heck, does it ever cool off in Texas?"

He grinned. "It doesn't usually get cold enough to snow."

"Fake snow, then. It could be mounded in corners with little signs pointing the way to the dessert tables and the bar and the auction itself… Ooh, write that down. We should have lots of different desserts. I bet Jillian at Miss Mac's Pie Shack would do the desserts for us and—" She paused and narrowed her eyes on him. "What're you smiling at?"

He shook his head. "Just that I'm sort of getting used to your monologues."

"Well," she said, "I talk to myself because I always understand me."

"Uh-huh." He walked to the kitchen island, hitched one hip against it and asked, "How do you know Jillian Navarro at Miss Mac's Pie Shack?"

"I was in town and hello. *Pie.* I stopped in to try some and got to talking with her, and her daughter is just adorable and her desserts are amazing."

"Right. So you're helping Alexis with the auction. Making friends all over town. Does that mean you've decided to stay in Royal after you get your money back?"

Shelby sighed. She'd been thinking a lot about just that. Stay or go. The truth was, she had nothing in Chicago to go back to. A few friends, some loyal clients, but nothing else. Here in Royal, she could start over. Build a new business. Make new friends. But even she didn't believe those reasons were the only ones she was considering staying for.

She'd like a chance with Caleb. But there was no guarantee that would happen and if she stayed and couldn't have him, would she be able to live with it?

"Honestly, I don't know," she said, looking up at him. "Until I get the money, I don't have to make that decision so I guess I'm putting it off."

He simply stared at her for a long minute or two and once again, Shelby was left wishing she could read what he was thinking. The whole quiet cowboy thing was irritating in the extreme when you wanted answers and got nothing but more questions.

Then his manner shifted. He straightened up, set his beer down on the counter and pointed at the window behind her. "Looks like we've got company."

Shelby turned in her seat in time to see Brooke Goodman get out of her car. Darkness was lowering over the ranch, but the porch light was bright enough to see that Brooke's light blond hair was lifting in the ever-present wind. She wore skinny black jeans, a dark red shirt with long sleeves and a pair of black sandals. She took a long look at the house, then turned back to her flashy red convertible and reached into the backseat.

When she lifted out one of Shelby's suitcases, Shelby gave a *whoop* of excitement. "She's brought my stuff!"

Jared's sister was the only one of the Goodman family that Shelby had actually *liked*. Brooke had been her one and only bridesmaid at the wedding that hadn't happened. And if she was here now, with her suitcase, maybe she was also going to deliver the money that was Shelby's.

She scooted out of the bench seat and headed for the door. "I'll go talk to her."

"Yeah," Caleb said, walking right behind her. "*We* should."

Shelby rolled her eyes. Whether he wanted her or not, the man couldn't seem to stop trying to protect her. But with Brooke, no protection was necessary.

She opened the door just as Jared's sister was lifting one hand to knock. Instead, she slapped that hand to her chest and gave a short laugh.

"Wow. You scared me."

"Sorry," Shelby said and reached out to hug her. "I'm so glad to see you, Brooke."

"I'm sorry it took me so long to get your things back to you," she said, as Caleb took the suitcase from her and pulled it inside. "There's another one in the backseat."

"I'll get it."

Meanwhile, Shelby steered Brooke into the great room and took just a second for a little self-congratulatory smile. She really had made a huge difference in this house. The room was open, welcoming. The ranch was now looking exactly like what it was, a luxury ranch house with eclectic details. She waved Brooke onto the couch and sat down beside her.

Brooke was petite and pretty and so nice it made up for the fact that she seemed nearly perfect. She was also a talented artist, though neither of her parents were supportive of her goals.

"Thank you for bringing my things," Shelby said.

"Don't thank me." Brooke took a breath and let it out in a rush. "I couldn't get your money. The family is still furious and it was all I could do to sneak your suitcases out."

Shelby felt a wave of disappointment rise up, then dissipate. She would get her money, it was just a matter of *when.* "It's okay. Really." She forced a smile. "This is all my fault, anyway. I should have called the whole thing off long before the wedding day."

Brooke shook her head. "Don't ruin it for me. You're actually my hero in all of this. You stood up to the Goodman family and that's something I've never been able to do."

Shelby knew that Brooke's dream was to go to Europe to study painting, view the old masters in person. But her parents had control over Brooke's inheritance and they refused to give her what her grandmother had left her.

"Brooke," Shelby said, reaching out to give her hand a squeeze, "just *do* it. Don't wait for your parents to agree. Just go."

The other woman sighed a little. "I can't touch my money unless my parents give permission or I'm married."

"Wow." Shelby sat back. "Couldn't you go anyway? Work to support yourself while you're there?"

"It sounds wonderful, but I'm not trained to do anything," Brooke said. "Unless someone wants me to arrange a sit-down dinner for thirty. I can do that."

"You're being too hard on yourself," Shelby said. "You're so talented. You have to do something with your art."

Brooke instantly brightened. "Actually, Alexis Slade asked me to do some painting at the TCC. I'm doing a mural at the day care and more in the public garden areas. It's not Europe, but it's exciting."

Shelby grinned. "What did your parents say?"

Brooke laughed. "They don't know."

Caleb walked back into the room and took a seat near the two women. "I put your things in your room, Shelby."

"Thanks. Brooke was just telling me—"

"What the hell?" Caleb cut her off, looking through the wide front windows at a long, black sedan hurtling down the drive and coming to a hard stop behind Brooke's car.

Both women turned to look and Brooke groaned. "Oh, God. That's my father. What's he doing here?"

"He probably knows you brought my things over," Shelby said, standing up. "I'm so sorry. You shouldn't have to get in trouble over me."

"Doesn't matter," Brooke said. She stood up, too, and all three of them watched as Simon Goodman stomped toward the front door.

He didn't bother to knock, just came inside and slammed the door behind him. "Brooke! Where the hell are you?"

She gave Shelby a sad smile. "Right here, Father."

Caleb took a step forward, automatically putting himself between Simon and the rest of the room. He stood there, Shelby told herself, like a soldier. Back straight, legs braced wide apart, arms crossed over his chest. He was a solid wall of protection and she felt a rush of warmth for him. He would always stand for someone he felt needed defending.

Simon Goodman marched into the room like a man on a mission. His features were thunderous, his dark eyes burning as he swept the room before landing on his daughter. "The minute I saw that woman's suitcases gone from the hall, I knew you were behind it."

"Father," Brooke said with calm, "these are Shelby's things. She deserves to have them."

"She deserves *nothing* from us," he countered and shifted his gaze to Shelby. "You've dragged my son's name through the dirt. And for what?"

Caleb speared him with a hot look. "You're going to want to watch what you say, Simon."

"It's all right, Caleb. I can handle this," she said, then looked at the older man vibrating with fury. "Mr. Goodman, I didn't mean to—"

"You didn't mean," Simon said with a harsh sneer. "Is that supposed to make this all go away? People are gossiping about my son and here you are, living with a rancher, no better than you should be."

Caleb took a step closer to him. "That's enough, Simon."

The older man glared at him. He wore a suit and tie, but his hair was disheveled as if he'd been electrocuted recently and his eyes fired with indignation.

"It's not enough. You were a guest at my son's wedding and left with the bride." Simon looked him up and down with one quick, dismissive glance. "What does that make you? Or *her*?"

"Now, just a minute," Shelby said.

"Father, you're making this worse."

"You keep your mouth shut," Simon snapped. "You're a damn traitor to your family."

"Hey, there's no need to punish Brooke," Shelby protested.

"Simon," Caleb warned, ice dripping from his words. "You should leave. Now. You don't need to be here."

"I'm here to deliver this tramp's money." He reached into his inner suit pocket and pulled out a check. Then he tossed it at her and watched as it fluttered to the floor.

"Pick it up." Caleb's voice was cold. Tight.

"Damned if I will," Simon said.

Brooke bent to pick up the check and instantly handed it to Shelby. "I'm sorry for all of this," she whispered.

"Sorry? You're sorry?" Her father's eyes wheeled. "This woman smeared your family, your *brother* and you would apologize to her?"

He looked back at Shelby, a sneer on his face. "There's your damn money." He shifted his gaze to Caleb. "I brought it because I had to see this tramp myself. To tell her that she should leave Royal because a life here will be a misery for her." He looked at her. "I'll see to it myself."

"You'll do *nothing*." Caleb moved in on the man and Shelby noticed how quickly Simon backpedaled.

Still, she didn't want to cause even more chaos in this house. This town. "Caleb, I told you I don't need to be defended."

"There is no defense for you, young woman," Simon blustered.

Caleb ignored him and focused on Shelby. "You think I don't know you can handle this? I do. But I'm damned if I'm going to stand in my own house and listen to insults."

"It doesn't matter," Shelby insisted. "Not to me. Not anymore."

Brooke put one hand on her arm and shook her head slightly, as if silently telling Shelby to let Caleb handle it.

"It matters to me," Caleb said. "I've seen more of the Goodmans in the last week than I have in the last year and I can truly well say that but for Brooke, I've had more than enough."

"You would insult me? Your father wouldn't stand for this," Simon said.

"Well then, that convinces me I'm doing the right thing." Caleb took another step closer to the other man. "You're fired."

"What?" He genuinely looked surprised.

"Should have done it years ago, but it's done now."

"Caleb," Shelby said.

"You're going to let this woman ruin a good working relationship?" Simon was clearly stunned at the idea. "Are you blind, boy? She's just a city girl come looking for a rich cowboy. She turned my boy loose and she's aiming at you, now."

"Oh, for…" Shelby muttered.

Caleb never glanced at her. "You should leave, Simon. Your business is done here."

"You'll regret this, boy."

"Not a boy," Caleb reminded him. "And the only thing I regret is waiting so long to fire your ass."

"Brooke," Simon ordered, "you go get in your car. We'll not stay and be insulted."

"Brooke," Shelby said quietly, "you don't have to go."

"Now," Simon roared.

"It's better if I go," Brooke said. "Don't worry. He's all thunder, no lightning. I'll talk to you soon."

Simon stomped from the room and Brooke was just a step or two behind him. She turned at the threshold and gave them one small smile before following her father out to the yard.

Caleb and Shelby stood side by side, watching as the Goodmans drove off. Shelby was more than a little rattled by the encounter, but her suitcases were in her room and she held a check in her hand. She glanced down at it, making sure the total was right. It was.

Caleb looked at it, too, then caught her gaze with his. "So, guess there's nothing holding you here now, right?"

She lifted her gaze to his and wanted to wail when she saw the blank look in those icy-blue eyes. Just a moment ago, he'd stood in front of her, defending her. Now it was as if he'd erected a wall between them, closing her off, turning her back into the outsider she had been when she'd first come here.

"I don't know," she said simply. "I don't know what I'm going to do."

"Come on, Shelby." He shook his head, his gaze locked with hers. "We both know what you're going to do."

"No—" She didn't. How could she know when everything inside her was in turmoil?

"You'll go back to Chicago, now that you've got the means to do it," he said in a clipped tone that carried a sheen of ice. "Your reason for staying's gone. Probably best all the way around. No point dragging this out, is there?"

God, it was as if he'd already said goodbye and watched her leave the ranch. Was it so easy for him, then? To let her go? Would he not miss her? Even a little? "Caleb…"

He spoke up quickly as if he simply didn't want to hear whatever she might have said. "I don't blame you for leaving. Royal's not your home. Nothing holding you here anymore. Sorry you had to go through all of that, but at least it's finished now." He took a step back from her.

"I've got things to check on," he muttered. "Don't wait on me for dinner. Don't know when I'll be back."

Shelby watched him go and knew he was doing more than walking out of the room.

He was walking out of her life.

Ten

Two days later, Shelby was still in limbo, and it was a cold, lonely spot.

Caleb had cut her out of his life with the smooth efficiency of a surgeon. Yes, she was still living at the ranch, but she might as well have been on the moon. Caleb didn't come to her in the middle of the night. They didn't share dinner in a quiet kitchen, telling each other stories of the day. She hadn't been back in *his* room since their first night together.

In the mornings, he left at first light, so she didn't even see him over the coffeepot. And Shelby tried to avoid the kitchen altogether now, since the sympathy in Cam's eyes simply tore at her.

"If you had any sense, you'd just leave," she told herself firmly.

She'd taken her check and opened a bank account in town. But that didn't necessarily mean she was going to stay, she reminded herself. She could always have the money wired to another account. In Chicago. Or maybe New York. Or even Florida. Somewhere far away from Texas so she didn't have to be reminded of what a nightmare the month of August had become.

"Sorry," Meg said as she hurried back into the twins' bedroom. "Sometimes I hate that phone."

"It's okay," Shelby said, putting on a smile and a lighthearted tone that she didn't feel. No reason to depress Meg. Especially since the woman was giving Shelby something to *do*. Something to focus on besides her own broken heart. "Gave me a chance to look around, get some ideas."

"Thank God," Meg said, doing a slow circle to take the room in.

Just like the main ranch house, Meg and Mitch's place quietly spoke of money. There was nothing overt, but the furnishings were all high quality and the house itself had obviously been built with care. Hardwood floors gleamed in slashes of sunlight that speared through wide windows. Heavy rugs dotted the floors, giving warmth to the space and the twins' beds were side by side, divided only by a child-sized table holding a grinning, cow-shaped lamp.

The space was huge and Shelby's imagination raced with ideas for making the space more like a child's dream room.

"You know, with the new baby coming, I really want to get Jack and Julie's room redone. And with the miracle you worked at the big house, who better to help me?" Meg walked over, picked up a pair of Julie's pink sneakers and stowed them neatly beneath the bed.

Shelby nodded thoughtfully as her mind whirled with idea after idea. "I love how it is right now. It's decorated beautifully."

"It is, but it's more adult pretty than kid pretty, you know?"

Shelby knew just what she meant. The furnishings were lovely, but there was nothing about the room that sparked a child's imagination.

Meg looked around again. "We had a designer come in originally, but—" she winced "—the woman didn't actually *have* children, so she set the room up as if kids never move or do anything. I mean, it's pretty and I do like it, but the toys and clothes and just the general flotsam created by two tiny humans is staggering. Even the housekeeper is ready to throw up her hands."

Shelby grinned. "Well, I don't have kids, either, but I know what I'd like. I think there are a few simple things we can do to make it all easier on you and them."

"I'm all ears," Meg assured her.

"Organization first, and then we can spruce it all up and make it more…fanciful."

"I like it already," Meg assured her.

Shelby walked to the wide walk-in closet and threw the doors open. "This for example. There's a lot of wasted space. On hangers, kids' clothes don't hang down very low. We can put a shelving system here and add wicker baskets on the bottom. That way the kids can put their own toys away in the baskets while you'll have the top shelf for shoes, sweaters, whatever else you need, but don't hang."

"I like it," Meg said, nodding as if she could see it.

"And, we can have beds made that come with storage beneath, so the twins can have their own treasure chests, keep things that are important to them stored away."

"Oh, they'd love that," Meg agreed.

Shelby gave an inner sigh. Those children were adorable and pulled on every one of her heartstrings. Along with giving her own biological clock a good, hard kick.

She shook the feeling off and concentrated on bringing her imagination to life. "And in the corner, we can put in a table and chairs, kid-sized, where Julie can practice her drawing. With a series of smaller shelves and small baskets there, we'd have a space for her paper and crayons and markers."

Meg grinned. "Oh, my God, this is great. Keep going!"

Laughing now, Shelby turned and pointed to the far corner. "This room is so big, we could build a playhouse there for both of the kids and make it like a tree house." She was thinking as she spoke and smiled when another idea hit her. "You know,

Brooke Goodman is an excellent artist. I bet she'd love to paint a tree mural on the wall and we could build the house to look as though it's hung on the tree branches. With little steps and ladders and secret passages... Oh, and maybe a place inside where they could nap."

"I love it. I love all of it," Meg said, wrapping her arms around her middle. "I can't even tell you. It's perfect. Honestly, Shelby, you're brilliant."

"Thank you, but sometimes, it just takes an outsider to look at a space and see it differently."

Meg frowned a little. "You're not an outsider, Shelby."

Shaking her head, she ignored that because the truth was that Caleb had cut her out. Pushed her out.

"I just love to bring a room together and make it functional, you know?" She looked around and could almost see what it would be like when it was finished. A sharp pang settled around Shelby's heart when she realized she most likely wouldn't see the completed project. How could she stay when Caleb was making it clear he didn't want her there?

"This is more than functional," Meg said. "You're talking about building a kid's dream room."

Shelby smiled. "For now. Then, when they want their own rooms, you could make this one a shared play space and decorate other bedrooms for them."

"God knows the house is big enough for it," Meg said, nodding. "And Mitch is already talking about adding on another wing. The Mackenzies are big on *wings*," she added with a laugh. "He wants a *lot* of kids, but then, so do I."

"It sounds wonderful," Shelby said and, though she thought she was being stiff-upper-lippy, Meg must have caught something in her tone.

"What's going on, Shelby?"

"Nothing. Really." Even she heard the lie and Shelby wished she were better at it.

"Is it you and Caleb?"

Shelby shook her head. There really was no point in pretending, when she'd have to leave the ranch soon. Everyone would know the truth then. "There is no me and Caleb."

"What? Why? Since when?" Meg walked closer. "I can see the way you look at each other. Your eyes practically devour him when he walks into a room. And he's clearly crazy about you, Shelby."

"No, he's not," Shelby said and looked down into the yard. From the kids' bedroom, she had a good view of the corral where Caleb was working with one of the horses. He held the reins as the huge, black animal trotted around the perimeter. Mitch and the three-year-old twins stood at the fence, watching, but Shelby couldn't tear her eyes away from Caleb.

Everything about that man called to her. Sadly, he obviously didn't feel the same about her. Otherwise, he never would have been able to simply ignore her existence as he had the last couple of days.

"What happened, Shelby?" Meg asked, her voice soft. "Did you guys have a fight?"

Shelby laughed, but it hurt her throat. "No, we didn't. That's the hardest part to accept. Nothing happened. Nothing at all. No fight. No huge, defining moment that tore us apart. It might be easier to take if there had been a big blowup." She sighed a little and kept her gaze locked on Caleb. "He just…shut down. Shut me out. The Goodmans gave me my money and Caleb assumed I'd be going back to Chicago. He actually told me it was probably for the best."

"Idiot," Meg muttered.

Shelby smiled sadly at the camaraderie. "After that, he simply closed himself off. For the last two days, he's ignored me completely. Avoided me. He won't even talk to me, Meg. I don't even know why I'm still here."

She turned to look at the other woman. "At this point, I think maybe Caleb was right and it would be for the best if I just left. For both our sakes."

"Oh, God, I was afraid of this." Meg sighed and moved up to stand beside her at the window. "This isn't about you, Shelby. This is about me."

Confused, she turned to look at her friend. "What do you mean?"

"God, it's like a Karmic circle."

"What are you talking about?" Shelby asked. Misery was stamped on Meg's features but her eyes simmered with a low burn.

"This is about me. And Mitch and what happened four years ago." Meg turned around to look at Shelby. "Once upon a time, I was engaged to Caleb."

Stunned, Shelby stared at her. She hadn't known what to expect, but this was still a shocker. Caleb was always so cool with Meg, it was hard to imagine the two of them engaged. "Really?"

"I know. Weird to think about now. It's funny, but Caleb never even really proposed." Meg sighed, reached up and tucked her hair behind her ears. "It seemed like a natural progression, you know? We'd known each other forever. He wanted family and so did I and..." She sighed. "That sounds so lame, but—"

"It's okay," Shelby assured her. Hadn't she done the same thing with Jared? Given in to her need for family, for home and then come to regret the decision? "Believe me, I understand."

Meg gave her a weak smile. "Thanks. Anyway, long story short—a few weeks before the wedding, Mitch and I discovered we loved each other. But what could we do? I was engaged to his brother for heaven's sake. Neither of us wanted to hurt Caleb, but that's what we did."

This explained so much, Shelby thought. Why Caleb would pull back every time a connection began to grow between them. And knowing this, she didn't have a clue how to fight it. How to get through to him and expect him to trust her.

"At the time, I tried to find a way to talk to Caleb, but he's so damn single-minded he wouldn't listen." She held up one hand. "Don't misunderstand, I'm not saying that any of this was his fault. Mitch and I were in love and it seemed like there was only one way to be together. So, the night before the wedding, Mitch and I eloped."

"Oh, God." Shelby shifted her gaze to the man in the middle of the corral.

"Yeah." Meg stood beside her. "I left Caleb a letter, trying to explain it all, but of course it wasn't enough. Apologies weren't enough. And for the last four years, Mitch and I have tried to make it up to him, but that's hard to do when the man won't acknowledge your presence."

"I know that, too," Shelby murmured.

"Caleb and Mitch kept working together, but they used to be close and that ended when we eloped. I still feel guilty about that. I know that it hurts Mitch daily. And I think Caleb misses his brother, too." Meg took a breath and sighed it out. "Just the other day, though, Caleb and Mitch talked and it might be getting better between them. But he'll never forgive me."

She turned, and her gaze locked with Shelby's. "So when you ran out on your wedding, it really hit home with him."

"Of course it did." Shelby's heart actually *sank*. She felt it drop to the pit of her stomach where it sat like an icy stone. This was why she couldn't get past the wall he'd built around himself. This was at the heart of the darkness she'd glimpsed in his eyes a few times.

No wonder he couldn't trust her. She understood how it had to seem to him. Shelby had done to Jared exactly what Meg had done to him. He'd already experienced betrayal and didn't want to risk it again.

"I'm so sorry, Shelby. He's being an ass because of something I did."

She wanted to agree. A part of Shelby wanted to give Caleb that out. Let him off the hook. But by doing that, she heaped guilt on Meg's head and she wasn't willing to do that.

"You know what?" Shelby said with a slow shake of her head.

"No. It's not your fault. You did the right thing four years ago just like I did the right thing. Caleb should know that."

"Yes, but—"

"No. If he doesn't want to trust me, then he has to do it for real reasons. For things I've done—well, okay I did run out on my wedding, so yeah. But I didn't do it to Caleb. Why should he expect that I'd be untrustworthy? I'm practically a golden retriever I'm so loyal."

"A dog?"

"And he should know that," Shelby said, getting angrier the longer she thought about it. "We've been together nonstop for nearly two weeks. And in dating time, that's like two years or something—"

"Well, two years is—"

"He should know me better," Shelby continued, talking to herself more than Meg. She stared out the window at Caleb's broad back and half expected him to turn around and look at her just from the power of her stare. "And if he doesn't know me better than this, then he should have *told* me what he was thinking. Heck, he's still mad at you and Mitch for not talking to him.

"Told me himself that I should have talked to Jared, but *he* doesn't have to talk. No, not the great Caleb Mackenzie. He gets to keep his secrets," Shelby muttered, warming now to her rant and letting it all out as she stared down at the man she loved. The man she was suddenly furious with.

"He just walks out and then ignores me. Does he tell me why? *No.* Did he hope I'd just go away? Slink out of town to make his life easier? Well, why would I do that? He should have talked to me, damn it. He's acting like a child and I don't like it one bit."

"Shelby—"

"Why should I go back to Chicago?"

"Who said you should?" Meg was watching her warily.

"Caleb tried, but why does he get a say in what I do when he won't even talk to me? No, I don't want to go back. I was going to anyway, because it was too hard to be here and not be with Caleb. But that would make it easy on him, wouldn't it? And why should I do him any favors? Why does he get it easy when *he's* the reason this is all happening?"

"Um," Meg said, "I don't know."

"If Caleb Mackenzie wants to ignore me, then I'm going to make him work for it." Shelby turned around and headed for the door, riding a wave of anger. "I'm staying in Texas. I'm staying in Royal. And I'm going to start up my business and I'm going to be so successful he'll hear my name everywhere he goes."

"That's great, but—"

Shelby stopped at the threshold and looked back at her friend. "The good news is, I'll be here to help you make this room fabulous. And I'm going to help Lucy Curran, too. And help Alexis run the auction. And we'll design your new baby's room together, too, and when you're ready to add on the new wing, we can plan it all out together."

"Yay?" Meg said, clearly a little shocked at how quickly Shelby had moved from misery, to sympathy to fury. "Um, where are you going now?"

"To tell that stoic cowboy that he loves me. And to let him know that if he can't trust me, then it's his loss." She didn't wait to see if Meg had a response.

Shelby took the wide staircase at a fast clip, crossed the elegantly appointed hall and went out the front door. She walked straight to the corral and paused only when the kids rushed up to her.

"Sheby!" Jack looked up and shouted, "I get a puppy!"

Shelby's heart melted a little at the way Jack mutilated her name.

Julie was there, too. "*We* get a puppy! He's mine, too."

"Is not."

"Is, too."

Mitch came over, scooped up both kids into his arms and grinned at Shelby before telling his kids, "It's my puppy! Let's go find Mom so we can go get that poor dog that's going to be killed with love."

"Yay!" The twins shouted in excitement as their father carried them off to the house. Then she turned back to Caleb, still in the corral, busily ignoring her.

Now that she knew what was behind his behavior in the last few days, she was torn. She loved him. And she was furious with him. She wanted to kiss him and kick him. Shelby wondered if most women felt that way.

"Caleb!"

He glanced over his shoulder at her. "I'm busy."

"That's too bad," she said and kept walking. She was wearing her pale green camp shirt, white capris and completely inappropriate sandals to be walking through the dirt, but that couldn't be helped. She wasn't going to stop now.

Opening the corral gate, she started inside when Caleb shouted, "Stay outside! I don't want you near this horse, he's still a little wild."

Well, that stopped her cold. She was angry and ready for a come-to-Jesus meeting, but she didn't want to be killed by a horse, either. "Fine. Then you come out. We have to talk."

He glared at her for a long minute and she wondered how she could be both angry and attracted at the same time. The look on his face was fierce and it didn't bother her a bit. If anything, it made her insides churn with the kind of longing that had been eating at her for the last few days.

She watched as he released the lead from the horse's bridle, then turned him loose to race crazily around the corral. Caleb walked to the gate and opened it, closing it again securely behind him. Then he didn't glance at her before heading for the barn.

Shelby was just a step or two behind him. "Will you stop so we can talk?"

"Whatever we have to say to each other is going to be private," he growled out, "not said out in the yard where every cowhand nearby can listen in."

"Oh. All right."

In the shadowy barn, Caleb finally stopped, turned around to look at her and said, "What is it?"

Huh. Now that she had his complete attention, she hardly knew where to start. But that irritated gleam in his eyes prompted her to just jump in, feetfirst. "Meg told me what happened four years ago."

"I'm not talking about that," he said and turned away.

She grabbed his arm and he stopped. "Fine. We don't have to. But we do have to talk about the fact that it's the reason you're shutting me out."

"Don't be ridiculous."

"I'm not. You don't trust me, Caleb." It broke her heart to say it, to read the truth of it in his eyes as he looked down at her. "Because I did to Jared what Meg did to you. So you're thinking that I'm completely untrustworthy. But I'm not. I did the right thing in walking away. It wasn't easy, but I did it."

"I didn't say I don't trust you."

"Oh, please, you didn't have to," she countered, waving him into silence. Horses in their stalls moved restlessly. The scent of straw and wood and leather surrounded them and she knew it was a scent she would always associate with Caleb.

"I understand why you feel that way, but you're wrong."

"Well, thanks. Now I'm going back to work."

"I'll just follow you until I say what I have to say," she warned.

He believed her and sighed irritably as he crossed his arms over his chest. "Fine. Talk."

"You love me, Caleb."

He blinked at her. "What?"

"You love me and you don't want to and that's sad for both of us because we're really good together. I mean, I know we've only known each other a little while but like I told Meg, we've been together nearly every second, so that's like two years' worth of dates and really, does it matter how long you know a person before you love them?"

She answered her own question. "It really doesn't. The love is either there or it's not and it is. For you. And for me. And you don't want to admit it because you're scared."

"Scared?" He laughed, dismissing the very idea.

But Shelby knew him well enough to see the truth in his eyes. "Terrified. You know, I was going to leave Royal. Because I knew you didn't want me here anymore so I thought it would be best if I just left. Make it easier on you—"

He opened his mouth to speak but she cut him off.

"—but I don't want to make it easy on you. You *should* suffer because I'm here in town but not with you. Because it'll be your own fault because you're too stubborn to see that what Meg did four years ago was right. And what I did was right, too. Doing the right thing isn't always easy, Caleb. But it's necessary. I still believe that. And did you ever think that maybe fate brought me here to Texas so that I could realize a mistake and find *you*?"

"Fate?"

She kept going. "Just so you know, I'm opening my business in Royal and I'm going to work for Lucy Curran. And Alexis. And I've got a job working with Meg, too, so I'll be here at the ranch. A lot. So get used to seeing me. And not having me."

Her heart was breaking, but she also felt good, telling him exactly what she was thinking, feeling. How could she have fallen for a man so stubborn? So resistant to the very idea of taking a chance again?

"You should know that I love you, but I'm going to try to get over it." She turned around and headed for the door, determined to get out before she cried. After that wonderful speech, she didn't want to ruin it all by looking pitiful. Which is just how she felt, beneath the simmering boil of anger.

"Where the hell are you going?" Caleb shouted.

"To Royal," she called back. "I'm going to buy a house."

* * *

An hour later, Caleb was still thinking about what she'd said. And how she'd looked, facing him down, challenging him, calling him a damn coward.

Was she right?

She was staying in Royal. She'd be right there. In town. Every day. And she wouldn't be with *him*. Is that what he really wanted? Caleb had spent the last two days ignoring her, avoiding her, because he thought it best to get used to being without her. So it wouldn't hit him so damn hard when she left for Chicago.

But she wasn't leaving.

And he missed her already, damn it.

"Uncle Caleb!" Julie's voice and the clatter of tiny feet stomping into the barn.

"Look! A puppy!"

Grateful for the distraction from his own thoughts, Caleb looked up to see the twins rush inside, a black Lab puppy in Jack's arms. A local rancher's dog had had another litter and Mitch had been determined to get one of the pups for the twins. Looks like that, at least, had gone well.

Meg was right behind the kids, though, so his smile didn't last long.

"He's a girl," Jack said proudly.

"She don't have a name," Julie announced.

"Doesn't," Meg corrected. "You kids set the puppy down, but keep an eye on her while I talk to your uncle, okay?"

As the kids settled in to play with the puppy who was busy peeing on the straw floor, Caleb drew a sharp breath and narrowed his eyes on her. Setting things right with Mitch had been one thing. But he didn't know that he was ready to talk to Meg about any of this. Hell, he'd had too much already of strongwilled women. "I'm busy, Meg."

"You're always busy, Caleb. But this little chat is long past due." Meg reached out and stroked the long nose of a mare who'd stuck her head through the stall door hoping for attention. "I told Shelby she could use my car, so she's in Royal right now, looking for a place to buy. Or rent."

"She told me."

"Uh-huh, and you're still standing here, so I'm guessing you didn't listen to anything she said any more than you've ever listened to me." She gave him a look he'd seen her pin the twins with and he didn't much care for it.

Then he glanced at the kids shrieking and laughing with their pup. "Now's not the time for this."

"Now's the perfect time," Meg corrected. "I knew you wouldn't be rude to me in front of the twins."

"So you used them."

"You bet," she agreed. Laying one hand on his forearm, Meg leaned into him and said, "You're a good man, Caleb. But you're being deliberately deaf and blind."

"Butt out, Meg," he warned quietly.

"No, I've done that for too long." Smiling sadly, she said, "We were friends once, Caleb. Good friends who made the mistake of thinking that meant a marriage would be good for us, too.

"We were wrong. I'm sorry I hurt you when I ran out on the wedding, but can't you see now that I did the right thing? For all of us? You and I are too much alike, Caleb. We're both so damn quiet usually that we never would have spoken to each other."

He thought about that for a second and had to agree. Mitch was the louder brother and he kept Meg laughing. Just as Shelby did for Caleb. Already, he wasn't looking forward to the silence that would greet him in the house every day once Shelby left for good. Hell, the last two days had been bad enough, even knowing she was there.

"Damn it, Caleb, everyone can see that you feel for Shelby what I feel for Mitch." Meg looked up at him, serious and determined. "You and I would have made each other miserable. But you're happy with Shelby. The two of you just *work*."

He sighed, looked over her head at the slash of sunlight outside the barn. In his mind's eye, he could see Shelby in those foolish sandals, marching through the dirt and straw, her chin held high, riding the mad she had for him. He saw her in Houston, wearing that blue dress, laughing up at him.

And he saw her in bed, hair a wild tumble, her eyes shining and a soft smile on the lips he couldn't taste enough.

"Don't hold what I did to you against Shelby, Caleb," Meg was saying. "Don't cheat yourself out of something spectacular because you're holding on to old hurts. Oh, and by the way, I'm glad you and Mitch worked things out. He's missed you, you big jerk. I've missed you."

He blinked at her and laughed. She was standing up for Mitch as he stood up for Shelby and Caleb realized that she was right. Had been all along. Yeah, he wished they had handled it better, but Mitch and Meg were good together. As he and Shelby were.

For the first time in four years, he could look at his sister-in-law and not be reminded of betrayal. Which told him that he was the only one who had been preventing his family from healing. Maybe Shelby had a point. He'd never thought of himself as a coward, but what else could you call a man who refused to forgive? Refused to trust? Refused to grab his future because of his past?

He'd hated the thought of Shelby moving away from Royal, going back to Chicago or wherever. But he hated even more the idea that she would be living in town without him. He couldn't stand the thought of being without her damn it and she was right. He did love her. He just hadn't wanted to admit it, even to himself.

Idiot.

"I hate lectures, Meg. You know that."

"Yes, but—"

"Especially," Caleb added, "when you're right."

"I am?" A slow, self-satisfied smile curved her mouth.

"Don't gloat," he said, giving her a one-armed hug that eased away the last of the pain, the last of the aloofness he'd treated her with for too long.

When she hugged him back, Caleb relaxed. "Hell, I have been blind. I see how good you and Mitch are together, Meg. And I'm glad of it."

She tipped her head back and smiled, her eyes shining.

"Don't cry."

"Absolutely not," she said, shaking her head as a single tear dripped down her cheek. "Pregnant hormones. I'm good. So what're you going to do now?"

Only one thing he could do. "I'm going to Royal and I'm going to bring Shelby back home. Where she belongs."

Shelby liked the condos well enough, she thought as she walked down Main Street. But after living at Caleb's ranch, they all felt small, confined. There was no view of ranch land or ancient oaks. There were no kids playing in the yard and mostly? There was no Caleb.

"You're going to have to get used to that, though," she muttered. She walked past Miss Mac's Pie Shack and waved to Jillian through the glass.

Across the street, she saw Lucy Curran and waved to her, as the woman hurried to her truck. Alexis Slade was heading into the TCC and Shelby realized that Royal had become home to her. She had friends here. Work here. She would be fine. She'd get over Caleb. Eventually.

"Shouldn't take more than ten or twenty years," she told herself.

Stepping up her pace, she hurried along to the TCC. If nothing else, she could go inside and tell Alexis that she was going to be staying in Royal, so she'd be available to help with the bachelor auction. "Keep busy, Shelby. That's the key. Just keep busy."

She heard the roar of the engine before she looked up to see it. Caleb's huge black truck came hurtling down Main Street and careened into the TCC parking lot.

Shelby's heart was pounding hard in her chest even before Caleb shut off the engine and leaped out of the truck, slamming the door behind him. Her mouth went dry and her stomach started spinning. He stalked toward her and his features were tight and grim.

"Caleb, what're you doing here?"

He moved in close, grabbed her upper arms and lifted her up onto her toes, pulling her face within a kiss of his. "Damn it, Shelby, what the hell do you mean you love me but you'll get over it?"

Surprised, she could only stare up at him as he loomed over her. The brim of his hat shadowed his face, but his eyes, those icy-blue eyes, were on fire. "Just what I said. I'm not going to be in love all by myself, how stupid would that be? So I'll just work on getting over you and——"

"*Stop,*" he ground out. "Just stop and let me talk for once. There's a lot to say. A lot I should have said before now." He eased his grip on her arms, but he didn't let her go. "First things first, though. You're not in love alone. I love you, Shelby."

Her breath caught and she felt tears sting her eyes.

"You sneaked up on me," he said, his gaze moving over her face as if etching her features into his mind. "Before I knew it, I was loving you and trying not to."

"Great," she murmured.

He grinned, then sobered. "You're right you know, the time we've spent together is as good as two years of dating. I know you, Shelby," he said, his fingers gentling his hold on her but not letting go. "I know I can trust you. I know that. I was just…"

"A big stoic cowboy?" she finished for him.

"Yeah, I guess," he admitted wryly. His hands slid up her arms to cup her face as his voice deepened and the fire in his eyes became a low, simmering burn. "The point is, I didn't want another woman in my life. I was so mad at Meg and Mitch and never took the time to notice that she was right to do what she did. Just like you were."

"Oh, Caleb…" He couldn't have said anything that would have touched her more.

"Not finished," he warned and gave her that half smile that never failed to tug at her heart. "I don't want you to ever get over loving me, Shelby. I need you too badly."

"I didn't want to get over you," she said softly, as she sensed that all of her dreams were coming true. "I love you, Caleb. I always will."

"I'm counting on that darlin'." He gave her another half smile. "I was an idiot. I didn't want to risk love again. Thought it was just too dangerous to even try. Since you, though, I realized that losing you would be the real risk—to my heart and my sanity. How the hell could I live in a quiet house? I'd miss those rants of yours."

"I'm going to choose to be flattered," she said, smiling up at him because her heart was racing and her hopes and dreams were about to come true, right there on the busy Main Street of Royal, Texas.

"Good. That's how I meant it." Caleb shifted one hand to cup her face and he said, "I love you, Shelby. Don't think I'll ever get tired of saying it. I know I'm not easy to live with—I tend to go all quiet and pensive—but I think you're tough enough to pull it off."

"I really am," she promised. "When you get too quiet, I'll just follow you around, or ride a horse out to find you and I'll stick to you until you talk to me again."

"You won't have to follow me, Shelby," he said, his gaze locked with hers. "We're going to be side by side. And we're going to have a hell of a good marriage and we'll make a lot of babies, fill up all those empty rooms with laughter and love. Because that's what you deserve. It's what we *both* deserve."

"It sounds perfect," Shelby said. "And I think we might have already started on those babies. Skipping a few days of pills probably wasn't a good idea."

His eyes went wide and bright and his smile was one that lit up every corner of her heart. "Yeah? That's great, because you know Meg's pregnant again, so they're three ahead of us."

"We'll catch up," Shelby said.

"Damn straight we will." Caleb leaned down and kissed her, hard and long. When he lifted his head, he said, "Let's go."

"Where?" she asked, a laugh tickling her throat.

"Down to the jewelers," Caleb said firmly. "We're picking out a ring. Biggest one he's got, because I want everyone who sees it to know you're mine and I'm yours."

"You don't talk a lot," Shelby said with a sigh, "but when you do, you say just the right thing."

"There's just one more thing I have to say," Caleb whispered.

"What's that?" What more was there? He'd already given her the dream. Home. Roots. Family. *Love.*

"Shelby Arthur," he said softly, "will you marry me tomorrow?"

She sighed, filled with the love she'd always longed for and looked up into icy-blue eyes that would never look cold again. Then she grinned and asked, "Why not tonight?"

Caleb picked her up, swung her around, then planted another kiss on her mouth. "That's my girl."

* * * * *

Most Eligible Texan

Jules Bennett

USA TODAY bestselling author Jules Bennett has published over sixty books and never tires of writing happy endings. Writing strong heroines and alpha heroes is Jules's favorite way to spend her workdays. Jules hosts weekly contests on her Facebook fan page and loves chatting with readers on Twitter, Facebook and via email through her website. Stay up-to-date by signing up for her newsletter at julesbennett.com.

Books by Jules Bennett

What the Prince Wants
A Royal Amnesia Scandal
Maid for a Magnate
His Secret Baby Bombshell
Best Man Under the Mistletoe

Mafia Moguls

Trapped with the Tycoon
From Friend to Fake Fiancé
Holiday Baby Scandal
The Heir's Unexpected Baby

The Rancher's Heirs

Twin Secrets
Claimed by the Rancher
Taming the Texan

Texas Cattleman's Club: Bachelor Auction

Most Eligible Texan

Visit her Author Profile page at millsandboon.com.au, or julesbennett.com, for more titles.

Dear Reader,

Who doesn't love the Texas Cattleman's Club series? I mean, come on. This ongoing story line is absolutely amazing as a reader. And as an author? I admit I get a little giddy when I'm asked to do another.

Matt and Rachel have a special history—and by special, I mean Matt has the hots for his late best friend's wife. When Rachel asks him to be part of the bachelor auction, he agrees...secretly hoping she'll be his highest bidder.

Single mom Rachel is trying to get her life back together since the death of her husband. What she doesn't have time for is unwanted passion toward her best friend. He's just been named one of the most eligible bachelors in Texas, so why would he ever be interested in someone who doesn't have a steady job and is raising a baby?

Friends to lovers is one of my absolute favorite tropes. Throw in the late husband/best friend story and I'm skipping my way from chapter one to the end!

I hope you all enjoy Matt and Rachel as much as I do!

Jules

To single parents trying to push through
from one day to the next.
You are somebody's hero and you've got this!

* * *

Don't miss a single book in the
Texas Cattleman's Club: Bachelor Auction
series!

Runaway Temptation
by *USA TODAY* bestselling author
Maureen Child

Most Eligible Texan
by *USA TODAY* bestselling author
Jules Bennett

Million Dollar Baby
by *USA TODAY* bestselling author
Janice Maynard
(available November 2018)

His Until Midnight
by Reese Ryan
(available December 2018)

The Rancher's Bargain
by Joanne Rock
(available January 2019)

Lone Star Reunion
by Joss Wood
(available February 2019)

One

An entire morning of pleasure reading plus an extra-large pumpkin-spice latte with a healthy dose of whip? Hell yes, sign her up.

Rachel Kincaid spotted The Daily Grind across the street and nearly skipped to the door. She had two weeks before she had to dive back into her textbooks and this was her first time out alone since giving birth eleven months ago.

Part of her felt guilty for leaving her precious Ellie, but on the other hand, she knew her baby was in the best hands back at the Lone Wolf Ranch under the care of her friend, Alexis Slade, and the host of staff members they had. The chef had taken quite a liking to Ellie and was always fussing over her.

Alexis had graciously invited Rachel and Ellie to stay in her Royal, Texas, home and Rachel desperately needed the gal-pal time. Alexis and her grandfather Gus had gone out of their way to make the two of them feel like part of the family.

Rachel stepped up onto the curb and pulled her cell from her boho-style bag. She'd just shoot off one quick text to make sure everything was okay. Although she was most definitely looking forward to this break, she was still a fairly new mom and a bit of a worrier when it came to her baby girl.

Just as she pulled up the text messages, Rachel plowed into the door.

No, not a door. A man. A broad, strong, chiseled man.

Large hands gripped her biceps, preventing her from stumbling backward. Rachel jerked her gaze up at the stranger she'd slammed into.

Familiar dark blue eyes stared back at her, no doubt mirroring her own shock.

"Matt?"

"Rachel?"

The last time she'd been in Matt Galloway's arms had been at Billy's funeral, and that had been just over a year ago. Other than a handful of texts immediately following, she hadn't heard a word from her late husband's best friend.

The pain from the void thudded in her chest. Matt had been her friend, too, and she'd wondered where he'd disappeared to. Why he'd dodged her for so long.

"What are you doing in Royal?" she asked, pushing aside the heartbreaking thoughts.

Last she knew he was still in Dallas making millions and flashing that high-voltage smile to charm the ladies.

Matt released her and stepped back.

"Hiding out," he stated with a laugh. "I'm taking a break from the city for a bit and staying out of the limelight."

Rachel couldn't help but smile. "Ah, yes. I recall you being dubbed Most Eligible Bachelor in Texas. What's wrong, Matt? Don't want all the ladies chasing you anymore?"

Matt never minded the attention he received from beautiful women. In fact, Rachel had been interested in him at one time, but then Billy had asked her out, whisked her off her feet and, well…that was all in the past. She was moving forward now.

"Come in," he said, gesturing toward the door. "I'll buy you a cup of coffee."

"Just like that? As if the past year of silence hadn't happened?"

The words escaped her before she could stop herself. But damn it, she'd needed him and he'd vanished. Didn't she deserve to know why?

Honestly, such a heavy topic was just too much to handle this early in the morning running on little sleep and no caffeine.

"You know, never mind," she amended, waving her hand through the air as if she could just erase the words. "It's good to see you again, Matt."

She wasn't sure what to feel or what memory from their past to cling to, as there were a great many. From meeting him and Billy for the first time at a college party, to the fun times they all had together, to the tragic death that had forever changed the dynamics between them.

Rachel pasted a smile on her face, though. She needed a day out, and running into Matt might just be what the doctor ordered. Even though he'd hurt her, she'd missed him, and she knew Matt well enough to know he had a reason for staying away. She just couldn't fathom what could keep him at such a distance for so long.

"I don't do coffee," she stated as she passed him to enter The Daily Grind. "But you can buy my glorified milkshake."

Matt placed a hand on the small of her back, a simple gesture, but one that had her inwardly cringing. Not because she didn't want Matt to touch her, but because the electric tingle that spread through her was so unexpected. No other man had touched her in so long...

She wasn't affected by him, she told herself. He was her friend, for pity's sake. No, the reaction only came from seeing him again and the lack of human contact...the lack of *male* contact.

Ugh. This was so silly. Why was she letting such a simple gesture from Matt occupy so much of her mind?

"You're going to get something pumpkin-spice with whip, aren't you?"

Rachel smacked his chest as she made her way toward the counter. "Listen, I won't judge you and you won't judge me. Got it, Mr. Eligible Bachelor?"

Matt shook his head as he placed his order for a boring black coffee. Once Rachel placed her own order, the two of them found one of the cozy leather sofas in front of the floor-to-ceiling glass window.

The shop wasn't too busy this morning. A few people sat on stools along the back brick wall, and the bar top that stretched along the brick had power stations, so those working had taken up real estate there.

Even though they were seated in the front of the coffee shop, Rachel and Matt had just enough privacy for their surprising reunion. She still couldn't believe he was here in Royal. Couldn't believe how handsome and fit he still looked. Okay, fine. He was damn sexy and she'd have to be completely insane to think he'd ever be anything but. The past year had been nothing but kind to Matt, while she figured she looked exactly how she felt: haggard and homely.

Rachel eased back into the corner of her seat and smoothed her hands down her maxiskirt. She wasn't sure what to say now, how to close the time gap that had separated them for so long.

More importantly, she wasn't sure how to compartmentalize her emotions. Matt had been her friend for years, but seeing him now had her wondering why she felt…hell, she couldn't put her finger on the exact emotion.

"What are you doing in Royal?" Matt asked, resting his elbow on the back of the couch and shifting to face her. "You're not hiding from some newly appointed title by the media, too, are you?"

Leave it to Matt to fall back into their camaraderie as if nothing had changed between them over the last year. She'd circle back to his desertion later, but for now she just wanted a nice relaxing chat with her old friend.

"Afraid I'm not near as exciting as you," she stated with a smile. "I'm visiting Alexis Slade, my friend from college."

"I'm familiar with the Slade family. Are you alone?"

"If you're asking if I have a man in my life, no. I'm here with my daughter."

Matt opened his mouth, but before he could say anything, the barista delivered their orders and set them on the raw-edged table before them. Once they were alone again, Rachel reached for her favorite fall drink.

"I didn't mean to pry," Matt muttered around his coffee mug. "I don't have any right to know about your personal life anymore. How are you, though? Really."

"I'm doing well. But you're not prying. We've missed a good bit of each other's lives." She slid her lips over the straw, forcing her gaze away when his dark blue eyes landed on her mouth. "Ew, what is this?"

Rachel set her frosted cup back on the table. "That's not a pumpkin-spice latte."

Matt laughed. "Because that's not what you told them you wanted."

"Of course it is," she declared, swiping at her lips. "I always get the same thing at any coffee shop, especially in the fall. I'm a creature of habit and I'm pumpkin-spice everything."

"That I definitely recall." The corners of his eyes crinkled as he laughed. "But at the counter you ordered a large iced nutmeg with extra whip and an extra shot."

What the hell? Bumping into Matt had totally messed up her thought process. Maybe it was the strength with which he prevented her from falling on the sidewalk, or the firm hand on her back as he'd guided her in. Or maybe she could chalk this up to good old-fashioned lust because she couldn't deny that he was both sexy and charming.

And her late husband's best friend. There could be no lust. Not now. Not ever.

"I'll go get you another." He came to his feet. "Tell me exactly what you want."

"Oh, don't worry about it. I'm just not used to leaving the house alone—I guess it threw off my game."

Yeah, she'd go with the excuse that she was used to carrying a child and a heavy diaper bag. No way would she admit that Matt's touch, Matt's intense stare, had short-circuited her brain.

He pulled out his wallet. "Better tell me your order or I'll make something up. Do you really want to risk another bad drink?"

Rachel laughed. "Fine."

She rattled off her order and watched as he walked away.

Nerves curled in Rachel's belly. She shouldn't feel this nervous, but she did. At one time, Matt had meant so much to her—he still did. Yet she had no clue what to talk about and she certainly didn't want the awkward silence to settle between them.

One thing was certain, though. Matt hadn't changed one bit. He was still just as sexy, just as charismatic as ever. And he was the Most Eligible Bachelor in Texas. Interesting he came back into her life at this exact time.

Matt took his time getting Rachel's drink. He opted to wait at the counter instead of having the barista deliver it. He needed to get control of himself, of his thoughts. Because Rachel Kincaid, widow of Billy Kincaid, was the one person he'd thought of a hell of a lot over the years...and even more so this past year. Yes, he'd deserted her, but he'd had no other choice.

And now she'd want answers. Answers she deserved, but he wasn't ready to give.

He'd thought for sure the absence would get his emotions under control. He'd been hell-bent on throwing himself into his work, into a new partnership with his firm, and forging more takeovers in the hopes that he'd get over the honey-haired beauty that had starred in his every fantasy since they'd met.

Unfortunately, that hadn't been the case. Perhaps that's because he'd kept track of her. That sounded a bit stalkerish, but he'd needed to know she was alright. Needed to know if she was struggling so he could step in and help. From what Matt could tell, Billy's parents, plus his brother and his wife, had made sure Rachel had all she'd needed. Insurance money only went so far, but Billy came from a wealthy family.

Rachel had sold her Dallas home, though. She'd moved out and now she was here. So what was her next move? Did she have a plan? Was she going to return to Dallas?

Insurance money would run out at some point and so would her savings. Matt couldn't just let this go, not when she might need him. She'd be too proud to ever ask for help...all the more reason for him to keep an eye on her.

So many questions and he'd severed all rights to ask when he pushed her from his life. But for his damn sanity and out of respect for Rachel, he'd had no other choice.

Matt had known she'd had a little girl. She was a few months pregnant at the funeral and had already started showing. He recalled that slight swell against him as he'd held her by the graveside.

He'd honestly had no idea she'd be here in Royal, but like the selfish prick he was, he wasn't a bit sorry he'd run into her. Now was the time to pay his penance and admit he'd dodged her, admit that he needed space. But one thing he could never admit was his attraction. That was the last thing Rachel needed to be told.

"Here you go," the barista said with a smile as she placed the new frothy drink on the counter.

Matt nodded. "Thanks."

The second he turned back toward Rachel, the punch of lust to his gut was no less potent than it had been the first time he'd seen her all those years ago. She'd always been a striking woman, always silently demanded attention with just a flick of her wavy blond hair, a glance in his direction. Hell, all he had to do was conjure up a thought and she captivated him.

And nothing had been as gut-wrenching as watching her marry his best friend...a man who hadn't deserved someone as special as Rachel.

Rachel was, well, *everything*. But she wasn't for him.

Matt wasn't sure what was worse, staying in Dallas dodging paparazzi over this damn Most Eligible Bachelor in Texas title or being in this small town face-to-face with the one woman he could never have—the only woman he'd ever truly wanted.

A group of college-aged kids came through with their laptops and headed to the back of the coffee shop. Their laughter and banter instantly thrust him back to that party where he had first met Rachel. He'd flirted a little and was about to ask her out when Billy slid between them and whispered, "Mine," toward Matt before whisking her away.

If only Matt had known how things would go down between Billy and Rachel...

"One extra-shot pumpkin-spice latte with a side of pumpkin and pumpkin whip on top." Matt placed the drink in front of Rachel and made a show of bowing as he extended his arm. "Or something like that."

Rachel's laughter was exactly the balm he needed in his life. "Thank you, but that wasn't necessary."

"Was the bow too much?"

He took a seat next to her and couldn't take his eyes off the way her pretty mouth covered the pointed dollop of whip or the way she licked her lips and groaned as her lids lowered. Damn vixen had no idea what she could do to a man. He wondered how many others she'd put under her spell.

"So, tell me all about this newly appointed title." She set her drink on the table and tore the paper off her straw. "Are we going to get bombarded by squealing fans or camera flashes?"

"I sure as hell hope not." Matt grabbed his mug and settled

back into the corner of the sofa. "And I'd rather not discuss all of that. Let's talk about you. What are you doing here in Royal? Other than staying with the Slades."

Rachel held on to her cup and crossed her legs. The dress she wore might be long, but the thin fabric hugged her shapely thighs and shifted each time she moved. And from the way she kept squirming, she wasn't as calm as her smile led him to believe.

"I'm working on finishing my marketing degree online and figuring out where to go from here."

Matt didn't like that there was a subtle lilt leading him to believe she wasn't happy. The thought of her not moving on to a life she deserved didn't sit well with him. Not one bit.

"How much longer do you have?" he asked.

Rachel slid her fingertip over the condensation on her glass. "One more semester and I'm done. The end can't come soon enough."

And being a single mother no doubt added to her stress. Surely she wasn't strapped for cash. Her in-laws alone should've covered anything she needed that Billy's finances couldn't.

She'd been working on her degree when they'd met, but once she and Billy married, Billy had talked her out of finishing. Matt was damn proud she was doing this for herself.

He had so many questions, yet none of them he should ask just yet. Even though she smiled and laughed, he'd seen the hurt in her eyes, the accusation in her question when they'd been outside. Rachel deserved her answers well before he was allowed to have his.

Matt wasn't going to leave Royal without making sure Rachel and her daughter were stable and had what they needed, at least until she got on her feet.

Well, hell. Is that why they were here? Because she didn't have a place to stay? What about the home she and Billy had?

"How long are you hiding from your fan club?" she asked, pulling him back to the real reason he was in town.

Matt clenched his jaw. He wasn't about to get into all the issues he had going on. The disagreements with his partner, the negotiations he had still up in the air, the fact he wanted to sell his 51 percent and start his own company. There really was no way to just sum up in a blanket statement all he had going on.

He would much rather keep their unexpected reunion on the lighter side. And now that they were both in Royal, Matt sure as hell planned to see her again. Fate had pushed them together for a reason and he couldn't ignore that.

"I'm going to be here awhile. My grandfather's old estate is on the edge of town. It's sat empty for several years. Figure I should think about having it renovated and perhaps selling. For now, I'm staying at The Bellamy."

The five-star establishment had been recently renovated into a luxurious hotel. Matt had requested the penthouse and had paid extra to have it ready on the same day he'd had his assistant call for the reservation. Money might have gotten him pretty much everything he wanted in life, but there was still a void. Something was missing and he had no clue what it was.

Rachel slid those plump lips around her straw again and Matt found himself shifting in his seat once more. He'd been in her presence for all of ten minutes and it was as if no time had passed at all. He still craved her, still found her one of the most stunning women he'd ever known. Still wondered what would've happened between them if Billy hadn't been at that party.

Actually, there wasn't a day that went by that he didn't wonder. If he were being honest, most of the women he'd hooked up with were just fillers for the one he truly wanted.

Matt set his mug on the table, then leaned closer to her. "Listen, Rachel..."

"No." She held up her hand and shook her head. "Let's not revisit the past. Not quite yet."

He stared at her for another minute, wanting to deal with the proverbial elephant in the room, and yet needing to dodge it at the same time.

Finally, he nodded. "Since we're both in town for a while, I'll treat you to dinner tonight."

Rachel laughed. "I'm not the carefree woman I used to be, Matt. I'm a single mother with responsibilities."

"Bring your daughter."

Where had that come from? He'd never asked a woman and her child on a date. Had he ever even dated a woman with a kid?

He hadn't. But none of that mattered, because no other woman was Rachel. Besides, he wanted to see Billy's daughter. His best friend might not have been the world's greatest husband, but he was a good friend and his child would be the last connection to him.

Rachel's smile widened as she reached out and gripped his hand. "It's a date."

Matt glanced down at their joined hands and wondered why he'd just jumped head first into the exact situation he'd been running from. If he stayed around Royal too long with Rachel, he didn't know how long he could resist her...or if he'd even try.

Two

"From the way you're eyeing those photos, maybe you should consider bidding on your own bachelor."

Smiling, Rachel glanced up from the glossy images all spread out across the farm-style kitchen table to look at Alexis. Each picture featured a single man in Royal who had agreed to step up to the plate and be auctioned for a good cause. All funds would go toward the Pancreatic Cancer Research Foundation, but each woman writing the check would be winning a fantasy date with one hunky bachelor.

Rachel and Alexis were still searching for someone who could be the "big draw" or headliner.

"I think I'll just stick to the marketing and working behind the scenes and not worry so much about getting my fantasy date." Rachel blew out a breath and flattened her palms on the spread of photos. She did some quick figures in her head of what she could donate and still live off of until she completed her degree and got a paying job. "Don't worry, I'll still write a check for the cause. There are so many great guys who agreed to help... I'm just not sure which one we should use as the main event."

Alexis dropped to a chair next to Rachel and started sliding the images around. She picked up one, then set it aside, picked up another, dismissed it, too. There were so many options, from doctors to lawyers, ranchers to pilots. Royal had quite the variety of upstanding men. How were all of these hotties still single?

"The problem is these guys are all fabulous," Alexis stated, her blue eyes searching all of the options. "You can't go wrong with any of them. We do need the final man to be someone spectacular, someone the ladies won't mind writing an exorbitant amount for."

A small white paper with handwritten notes was paper clipped to the top right corner of each picture. The brief stats gave basic details of the bachelor: name, age, occupation. The overwhelming response from handsome, eligible men to help with the charity auction was remarkable. The Pancreatic Cancer Research Foundation would no doubt get a fat check afterward.

Gus and Alexis had done all the grunt work lining up the bachelors and it was Rachel's job to make sure word got out and women flocked with full purses to the biggest event of the year.

"We need to get these framed," Rachel murmured, thinking aloud. "They need to be propped on easels and in sturdy wood frames to showcase all this glorious masculinity."

They'd have to strategically set them around the outdoor garden area at the Texas Cattleman's Club so the women could come early and get an idea of who they wanted to bid on. Once Rachel went to the site, she could better plan all the details of how to arrange things.

She had already made a mock-up of the programs that would be handed out at the door. The program featured the bachelors with their regular posed image, plus she'd requested something playful or something to show their true personality.

"I have a spreadsheet of the order I think they should go in," Rachel stated. "Sorry, I know that's not quite marketing, but I was up late last night and started thinking of the best way to advertise and then I started numbering them and—"

"I get it. Your OCD kicked in and you ran with it." Alexis reached for her girlfriend's hand and squeezed. "I'll take any help I can get, and having you stay here is just like being in college. Well, with a child and less parties, but I love having you at the ranch."

Rachel loved being here, as well. She had been feeling adrift, but when Alexis had invited her to Royal, she figured this was just the break from life she needed. Who knew? Maybe Royal would become home. The big-city feel with the small-town attitude of everyone helping each other was rather nice.

Plus, there was the bonus of her best friend living here. Ellie seemed to have taken to Alexis and Gus.

"Lone Wolf Ranch is gorgeous," Rachel said, beaming. "I'm still excited you asked me to help with this auction. I think it's going to pull in more money than you ever thought possible."

Alexis pulled her hand away and blew out a sigh. "I don't know. I've set a pretty large goal. This fund-raiser means more to me than just money. I want to honor my grandmother's memory and make my grandfather proud of me at the same time. They did so much for me growing up."

Rachel knew this was so much more than a show or a popularity contest. Alexis lost her grandmother to pancreatic cancer and all of the funds from The Great Royal Bachelor Auction would go straight to the foundation in loving memory of Sarah Slade.

"She would definitely be proud of you," Rachel stated. "You're doing great work."

"I think you're doing most of it. I'd seriously be overwhelmed without you."

Rachel pulled all of the photos into a stack and neatened them up with a tap onto the table. "I'd say we make a great team."

The back door opened and Alexis's grandfather, Gus Slade,

stepped inside. He swiped the back of his arm across his forehead and blew out a whistle.

"An old man could get used to walking in his back door and seeing two beautiful ladies."

Rachel flashed him a grin. If Gus was about thirty years younger, she'd make him the headliner for the auction. The elderly widower was quite the charmer and his dashing good looks and ruggedness would make him a surefire hit. No woman could resist his thick silver hair and broad shoulders. The weathered, tanned skin and wrinkles around his blue eyes only added to his masculine appeal. Why couldn't women age as gracefully?

"Where is the youngest lady?" Gus asked as he headed to the fridge and pulled out a bottle of water.

"Ellie needed a nap," Rachel replied. "She was rather cranky."

"She's a sweetheart," Gus defended. "I get a little cranky when I need a nap, too."

Rachel's heart swelled at how easily Alexis and her grandfather just took in two stray guests as if they were all one big happy family. Rachel had only been in Royal a short time, but she already felt like this was home. She hadn't really had a sense of belonging since Billy's death. Staying in Dallas in their home hadn't felt right. Especially considering the house they'd lived in had been purchased without her approval. He'd surprised her with it and she'd never really liked the vast space. The two-story home had seemed too staid, too cold.

She'd sold that house not too long ago and moved to a small rental house, much to the shock of Billy's family. Speaking of, life had been even more stressful with her in-laws hovering and making it a point to let her know they'd be willing to keep Ellie for a while so Rachel could finish her degree.

Then Billy's brother and his wife offered to take Ellie to make Rachel's life "easier." What the hell? She didn't care about easy. She cared about her child and providing a stable future.

Ellie was the only family she had and Rachel wasn't going to be separated from her for any amount of time. She'd give up her degree first. Ellie was her world...a world Rachel hadn't even known she'd wanted until the time came.

Billy hadn't wanted children and they'd both been taken by surprise when Rachel had gotten pregnant. Rachel had slid into the idea of motherhood and couldn't imagine a greater position to be in. Billy, on the other hand, hadn't gotten used to the idea before his death. In fact, that was one of the things they'd argued about right before he'd left that fateful day.

Rachel didn't have many regrets in life, but that argument still haunted her.

"Well, I hope you both are saving your appetites for a good dinner tonight." Gus's statement pulled Rachel from her thoughts. "I've got the chef preparing the best filets with home-made mashed potatoes and her special gravy, and baby carrots fresh from the garden."

All of that sounded so amazing. Any other night Rachel would welcome all those glorious calories. In fact, she'd enjoyed each meal their chef prepared over the past several days. If she hung around much longer she'd definitely be packing on the pounds.

"I actually have plans."

Alexis and Gus both turned to her like she'd just announced her candidacy for president. Rachel couldn't help but laugh at their shocked faces.

"I ran into an old friend earlier at Daily Grind and he asked to see me tonight. I'll be taking Ellie, so don't worry. You won't be babysitting."

Alexis waved her hands and shook her head. "Hold up. Forget the babysitting, which I'd happily do. You said *he*. You're going on a date?"

Rachel cringed. "No, not a date. Matt is an old friend."

"Matt who?" Gus asked, his brows drawing inward like a concerned parent.

"Galloway."

Gus's features relaxed as he nodded. "Businessman from Dallas, also a member of TCC. So, he asked you on a date?"

"No, it's not a date," she repeated, feeling like perhaps she shouldn't have disclosed her plans.

"Matt Galloway. Oh, I remember him," Alexis murmured. "A businessman from Dallas sounds perfect. How old is he now? Early thirties, right?"

"A few years older than me. Why do you say he's perfect?"

Alexis's smile beamed and she merely stared. Then Rachel realized exactly where her friend's thoughts had traveled.

"No." Rachel shook her head and gripped the stack of photos. "We have our guys and I'm not asking my friend to do this. I couldn't. We just reconnected after a year apart and he was one of Billy's best friends. It would just be too weird."

Not to mention her heart rate still hadn't recovered from their morning together. Part of her felt guilty for the way she'd reacted. Yes, her husband was gone, but was it okay to already feel a flicker of desire for another man? And one of her friends at that. Surely her sensations were all just heightened over their reunion. Rachel was confident the next time she saw Matt it would just be like old times when they hung out as pals.

And if that attraction tried to rear its ugly head, Rachel would just have to ignore it. A romantic entanglement between the two of them was *never* going to happen. Besides, even though a chunk of time had passed, Rachel still considered Matt someone special in her life. So, no. She couldn't ask him to put himself up on the stage…especially considering he was trying to stay out of the public eye.

"You didn't tell me he was named Most Eligible Bachelor in Texas," Alexis exclaimed.

Rachel blinked and focused on her friend who had her phone in hand, waving it around. An image of Matt in a tux on the red carpet posing in front of some charitable gala had Rachel sighing.

"No, I didn't tell you that. One of the reasons why he's in Royal is to lie low."

"Rach, no guy can look like this and have women ignore him. It's not possible."

"Looks like a perfect candidate for you to bid on, Lex," Gus chimed in with a nudge to his granddaughter. "You're putting in all this work—you should pick out a date, as well."

The idea of her best friend and her other friend hooking up hit the wrong chord in Rachel. But what could she say? She had no claims on Matt, and Alexis was single. They both could do whatever they wanted...but Rachel wasn't so sure she'd like it.

"Poor guy," Gus added, leaning over to look at the photo. "It's hell when the women are all over you and you have no place to hide. I feel his pain."

Alexis rolled her eyes and laid her phone down on the table. "Ignore him. He's a romantic. But let's focus on Matt. Seems like he's the perfect big name for our auction needs. Figured I'd look him up really quick and see how we can market him."

As if he were cattle ready to go to the market. Rachel was fine discussing the other bachelors; in fact, she rather enjoyed using her creativity and schooling to make each guy stand out in a unique way. But something about the idea of Matt up for grabs really irritated the hell out of her.

Perhaps it was because Rachel knew for a fact that the female attendees would bid high on the very sexy, very wealthy Matt Galloway, but she didn't want to give them the opportunity.

First, she'd feel like a jerk asking him when he'd been upfront as to his reasons for being in Royal. He was dodging this new title and clearly not comfortable with the added attention.

Second, the idea of women waving their paddles and tossing money for a fantasy date with Matt...well, she was jealous. *There.* She admitted it—if only to herself.

Why was she suddenly so territorial? She'd always found Matt attractive, always respected and admired him. How could she throw him into the lion's den, so to speak, and expect not to have strong feelings on the matter? They were friends. She should feel protective, but there were other feelings swirling around inside her, and none of them remained in the friend zone.

"Tell me you'll at least think about it."

Rachel met Alexis's pleading gaze. She was here to help her friend—they were actually helping each other—and this auction was a huge deal to the Slade family. How could Rachel say no when Alexis had opened her home and heart to Rachel and Ellie?

"I'll see what I can do," she conceded with a belabored sigh. "But I can't promise anything and I won't beg."

Alexis squealed. "All I ask is you try."

Gus rested a large, weathered hand on Alexis's shoulder. "My granddaughter is all Slade. When she wants something, she finds a way to make it happen. So, which guy are you bidding on, Lex?"

Alexis rolled her eyes. "Stop trying to marry me off. I'm working on raising money, not finding a guy to put a ring on my finger."

Rachel scooted her chair back and came to her feet. "Well, I'm pretty determined to help bring in all the money possible, but I won't make Matt feel uncomfortable."

"I understand," Alexis said, nodding in agreement. "But, I'll wait up so I can hear all about your date and see if he agreed to be auctioned."

That naughty gleam in her friend's eyes was not going to last. If Alexis knew all that Rachel, Matt and Billy had been through, she'd understand just how delicate this situation was. But she wasn't wanting to get into all of that now. She didn't want to revisit the ordeal that was her marriage and the gap of time she'd missed Matt.

"Feel free to wait up, but I assure you I won't be out long. I have a baby, remember? Early bedtimes are a must."

"Why don't you leave her here?" Gus suggested. "It's nice having a little one around, and she's no trouble."

Alexis stood up and patted her grandfather's shoulder. "If that's a hint, relax. It's going to be a while before I give you a great-grandchild. I'm a little busy in case you haven't noticed."

Rachel didn't miss the way Alexis's eyes landed on the top photo...which featured the very handsome Daniel Clayton.

Alexis Slade and Daniel Clayton had once been quite an item, but they'd fallen apart and Rachel still didn't know what had happened. Whenever Rachel brought up the topic, her friend not-so-subtly steered their chat in another direction. Eventually, Rachel would find out what was going on between her friend and the mysterious ex.

"What time is your date?" Alexis asked.

Resigned to the fact nobody believed her about the nondate, Rachel shrugged. "We kept it open. He realizes I need to be flexible with a little one. I'll head over to his hotel room later. Once Ellie wakes, I need to grab a shower and we both need to get ready."

"What are you taking?" Alexis asked.

"Taking?"

"A bottle of wine? A dessert? I'm sure we have something the cook has whipped up. She always has breads."

Rachel shook her head. "I'm not taking anything. You're letting that romantic streak show."

"Just trying to help," she muttered.

Rachel patted her friend's arm. "I know, but I've only been a widow for a year. I'm not ready to rush into anything."

Her marriage had started out in a whirlwind of lust and stars in their eyes. Rachel and Billy had lived life to the fullest and loved every minute of it. Then the pregnancy had slid between them and continued to drive a wedge through their relationship. They'd built something on top of shaky ground and hadn't realized until after the fact.

Unfortunately, Rachel would never know if their marriage would've worked itself out. Would Billy have ever settled down and stepped into the role of loyal father and devoted husband?

Pain gripped her from so many angles, but she had to keep pushing forward for her sake as well as Ellie's. Rumored infidelity and ugly arguments weren't how she wanted to remember her late husband.

"I'm going to go check on Ellie," Rachel told them. "She should be waking soon. Lex, I'll get you a list of the order I think we should use for the auction. If Matt isn't onboard, then Daniel might be our best bet as the big-name draw."

Her friend's lips thinned, her jaw clenched. Gus blew out a breath that Rachel would almost label as relief, and he had a satisfied grin. Whatever was going on with Daniel and Alexis—or wasn't going on—was quite a mystery.

One thing was certain, though—Alexis was not a fan of having Daniel up on the auction block. Ironically, Rachel still wasn't too keen on the idea of Matt being up there, either.

Because if that came to pass, one or both of them might just have to grab a paddle and place their own bids.

Three

Matt tipped the waitstaff a hefty amount for their quick, efficient service and for meeting his last-minute demands. He hadn't known what to have for dinner for Rachel, let alone an infant.

Infant? Toddler? What was the right term for an eleven-month-old? He knew nothing about children and had never taken to the notion of having his own, so he'd never bothered to learn.

But he was interested in Rachel, and she and Ellie were a package deal that he didn't mind. No matter the years that passed, no matter the fact she'd married his best friend, nothing at all had ever diminished his desire for Rachel. He'd hid it as best he could, often gritting his teeth and biting his tongue when Billy would be disrespectful to Rachel's needs.

Once Rachel got pregnant, the two started fighting more, and Billy's answer was to get out of the house so they both could cool off. Those times when Matt and Billy were at the Dallas TCC clubhouse shooting pool and drinking beer or even out on Matt's boat on the lake, Billy never did grasp that running didn't solve the problem. He never once acted excited about the pregnancy. He never mentioned how Rachel felt about being a mother. Billy's life didn't change at all and Matt knew Rachel hurt alone.

He also knew she'd been excited about the pregnancy, but how much could she actually enjoy it knowing her husband wasn't fully committed?

Whenever Matt would mention anything to Billy about Rachel, the other man always told him to mind his own business and that he didn't know what marriage was like. Valid point, but Matt knew how to treat a woman and he damn well respected Rachel.

Matt stepped back and surveyed the dinner he'd had set up on the balcony. His penthouse suite at The Bellamy had a sweeping view of the immaculate grounds, yet was private enough he felt comfortable bringing Rachel out here to talk.

He hoped this setting was okay. For some asinine reason he was a damn nervous wreck. What the hell? There had never been a woman to make him question himself or his motives. Even when he and Rachel had been friends before, the main emotion that always hovered just below the surface had always been forbidden desire.

But she was a different woman now. She was a single mother seeking out a fresh start, not some short-term fling with her late husband's best friend. And he wasn't looking for anything more than exploring the connection and seeing if this was just one-sided.

Matt needed to curb his desire. She wasn't coming here for a quickie. He'd invited her as a friend...and unfortunately, he feared that was the category she'd try to keep him in. Being near her again only put his desires right on the edge, and he had to retain control before he fell over the line of friendship and pulled her right with him.

Even now that she was single, he still had no chance with her because he was known as a ladies' man, the Most Eligible

Bachelor in Texas, and Rachel was a sweetheart who wouldn't settle for anything less than happily-ever-after.

Damn that title. It had been nothing but a black cloud over him since he'd been given the title some men would happily flaunt. He was not one of those men. He hadn't even been able to go on a damn date back in Dallas without a snap of the camera or someone coming up to him asking for his autograph.

The final straw had been when he'd come home to his penthouse and a reporter was lurking outside his door. He'd fired his security guard promptly after that irritating inconvenience.

The one woman he wanted could never be his, even temporarily. Perhaps that was his penance for lusting after his best friend's wife.

Matt looked at all the items he'd ordered. He might not know much about children, but he'd paid his assistant a nice bonus to make a few things happen within the span of a few hours and by just making some calls. Even from Dallas, the woman was working her magic here in Royal and had baby things delivered in record time. That woman definitely deserved a raise. She saved his ass on a daily basis.

With one last glance, he started having doubts. The balcony ledge went up waist-high on him, the wrought iron slats were about an inch apart. There shouldn't be a problem with Ellie out here, especially with all the other paraphernalia to keep her occupied, but seriously, what did he know about this? Did she walk or crawl? Did she look like Rachel or Billy?

Nerves pumped through him and he didn't like it. Not one bit. Matt never got nervous. He'd handled multibillion-dollar mergers and never broken a sweat, so it baffled his mind as to why he was getting all worked up.

Besides, what did he think would happen here tonight? Did he truly believe they could pick back up where they'd left off before Billy died? He'd deserted her due to his own selfish needs and worry he wouldn't be able to control those wants. He'd had to push her away for both of their sakes.

Surely he wasn't so delusional to think that she'd…what? Want to tumble into bed with him? He'd be a complete liar if he said he hadn't fantasized about her since the moment they'd met. There was probably some special pocket of hell for men like him, coveting his best friend's wife.

But Rachel had always been different. Perhaps it was her beauty or the way his entire body tightened with desire when she was around. Maybe it was the way she could go up against anyone in a verbal sparring match that he found so sexy.

Hell, he had no idea. What he was sure of, though, was that having her come to his suite and bring her child along might have been the worst idea he'd ever had.

No, the worst idea he'd had was letting Billy ask Rachel out first. That was where Matt had gone wrong from the start.

The bell chimed throughout the suite and he raked a hand over his cropped hair as he crossed the spacious room. There was no going back now, and he wasn't about to keep second-guessing himself. Rachel was a friend; so what if he had her over for dinner?

Yet you want more.

He wished like hell the devil on his shoulder would shut up. Matt was well aware of exactly what he wanted from Rachel, but he respected her enough not to seduce her.

With a flick of the lock, Matt pulled the door open and every single best intention of keeping his thoughts platonic vanished.

The formfitting blue shirt that matched her eyes hung off one shoulder. Those well-worn jeans hugged her shapely hips, and her little white sneakers had him immediately thinking back to the younger version he'd first met. But this grown-up Rachel had a beautiful baby girl on her hip…a baby that was a mirror image of her mother right down to the prominent dimples around her mouth.

Matt had always been fascinated by Rachel's mouth and those damn dimples. Every time she smiled, he'd been mesmerized.

"Come in."

Geesh, he'd been staring and reminiscing like some hormonal teen. He was a damn grown man, CEO of a billion-dollar company, and he stood here as if he'd never seen an attractive woman before.

"Wow, this is one snazzy hotel."

Rachel moved into the living area and spun in a slow circle. Her daughter still clutched her little arms around her mother's shoulders.

"I thought the outside was impressive," she stated. "But this penthouse suite is bigger than the apartment I'd been renting."

Matt frowned. Why the hell had she lived in such a small space to begin with? He understood her emotional reasoning for selling the home she and Billy shared, but why an apartment? Could she not afford another home?

He had no right to ask about her financial standing, but that's exactly what he wanted to do. Obviously this wasn't something he'd get into with Ellie here.

"I figure this is a good place to hide while I'm in town," he joked. "I can work from the offices at the TCC clubhouse and come back here and enjoy the amenities of the gym and sauna, and having dinner here is no hardship."

Rachel patted her daughter's back. "Then you can stay up here on the balcony and look down on the peons and paparazzi?"

"Something like that," Matt laughed. "Actually, I had our dinner set up out there if you'd like to head out. The view is breathtaking."

Rachel moved toward the open French doors. "I don't know if it's safe to have Ellie out here."

As she stepped outside, she gasped as she took in everything he'd done. "Matt, my word! What didn't you think of?"

Matt shrugged, wondering if he'd gone overboard. Hell, he hadn't known what to do, so in those instances his default was always to do everything. His motto had always been "Better to have too much than not enough."

"I wasn't sure if she used a high chair," he stated, stepping over the threshold to join her. "When I called my assistant for reinforcements, I told her to ask for the works. The guy came to set all of this up and asked how many kids I had."

Rachel laughed as she turned and surveyed the spacious balcony. Matt couldn't take his eyes off her or her daughter. He wasn't even sure how to feel looking at Billy's child, but when he saw that sweet girl, he really only saw Ellie.

Guilt slithered in slowly from so many different angles. He shouldn't still have been lusting after his late friend's wife, but there was clearly no stopping that. But he also shouldn't be wanting to get closer to Rachel knowing full well that he wasn't looking for a family or any type of long-term commitment.

Being married to a career didn't leave much time for feeding into a relationship. Besides, he couldn't lose Rachel as a friend. The risks were too high that that was exactly what would happen if he pressed on with his pent up desires.

Rachel still hadn't said anything as she continued to take in everything. One area of the stretched balcony looked as if a department store had set up their latest display of baby gear. High chair, Pack 'n Play, play mat, toys, stationary swing...

"I don't know the age for any of this stuff, so if you need something else let me know and I'll call—"

"No." Rachel turned back around to face him, her eyes filled with unshed tears. "This is... I don't even have words. You invited me for dinner and thought of everything for Ellie."

His gaze darted to the child in question. Her wide brown eyes, exactly like Rachel's, were focused on him. She clutched a little yellow blanket against her chest and huddled against her mother for security. Something shifted inside Matt, an unknown emotion he couldn't label and wasn't sure he wanted to explore.

"She's beautiful." Matt turned his gaze back to Rachel as a shimmer of awareness flowed through him. "Just like her mother."

She blinked and glanced away, never one to take a compliment. That had never stopped him from offering them. Even when the three of them had all hung out, back in the day, Matt would tell her she looked nice or he liked her hair. There hadn't been a time he recalled hearing Billy compliment his wife, and Matt hadn't been able to help himself. Billy had been a great friend, yet from everything Matt could tell, he had been a lousy husband.

But really, all of this was a moot point. Because regardless of the state of their marriage, Matt knew he shouldn't be trying to make a play for Billy's wife. He had regrets in his life, but this might be the most asshole-ish thing he'd ever done. Still, Matt had never backed away from what he wanted…and he wanted the hell out of Rachel Kincaid.

"Who else is eating with us?" Rachel asked as she stared at the spread he'd ordered.

"Just us. I ordered all of your favorites. Well, what I remember you ordering in the past, but I didn't know what you were in the mood for."

Rachel wrinkled her nose. "I'm a boring creature of habit. I pretty much stick with pizza, pasta or any other carb. This all looks amazing."

He took a step forward and offered a smile. "You're not boring," he corrected. "There's nothing wrong with knowing what you want. I'm the same way. I see something I want, I make it mine."

Damn it. He needed to calm the hell down. Hadn't he told himself to get control over his desires?

But saying and doing were clearly two different things because he couldn't stop himself. Rachel pulled out emotions in him he couldn't even describe.

Her eyes widened. "Are you talking about food or something else?"

Matt shrugged, forcing himself to take a step back and not get her any more flustered. "We'll discuss food. For now."

Rachel moved to the Pack 'n Play and sat Ellie down. The little girl whimpered for a moment before Rachel pulled a doll from the diaper bag on her shoulder. Damn it, why hadn't he taken that from her?

"Let me help." He took the bag from her shoulder. "Damn, woman, what do you have in here?"

Rachel straightened and turned. "It's amazing how one little person can need so many things. Diapers, wipes, butt paste—"

"Pardon?"

She laughed and went on. "I have an extra change of clothes in case of blowouts, food, snacks, toys, pain reliever for her swollen gums..."

"I don't know if I want any more information about the butt paste and blowouts." Matt set the diaper bag next to the door. "I'll fix you a plate. The restaurant downstairs serves some of the best food I've ever had and I've been all around the world. I ordered their rosemary bread because when I called, they said they'd just taken it from the oven."

"Well, you clearly know me," she said with a wide smile that punched him with another dose of lust. "If it's carbs, I'm in."

"Do you still have a love for key lime pie?"

Rachel rolled her eyes. "If you mean do I still inhale it like it's my job, then yes. I don't even care about the added pounds. Key lime pie is so worth it."

"You're still just as stunning as always, Rachel. No pounds could change that."

She crossed her arms over her chest and tilted her head. "I'm starting to see why you were the recipient of the most prestigious bachelor title. You're still quite the charmer."

He might try to charm other women—well, he didn't try; he flat-out *did* charm them. But with Rachel, he wasn't trying. He always spoke the truth, always wanted her to know her value and how special she was.

If you cared so much, you wouldn't have let a year pass since seeing her.

"I've missed you," she stated, as if reading his mind. "I miss our friendship."

Friendship. Yes. That's the only label their relationship could have, because she was a widow, a single mother and she wasn't looking to jump back into anything. Honestly, he wasn't looking to fill the role of Daddy, either, but that didn't stop the fact he wanted Rachel as more than a friend.

Likely she'd thrown that out there as a reminder, but he dismissed the words. He'd respect her if she flat-out wasn't interested, but he had to know. He had to know if she was interested in him. He needed to find out if she burned for him as much as he for her. Would she even want to attempt anything physical knowing he wasn't ready for anything more?

Why did this all have to be so damn complicated? Oh, right. Because he'd spent years building and attempting to ignore these emotions.

"I'd better eat before she starts fussing," Rachel told him as she went to take a seat. "There's always a small window of opportunity and I rarely get warm food because I feed her first."

Matt urged Rachel toward the table and pulled her chair out. "If she fusses, I'm sure I can hold her and entertain her while you finish, or I can feed her. Regardless, you are eating right now while it's warm, and there will be no arguments."

Rachel looked up at him and quirked one brow. "You ready to play Uncle Matt?"

Ouch. That stung. He wasn't sure what he wanted to be called...then again, he hadn't given it much thought. He was having difficulty processing much of anything with that creamy shoulder of Rachel's on display and her familiar floral fragrance teasing his senses.

"I win over billion-dollar mergers before breakfast," he joked. "I'm pretty sure I can handle a little person."

Rachel snorted. "Don't get too cocky. It's harder than it looks."

"I never doubted that for a minute," he corrected. "Now eat. There's plenty."

Once she took a seat, Matt eased it closer to the table. He

immediately started filling her plate with rosemary bread and Alfredo over penne and chicken, then filled her glass with pinot grigio.

"You put all of this together pretty quick considering you just asked me today."

Matt set her food in front of her before taking a seat across the table. "Just a few calls and the right connections. Why wouldn't I go all out for a friend I haven't seen in a year?"

Her stare leveled his. "I'd think a cup of coffee or a stroll in the park would've sufficed."

Matt reached across the table and squeezed her fingers. Her eyes immediately darted to their joined hands. "You have every right to be angry with me."

"I'm not angry," she retorted.

Matt raked his thumb across the silky ridge of her knuckles before easing back. He noticed she didn't wear her wedding band any longer and part of him swelled with approval and excitement.

"Hurt then. You can't lie to me, Rachel. Billy's death did something to both of us."

Like the fact he couldn't be the one to console her. He simply...damn it, he couldn't. He'd wanted too much for too long so he'd had to let her go and pray someone else offered the comfort she needed. Because if he'd had to hold her day after day, night after night until her pain had eased...

"I was hurt," she admitted. "I still am, actually. Care to tell me why you just disappeared?"

"I texted."

Such a lame defense, yet the words left his mouth before he could stop himself. Out of everything and everyone in his life, Rachel was the one he'd barely been able to control himself around.

"I don't really want to dredge up the past right now. I want answers from you, but let's not do it tonight." She picked up her fork and offered a typical dimpled smile. "Billy was a big part of my life, but I've worked hard at moving on. I'm trying to make a future for Ellie and me. Always looking back isn't the way to do that."

He had to hand it to her. She'd hurt from her husband's death, from Matt's absence, from being thrust into being a single mother, yet she forced herself to trudge on.

"So, you're finishing your degree," he started, hoping to keep the topic on her life. "Where do you go from there?"

Rachel stabbed a piece of pasta and lifted a shoulder. "Right now I'm helping Alexis with the charity auction for the Pancreatic Cancer Research Foundation."

Impressed, Matt nodded in silent admiration. "What's the auction? Do you have donations from area businesses?"

Rachel dropped her fork, pulled the napkin from her lap and dabbed the corners of her mouth. "We're auctioning men."

Matt stilled. "Excuse me?"

Those bright, beautiful eyes locked on his across the table. There was that mischievous gleam he'd seen from her in the past. He wasn't sure he wanted to know more.

"We're having a bachelor auction. Care to be Bachelor Fifteen?"

Four

Way to go. Nothing like blurting out her thoughts without easing into the request. Granted she'd promised Alexis she'd ask Matt for the favor, but Rachel probably could've done a better lead in.

"Bachelor Fifteen."

The words slid slowly through his sultry, kissable lips as he set his fork down and continued to hold her gaze without so much as blinking. She really needed to not stare at his mouth, and she absolutely should not be imagining them on hers.

Rachel cringed. "So, we need another bachelor and we were wanting one that would be fairly popular, and you came to town, we're friends, you've got that new title and..."

He sat still as stone.

"I'm rambling," she muttered. "You don't want the hype or the press. I get it. Forget I asked."

Rachel focused on the potatoes on her plate. Carbs were always the answer, especially when she'd just verbally assaulted their friendship.

"Is that why you came?" he asked.

Rachel immediately met his gaze. "What? No. I wanted to see you. I wanted you to meet Ellie. Earlier I was working on the auction and Alexis and I started talking and your name came up."

Matt offered that cocky, familiar smirk. "Is that right?"

He was clearly intrigued by the idea of being the topic of conversation, but she wasn't about to feed that ego.

"But don't feel obligated to agree just because we're friends. In fact, forget I asked."

Rachel started to reach for her sweet tea just as Ellie let out a cry of frustration. Pushing back in her chair, Rachel came to her feet, but Matt was quicker. He stood and crossed to the Pack 'n Play, reached down and lifted Ellie out.

Unable to look away, Rachel stared at the way Matt's large hands held on to her daughter. Ellie's little mouth slid into a frown as she stared at the stranger. She reached up and patted her tiny fingers against his mouth.

"Here, let me take her."

Matt shook his head as he made his way back to the table. "She's fine. Enjoy your dinner and we can discuss this auction some more."

Rachel eased back into her seat as Matt sat back down in his own chair. Immediately Ellie's arm smacked Matt's glass over, spilling his drink into his plate of food.

"I'm so sorry." Rachel jumped up and grabbed her daughter before handing Matt her cloth napkin. "Let me go inside and get a towel. Go finish my plate and I'll get this cleaned up—"

Matt grabbed her arm. "Relax. Nobody's hurt here and it's just a spill. Maybe we should go inside where Ellie can play on the floor and we can sit on the sofa and have dinner?"

Rachel wanted to gather her child and their things and leave to save further embarrassment, but she knew that would be rude after all the trouble he'd gone to. So against her better instincts, she nodded.

"I think she's getting hungry," she replied. "Let me feed her and then I'll help clean and carry things inside."

"Take care of her. I'll take care of everything else."

Rachel stared for a moment until she realized he was serious. She couldn't help but think back to Billy, who hadn't wanted kids, who'd been flat out angry over the pregnancy. Yet here was Matt offering to care for Ellie while Rachel did something as simple as eat her dinner.

She shouldn't compare the two men. Sure they were friends, but they'd always been opposite. Billy had been the adventurer, the wanderer, which had been the initial draw for Rachel.

Matt was just around for a good time. He was content in Dallas, happy with life and work. He was well-grounded and only got away to travel to Galloway Cove.

Who wouldn't be happy owning their own island? At this point in her life, Rachel just wanted to own her own home, not the house Billy had bought and not some place her in-laws wanted her to have. She wanted to do life her way.

Several moments later, Ellie had been fed. After cleaning her up, Rachel scooted the coffee table off to the far wall and left an open area for Ellie to play in without hitting her head on the furniture.

Matt came back in and quickly had their food all set up, acting as if an infant hadn't just turned his steak and potatoes into tea soup.

"I'm really sorry about that," Rachel offered as he sat on the sofa next to her.

"Why do you keep apologizing? Just because I don't have children doesn't mean I'm going to get angry over an accident."

Rachel glanced down to Ellie who was quite content plucking the nose on the stuffed toy monkey. "I just never know how people will respond. Some people don't like children."

"I've never really seen myself in the role of a father, but I like kids. I mean, I highly doubt she knocked my glass down on purpose."

Rachel settled her plate into her lap. "You can eat at the table, you know. You don't have to sit here with me."

All of this was too familial, and being in a situation like this with Matt only made her fantasize about things she could never have…at least not with this man.

"Tell me more about the auction," he said, ignoring her previous statement.

"Matt, really—"

"Tell me."

His gruff command had her pulling in a deep breath. "Alright. The bachelor auction is going to raise funds for the Pancreatic Cancer Research Foundation. Alexis's grandmother and Gus's wife passed away from that. When Alexis invited me to come visit, I offered to help with the auction. I'm not quite finished with my marketing degree, but I'm thrilled to be doing something along the lines of where I want to be. Not only am I helping the cause—this will look great on a resume when I finish my degree."

"They're lucky to have you working on this," Matt stated with such conviction she turned to him in surprise .

"You have a lot of confidence for someone who hasn't seen me in a year."

Matt finished chewing before he replied. "I know you, Rachel. Maybe better than you know yourself. You're determined, headstrong and always looking out for everyone but yourself."

His blue eyes locked with hers, causing a warm melting sensation to spread through her.

"Alexis couldn't have chosen a better person for the job. You don't need a degree to have compassion."

She wasn't even sure how to respond to such praise. She hadn't been looking for a compliment. They finished their dinner in silence and Ellie played without interruption.

"Let me take the plates to the kitchen," Rachel said, reaching for Matt's empty dish.

"I've got it."

"You've done enough. I can take care of this."

His suite at The Bellamy was absolutely dreamlike. Rachel couldn't imagine being a guest here. She'd never want to leave.

"I invited you."

Matt took the dishes and headed toward the open kitchen area. Having a sexy man do domestic chores was something no woman could look away from. Added to that, the thin navy sweater he wore stretched beautifully across his broad shoulders, captivating her attention.

"You're not doing anything except telling me more about the auction," he stated. "What do I have to do as Bachelor Fifteen?"

Rachel laughed, more out of shock than humor. "You don't have to put yourself up for auction. We have guys who will bring in the goal Alexis is hoping to raise."

To Rachel's surprise, Matt didn't sit back on the sofa with her, but on the floor with Ellie. With one hand propped behind him, he rested his other arm on the knee he'd drawn up.

"So when a woman wins her dream guy onstage, or however you're doing it—"

"In the gazebo at the TCC clubhouse," she interjected.

He nodded. "Fine. So when a lady's knight in shining armor steps from the gazebo and they gaze into each other's eyes, then what?"

Rachel eased down to the floor as well and couldn't help but laugh. "It's probably not going to be that dramatic. But, the ladies are bidding on a fantasy date. Whatever that might be. One of our bachelors is a pilot, so the winner could also choose to be flown in his private jet to a nice dinner. All of the guys bring something different to the table, which is exactly what we want so we can appeal to a variety of women."

"And their checkbooks."

Rachel smiled and nodded. "Exactly."

"How many bachelors have an island?"

"None."

"Then count me in."

Rachel jerked back. Ellie crawled to her and climbed onto her lap. "Just like that you're offering yourself up?"

"It's one date, Rachel. I'm not marrying anyone. If it's for a good cause, and it is, I'm willing." He handed Ellie her monkey when she wobbled closer to him. "I'll match the donation of the bid made on me, as well."

She couldn't believe how easy this was. "You could just write a check if you're only wanting to help financially."

"Sounds like you don't want me to be on the auction block," he threw back with a quirked brow.

That's precisely what she sounded like because that's exactly how she felt. But she had no right, and she truly had no motive to keep him all to herself. Matt didn't belong to anyone, especially not his best friend's lonely widow.

"I just want you to be fully aware of what you're getting into."

His eyes held hers and they did that thing again, that thing where he seemed as if he could look right into her soul and grab onto her deepest thoughts. However, it was best for them both that he couldn't see her true feelings.

"I think I can handle myself," he murmured. "Will you be bidding?"

Rachel's heart thudded in her chest. She honestly hadn't given it much thought until the idea of Matt being up for grabs came to light. Could she actually bid on him? What would he think? Would he think she was trying to date him? That she wanted to start something beyond friendship? Or would he think she was saving him from the other women waving their paddles?

"Do you want me to bid on you?"

Why did her voice come out so husky like some sultry vixen? Because she certainly was no seductress. For pity's sake, her child had fallen asleep on her lap and Rachel was acting like some love-struck teen.

Matt lifted a shoulder. "What would your dream date be? We might be able to work out a deal and both get what we want."

What did that mean? Did he want a date with her?

Why the hell was this all so confusing now? When she'd been married to Billy and they'd all gone out with friends and had a good time, she and Matt would joke and laugh and there was never this crackling tension.

Crackling tension. What a great way to say sexual energy, though she had no idea if this was all one-sided or not. Or had this been there before and she'd never noticed? Surely she would've sensed it if Matt had been interested.

"I don't know what my dream date would be," she admitted. "I've never thought about it."

Matt reached over and Rachel thought for sure he was reaching for her, but he slid a wisp of a curl from Ellie's forehead. Rachel's heart flipped. She had no idea what to expect with Matt and his reaction to Ellie, but he'd put her needs ahead of anything else. The baby items on the patio had to have cost a ridiculous amount, and now he sat here acting so caring and doting toward her little girl as if this were the most natural thing in the world.

He settled his hand on her knee and Rachel realized he'd slid even closer. "What about a day out on my boat? You could relax and do nothing but get a suntan and snap your finger for another fruity drink."

Rachel tipped her head and smiled. "Do you honestly think I could relax and do nothing? When have you ever known me to laze around?"

Right now, though, it was getting rather difficult to think of anything because all she could concentrate on was his large, firm hand on her knee. Forget the fact a good portion of her lap had gone numb from Ellie's weight; she could most definitely feel Matt's searing touch.

"Okay, then, maybe a trip to Galloway Cove. You could swim, have dinner on the beach, get a massage from one of my staff."

Rachel shook her head. "I'm pretty sure I won't be bidding. First of all, I'm not sure I could afford you once the ladies see your credentials. And second, I couldn't leave Ellie for an entire day."

"If you bid on me and win, Ellie could come, too. I have on-site staff at every single one of my homes."

Of course he did. Billy had come from money, but that was nothing compared to the lifestyle Matt lived. Billy partied with his money, but Matt invested. He had homes, jets, an island and who knew how many cars. Most likely he had businesses on the side from the company he ran. Men like him never had just one business going because that wouldn't be smart. And Matt was one of the most intelligent people Rachel had ever known.

"I think I better just write a check to the foundation and stay behind the scenes."

Matt's thumb stroked over her knee. Back and forth, back and forth. The warmth through the fabric of her capris ironically sent shivers through her.

"Matt," she whispered, not knowing what to say but realizing this moment was getting away from them.

"What if I want you to bid on me?" he asked, never looking away from her. "Maybe I want to give you that day you need. Perhaps it's time someone makes you take time for yourself."

Rachel didn't know what to say. She'd seen Matt charm women in the past, but she'd never been on the receiving end. He was dead serious that he wanted her to bid on him. But if she did that, if they went off on some fantasy date, Rachel couldn't guarantee that she'd be able to avoid temptation. Matt had always held a special place in her heart, but she was seeing him in a whole different light now. Getting mixed up with him on a physical level would only end in heartache...and she had plenty of that to last a lifetime.

"You don't have to answer now," he added. He hadn't eased back, nor had he removed his hand. "But I'm all in under one condition."

She was almost afraid to ask.

"And that is?"

That cocky, signature Matt Galloway grin spread across his face. "You're the only one I'm dealing with. As in the photos that need taking and anything else that is needed from me for the auction itself. You're it for me."

That last sentence seemed to spear straight through that tough exterior she'd shielded herself with. Matt had that power, a power she'd always known he possessed, but she'd never fully realized the impact he could have on her until now.

"I'm not exactly a professional photographer," she reminded him.

"I recall your hobby behind the lens and I would bet anything you've kept up with it, especially to take pictures of Ellie." He slid his hand away, but eased forward until their faces were only a few inches apart. "Do we have a deal?"

Rachel simply nodded, unable to speak with him so close. She wasn't sure what she was getting herself into, but Alexis would be thrilled to have Matt as the headliner. Wasn't that the goal?

Five

Gus closed the tack box and blew out a sigh. He'd worked hard today, but he wouldn't have it any other way. Lone Wolf Ranch gave him the reason to get out of bed each day, especially since his beloved Sarah had passed. That made two women in his lifetime who had left an imprint on his heart. There was only so much heartache a man could take, and Gus had met his quota.

From here on out, he planned on devoting his every single day to his livestock, his ranch and his granddaughter. There was no way in hell his sweet Alexis could hook up with Daniel Clayton. That boy was nothing but trouble and the grandson of Rose Clayton... Gus's first love.

The Claytons were dead to him. He'd rather give up his ranch than see their families merge...and he sure as hell wasn't giving up his ranch.

The years he and Rose spent together all seemed like a lifetime ago. In fact, it was. They'd been in love and Gus had worked his ass off to make sure he was ready for marriage before he set out to get approval from Rose's father.

Gus had never been so nervous, so excited, so ready to spend his life with the woman of his dreams. But when he'd come back, he'd discovered his beloved Rose had been married the year before to a man handpicked by her father.

Gus wasn't going down that road in his mind again. He'd traveled that path too many times to count, too many times wondering what the hell had happened. But in the end, he'd married Rose's best friend, Sarah, and they'd had a beautiful life together until she passed.

The rap of knuckles on wood had him turning from the stalls. Outlined in the doorway of his barn with the sun setting against her back stood Rose Clayton. He might as well have conjured her up from his thoughts. Lately his mind had been focused on her more than it should, but that was only because they were conspiring with each other...not that they were reconnecting. That love story had ended long ago.

"I hope this isn't a bad time," Rose stated, stepping into the barn.

She always appeared as if she were going to a tea party at the country club, but as she strode through the barn filled with the smell of hay and horses, Gus got a lump in his throat. She looked absolutely beautiful here. Her pale pink capris and matching jacket with a crisp white shirt and gold necklace created quite the contrast to his filthy work clothes. She'd always been that way, though...a vast juxtaposition from him.

Damn it. He needed to focus on the present, and not waste his time dwelling on nostalgic memories.

"I'm just finishing up for the day," he replied, adjusting the tip of his Stetson. "You're lucky Alexis isn't around or she'd wonder what you were doing here."

"I actually just saw her getting out of her car in town so I knew it was a safe time."

The way she looked at him as she moved through the open space, the way she spoke so softly, all of it was so Rose. Everything about her was precise, well-mannered, captivating.

And he'd always been the man who wasn't good enough for

her. Being pushed from her life was the last time he'd ever allowed anyone to make him feel inferior.

But he could look and even admit that she was more stunning now than she'd been forty years ago.

"I was wondering how the auction is shaping up," Rose stated, clutching her purse with both hands. "I hadn't heard from you in a few days and I didn't know what Alexis has said."

Why did Rose seem so nervous? She typically had confidence he admired, even though they weren't friends—more like sworn enemies.

"Alexis and her friend Rachel were going over the list of names the other day. Daniel still hasn't fully committed even though he did allow us to put him on the roster. He told Rachel he was still on the fence, so you'll have to nudge him." He released a breath. "Rachel is doing the marketing and has all of his information and the headshot that you sent anonymously, but we'll need him to actually sign the contract."

Rose sighed. "That's what I was afraid of. I've told him he's a perfect bachelor. What woman wouldn't want to go out with a successful rancher? He has his own jet—he could take his fantasy date anywhere."

"But his fantasy date is my granddaughter," Gus reminded her tersely.

Rose pursed her pale pink lips and nodded. "I'll talk to him tomorrow."

"Alexis didn't seem all that pleased to see his name on the list when Rachel was going over it the other day."

"He'll be on that stage," Rose assured him. "We just have to make sure Alexis isn't the one bidding on him."

Gus smiled. "Oh, I'll have her busy when it's his turn. If I have to make up some backstage disaster, Alexis will not bid on Daniel. I've mentioned a few bachelors to her, but I'm pushing her toward Matt Galloway, Rachel's friend from Dallas. He seems perfect for my Lex."

Rose stared at him another moment before giving a curt nod.

When the silence settled heavy between them, Gus propped his hands on his hips and tipped his head.

"Something else on your mind?" he asked.

She opened her mouth, then shut it. After a moment, she finally said, "No. That's all. I just want to keep this communication open if we're going to make sure this goes off exactly as planned."

Gus didn't believe her one bit. She could've called or texted. Showing up here was rash and dangerous. They might have ended things decades ago, but he still knew when she was lying.

"Rose."

"Were you happy?"

The question came out of nowhere and left him speechless for a second. From the soft tone, the questioning gaze, he knew exactly what she referred to.

"Of course."

He never understood the term *sad smile* until now. The corners of Rose's mouth tipped up, but her low lids attempted to shield the pain in her eyes.

"That's all I ever wanted," she whispered.

Gus started to take a step forward, but Rose eased back and squared her shoulders. That fast she'd gathered herself together and whatever moment had just transpired had vanished.

"I'll keep you posted about Daniel."

When she turned to go, Gus couldn't stop himself. "You were happy with Ed, weren't you?"

Rose said nothing as she slowly turned and offered him that same less-than-convincing smile. Then she walked away. Not a word, not a nod of agreement. Nothing but sadness.

What the hell had just happened? What was this cryptic visit all about?

Any time he'd seen Rose and Ed over the years he'd always assumed they were a happily married couple. Sure Gus had been brokenhearted when he and Rose split, but he'd moved on and so had she. They'd turned into totally different people, created their own families and lives.

Gus never got over his bitterness toward how he was treated, how Rose so easily threw aside what they'd had. But marrying Sarah had been the right thing. He'd loved her with his whole heart and still mourned her loss.

And he'd be damned if Alexis and Daniel tried hooking up again. The last thing the Slades and the Claytons needed was to circle back together. He didn't want Rose in his life in any capacity. That might be harsh and rude, but the Claytons weren't exactly friends.

There was a nice young man out there for Alexis... Daniel Clayton just wasn't him.

"Where's Alexis?"

Rachel glanced around the garden area at TCC, but only saw Gus striding toward her. The wide hat on his head shadowed his face, but she could still catch that smile.

"She couldn't make it, so I told her I'd come help."

"Really?" Rachel asked, then shook her head. "Sorry, that was rude. I'm just surprised you'd want to discuss flowers, seating arrangements and how we'll be setting up the stage."

"This charity is dear to me," he told her as he wrapped an arm around her shoulder. "I'll do anything to help the cause."

After a quick pat on her back, Gus dropped his arm and spun in a slow circle. "Well, this place could use some maintenance."

Rachel had had those exact thoughts as she'd stepped outside. She and Alexis had planned on meeting here so they could figure out various parts of the auction. Rachel was hoping to get some photos to help use for the promotional side of things. Like maybe one of the empty area where the bachelors would be on display. She could use a simple photo like that and change out different catchy phrases for social media.

Unfortunately, Rachel wasn't so sure the gazebo was the best place to show off the hunky men.

"I don't even know where to start," Rachel murmured.

Gus pulled in a deep breath and adjusted his hat. "Well, first thing we're going to do is get a professional in here. You tell me what you want, and I mean every bloom and color, and I'll see that it happens."

Gus Slade wasn't joking. His matter-of-fact tone left no room for argument and she certainly wasn't about to turn away the help.

"I think everything out here needs to be dug up," she stated, waving her hand over the overgrown, neglected landscaping. "The gazebo could use a fresh coat of paint, too. Keep it white, definitely, and add some nice fat pots at the entrance. Something classy, yet festive. Maybe whites and golds—or should we add some red in the mix? I love the idea of the clean look with white and gold. Oh, poinsettias. We would definitely need those, too."

Gus laughed. "Honey, you better write all that down. I'll make some calls and get a crew out here. We'll get this place fixed up in no time."

"Hopefully they can make it magical on short notice. We only have a few months to get everything ready, and I'll still need to get some pictures to advertise after the work is done."

She wanted to showcase the auction site and make a fairy tale–like poster to entice women and pique their interest before revealing the bachelors. She figured she would do one bachelor per day on their social media sites; that way each man got his proper attention.

Gus rocked back on his heels and pulled his cell from his pocket. "Money can make a whole host of things happen when and how you want it. I'll make a couple of calls right now. Hang tight."

Rachel walked around, making mental notes. She took some random pictures on her phone to use for reference later. In her mind, she could easily see the grand garden area filled with a perimeter of festive blossoms, with white chairs lining the middle. She wasn't sure if any woman would be able to sit once the excitement of bidding started, but there was also a good possibility of some ladies getting weak in the knees. Their bachelor lineup even had Rachel ready to wave a paddle.

"All set."

Rachel shifted her focus back to Gus. "You found someone to come already?"

"I left a message with Austin Bradshaw. He did some work for me a few years back and there's nobody else I'd trust to do this job. I know he's good and he'll make sure it's done in the time frame I want."

If Gus was that confident, and footing the bill, Rachel was definitely onboard. Alexis would be thrilled, too.

"I can't thank you enough." Rachel patted his arm, then adjusted her purse on her shoulder. "So, I'll go back to the ranch and draw up the list in detail. I took some photos so I can remember exactly what I want, and where. I'll get that to you this evening."

"Sounds good. I'm sure I'll hear back from Austin today." Gus narrowed his gaze and grinned. "Do you have your sights set on any bachelors? You've seen each one, so you have an edge on the competition. Daniel Clayton has his own ranch. You seem to love that lifestyle."

First of all, the auction was only bidding for a date. Second, Rachel was pretty sure Alexis would have something to say if her best friend bid on Daniel.

And third...there was only one man from the entire group she'd want to bid on, and she was still torn over what to do on that. Matt had flat out asked her to bid on him. She wasn't sure what to make of his demand, but she certainly wanted to take as much as she was able to from her savings and do just that. If she already had her degree and a job, she'd be able to donate more, but she certainly could spare some to a worthy cause.

"Ah, so there is a man," Gus drawled out. "Well, he's a lucky guy. And who knows, maybe a date will turn into more."

Rachel laughed and shook her head. "You're a hopeless romantic, Gus. But I'm a widow and a single mother. I'm not ready to jump into the dating pool, let alone make another trip down the aisle."

The older gentleman opened his mouth to speak, but his cell chimed from his pocket. "Hold that thought," he said, pulling the phone out.

Yeah, she wasn't about to keep that topic open. She couldn't bring herself to fully think what would happen if she actually bid on Matt.

A shiver crept over her and she could chalk it up to nothing but pure desire. When she'd had dinner in his suite the other night, she was certain he would've closed the gap between them and kissed her. She'd seen the passion in his eyes and she hadn't missed the way his eyes dropped to her mouth and lingered.

Rachel wrapped her arms around her midsection and attempted to cool her heated thoughts. This kind of thinking was counterproductive, not to mention dangerous. She needed Matt to remain a friend, nothing more. She'd loved him like that for years. Yes, she was still hurt and she still deserved an explanation as to why he vanished, but this was Matt and she couldn't stay mad at him. She realized he'd been hurting, too, when Billy passed.

"That was Austin," Gus said. "He said he'll meet me out here tomorrow morning and look over your list. He'll start as soon as he gets all the supplies in."

"Wow," Rachel exclaimed. "That was fast."

Gus shrugged. "He's pushing a few jobs back for this. I just need to clear everything with the TCC board, but that won't be an issue."

Gus Slade was one powerful man who got what he wanted, when he wanted it. He reminded her of another strong man.

Rachel sighed. Did every thought lately circle back to Matt? Because every time her mind headed toward him, she got that tingling sensation all over again. Hard as she tried, there was no controlling her imagination or this new ache that seemed to accompany each thought of him.

"I truly appreciate this," she told him. "Alexis will be so thrilled."

"You're doing so much more than just marketing," Gus added. "We need to be thanking you."

"Just give me a good reference when I get my degree and need a job."

"Consider it done."

Gus wrapped his arm around her shoulder and started walking back toward the entrance to the clubhouse. "What do you say we grab some lunch? My treat."

"I really should get back to Ellie."

Ellie had been left with a member of Gus's staff. Each person at Lone Wolf Ranch absolutely doted over Rachel's daughter, so there was no doubt she was in good hands.

"Another hour won't matter," Gus stated. "Call and check on her if it makes you feel better."

Rachel nodded. "You're spoiling me and I might never leave."

As he led her toward the restaurant inside TCC, Gus laughed. "You have an open invitation to stay at Lone Wolf as long as you like."

Her in-laws probably wouldn't like that idea, but the longer Rachel stayed in Royal, the more she felt like she'd finally come home.

Six

Matt glanced at the Halloween-costume party invitation that had been hand delivered to his suite. The board at TCC was hosting the festive event and apparently the entire town was invited.

What the hell would he do at a costume party? Was there a man in his right mind who actually wanted to dress up?

Granted he could always go as a disgruntled CEO or aimless wanderer since he had no clue what the hell he wanted in his life right now. Something was missing, something that his padded bank account couldn't buy. Being back in Royal stirred something in him he hadn't felt in a long, long time. There was a sense of community here and people always looking out for each other...something he didn't see in Dallas.

Tossing the invitation on the counter, Matt grabbed his keys and headed to the elevator just off his living area. He planned to do a drive-by of his grandfather's place today to see exactly what he was dealing with, and then he had to pick up Rachel so she could take some pictures of him for the auction.

Whatever possessed him to agree to such madness? Auctioning himself off sounded absurd, and he preferred to choose his own dates, thank you very much. It wasn't like he had trouble finding female companions. So how did he end up here?

Oh, that's right. Rachel had asked. Things were as simple and as complicated as that. He couldn't say no to her, no matter what she wanted. Rachel was...well, she was special and she deserved better than the thoughts and fantasies he'd been harboring for years.

More times than he cared to admit he'd imagined her in his bed, all of them from the island mansion to his Dallas home. He'd pictured her swimming in the ocean wearing nothing but his touch and a sated smile.

Matt attempted to shove thoughts of Rachel from his mind as he drove toward his grandfather's old farm. The place had sat empty for years. After Matt's parents had passed, the land had been willed to him. He had been too busy in Dallas to deal with it, but now, well, he could sure as hell use the outlet.

He and his partner weren't seeing eye to eye, and that was partially due to Matt not being happy in the place he was at in his life. Every day he went to work, and no matter how successful he was, there always seemed to be a void.

Maybe finding a contractor and pushing through some renovations would help. It certainly couldn't hurt.

Matt pulled into the drive overgrown with grass and weeds. The white two-story farmhouse sat back, nestled against the woods. The old barn off to the right actually looked to be in better shape than the house itself.

Swallowing the lump of emotion, Matt stared at the front porch that looked like a good gust of Texas wind could knock it down. He recalled spending his summers with his grandfather, learning all about farm life, about hard work and seeing it pay off. Matt owed everything to that man. Without Patrick Galloway, Matt wouldn't be the successful oil tycoon he was today.

As a young boy, he hadn't realized all the life lessons being instilled, but now looking back, there was no doubt he was being shaped.

Matt smiled as he continued to look at the porch. The creaky swing that hung on one end was gone, but he could easily see it in his mind. His grandfather would sit there and play the harmonica while Matt sat on the top step with two sticks and played faux drums.

Damn it. He missed the simpler times. He missed his parents, his grandfather, those carefree summer nights followed by sweat-your-ass-off workdays.

He'd call a contractor tomorrow. This wasn't something he was going to leave to his assistant, though she was fabulous. Matt planned on handling every bit of this personal project himself.

His cell rang through the speakers of his truck, but he ignored the call when his partner's number flashed on the screen. Matt would call him back later. Right now he wanted to get to Rachel and get this photo shoot over with. She'd requested he wear a suit so she could capture him in his element. Although it was true that business attire was part of his daily life, he'd like to be a bit more casual for this shoot.

Then again, this wasn't his charity and he wasn't the one bidding. Good grief. He was honestly going to stand on a stage and watch women waving paddles around just to go on a date with him.

There was only one woman he wanted to win that bid. He'd have to do some convincing, though. Rachel had seemed a little hesitant and he couldn't blame her. He'd up and deserted her after Billy's funeral, then he'd dropped back into her life unexpectedly, and followed that by making it clear he wouldn't mind kissing her.

Yeah, he saw her lids widen and heard her breath hitch when he inched closer as they sat on the floor of his suite. Had Ellie not been between them, Matt would have pulled Rachel to him and taken a sample of something he'd coveted for far too long.

Just one taste. At least that's what he told himself he needed to get over the craving.

Matt pulled out of the drive and headed toward Lone Wolf Ranch. Ten minutes later, he was turning into the sprawling estate with a wrought iron arch over the entrance. This was Royal, small town charm mixed with money, lots of it, and a big-city feel. Matt could easily see the pull to live here, and he was banking on that for when he renovated his grandfather's farm. The real estate market was booming and he knew he'd have no trouble selling.

The thought didn't settle well with him, but he didn't need the place. He had his ten-thousand-square-foot home in Dallas and his own island, for pity's sake. He traveled when and where he wanted. He couldn't hold on to the old farmstead simply for nostalgia.

As he approached the massive main house, Rachel came bounding down the stairs. She smiled and waved. There was no denying the punch of lust to the gut. She wore another one of those long, curve-hugging dresses that she probably thought was comfortable, but all he could think was how fast he could have that material shoved up to her waist and joining their bodies after years of aching to have no barriers between them.

There wasn't a doubt in Matt's mind that the real thing would put the fantasy to shame.

Damn. He seriously needed to get a grip.

Rachel opened the truck door, and had he not been imagining her naked he would've gotten out and opened her door for her.

"Hey." She hopped in and set the camera bag between them. "Are you ready for this?"

A day alone with Rachel? Hell yeah.

"I guess so." He turned toward her slightly. "This suit okay?"

He absolutely relished the way her eyes raked over him. Sure his ego was larger than most, but the only woman he wanted was looking at him as if she wanted him right back.

"It will do."

Leave it to Rachel to knock him down a peg. With a low chuckle, Matt put the truck in gear and headed back down the drive.

"So, where are we going?" she asked.

He'd insisted on the location of the shoot as well as her being the photographer. If he'd told her ahead of time where he was taking her, she would've balked at the suggestion.

"I'll keep it a surprise for now."

Rachel clicked her seatbelt into place and settled back in the seat. "As long as I'm back in time to give Ellie a bath. I was actually ordered by Alexis to go have fun. She thinks we're dating."

Interesting. "What have you been saying about me to your host family?"

Rachel laughed, the sultry sound flooding the small space. "Gus is a romantic at heart and Alexis, well, she's just excited I'm talking to any man."

Matt gripped the steering wheel. "Surely you've been on a date in the last year."

"Why would you think that?"

He pointed the truck toward the edge of town, heading for the airstrip. "Because you're a beautiful, passionate woman, Rachel."

"I'm a widow and a single mother."

Gritting his teeth, Matt weighed his words carefully. "So you've reminded me before, but that doesn't mean you don't get to have a social life. Do you plan on staying single until Ellie moves out of the house?"

Rachel blew out a sigh and turned to face the side window. "I don't want to argue with you, Matt. It's not like I can just pick up and date anyone I want. I have a child to think about now and she has to come first. We're a package deal, so I can't just bring men in and out of her life."

He didn't say another word, because he also didn't want to argue, but there were plenty of thoughts circling around in his mind. Maybe he didn't want a ready-made family and marriage and picket fences, but he wanted Rachel. He wanted to prove to her that she was still alive, that just because her life had changed dramatically didn't mean she had to give up her wants and needs.

Maybe this bachelor auction was exactly what he needed to make his case. If he was going to put himself on display like a piece of meat, he was sure as hell going to use it to his advantage. Rachel was about to come to grips with the fact that she could still be a mother *and* a woman. A passionate, desirable woman.

"What are we doing here?"

Rachel stared at the small airstrip and the private plane with a man dressed all in black waiting at the base of the stairs. For the past ten minutes, she and Matt had ridden in silence. He simply didn't understand where she was coming from in regard to her dating life and she wasn't going to keep explaining her situation.

"You wanted pictures, right?" He pulled the truck to a stop and killed the engine. "We're going to Galloway Cove."

She jerked in her seat and faced him. "What? But, you're in a suit and I thought we were doing office-type images since you're a CEO."

Matt shrugged. "You want me in the auction, I'm calling the shots on how I'm portrayed. Don't worry, there's an office in my beach house."

He hopped out of the truck without another word and circled the hood. When he opened her door, Rachel still couldn't believe he was taking her to his island for the photo shoot. She couldn't be alone with him on a secluded island. That screamed *cliché* with all of these newly awakened emotions she had toward him. Was he purposely trying to get her alone?

Anticipation and nerves swirled together deep in her gut. Was he trying to seduce her?

"Why don't we just take some of you standing in front of

your plane?" she suggested, trying not to sound as flustered as she felt. "That would fuel any woman's fantasy for the auction."

Because this suit was totally doing it for her.

Matt's striking blue eyes held her captivated as he leaned closer. "Maybe there's only one woman I want to fantasize about me."

Even with the truck door open, there still didn't seem to be enough air to fill her lungs. This was Matt, her friend. Her very sexy, very dynamic friend whose broad shoulders filled out his suit to the point it should be illegal for him to walk around in public.

The stirrings of desire hit her hard. Harder than when she'd wanted him to kiss her in his penthouse suite. Why now? Why did he drop back into her life and make her question the direction she was moving? She didn't have time for desire or kisses or hot, sultry looks from a man who used to be her rock. She wasn't looking for anything akin to lust or attraction right now. Like she had the time to worry about another relationship.

His dark blue eyes slid from her eyes to her lips.

"Don't do that," she scolded.

His mouth kicked up in a cocky smirk. "What's that?"

"Try to be cute or pretend like you want to kiss me."

Matt laughed. "Leave it to you to not skirt around the situation. I'm not pretending, Rachel. I plan on kissing you. You won't know when, but that's your warning."

Well, hell. Apparently the gauntlet she just threw down had awakened the beast. The real question was, how long had he been lying in wait?

Matt leaned across the seat, his solid chest brushing hers, his lips coming within a breath. Rachel inhaled, the subtle movement causing her sensitive breasts to press further against his hard body. She hadn't been aroused like this in so long, she couldn't trust her judgment right now. Her mind was all muddled and her hormones were overriding common sense. But she had to remain in control…at all costs.

"Relax," he murmured.

The click of her belt echoed in the cab of the truck and Matt eased away, taking her hands in his to help her out. He reached back in for the camera bag and flung it over his big, broad shoulder before closing the door.

Finally, she could breathe. Even though he was holding her hand as they walked across the tarmac, Rachel could handle that.

What she could not handle, however, was that promise or threat or whatever he'd issued when he'd warned her of the kiss. The way he'd looked at her, rubbed against her and put naughty, *R*-rated thoughts inside her head.

They shouldn't be kissing. What they needed to do was get photos and focus on the auction...an auction where other women would be writing big fat checks to score a date with this handsome, prominent bachelor. He wasn't hers...not in that way.

"I'm not going to bid on you," she stated, as if that was her mega comeback for the way he'd got her all hot and bothered in the truck, and then strolled along as if nothing had changed between them. "You need to get that through your thick head."

"Of course you will."

Rachel jerked her hand from his and marched onward toward the steps of the plane. Arrogant bastard. Why was she friends with him again?

The pilot smiled and nodded as he welcomed her on board. Rachel climbed the stairs and was stunned at the beauty and spaciousness of the plane. She'd known Matt had his own aircraft, but she'd never been inside it. She'd never been to Galloway Cove, either. When they all hung out, Billy, Matt and her, Matt usually came to her house or they all met at their favorite pub in Dallas.

But Rachel wasn't going to stroke his ego anymore and comment on the beauty of the details or even act like she was impressed.

She went to the dark leather sofa that stretched beneath the oval windows, took a seat on one end and then fastened her safety belt. Matt and the pilot spoke but she couldn't make out their words. Didn't matter. She knew where they were going, knew Matt's intentions, but that didn't mean she would give in. He still owed her answers, and being on a plane with nowhere for him to run was exactly where she planned on getting them.

Rachel shifted and kept looking out the window as Matt came back and took a seat—of course on the same sofa, but at least on the opposite end. It took all of her willpower not to just bombard him with all the questions she'd been dying to ask since he'd disappeared from her life. But she would. She wanted him to get nice and comfortable with his situation first. He thought he was calling the shots, but she was about to flip their positions.

Seven

Rachel had been quiet during takeoff. Too quiet. Her gaze never wavered from the window. The flight took about an hour and a half from Royal and Matt had to admit, he was worried.

She was plotting something. She was pissed, if the thin lips and the sound of her gritting teeth was any indicator. Perhaps he'd been too forward earlier, but damn it, he'd held out for years and he was done skirting around his attraction. She deserved to know how much he wanted her. He couldn't go at this any slower. At this rate they'd be in a nursing home before he got to first base.

He might want nothing more than to see where this fierce physical attraction went, but perhaps she was on the same page. He knew she was more of a happily-ever-after girl, but perhaps she wanted to just have a good time and not think about commitments for a while.

That was plausible…right? Or was he just trying to justify his actions to himself so he didn't feel like an ass for making a move on his late friend's wife?

"Why don't you just say what you're stewing about and let's move on?" He couldn't stand the damn silence another second.

She didn't move one bit, except her eyes, which darted to him. Oh, yeah. She was pissed.

"Fine. Start with Billy's funeral and your immediate absence after."

Hell. He'd known this was coming—he'd rehearsed the speech in his head over and over. However, nothing prepared him to actually say the words aloud.

"I know you were hurting—"

"Hurting? You *crushed* me," she scolded. "Billy's death tore me apart and I needed you. I was pregnant, scared, facing in-laws who were smothering me, and I just wanted my friend."

He'd crushed her. That was a bitter pill to swallow and he had no excuse other than he was selfish and trying to do what he thought was best at the time. But she'd needed him, and he worried more that he'd take them into unknown territory while she was still vulnerable. He'd been a total prick, but hindsight was a bitch.

"I texted." That was lame even to his own ears. "I just… I needed space."

She turned her attention back to the window. "An entire year," she murmured. Then she shifted in her seat to fully face him, anger and pain flooding her eyes with unshed tears, and she might as well have stabbed him and twisted the knife.

"Would you have contacted me had we not run into each other? Or were you only friends with me because of Billy?"

"No." She had to know that above all else. "What you and I shared had nothing to do with Billy."

And everything to do with him.

"I would've reached out to you, Rachel," he said softly. "I missed you."

"Well, that's something," she whispered, almost in relief.

Matt immediately unbuckled his belt and slid closer, taking her hands even though she tried to pull back. "Look at me, damn it. Did you honestly believe that because he died I was just done with you? With us?"

"What else was I supposed to think? I mean, we were close for so long and then I didn't see you. I went by your house and your housekeeper told me you were on vacation. You answered my texts in short sentences as if I was bothering you. Then... nothing."

Yeah, because he'd hidden away at his home on Galloway Cove until he could go back to Dallas and not risk telling Rachel how he'd felt for years. There were things about Billy she didn't know, and it had taken all of his strength to keep those secrets to himself. But those last few days of his life, Billy hadn't only argued with Rachel. He and Matt had finally had it out and Matt had issued an ultimatum. Rachel didn't deserve to be treated like she wasn't the most important thing in Billy's world. Billy accused Matt of always wanting her, and fists started flying.

"Matt?"

He blinked away from the memories and squeezed her hands. He couldn't tell her about all of that. He sure as hell wasn't going to tell her when Billy died, because she was suffering enough. What would the point be in telling her now that her husband had been unfaithful? There was no reason at all to drudge up the past and make her feel even worse.

"I had to get away," he croaked out, cursing himself for showing weakness. He swallowed the lump of guilt and the ache that accompanied his desire for her. "I knew Billy's parents and brother would watch out for you. I needed some time to myself."

"I still don't understand why so long." She stared back at him, studying his face as if truly trying to understand his way of thinking. "I missed you."

There was only so much a man could take, and those last three words sliced through his last thread of control.

Matt gripped her face between his hands and covered her mouth with his. For a half second he had a sliver of fear that she would push him away. She didn't pull back, but she stiffened, hopefully from shock and not from repulsion.

Yes. That's all he could think as he slid his tongue through the seam of her lips. He'd been right. The real thing didn't even compare to his fantasies. Not only that, no other woman had ever made him so damn achy and needy like Rachel.

The second she relaxed, Matt shifted his body to cover hers as she leaned against the back of the sofa. Her hands came up to his shoulders, her fingertips curling around him as if to hold him in place. Like he was going anywhere after finally getting her in this position. If only he could shut out the rest of the world and stay like this with her until he'd finally exorcised her out of his system.

Matt wanted to rip her dress off, discard this ridiculous suit and lay her flat out, taking everything he'd craved for damn near ten years.

But he couldn't. He respected Rachel, and a kiss was one thing, but taking it to the next level was another. And if that was the route they were going to go, he wasn't dragging her. No, if she wanted him, she'd have to show him.

At least now she knew where he stood.

Matt pulled back, still keeping her face between his palms. He rested his forehead against hers and fell into the same breathing pattern as her.

"Well, you did warn me."

He laughed. He couldn't help it. "I won't apologize."

Rachel tipped her head back. Heavy lids half covered her expressive eyes, and her lips were plump and wet from his passion. She stared at him for a moment before she seemed to close in on herself, blinking and pulling in a deep breath.

"I didn't ask for an apology," she stated. "We kissed. It's over. We're friends, so this shouldn't be a big deal."

Processing her words, Matt slowly released her and sat back. *Shouldn't be a big deal?* He'd waited to touch her, to taste her for a damn long time, and she just brushed it aside as no big deal? It sure as hell was a huge deal, and she knew it.

"I told you before you're a terrible liar."

Rachel's eyes widened a fraction before she eased away from him and came to her feet. Considering there was nowhere for her to escape, he sat and watched as she paced. She not only paced—she held her fingertips to her lips. The egotistical side of him liked to think she was replaying their kiss—he sure as hell was.

"Let me get this straight." She paced toward the kitchen, then back toward him. "We've been friends since college. I marry your best friend. He passes away. I don't hear from you for too damn long, and now you want to…what? What is it you want from me?"

Everything.

No. That wasn't true. He didn't want marriage or children. He'd never considered any of that part of his life plan. Billy hadn't, either, but when he'd married Rachel, he'd been in love. It was the whole family thing that had put him off-kilter.

"Maybe I want to prove to you that you're ready to get back out in the world and date." The thought of her with another man prickled the hairs on the back of his neck and made him fist his hands in his lap. "You returned that kiss, Rachel. Don't tell me you don't have needs."

She snapped her attention back to him, crossing her arms over her chest. "My needs are none of your concern."

They were every bit his concern.

"Sit down," he demanded. "You're making me dizzy watching you pace back and forth."

She narrowed her eyes before turning and taking a seat in one of the two swivel-style club chairs on the opposite side. She crossed her legs and adjusted her dress over her knees, but that did nothing to squelch his desire.

Matt still tasted her on his lips. He still felt her grip on his shoulders. What would she be like when she fully let her guard down and let him pleasure her? Because that moment would happen. Right now she had to get used to the kiss—there would be more—and then he'd slowly reawaken the passion he knew was buried deep inside.

Matt's single-story beach home with its white exterior and white columns along the porch might have been the most beautiful thing Rachel had ever seen. The lush greenery looked like a painting, and the various pieces of driftwood in the landscaping were the perfect added touch.

Rachel could easily see why he kept this island a secret. Some men would've thrown parties here at the opulent beachfront home, but Matt kept his life more private.

And that privacy was one of the main differences between him and Billy. Her late husband liked to live large, celebrate life every single day by going on adventures or partying.

It was difficult not to compare the two friends, especially now that she'd kissed Matt. No. Correction. He'd kissed her. And boy did he ever kiss. That man's mouth was potent enough she was still tingling. What the hell would happen to her if he actually got his hands on her?

The idea had hit her the moment he'd touched his mouth to hers and part of her had wanted him to take things further.

Which was why she'd had to sit on the other side of the plane for the duration of the flight. Her mind was clouded, that's all. She didn't want her best friend…did she?

Being on the other side of the plane hadn't stopped Matt from staring at her, looking like the Big Bad Wolf deliciously wrapped in an Italian suit. Predators apparently came in all forms and hers was billionaire oil tycoon posing as her friend. Because the way he'd stared made her feel like he could see right through her clothes to what lay underneath.

If he saw her saggy tummy and stretch marks, maybe he wouldn't be so eager. She wouldn't change her new mommy body for anything, though. Ellie was the greatest thing that had ever happened to her.

"Where do you want me?"

That low, sultry tone wrapped Rachel in complete arousal. Damn that man for making her want, making her think things she really shouldn't. She was human, after all, and she couldn't turn off her emotions or her needs. Surely there was some unwritten rule about lusting after your late husband's best friend.

Rachel turned from the wall of windows facing the stunning ocean view and met Matt's gaze from across the living room. He'd told her to look around and see which room would be best, and that had been nearly a half hour ago. She wasn't sure where he'd gone or what he was doing, but even her time alone in this stunning house hadn't cooled her off from that most scintillating plane ride.

"I thought you were calling the shots," she tossed back. "Granted the other guys I photographed didn't care where I put them."

Matt's eyes narrowed. "I thought you weren't comfortable taking my picture for this. You didn't say you'd done the others."

Rachel shrugged. "It saved money and I enjoy it. I never said I didn't want to take your picture, by the way. I simply said I wasn't a professional. You should've asked someone else."

One slow, calculated step at a time, Matt closed the distance between them. "And why is that, Rachel? Afraid of what you're feeling?"

She swallowed and tipped her chin. "I'm not afraid of anything. Now back off and stop trying to seduce me."

He reached out and smoothed her hair from her face before dropping his hand. "I'm not trying to seduce you. When I seduce you, you'll know it."

When.

The bold term had anticipation and arousal pulsing through her. This was getting them nowhere except dangerously close to the point of no return for their friendship.

"Are you willing to throw away our friendship for a quick romp?" she countered.

"Oh, honey. It won't be quick. I assure you." He stepped back and spread his arms wide. "Now, where do you want me?"

Why did he keep phrasing it like that?

Focus.

Rachel clutched the camera bag on her shoulder and nodded toward the hallway. "Let's start in your office. We'll do some professional shots and then I'll have you take off the jacket and tie, and roll up your sleeves and we'll do some casual ones outside. You've got such gorgeous landscaping and pool, it would be a shame not to grab some there."

"What about the waterfall?"

Rachel shook her head in amazement. "You have a waterfall? I seriously need to get my own island."

Matt laughed. "I'll show you when we're done. Maybe you'll want some shots there, as well."

A photo of this rich, gorgeous oil tycoon posing in front of a waterfall...yup, that would certainly have all the ladies drooling. Not her, of course, but the others who were bidding.

"You might just decide to bid on me yet," he drawled.

"Don't get too cocky."

"If I wasn't cocky, I wouldn't have gotten where I am today. And I prefer to use the term *confident*."

Rachel rolled her eyes and headed toward the other end of the house, where the office was. "And I prefer to leave our friendship intact, so keep those lips to yourself."

"Whatever you want," he murmured as she passed by. But his low, seductive tone indicated she'd want something else entirely, and damn it, he was right.

Eight

Rachel was going to need to take a dip in the pool to cool off. Mercy sakes. She'd thought Matt adorned in a three-piece suit, leaning against his desk with his arms crossed over his massive chest, flashing an arrogant smirk at the camera was sexy, but that was nothing compared to the images she currently snapped of him in the waterfall.

As in, *in* the waterfall. He'd rolled up his pant legs to his calves, folded his shirt sleeves onto those impressive forearms, and then untucked and unbuttoned the damn thing.

Oh, he was playing dirty and he knew it. It would serve him right if she let some wealthy socialite bid on him and then make him fulfill some fantasy date.

But would he kiss that faceless woman good-night? Would he pour every bit of his body and soul into that kiss like he had with her?

Jealousy didn't sit well with Rachel. She'd experienced it with her own husband in the final days of their marriage when she suspected infidelity, and she sure as hell didn't want to experience it again. Matt was a ladies' man, his newly appointed title made that crystal clear. No way would she ever want to get involved with a player again, and she wasn't sure if she'd ever be ready for another committed relationship.

"I think we have enough," she shouted over the cascading water.

Matt raked his wet hands through his hair, making the black strands glisten beneath the sun. In an attempt to ignore the curl of lust in her belly, Rachel scrolled through the images she'd taken over the last couple of hours.

The only problem she saw with each picture was that each one was absolute perfection, which said nothing of her photography skills and everything of the subject on the other side of the lens.

"Put your camera down."

Rachel glanced up. Matt still remained in the water, the bottom of his pants soaked, his shirt clinging like transparent silk against his tanned, muscular chest.

"What?"

"Get in the water. Work is over."

"Then we should head back."

She could *not* get into that water with him. Then her clothes would get clingy and he'd probably touch her or kiss her again, and at this point she wasn't sure she would be able to ignore the aching need. There wasn't a doubt in her mind Matt would set her world on fire; it was everything that came afterward that worried her.

She'd been without a man for so long...*too long*. She simply couldn't trust her erratic emotions right now.

Matt stalked toward her like some god emerging from the water. Droplets ran down his exposed skin and she was so riveted she couldn't look away. Part of her even imagined licking each and every one, and that only added fuel to the proverbial flames.

How had he put this spell on her and why was she letting

him? Oh, right. Because she was on a slippery slope and barely hanging on.

When he reached for her hand, Rachel set her camera down on a rock. He urged her forward.

"I can't get wet," she protested, though her feet were following him. "I don't have extra clothes."

He walked backward, his eyes never wavering from hers. "Take off your dress and we won't have a problem."

"You're not getting me out of my clothes."

The smirk, that raised brow, the way he kept walking her toward the water's edge…damn it. He took her statement as a challenge.

"Matt, we can't do this."

Cool water slid over her toes, over her ankles, soaking the bottom of her dress. She was losing a battle she wasn't sure she ever had a fair fight in.

"No one is here to tell us not to."

"I'm telling us not to," she argued. "This isn't right."

"Says who? Tell me you're not attracted to me, Rachel. Tell me you didn't kiss me right back and you haven't been thinking of it every second since."

She chewed on her bottom lip to prevent a lie from slipping out…and also to hold the truth inside. But her silence was just as telling as if she'd admitted her true feelings.

"It's just water," he crooned. "Nothing to be afraid of."

"I told you before, I'm not afraid." She pulled her hand from his and lifted her dress, bunching it in her fist at her side. "Is this how you get all your women? You use that sultry voice, that heavy-lidded gaze and…" She waved up and down at his bare chest.

"All of my women?" he repeated. "Watch it, Rachel. I'll start to think you care about my sex life."

She'd never given it much thought before now. And in the past several hours, Matt and sex had consumed nearly all of her thoughts.

Without thinking, she pulled from his grasp and leaned down, scooped up some water and splashed him right in the face. He sputtered for a second before flicking the excess away. Rachel couldn't help but laugh at his shocked expression, but then that surprise turned to menace.

"You think that's funny, do you?"

In a lightning-flash movement, he scooped her up into his big, strong arms and headed toward the waterfall.

"No!" she squealed. "Don't drench me, Matt, please. I'm sorry! I'll do anything, just don't—"

Water covered her entire body, chilling her instantly. Rachel squeezed her eyes shut and held her breath as she wrapped her arms around Matt's neck and clung tight. She turned her face toward his neck, trying to shield herself from the pounding spray. A moment later, he shifted and the water was behind her.

Rachel blinked the water from her eyes and glanced up. Matt stared down at her with even more raw, elemental desire than she'd ever seen. Billy had never looked at her that way...no one had.

Easing her to her feet, Matt kept an arm banded around her waist and cupped the side of her face with his other hand. Rachel's heart pounded in her chest. She needed to stop this before things went any further, but she hadn't done a very good job at stopping the progress up to this point.

"I want you," he muttered against her mouth. His words were barely audible over the rushing waters.

"I know."

He tipped her back, leaning over her, still very much in control over her body...physically and emotionally. Those blue eyes locked on hers.

"Tell me no and we'll walk out of here and get back on the plane. My pilot is there and ready when we are."

He'd just handed over total control to her and with one word she could end it all...or take what he'd presented to her wrapped in a delicious package.

And there was really no decision to be made here. Because, in the end, she wasn't going to deny herself. She had basic needs—there was nothing shameful about that. Besides, this was Matt. They were friends; he wasn't looking for more and neither was she.

One time. Just this once, be selfish.

Rachel gripped his face and pulled his mouth down to hers. In the next instant, Matt wrapped his arms around her waist, filling his hands with her rear. The warmth of his touch through the cool material warmed her instantly.

She slid her hands through his wet hair, clutching onto him as he continued to tip her backward. There was no way he'd let her fall, though. His grip was too tight, his mouth too powerful, his need practically radiating from him. She wasn't going anywhere.

His hips ground into hers and the thin layer of wet clothes might as well have been nonexistent. Except it was and proved to be a most frustrating barrier. She'd never felt this overwhelming need before, never had the feeling of all-consuming passion, like she couldn't control herself.

It had never been this way with Billy.

No. For right now she was going to be completely closed off from reality and anything that threatened to steal her happiness. Damn it, she was going to take what she wanted...what Matt wanted. How long had he desired her? Did seeing her again spark something inside him?

Oh, my. Had he wanted her before?

"You're thinking too hard," he rasped against her mouth.

His hands came to her shoulders and gripped the straps of her maxi dress. He yanked them down, the clingy material pulling the cups of her bra as well, instantly exposing her breasts.

She didn't have time to worry about her body or what he thought, because his mouth descended downward and Rachel arched against him as he drew one tight nipple into his mouth.

"Matt," she moaned.

"Say it again," he demanded. "I want my name on your lips."

She didn't think he'd heard her over the rushing water, but she definitely heard him. From the command, she had to guess that he was just as turned on as she was at this point.

Rachel yanked on the material of his shirt, but it clung to his biceps. He eased back just enough to remove the garment and toss it in the general direction of the shore.

Instantly her eyes went to the ink over his shoulder. She traced her finger over the eagle's wings that spanned around to the back.

"This is new."

When he trembled beneath her touch, she wondered just how much control she had here. More than she'd initially thought.

When her eyes darted to his face, she noted the clenched jaw, the heavy lids, the blue eyes that had darkened with arousal.

So much hit her all at once that it was like truly seeing Matt for the first time...and recognizing the secret yearnings he'd kept locked up inside for so long. "I never knew."

"Now you do."

Yeah, she did. And she'd have to worry about that later. Her body was humming and zinging and doing all of the other happy dances that accompanied the heady anticipation of having really great sex. But she'd never been this charged before, never wanted a man so bad. Knowing that he wanted her just as much...well, that only fueled her desire.

With more confidence than she'd ever had, Rachel pushed her dress all the way down until it puddled around her waist. She shimmied just enough to let it fall before she stepped out of it. With her bra barely covering her and her panties beneath the surface, she felt more exposed than ever.

Who the hell had sex outside in the middle of the day? The sun shone bright down on the pair, the water rushed beside them and a butterfly had literally just flown by. It was as if she'd already bid on her best friend and was living out the fantasy date she never knew she even wanted.

On a growl, Matt picked her up and headed toward the shoreline. Her legs instantly wrapped around his waist. This was seriously happening. If she deliberated too much about all the reasons this was a bad idea, she might back out, so she cleared her head of all rational thought.

Matt sat her down once again, this time her toes landing on the lush ground cover that ran along the edge of the waterfall. In seconds he'd discarded his clothes, and Rachel was too busy admiring the mouthwatering view to realize he'd gripped the edge of her panties. The material fell away as he gave a yank and they ripped clear off her body.

"Matt," she cried.

"I'm done waiting."

He enveloped her into his arms, gently taking her to the ground, but he rolled beneath her so that she was on top. Instantly her legs straddled his hips. Her hands went up, ready to cover her torso.

"No," he commanded as he took her hands away. "I want to see all of you. Don't be ashamed of something so beautiful."

Beautiful? Not how she'd describe her post-pregnancy body, but the way Matt's eyes caressed her skin had her almost believing him.

We don't have protection. The thought slid into her mind and she wondered if he'd stop. "I'm on birth control even though I haven't been with anyone since Billy, and even that was a couple months before his death."

The night Ellie had been conceived, actually. But that was a story she didn't want to plunk down right here between them.

"I've never been without protection, Rachel. I know I'm clean, but this is your call."

He gripped her hips, whether to hold her away or encourage her to hurry and make up her mind, she didn't know. But she was sure of this, of him.

Without a word, she lowered herself and joined their bodies. His groan of approval had her smiling as she rested her hands on either side of his head. Matt nipped at her lips before pushing her back up.

"I want to watch every second of this," he murmured.

He might have seduced her, not that she'd put up too much of a fight, but he was handing over total control. Matt wasn't a man who liked to give up his power...which just proved how much he wanted her, wanted *this* to happen.

Rachel would have to analyze that from all different directions later. Right now, she only wanted to feel—and she certainly felt.

Matt's hands roamed from her hips to her breasts and back down. She shifted against him, finding that perfect rhythm. Never once did she shy away from his hot, molten gaze. She couldn't pinpoint that look in his eyes; she couldn't figure out what he saw when he stared at her so intently. But she did know she'd never felt like this, and she wasn't so sure she wanted this to end.

Matt tightened his hold on her as his hips pumped faster beneath her. That strong jawline of his clenched. Rachel leaned over him, her wet hair falling around to curtain them as she covered his mouth.

Then the dam burst. Matt's hands were all over her as he pushed up to a seated position. Her legs curled around his back and her hips continued to rock against his. When the climax spiraled through her, Rachel tore her mouth away, clutched onto his shoulders and arched back.

He murmured something, but she couldn't decipher the words. She clung to him as wave after wave crashed over her. Before she came down from her high, Matt was clutching her against him, his hips stilled beneath her as his entire body tightened and he let the passion consume him, too.

Rachel circled her arms around his neck and buried her face against his moist, heated skin. As Matt's body relaxed, his fingertips started trailing up and down her back. She couldn't lift her head, couldn't face him.

What had they just done? Part of her mind said they'd both betrayed Billy, but the other part wondered how the hell she could ever be with another man after the way Matt made her feel.

At some point, she'd have to face him. More so, she'd have to come to grips with how this changed every emotion she had toward her best friend.

Nine

Matt had known she wouldn't want to talk. He'd sensed her emotional disconnect the moment their bodies calmed, even while she was still wrapped around him. They'd still been joined physically, but she'd checked out mentally.

What did he think would happen? That she'd flash that wide smile at him and ask him to take her back to the house for an encore?

Sex with Rachel was everything he'd ever wanted…and nothing like what he expected. No fantasy could've compared to having the real thing.

He stood in his living room and waited on her to dress. They'd walked back to the beach house in awkward silence and he'd given her that gap she'd obviously needed. Knowing Rachel, she was trying to analyze her new feelings, was trying to figure out if she'd just done something morally wrong against her late husband.

Matt had loved Billy like a brother, but Billy was gone. Life moved on and he was done waiting. He was done letting guilt consume him. But where did that leave the two of them?

As soon as they'd reached the house, Matt had taken her soaking-wet clothes and put them in his dryer. He'd told her to go shower in the master bath, which was a wall of one-way windows that overlooked the ocean. Surely the combination of the breathtaking view, the rain head and six jets would relax her.

He'd taken his shower outside surrounded by the lush tropical plants he'd had arranged perfectly to ensure privacy for guests...not that he'd invited anyone here. Galloway Cove was his haven, his private life away from the office and its demands.

Rachel was the only woman he'd ever brought here, and damn it if he didn't like seeing her walk around his private domain. There had never been a doubt in his mind who he would bring here. Having shown her his favorite spot on the island, having made love to her with the waterfall in the background...

Matt turned from the windows and curbed his desire. There was no way he could go into that bathroom and show her just how amazing they were together. She knew. He'd seen that look of passion, desire and want staring back at him earlier.

But she'd been in the bathroom nearly an hour. Her clothes had dried and he'd laid them on his king-size bed. Her delicate bra and that dress that drove him out of his mind were displayed for her to see. He owed her a pair of panties, though.

Matt pulled out his cell and attempted to clear his head by checking work emails. His partner had forwarded one where another firm had showed interest in buying them both out. He wasn't sure how he felt about that. True he wanted...hell, he wasn't sure *what* he wanted. He knew something was missing, and as soon as he could put his finger on that, he'd be better-off.

Selling his share of the company? He'd given his partner the chance to buy his half. But was Eric wanting to sell his own, as well? That was definitely something they'd have to discuss via phone because Matt wasn't about to email all of his thoughts.

Shuffling feet down the hallway had him shoving his phone and his business predicament aside. With his body still humming from being with Rachel, work wasn't relevant right now.

Never in his life had he ever put a woman, put *anyone*, ahead of his career. That's how he'd gotten to where he was, able to take off whenever he wanted, travel wherever, buy anything. Yet all of that still left him with an aching void.

And the only time he'd felt whole was when he was inside Rachel.

Raking his hands over his face, Matt blew out a sigh and wished like hell he could get a grasp on his emotions. He'd wanted Rachel physically for years. What the hell was all this other stuff jumbling up his mind for? He couldn't feel whole with her. She wasn't the missing link. Hell, he'd avoided her for a year to dodge all of the other mess that he worried would come with getting this close to her.

But he didn't have regrets about the waterfall, and he'd only just sampled her. He wanted more.

Rachel appeared at the end of the hall. Her steps stalled as she met his gaze from across the room. With her long blond hair down around her shoulders, her dress clinging to her luscious curves like before, he couldn't prevent the onslaught of a renewed desire even though he'd had her only a short time ago.

She looked the same, yet everything was different. If he wanted to get anywhere with her, to convince her that what they did was not wrong—but *inevitable*—he'd have to try to get her to open up.

"Do you want to talk, or just get on the plane and pretend like nothing happened?" he asked, knowing full well he'd never let her forget. What had happened here today was nothing short of phenomenal.

"I'd say it's best for both of us if we go back."

He started closing the gap between them, totally ignoring the way her eyes widened as he drew closer. "To Royal or to just being friends?"

Rachel tipped her chin, but never looked away. "Both."

"We'll talk on the plane."

He started to reach for her, but she held her hands up and

stepped back. "There's nothing to say. I was selfish and took what I wanted. We can't do it again."

Did she honestly think he'd let her just brush him aside like that? If she had feelings she wanted to suppress, well, that was her problem, but she was not going to pretend like he was nothing more than a cheap fling.

Damn it. Since when did he get so emotionally invested? He did flings; he did one-night stands. He moved on with a mutual understanding. But now? Rachel was a complete game changer for him and he had no clue how to proceed from here.

"Listen, I'm just as freaked out." He reached for her, grabbing hold of her shoulders before she could move away again. "You think I don't have feelings about what happened? You think I don't know you well enough to realize you're thinking you betrayed Billy? That we did something wrong?"

Rachel glanced away, but Matt took his thumb and forefinger and gently gripped her chin, forcing her gaze back to his. "I don't know if you're more upset over Billy or the fact that you slept with me. You're allowed to feel again, Rachel. I've wanted—"

"I know what you want." She jerked out of his hold. "I don't want to keep talking about it."

"Well, too damn bad," he threw back. "You deserve to know that I've wanted you for years."

Those bright eyes widened in shock. "Don't say that, Matt. You don't mean it."

"Like hell I don't. I've wanted you since I saw you at that party, before Billy interrupted us talking."

"So you just...what? Stepped aside and let your buddy ask me out? You let him *marry* me? You couldn't have wanted me that bad."

She had no idea. Hell, he wasn't sure he'd had any clue until he'd tasted her. Now he only wanted more. He'd had years to process this, but clearly Rachel was just now getting used to the idea of them being together.

Matt crossed his arms over his chest and took a step back. "Go get on the plane, Rachel."

"What?" she whispered.

"We're done here. I've given you enough to think about."

"No damn kidding." She threw her arms wide. "You've confused me, made me face things I never thought about before... what the hell do you want from me, Matt?"

Honesty was the only way. From here on out, he had to let her into his thoughts. She deserved that much.

"I don't know," he murmured. "I wanted you and thought maybe that would be the end of it...but I'm not done with you, Rach. Not even close."

Tears welled up in her eyes as her lips thinned. "I don't want a relationship. I've got a baby, a degree to finish, a life to figure out..."

"I'm not looking for long-term, either. I just know I couldn't take another day without you. I'm not sorry for what happened and I wish like hell neither were you."

"I never said I was sorry it happened."

Matt turned and headed toward the door. "You didn't have to."

"What are you going to be for the TCC Halloween party?" Alexis asked, smiling and waving around the invitation.

Rachel glanced up from the images of Matt covering her computer screen. For the past day she'd stared at these, not knowing which one to choose for the bachelor auction.

The petty, selfish side of her wanted to choose the worst one, but the realistic side had to admit there wasn't a single bad picture in the lot. He flashed that panty-melting sexy smile in each and every one. Not once had he blinked in an image. He was game on the second she'd started snapping.

"Rachel?"

She clicked to minimize the screen before she turned her focus to her friend.

"The party?" she asked. "Um, I hadn't thought about it. I saw the invitation on the kitchen island yesterday."

Before she'd left, before her entire life had changed. Before she'd boldly slept with her friend without putting up much of a fight. Despite what Matt thought, she wasn't sorry.

"Are you alright?" Alexis dropped the invitation to her side and stepped on into the office. "I didn't see you much yesterday evening, and the cook said you took yours and Ellie's breakfast up to her room."

Because she just wanted to spend her time with her daughter and not have any contact with people she had to actually talk to—not even Alexis. Rachel couldn't get a grasp on her thoughts and she hadn't slept. Today she looked like a zombie, and her hair wasn't faring much better.

"I'm just tired, that's all." She attempted a smile in an attempt to erase the worry lines between her friend's brows.

"Is the auction becoming too much?" Alexis took a seat on the leather sofa next to the desk. "Dad said he's got Austin starting on the landscaping and gazebo area. I can't wait to see how that turns out. Is there something I can do to lighten your load? Why don't you let me take care of Matt's pictures and getting them printed and ready?"

"No!" She hadn't meant to shout her answer. "No," she said more softly. "I've got it. I think I've narrowed it down to what we need."

She had to go with the one of him in the waterfall. The one right before he'd demanded she come into the water, the one where his eyes had started getting all heavy-lidded and molten with desire.

No woman could resist that—obviously she hadn't been able to. Isn't that what she wanted? Women to throw more money toward the charity? Alexis and Gus were counting on a big check, and Rachel was here to help.

So she'd offer up the man she wanted. There was no denying she wanted him again, and he'd made things perfectly clear he wanted her just as much. But they couldn't sleep together again. She couldn't even look at him on the plane ride home, let alone undress for him again.

Guilt had accompanied her onto the plane. Granted she and Billy had had a rocky relationship, she'd suspected infidelity and he'd pushed her away after discovering the pregnancy. Still, she had been willing to work on their marriage.

But then they'd had that terrible fight and then the accident... and then it was too late to fix their marriage.

"What's going on?" Alexis asked, easing forward on the edge of the sofa.

Even though Alexis was her best friend, Rachel didn't want to get into the events of yesterday. She had to try to figure out how to wrap her own brain around it first.

"I just want to make sure I get everything perfect for the auction," she stated, which was the truth.

Alexis raised her brows and tipped her head. "You're a terrible liar."

So Matt had told her more than once.

"I'm just dealing with a few things," she told her friend. "Nothing to worry about. I'm just not ready to talk."

"Well, I'm here whenever you need me. I can bring wine or ice cream or both. Both is always a good answer."

Rachel smiled. "Thanks. I know you're here for me."

With a nod toward the computer, Alexis came to her feet. "Pull those back up and let's see what we're dealing with. Because from the little bit I could see when I walked in, your Matt is one devastatingly handsome man."

"He's not mine."

Alexis made a sound of disagreement as she came around the desk and clicked on the mouse. "Wowza. Do you see how this man is looking at you?"

Rachel clenched her teeth and stared at the multiple images as Alexis scrolled through. "He's looking at the camera."

"He's looking like he wants to devour you." Alexis glanced

over her shoulder and met Rachel's eyes. "I'll assume this is what you're dealing with. Considering you two were at his private island all alone, I'd say you had a pretty good day."

"His pilot was there," she muttered.

Alexis laughed. "In the plane and paid a hefty sum to keep to himself."

Turning, she sat on the edge of the desk and crossed her arms. Her eyes held both questions and compassion.

"Stop staring at me," Rachel demanded. "I'm not talking about it."

"If a man looked at me like that and I was on his own island, you better believe I'd be talking about it."

Rachel pushed from her seat and shoved her hands in her hair, wincing when she encountered a massive tangle. "I need to go check on Ellie. She's resting."

"You have the monitor on the desk and there hasn't been a noise. Why are you running? Because of Billy?"

Because of Billy, because of Matt. Because the only other man in her life she thought she could depend on had turned out to be...more than she ever thought. Shouldn't she feel guilty simply over the fact that sex with Matt had been more amazing than anything she'd ever experienced in her marriage? Forget the fact that Billy had trusted them both?

Then again, she hadn't trusted Billy. Not in the end. Did he even deserve her loyalty at this point? He was gone and if this were Alexis telling her this story, Rachel would tell her friend there was nothing to feel guilty about.

But still, this wasn't Alexis.

"It's okay to have feelings for someone else," Alexis added. "You're young, you're beautiful, you're going to get a man's attention. What's wrong with your friend, the Most Eligible Bachelor in Texas? Honey, women would die to be in your shoes."

"Then they can have them."

Part of Rachel was glad her friend knew some of what was going on without her having to say things out loud.

"I need a break." She came to her feet and sighed. "What do you say when Ellie wakes up we go shopping? Maybe we can find some Halloween costumes for the party. Which is always difficult because I don't want to be a slutty Snow White or a clown. So…something in between?"

Alexis practically jumped with glee. "Yes. I want to go as a Greek goddess. Care to join me?"

Retail therapy to find a fun costume—sounded like the break from reality she needed. Royal had some adorable little shops, so surely they could find something to throw together. Since the party was adults only, Rachel didn't have to find Ellie anything, but she'd gone ahead and ordered her a little unicorn costume online for trick or treating.

For the rest of the day she wasn't going to think about Matt or the waterfall or the tumultuous feelings she had to face. Unfortunately, those emotions weren't going anywhere and she'd have to deal with them at some point. Damn that man for taking their relationship into unknown territory. She had absolutely no experience with flings or friends with benefits or whatever the hell this was called between them.

But she was certain of one thing. No way could she bid on him during the auction. A fantasy date with Matt Galloway was only asking for more trouble.

Ten

Matt walked through the old farmhouse, snapping pictures and making notes. He'd been here for hours, taking each room one at a time. There wasn't a spot in this place where he didn't see his grandfather or reflect on the memories of the greatest summers of his life.

This might not have been the grandiose spread that Lone Wolf Ranch was, but the small acreage and the two-story home still meant more to Matt than anything. More than his padded bank account, more than his private beach house on Galloway Cove and more than any relationship he'd ever had.

He'd already put a call in for a trust contractor to meet him at the end of the week and give an estimate of turning the whole place into something new. Matt wanted to keep the old elements as much as possible, like the built-ins and the old fireplaces, but breathe some new life into the home to make it market-able. Royal was a hot spot right now, so Matt had confidence the place would sell fast.

As he stepped back onto the porch, a lump caught in his throat. The thought of his grandfather's home going to someone else didn't sit well. Every time he thought of selling, well, he hated it. Maybe once an overhaul happened and most rooms seemed newer he would feel different. Perhaps then it would feel less like his family's farm and more just like a business transaction.

The wood plank beneath Matt's foot gave way and he jumped back just in time to save his leg from going through the porch. The damn thing was falling apart.

He rolled up the sleeves on his dress shirt and bent down to assess the damage. He recalled many times doing repairs with his grandfather. He'd always kept this place in pristine shape, and summertime was when he'd saved up all the projects to work on with Matt.

A few hours plus ruined clothes and shoes later, Matt had the porch torn apart and had found old, sturdy boards in the barn to prop up the porch roof.

He stepped back and pulled in a deep breath as he surveyed his destruction. Damn, even in the fall the hot Texas sun beat down on him. The moisture from all his sweat had his shirt clinging to his back.

Tires over the gravel drive forced his attention over his shoulder. Rachel's SUV pulled closer to his truck as he swiped his forearm over his forehead.

Confused, Matt crossed to her car. He hadn't spoken to her since yesterday and he honestly didn't think she'd come to him. Was she ready to discuss what happened? What it meant to their relationship?

When he got to the driver's side, the window slid down. Rachel offered a nervous half smile.

"Hey, there!"

Matt leaned down and spotted Alexis in the passenger seat. "Afternoon."

"It's evening now," she corrected with a laugh. "Looks like you ruined your clothes."

Matt glanced to his grimy shirt and back up. "Impromptu demo. What are you all doing out?"

"We went to find Halloween costumes for the TCC party," Alexis stated. "You'll be going?"

With a shrug, his eyes came back to Rachel. "How did you all end up here?"

She nodded toward the back seat. "Ellie fell asleep as soon as we were done shopping, so we took the long way home so she can get a little nap in."

There were various routes to get back to Lone Wolf Ranch. Interesting that she would choose this one.

"We saw your truck and pulled in," Alexis stated with a knowing grin. What had Rachel told her friend?

"Alexis insisted I pull in," Rachel corrected.

A whine from the back had Rachel jerking around and reaching toward the car seat. "It's okay, sweetie."

"Let me take her home," Alexis offered.

"What? No," Rachel insisted. "We're going now."

"Stay."

The word slipped through his lips before he could even think otherwise. From the shock on Rachel's face and the glee on Alexis's, he had to assume they were just as much caught off guard.

"Matt—"

Alexis was already out of the car before Rachel could finish whatever argument she had on her tongue. Matt reached for her door handle as Ellie's whines started getting louder.

"This is crazy," Rachel muttered. "I can take my own daughter home."

"You can," Alexis agreed as she took Rachel's hands to ease her from the car. "But let her come with Aunt Alexis. I'll give her a bath and read her a story. I'll even get her to sleep…you know, if you end up coming home late. Or even in the morning."

The little Matt had been around Alexis back in college, he'd liked her. Now he suddenly felt like he had an ally.

Matt couldn't smother his grin or stop the wink in her direction. She merely raised her brows as if they had some secret bond. Clearly they both wanted Rachel happy, which meant in this situation, Rachel didn't have a chance in hell of winning the argument.

The two of them had to talk and the opportunity wouldn't get any more obvious. Being a businessman, he took every open opportunity to further his steps toward his goals. And Rachel was one goal he wasn't about to get rid of. Now if he could just figure out what to do once he fully had her...other than the obvious need to fulfill.

"Take your time, Rach," Alexis practically sang as she slid into the driver's seat. "Don't worry about Ellie. She's in good hands."

Then Alexis closed the door and Matt reached for Rachel's hand. "Relax," he murmured against her ear. "I won't bite unless you ask."

Rachel threw a glance over her shoulder and rolled her eyes. "I won't ask."

Alexis pulled from the drive and Matt headed toward the house, assuming Rachel would follow since she had nowhere else to go.

He started picking up the mess he'd created, carrying the broken boards around back and stacking them in a pile against the barn. When he came back from his third trip, he laughed at the sight of Rachel still standing in the driveway with her arms crossed over her chest. She merely stared back at him and raised a brow.

"You find a costume for the party?" he called.

"Shut up."

She was crazy about him.

"I'm thinking of going as a fireman...if you want to hold my hose."

Well, that pulled a smile from her lips. "You're a jackass."

"No, but I do care about that frown on your face." He moved

closer to her so he didn't have to keep yelling. "Seriously, at this point I'll be going as a CEO because I have no idea what to wear."

"So you're going?"

He shrugged. "Why not? Sounds fun."

"You don't strike me as someone searching for fun by way of costume parties."

He laid a hand over his chest. "That hurts, Rachel. Maybe you've forgotten the time I dressed up as a pirate."

Rachel shook her head and snorted. "That doesn't count. You did it to get into that bar when we went to New Orleans for Mardi Gras. If I recall, that costume garnered you several beads."

He still hadn't disclosed how he'd acquired those, and at this point he figured it was best she not find out. He'd like to garner a few acts to get beads from Rachel. The images flooding his mind weren't so much fantasies now, but possibilities.

"Well, we got in where we wanted and a good time was had by all," he stated. "So, are you going to tell me your costume or not?"

"You'll see it at the party."

Was she flirting? Hell, he had no clue. For the first time in all the years he'd known her, he couldn't get a read on her thoughts.

"Want to walk through?" he asked, nodding toward the house.

Her eyes darted to the ripped-apart porch and the two-by-fours propping up the roof. "I'm not sure that's a good idea."

"There's a back door." He grabbed her hand without asking and urged her toward the house. He'd missed her touch. Even though he'd been with her not long ago, the span of time was still too much. "I'm going to have a contractor meet me at the end of the week and discuss renovations."

"So you were trying to save money by ripping into it first?" she joked.

"Not hardly." He led her to the back, where the weeds had nearly overtaken the back porch. "Watch your step."

After helping her up and safely inside, Matt closed the screen door at his back.

"I'm not going to be doing the actual work," he told her. "I was actually getting ready to leave earlier when the boards snapped on the porch. One thing led to another and time got away from me. Demo is a good source to work out frustrations."

"Maybe you should give me a sledgehammer, then."

Though humor laced her voice, Matt knew she was quite serious. "You're more than welcome to help. You might actually enjoy the manual labor."

She glanced down to her jeans and off-the-shoulder sweater that showcased one sexy shoulder. "I'm not really dressed for renovating today."

Matt held his hands wide. "Clearly I wasn't, either. You up for a little grunt work?"

What in the world had she been thinking? First, she let her friends steamroll her right out of her car and parenting responsibilities, then she'd gone into the house, and now she was sweating like she'd just run a marathon...which was absurd because she'd never run a marathon. Ever. Unless there was chocolate and wine at the end, and even then she'd have to think about it.

Rachel stepped back and surveyed the upstairs master bath. The rubble around her looked like a Texas tornado had whipped through, but her screaming shoulders reminded her she'd smashed everything to bits.

She hoped like hell Matt knew what he was doing by taking everything out. He claimed some of the things in the house, like the claw-foot tub in the guest bath and the old dumbwaiter, would be kept.

Propping the sledgehammer at her side, Rachel smiled. This had been therapeutic...no doubt about it. Maybe she should take up demo work instead of photography for her hobby.

"How's it g—" Matt stopped in the doorway of the bathroom

and blew out a low whistle. "Remind me not to piss you off. You do some serious damage with that thing."

Rachel couldn't help but smile, as she was rather proud of herself. "So, what now? I'm a sweaty mess and apparently I have a sitter. Where else do you want me?"

His eyes raked over her body, instantly thrusting her back to the waterfall and making her realize her poor choice in words.

"I already told you that was a onetime thing," she warned, though saying it out loud was more as a reminder to herself than for him.

"You did say that." He remained in place, but the way his eyes drifted over her again only reminded her of yesterday. "Tell me you haven't thought of what happened on my island, haven't played it over and over in your mind, reliving every moment, just like I have. Tell me you can just be done after one time."

Rachel started to argue, but dropped her head and blew out a sigh. "What do you want, Matt? Do you want me to admit that I couldn't sleep for thinking of you? Of us?"

She lifted her gaze, surprised to find him still in the doorway and not right up on her, crowding her and filling her mind with more jumbled emotions.

"Fine," she conceded. "You win. I thought of every single detail from start to finish and then I rewound my memory bank and did it all again. I've thought of you while I'm awake and you've even invaded my dreams. But you know what? Nothing will come of this. You live in Dallas—I'm probably staying in Royal. You're a career businessman and bachelor extraordinaire, and I'm—"

"A single mother and widow. You've reminded me." Now he stepped forward, but didn't touch her. "You want to know how I see you? As a passionate woman who is denying herself because of guilt and misplaced loyalty."

"How dare you," she scolded through gritted teeth.

"What?" he yelled back. "You need to know what I've kept

to myself for so long. Why I stayed away for a year. Why Billy was so unhappy."

Rachel shook her head and closed her eyes, as if she could keep the pain from seeping inside. "Stop it. Just stop."

"I've wanted you for so long." His voice softened, as did her heart at his raw tone. "I watched Billy marry you. I watched him flirt with other women. I watched him disrespect you behind your back toward the end of your marriage. When I confronted him, he told me to stay out of your relationship. When you got pregnant…"

Matt clenched his fists at his sides and glanced down to the floor. He cleared his throat before meeting her gaze again.

"I know," she finished. "He didn't want the baby. We fought all the time. But I wanted her. From the moment I knew I was expecting, my whole outlook on life changed and I was excited to be a mother."

"You're a damn good mom." He smiled as he reached out to her. Cupping her face in his hands, he stepped in to her. "It's time you take back your life. Isn't that your goal? You want to start over? Well, now is the time. You can be a mother, but you also need to move on."

"With you? You don't want a family, Matt. Remember?"

His jaw clenched as he studied her face. "You want honesty? I don't even know what I want. All I know is when I'm not with you, I want you. When I am with you, I want you. I want you, Rachel. Right now."

He crowded her in this tiny room full of rubble. Her body instantly responded—if she was honest, the tingling had started in the driveway hours ago.

"I won't pressure you," he added. "But you need to know where I stand for however long I'm in Royal."

Matt released her and turned, stepping over the mess and back into the master bedroom. Rachel remained still, her skin still warm from his touch, her heart beating fast, her mind rolling over everything he said, everything she felt.

She couldn't deny herself, couldn't deny how Matt had made her feel more alive in the past few days than she had in a long time. Did she want to throw that away because she was confused and scared about the future, or did she want to grab onto this bit of happiness?

Rachel climbed over the mess she'd made. "Matt."

He stopped in the doorway leading into the hall, but didn't turn. His pants were filthy, his dark hair was a complete mess and there was a tear in his shirt on the right sleeve. Her attire wasn't faring much better. They both needed a shower, they both were feeling emotionally raw and they both had no clue where this was going.

There were so many reasons she should let him walk right out that door. But she couldn't do it. Maybe it was time she learned by his example and simply take what she wanted.

"Why is it when I'm with you, my clothes end up ruined?"

Her shaky hand went to the zipper of her pants. As she drew it down, the slight sound echoed in the room. Slowly, Matt turned to face her.

Eleven

Matt couldn't move, he couldn't speak. Right before his eyes Rachel had turned into the vixen he'd always known her to be. He'd gotten a glimpse of her at Galloway Cove. But this, this woman before him doing the most erotic striptease he'd ever seen, took his breath away.

He didn't miss the way her hands shook. That slight uncertainty, even while her gaze had completely locked onto his, only added to his arousal. She might be nervous about her feelings, but she was taking what she wanted…and that was him.

Matt didn't even bother to be subtle when he ran his eyes over every gloriously exposed inch of her. When she stood before him completely bare, there was no way he could keep this distance between them.

"While you're here, I'm taking this." She shook her long, honey-blond waves back and offered a slight smile. "Whatever is going on, it's between us. I know you're not looking for a happily-ever-after, and honestly, I don't think those exist anymore."

Her words stirred something in his soul…something that irritated the hell out of him, but with a beautiful, naked woman standing before him, he wasn't about to start analyzing his damn feelings. There was only one thing he wanted to analyze right now and it was all of this soft, creamy skin exposed before him.

"If you're waiting on me to argue with your logic, you'll be waiting a long time."

Before he could wrap his arms around her, Rachel was on him. Damn, if that wasn't sexier than her standing naked before him. She threaded her fingers through his hair and covered his mouth with hers. Her sweet body pressed against his and he wished he could just get his clothes to evaporate so he didn't have to step from her arms, from her mouth.

"I'm filthy," she murmured against his mouth. "I probably smell."

He trailed his lips along her jawline and inhaled just below her ear. "You smell amazing and you'll taste even better."

Matt stepped back and stripped down to nothing. He wanted her glorious, silken skin against his; he wanted to be one with her and he damned any consequence that would come their way later.

With his hands full of the woman who'd been tantalizing him for years, Matt backed her up until they fell onto the old, squeaky bed.

He realized the mattress probably wasn't the most comfortable, so he rolled, pulling her on top. But when he looked up at her, she was all smiles, her eyes sparkling with happiness and desire.

"This damn thing is a brick," he growled. "Did I hurt you?"

She shook her head, her hair sliding around her shoulders. "It's not pain I'm feeling right now."

Just like yesterday, Matt held on to her hips as she settled over him. Would he ever tire of this view? All these years he'd wanted her, but he'd never thought of what he'd want once he had her...now he had his answer. He wanted more Rachel.

"I'm yours," she murmured. "Do what you want."

She was his. His.

No. That sounded permanent. What they were doing was…
Damn it. He vowed to worry about this later.

Matt sat up, thrusting his hands in her hair as he came to his feet. She instantly wrapped her legs around his waist and then he turned and held her against the wall.

"Now, Matt."

His name on her lips was all the motivation he needed. How long had he waited to hear such a sweet sound?

With a jerk of his hips, Matt joined their bodies, eliciting a long, low groan from Rachel. Another sweet sound he couldn't get enough of.

Rachel wrapped all around him as he set the rhythmic pace. She fit him perfectly—yesterday wasn't just a onetime epiphany. No woman had ever made him want like this, like he couldn't breathe if he didn't have her, like he didn't want to go a moment without touching her.

Matt reached around to grab her backside and moved faster. His mouth ravished hers as the all-consuming need filled him. He couldn't get enough…and wondered if he ever would.

Rachel's body arched against his; her mouth tore away as she cried out with her release. Matt couldn't take his eyes from her. Rachel coming apart all around him would forever be embedded in his mind.

His climax overrode any thoughts, but he never took his eyes from hers. She stared back at him now, a soft, satisfied smile on her face as his body trembled. Little minx knew exactly the power she held over him…and he wouldn't have it any other way.

Their sweat-soaked bodies clung together, not that he was in a hurry to release her.

"We need a shower," she mumbled, her head against his shoulder.

"If the utilities were on, we could make use of that bathroom downstairs."

He actually liked her soaking wet, wouldn't mind having her that way again. An image of her in his Dallas home filled his mind. He'd been to his island, now to his family's farmhouse. Where else could he take her?

Matt patted the glossy bar top to get the bartender's attention. He needed another drink and he wanted to try to make sense of these chaotic feelings swirling around his head. Wanting Rachel, having Rachel and then being confused as hell as to what he wanted now was tearing him up inside.

No, the answer couldn't be found in the bottom of his tumbler of bourbon, but it sure as hell didn't hurt.

"Hey, man."

Caleb McKenzie took a seat on the stool next to Matt. Caleb was another member of the Royal TCC and Matt had met him while they'd both been here using the TCC offices just a few weeks ago.

"What's up?" Caleb asked.

"Taking a break from work."

He'd been at his grandfather's farm for the past several days doing more demo work. His contractor had come by and they'd gone over each room in detail, but Matt was finding the demolition rather therapeutic. For now, he'd wait on hiring his contractor. Mainly because he was enjoying the manual labor and getting back to his roots. Another reason was that Matt knew his grandfather would be proud of his work, and that was more important to him than anything when it came to the farm.

He ordered another bourbon and Caleb requested a craft beer. After tipping his Stetson back, Caleb shifted on his seat and rested his elbow on the bar.

"I'm taking a break from wedding planning. Shelby probably appreciates the fact I'm letting her deal with choosing the exact shade of purple for the flowers."

Matt laughed. Caleb had dodged the auction block, but in the end, he'd landed his very own fiancée.

Matt wouldn't be dodging the charity auction, considering he wasn't engaged or looking to be.

"Oh, good. Glad I'm not the only one ready for a drink at twelve-oh-five."

Caleb and Matt turned to see fellow TCC member Ryan Bateman striding toward them. He took a seat on the other side of Matt and adjusted his Stetson.

"It's Friday," Matt stated. "Might as well kick off the weekend a little early."

"Hey, I heard you were the new recruit for the auction." Ryan let out a bark of laughter. "None of us are safe. You've been in town, what? Two weeks?"

The bartender set the drinks down and took Ryan's order. Matt curled his fingers around his tumbler and blew out a sigh. "Yeah, I was added most likely because this guy took himself off the market," he said, nodding toward Caleb.

"I'm a catch," Caleb drawled. "What can I say?"

"I just hope the fantasy date I'm supposed to go on involves steak," Ryan added as he took his beer from the bartender. "Other than that, I don't care."

Matt cared a hell of a whole lot about his fantasy date. If Rachel wasn't on the receiving end, he didn't want to be with anyone else. Sure he dated quite a bit over the years, but lately he wasn't wanting to get mixed up with anyone else. Besides, he knew exactly what she liked…in bed and out. Didn't it just make sense she bid on him? Damn stubborn woman putting an expiration date on their bedroom escapades…

Would she be jealous if he took another woman out? That wasn't a game he wanted to play, but if Rachel didn't bid, then he'd obviously have to wine and dine someone else.

"I have a buddy who would be a great candidate for the auction," Ryan chimed in. "Tripp Noble. That guy is down for anything."

Matt sipped on his bourbon, welcoming the slight burn as the liquid made its way through his body. "I'll let Rachel know. She's been working hard on the social media aspect and getting the headshots ready for the posters. I doubt it's too late to add another, especially if it brings more money."

"Did I hear you and Rachel were at Daily Grind the other day for a date?" Caleb asked, a knowing smile on his face. "You may be off the market, too, if you're not careful."

Matt shook his head in denial. Their coffee "date" had been their first encounter in a year. So much had happened since then and none of it was about to be shared here.

"I'm not looking for a wife," he explained, shaking his head. "I'm just stepping in to help the cause."

"I wasn't looking for a wife, either," Caleb threw back. "These are the mysteries of life."

Oh, there was no mystery for Matt. He wasn't getting married anytime soon. Maybe one day he'd like a family, but he hadn't given it much thought, and he was too busy now to nurse another commitment.

He tipped back the remainder in his glass and came to his feet. After throwing enough bills down to cover all drinks, Matt glanced between his two friends. "I'd best get back to work."

"Are you using one of the offices here today?" Caleb asked.

Matt nodded. "I'll be here another couple hours." Until he traded his dress clothes for jeans, a T-shirt and work boots and headed back to the farm. He needed to get a call into his partner, but Matt's assistant had told him that Eric was out until this afternoon.

It was time to make a decision on the sale of the business... or Matt's half, anyway. Considering he kept feeling a void in his life he couldn't quite describe, perhaps it was time to start liquidating things that didn't fulfill him anymore—like his partnership.

"I'll probably be here later this evening," he added. "The Bellamy has an amazing restaurant, but I'm thinking beer and billiards sounds more like what I need."

"If that's an invite, I'll be here, too," Ryan added. "I'll bring Tripp."

"Shelby is going to some makeup party, so I'm also free tonight," Caleb supplied, dangling the neck of his beer bottle between two fingers. "It's been a while since I played pool."

"Looking forward to crushing all three of you," Matt said with a smile.

"You want to put money on that?" Ryan asked, quirking his brow.

"I can get behind that." Matt adjusted the rolled-up sleeves on his forearms. "But don't whine when I take all your money."

The guys tossed back insults as Matt headed toward the hallway leading to the offices. He loved being a member of TCC in Dallas, but connecting with the guys in Royal made him feel even more welcome than at his regular clubhouse.

Royal was definitely a town anyone would be lucky to live in. But he wasn't so sure it was for him. First of all, once the auction was over and he and Rachel ended their...dalliance, Matt wasn't sure he could stay in a town where he saw her every day. Because he was absolutely positive she'd want to stay here for the long haul.

He and Rachel would go back to being friends, he'd go to Galloway Cove until he figured out what he wanted to fulfill him and Rachel would meet another guy and settle down, just like she was meant to do.

Without him.

A heavy dose of jealousy and fear came over him as he realized he didn't want to see her with another man. Hadn't the years of seeing and hearing her with Billy been enough?

So what now? How did he carry on with his life and career and attempt to figure out what was missing? How did he move on like Rachel hadn't touched something so deeply inside him?

Matt had never been this confused, this out of control of his own emotions. And he didn't like it, not one damn bit.

Twelve

Rachel tugged at her dress once more. Mercy sakes. Hadn't this dress been a few inches longer? She'd tried this on at the Halloween shop, but being in a dressing room and getting ready to leave your house were obviously two totally different scenarios.

Ellie was down in the family room playing with the chef, who seemed to be doubling as a nanny lately. Since the party was adults only, Gus and Alexis had both demanded Rachel make an appearance because she was working on the auction. Any way they could talk it up and promote it, they would.

So Rachel stood before the floor-length mirror and tugged at her flapper dress once more. Her only saving grace was the added fringe around the bottom. She just couldn't bend over. Or breathe. Or lift her arms.

Really, what could go wrong?

There was no plan B by way of costumes unless she went as a haggard mother, so Rachel blew out a sigh, adjusted her sequined headband around her forehead, then grabbed her matching black clutch from the dresser.

She did feel a little silly going out with a fringe dress,

bright red lips and these stilettos. She should be braless, in her sweatpants and getting ready to give Ellie a bath. That was her routine…save for a few nights ago when she'd been wrapped in Matt's arms once again.

Heat coursed through her and she shivered just as she had at his first touch. He'd been so thorough in their lovemaking—likely because he'd been waiting for so long to have her.

There was no denying that a good portion of her nerves had his name written all over them. He would be at the party and she had no idea how he'd come dressed. No doubt whatever he chose, he'd set her heart beating faster.

As soon as she hit the bottom steps, Mae stood there holding Ellie, who was already rubbing her eyes.

"I really appreciate this," Rachel said, giving Ellie a kiss on the forehead. Well, that was a mistake. Now the poor child had a perfect red lip outline. "Sorry about that."

Mae laughed. "No trouble at all. I'll clean her up, read her a story and get her in bed. She's such a sweetheart."

Rachel loved how this family had so easily taken them in. The family and the staff. They were all so close-knit, so bonded. That's what Rachel wanted for her daughter, for their new life.

"You look quite lovely," Mae stated, glancing to Rachel. "Is there some young man you're meeting at the party?"

"I'm going to talk up the charity auction." Though if she happened to see Matt, she wouldn't mind sneaking off for a kiss or two. "I don't plan on staying for the entire event, so I shouldn't be long."

"Oh, please." Mae patted Ellie's back. "You're young and stunning and dressed up. Stay for the whole thing. I assure you we are all fine here, and if anything arises, I'll call you."

Rachel smiled. "Thank you. For everything you're doing for us."

"No thanks necessary." Mae started up the steps. "You go have a good time and don't worry about a thing here."

Gus came down the hallway dressed as a pirate in all black complete with eye patch and parrot on his shoulder.

"Well, look at you." Rachel crossed to him and smiled. "You look great."

Alexis came from the back of the house, where her room was, and Gus turned, then glanced back to Rachel. "I'll be walking in with the most gorgeous ladies there tonight. How did I get so lucky?"

Alexis looked absolutely stunning in her white one-shoulder dress with gold sandals, and gold ribbons holding her hair back. The goddess look definitely suited her.

"We're the lucky ones," Alexis stated, giving her grandfather a kiss on his cheek. "Nothing better than a rogue pirate. Are we all ready?"

Rachel nodded and when she stepped outside, the car had been brought around for them. Anticipation curled through her. Even though she wasn't used to being this fussed up, she couldn't deny her excitement about the party or seeing Matt. Being lovers aside, she was glad he'd come back into her life. She'd missed him. But knowing why he stayed away…well, that still left her confused and a little hurt. She wished he'd been up-front with her, but at the same time, she couldn't fault him. Had he come forward after Billy's death and told her he'd had feelings for her, Rachel highly doubted she would've believed him. She certainly wouldn't have been in the frame of mind to hear such things.

Matt was special. What they had was special. She had no clue where they were going, if anywhere, but for the first time in a long time, she was going to enjoy herself and have a good time.

When they pulled up to TCC, the valet opened their doors and greeted them. Rachel went first and stepped into the lobby. The entire place had been decked out with pumpkins, lights, faux spiderwebs and a witch's cauldron, and the entry to the bar and billiards room had a fog machine to really set the stage and showcase guests as they entered.

Searching the sea of costumes, she didn't spot Matt. There were so many faces she recognized, mostly the men she'd photographed, but disappointment settled in. He'd said he was coming, so he'd be here, right? Besides, she was here to chat up the upcoming auction. That was her main focus.

Rachel maneuvered through the crowd, passing a Queen of Hearts, a couple dressed as Belle and the Beast, and another couple dressed as eggs and bacon. Everyone looked so amazing, and suddenly she didn't feel so insecure in her dress, especially considering the lights were low and there were so many people around. The music blared from the DJ's stand at the far end of the room and there were several people on the dance floor already.

This was definitely a fun, festive party. Somehow, though, she'd lost Gus and Alexis. Rachel sighed and eased her way around people to squeeze into a slot at the bar. A nice glass of wine would hit the spot. She rarely drank, but she'd love to have a nice white.

"Buy you a drink?"

Rachel glanced over her shoulder. Matt had a wide grin on his face and had donned a fireman's costume sans the big coat. The red suspenders over the white T-shirt really accented just how in shape he truly was. Granted she'd seen, felt and tasted those fabulous muscles, but now they were all on display.

"I thought you were joking about the costume," she told him.

He raised a brow and leaned in closer. "Want to play with my hose?"

She couldn't decide to laugh or roll her eyes...so she delivered him both. "That line was terrible the first time you said it. Move on."

"That was pretty lame," he admitted. "But, do you?"

"Shut up."

She laughed again as she turned back to the bar and waited for her drink. Matt ended up with a bourbon and paid for both drinks before taking her hand and leading her toward the opposite side of the room from the music. He found a table in the corner that was empty. A slow song had come on and most couples were dancing.

"You look so damn hot."

Rachel crossed her legs beneath the table and toyed with the stem of her glass. "Thank you. I wasn't sure about this costume, but Alexis refused to let me try anything else on."

His eyes dropped to her lips, her chest, then back up. "Remind me to buy her a drink, too."

Rachel had to admit she was glad she'd bought this costume now. The way Matt looked at her was well worth whatever she'd spent. She hadn't realized she was worried what he'd think until now. Pleasure rolled through her at the fact she might just have the upper hand here.

"That's some getup you have, too."

This fireman's costume was sexy as hell. His dark hair and dark lashes eluded to a man of mystery, but she knew all about Matt Galloway. Knew he'd do anything for her, including sacrifice his feelings for nearly a decade. And she also knew he was fabulous with her daughter and that before ever meeting her, he'd put her needs ahead of everything else.

"I borrowed all this from a friend," he stated, then inched closer as his gaze dropped to her lips. "I've missed you."

Her heart fluttered in her chest. Those three words held so much potential. She wasn't sure what to ask as a follow-up. Had he missed her in general or missed her as in he was just horny? Was there a tactful way to ask?

He curled his fingers around his tumbler and settled his free hand on her thigh. Instant warmth and tingles spread through her. Damn it, she'd missed him, too. She didn't want to get too attached, not in any way other than friends. But when he touched her, when he looked at her, she couldn't help but want so much more.

And that was dangerous ground for her to be treading.

"How's Ellie?"

Surprised at his question, and touched that he was even asking about her daughter, Rachel replied, "She's good. I'm trying to plan a first birthday party for her and work on the auction, so things are a little hectic. I know she won't remember the party and we aren't even in our own home, but I'd still like to do something special."

"Has she been to a beach?"

"What?"

"Why don't we take her to Galloway Cove? She can play in the sand, splash in the ocean, put her face in a cake if that's what you want. We'll take my jet and there will be no pressure on you to do something extravagant. I can have my staff on hand to do whatever you want or I can tell them to leave us. Totally your call."

Rachel blinked. Was he serious? Spending her daughter's first birthday with Matt on his island seemed way, way too familial.

"I didn't think you wanted more with me than…"

Matt smiled and inched closer, his hand sliding higher up her thigh. "Sex? I definitely want that, but we're also friends. Why wouldn't I want to help ease your worries and spend more time with you?"

Rachel shook her head. "I don't know."

"Think about it."

Now that he'd planted the seed, she had no doubt that's all that would occupy her spare thoughts. Part of her wanted to jump at the chance to take a relaxing, fun trip with Ellie to celebrate her first birthday. But the realistic side kicked in and sent up red flags telling her that might not be the best idea.

Rachel caught a flash of white from the corner of her eye. Alexis headed out a side door leading to the hallways and about a second behind her was a man wearing a black Zorro mask. Interesting. Who was Alexis slipping away with? Rachel didn't need to ask, honestly. Her friend wasn't so discreet at keeping the secret of the man she was infatuated with.

Well, maybe others didn't notice, but Rachel knew her friend pretty well. Whatever Alexis wanted, Alexis would get.

"Dance with me."

Matt came to his feet and pulled Rachel up with him.

"I figured you'd want to stay hidden in the corner and make out," she joked as they headed for the dance floor.

He slid his arm around her waist and whispered into her ear, "Maybe I want to feel that beautiful body against mine instead."

Oh, when he said things like that he made her wonder how she never realized how he'd felt. Granted he'd stayed away from her for the past year because he'd worried about her emotions and his restraint. That right there told her how much he cared. She had been upset at first, and she still hated that she'd missed an entire year with him, but he'd been trying to protect her from getting caught up in more emotional upheaval.

Damn it. She was falling for him. There was no denying the glaring fact staring her in the face. At this point all she could do was hope his feelings started shifting, as well. If he'd cared about her for so many years, then perhaps he would want more.

Rachel sighed. She couldn't get her hopes up or hinge her future happiness on a man who clearly wasn't in it for the long haul. Above all else, she had to protect her little family and do what was right for them.

Before they hit the dance floor, Rachel pulled away. Matt glanced back at her and she merely nodded her head toward the side exit. Once she slipped out, Matt joined her.

"What's wrong?" he asked.

The thumping bass from the music inside pounded through the night. "I don't think it's a great idea for us to be seen dancing together. Talking is one thing, but grinding on the dance floor is something else entirely. You are the main event for the auction."

Her heart ached the moment those words left her mouth. But the truth was he was the big draw, and it was her job to promote the auction and help bring in as much money as possible.

Matt Galloway would give some other lucky lady a very nice fantasy date.

"I think we need to call this quits after the auction, too." She had to guard her heart and try to keep some semblance of control here.

Matt crossed his arms over his broad chest, which only went to showcase his perfectly sculpted biceps straining against the short sleeves.

"And why is that?" he tossed back. "You think whoever bids on me will, what? Steal my heart or make me forget you?"

That was precisely what she thought, but she sure as hell wasn't about to express her insecurities.

"I think that for as long as this lasts, we should enjoy it," she corrected, closing the distance between them. "Then when the auction comes, we go back to Matt and Rachel. Friends."

"Friends."

The word slid out like he had sandpaper in his throat. His arms snaked around her waist and a second later she was flattened against his chest.

"You're bidding on me."

With her palms resting on his chest, Rachel shook her head. "I'm not. You know I'm right about this. The sex is muddling your mind, but I'm a package deal and you're not looking for a family. You're not even looking for a girlfriend, so we need to put a stop date on this."

Or else my heart will get broken yet again.

His lips thinned as he stared down into her eyes. "Fine, but you're all mine until then."

Matt's mouth covered hers. A whole host of emotions swept through her and she couldn't decide if it was because of the kiss or the promised threat of being his. Matt clearly had territorial issues...another aspect that aroused her for reasons she couldn't explain.

Oh, wait. She could. Never in her life, not even with her husband, did she feel this wanted, this valued. Matt made no qualms about his current feelings. But what would happen later? When he was done with the good times and the sex? She had to be the one to put an ending to this story.

Rachel lost herself in his kiss, wrapping her arms around his neck and threading her fingers through his hair. She was a woman with wants and desires, and Matt was all too eager to help her check those boxes. She couldn't stop this onslaught of emotions even if she wanted to.

His hands settled on her ass as he squeezed and had jolts of arousal spiraling through her.

The sound of a car door slamming had Rachel pulling back and glancing around. Nobody had pulled into this side lot. She took the moment to pull in a deep breath. When she glanced back to Matt, he had red lipstick smeared all over his mouth.

Reaching up, she swiped the pad of her thumb below his bottom lip. His tongue darted out and Rachel stilled, her eyes locked on his.

"Come to my suite tonight," he told her in that husky voice that practically melted her clothes right off. "I need you, Rachel."

"I can't. I have a baby back at Lone Wolf Ranch."

"Then I'm coming to you," he threatened. "I have to be with you. So either get Ellie and bring her—I still have that baby equipment from our dinner—or I'll climb up the damn trellis and come into your bedroom."

She had no problem imagining Matt scaling his way into her bed. "There's no trellis outside my window," she joked, trying to lighten the moment before she stripped him out of this damn costume and begged him for anything he was willing to give.

His hands gripped her backside, grinding her hips into his. "What's your decision?"

As if she had one. She wanted him; he wanted her. This was an age-old song and dance. But nothing about this was typical or normal or...hell, rational.

"You better come to me. Ellie will be asleep when I get home."

"Then leave a door unlocked or meet me out back and sneak me in." He nipped at her lips. "And I'm staying the night."

Oh, mercy. She'd just made a booty call date with her best friend and she was sneaking him into her temporary housing. Classy. Real classy.

Her hormones didn't seem to care, though. The anticipation of the night's events only had her body humming even more.

What was she going to do when it was time to call it quits?

Thirteen

"Where the hell are they?" Gus demanded.

Rose shook her head and sighed. "They've both been missing from the party for nearly an hour."

Alexis and Daniel had snuck out. There was no other way to spin this. They were purposely trying to sabotage the auction and totally go against their family's wishes. Gus couldn't stand the thought of a Clayton stealing his sweet Lex away.

Gus turned back to Rose. He'd sent her a text to meet him in the back gardens on the other side of the clubhouse and away from the party so as not to be seen. He'd gone out and she'd come about five minutes later.

As he stared at her, with the moonlight casting a glow over this elegant, vibrant woman, Gus couldn't ignore the punch of lust to his gut. He'd had that same heady reaction multiple times when they'd been younger, but he couldn't afford that now. Those days were gone, decades had passed. Lives had been changed.

Besides, he flat-out didn't want to feel anything for her.

Things were much simpler if he could just go on thinking of Rose Clayton as the enemy.

But she'd come to the party dressed from the Victorian era and he couldn't deny how stunning she was. Even though they weren't together, never would be and he still had that anger simmering inside of him, he could freely admit she was just as breathtaking as ever. The dip in her waist only accented the swell of her breasts practically spilling over the top of her emerald-green dress.

Damn it. He needed to focus and not think of her tempting body...or her at all. One wrong turn in his thoughts and he'd fall down that rabbit hole of memories he'd vowed never to rehash.

"So what do we do?" she asked. "I called Daniel, but he didn't pick up."

"I did the same with Alexis."

Rose smoothed her white curly wig over one shoulder. "On the upside, he has agreed to be in the auction. Just make sure you get your granddaughter out of the way of bidding when he hits the stage."

"I know my part," he growled, frustrated over the missing couple and agitated with himself for that niggling of want toward Rose. "Alexis won't be around even if I have to fake a heart attack."

Rose's eyes widened. "Don't joke about something like that."

Was that...care in her tone? *Whatever.* He wasn't giving that a second thought right now. He had a mission and he couldn't deviate from it.

"I'll text Alexis and tell her I'm not feeling well," Gus stated, pulling his phone from his baggy pirate pants. He hated this damn costume. He'd rather have dressed up as a rancher, but Alexis had forbidden him to wear his everyday clothes. "We came together so I'll have her meet me in the lobby. Surely that will get a response."

Rose nodded. "Good."

Gus shot off his text and held his phone, waiting. Silence curled around him and Rose, and the tension seemed to grow thicker with each passing second. There was so much he wanted to say, so many things he'd bottled up over the years, but what would be the point? Yes, he wanted answers. Hell, he *deserved* answers. But learning the truth of what happened all those years ago didn't matter now. Nothing mattered but stopping their grandchildren from falling in love...or whatever the hell they called it. The thought of his sweet granddaughter hooking up with a Clayton irritated the hell out of him.

Alexis deserved better and he was going to steer her in the direction her life needed to go. If that was meddling, well then he wasn't the least bit sorry. He only wanted what was best for her, and that certainly wasn't Daniel Clayton.

The phone vibrated in his hand. "She's going to meet me in the lobby in ten minutes."

Rose's shoulder sagged a bit, as if she'd been holding her breath. Considering they were both on the same page as to how much they *didn't* want Daniel and Alexis together, he was kind of glad Rose was his partner in crime here.

"I'll slip out and go back to the party," she told him. "Don't come out yet."

"I know how to do this," he snapped.

Rose jumped and guilt instantly flooded him. Damn it. Working with her was just supposed to be a way of keeping their families distanced for good. Instead, the more time he spent with her, the more his mind kept playing tricks on him and making him believe he was intrigued once again by her.

But that was absurd. Rose had been his first love; it was probably some residual emotions that had simply never gone away. He simply hadn't been around her this much in...well, decades. That's all. He was just mesmerized and captivated momentarily by her timeless beauty and her tenacity. Then he remembered it was that beauty and tenacity that had pulled him in and spat him out so long ago.

"Good night, Rose."

He dismissed her, feeling like an ass but needing to get out of here. Just as he started to pass, Rose reached out and put her hand on his arm. Gus stiffened at her unexpected touch. He didn't look over at her—he couldn't.

"We don't have to be enemies," she murmured softly.

Gus swallowed and fisted his hands at his sides. Nothing he said at this point would be smart. What could he say? They were enemies, after all, and that was all on her.

Choosing to remain silent, he kept his eyes on the exit and walked away. Whatever was going through her mind, he didn't want to know. They couldn't get distracted by anything, sure as hell not each other.

Gus pushed Rose from his mind and headed toward the lobby. He had to get Alexis out of here and away from Daniel. There wasn't a doubt in his mind that the two had snuck off together. If his granddaughter knew he had concocted the auction to keep her away, she'd never forgive him. Which was why she could never find out and why he needed to limit his face-to-face time with Rose.

And that was just one of the many reasons he had to curtail his alone time with the woman who had once crushed him.

How long should she wait? More importantly, why had she agreed to this preposterous plan of letting Matt into Lone Wolf Ranch?

Rachel sat on the back porch swing and blew out a sigh. She hadn't agreed—not in words, anyway. She'd kissed and groped all over the man instead. Clearly giving him the silent answer he wanted.

Clutching the baby monitor, Rachel pushed off the floor of the porch with her toe to set the swing in motion. There was something so calming, so soothing about country life. To hear the crickets, to see the bright stars, to know that your neighbor wasn't right on top of you was so freeing, and she valued the privacy. She really should start looking for a home of her own. She loved Royal and knew now with 100 percent certainty that she'd be setting her roots here. Ellie would love the park, love the farms, the community.

Rachel couldn't deny she also wanted a bit of distance from her in-laws. First, they'd wanted her to move in with them so they could care for her and Ellie. Then they'd wanted her to let Ellie stay there so Rachel could finish school and find a home. Her mother-in-law had called this evening, but Rachel had let it go to voice mail. She knew they meant well, and understood that they would forever grieve Billy's death, but when Rachel spent any time with them, she got sucked into that black hole, and she couldn't afford that...not if she wanted to move on to the life she and her baby needed.

An engine caught her attention and for a split second Rachel thought Matt was here. But the headlights and sound came from the direction of the barn where the hay was stored.

Confused, Rachel kept her gaze on the vehicle as it slowly came down the drive toward the exit. There was no mistaking that truck. She'd seen it before.

As the vehicle passed the house, she got a glimpse of a profile and, yup. That was definitely Daniel Clayton. Rachel bit the inside of her cheek as her gaze went back to the darkened barn. Looks like she wasn't the only one sneaking around to be with a man tonight. Rachel just hoped Matt wasn't spotted by Alexis. That was a conversation she didn't want to have with her roommate.

The low rumble of another vehicle approaching had her heartbeat kicking up. Matt pulled his truck around the back of the house and parked like he had every right to be here. Something about his arrogance—or confidence, as he'd called it—only intensified her attraction.

Why did this have to be the man to get her attention? Why was she able to push anyone else aside, but Matt Galloway demanded her everything and suddenly she had no control? As he closed the distance between them, the shadows surrounding him only added to the intrigue. Considering he'd had a thing for her for years and she'd just discovered it, she wondered if there was anything else he kept from her.

Rachel came to her feet. Without a word, he mounted the steps and she held the door open. Moving quietly through the house, Rachel took his hand and led him toward her own suite she'd been given. Thankfully, it was away from the other bedrooms and large enough to have a sitting room.

As soon as she entered, she turned the baby monitor off, since the crib was in the far corner near the sofa. The bed was on the other side of the suite, but Rachel wasn't comfortable doing this with her baby in the room because…well, because.

She hadn't thought this through very well. Obviously her need for this man had overridden any common sense on the realities of her sleeping situation…not that Ellie was old enough to know if there was a man in her mother's bed, but still.

Rachel held a finger to her lips, grabbed the monitor and urged Matt into the bathroom. She flicked on the light and slid the pocket door closed once he was inside.

"I guess I wasn't thinking that I share a room with her." Rachel shook her head and let out a humorless laugh. "If you want to go, I completely—"

His mouth was on hers, his arms wrapping her up and hauling her against his hard body. Rachel melted. Or, she felt like she had. The more time she spent with Matt, the more she wanted…well, everything.

His hands were all over her at once, stripping her clothes away before pulling his own off. Stepping over the pile of unwanted garments, Matt tugged her toward the wide glass shower.

How could she want him this much when she'd already been with him twice? When would this ever-pressing need go away?

Rachel wasn't sure, but she knew she needed to enjoy this while it lasted...because the end wasn't far off.

Fourteen

"Did you have a sleepover last night?"

Rachel glanced up from the office she'd been using at Lone Wolf Ranch. Alexis stood in the doorway with a wide smile on her face.

"Hey, I'm not judging," she immediately added before stepping in and closing the door. "I just saw a truck in the drive before I went to bed, and then this morning I heard it leave."

Ellie held on to her baby-doll stroller and pushed it around before falling back onto her diapered bottom. She'd just started walking, so there were still a few tumbles.

"I'm not the only one who had an evening visitor."

Alexis pursed her lips and took a seat on the sofa near the window. "I didn't come to talk about me. I'm here for you. Tell me that was Matt Galloway. I'm not even upset that we'll have to take him off the auction block. I'm just so happy you're dating...or whatever."

Off the auction block? Rachel wasn't going that far, and Matt never acted like he wasn't ready to strut his stuff—he just wanted her to bid on him.

Rachel really didn't have any reason to hide her current situation from Alexis. It wasn't like Alexis was going to wave her paddle when Matt came onstage or run out and tell anyone. She sure as hell wouldn't tell Gus, because her grandfather wanted Alexis to bid on Matt. Mercy, this was one complicated web they were all ensnared in.

Besides all of that, Alexis definitely only had eyes for one man, and it wasn't Matt.

"Things are complicated." Understatement of the year. "But, he's still in the auction."

"What on earth for?" Alexis jerked back, almost appalled at the statement. "He's clearly interested in you."

"We've snuck around a little," Rachel admitted. "But, like I said, things are complicated."

Alexis let out a little squeal. "I knew it! And, honey, there is nothing complicated about that man. He's obviously infatuated."

Sex was one thing, her strong emotions were another…and she had no clue how he truly felt. All Rachel knew was that he'd be going back to Dallas soon and they'd return to the friend zone. Would he put more time between them like he had before? Because she didn't want to lose him. If she could only have him as a friend, then she'd take it.

Falling in love had never been part of the plan…not that there had been a plan. Every bit of her reunion with Matt had been totally unexpected, yet blissfully amazing.

"You're falling for him." Alexis moved her legs up onto the sofa when Ellie toddled by. "I can see it plain as day."

"Don't be absurd," Rachel denied. She wiggled her mouse to bring her screen back to life so she could finish the social media graphics for the auction. "Matt and I have been friends for years. He was Billy's best friend. He's still going to be the headliner for the auction, so don't worry."

"Oh, I'm not worried about that. Because you'll be bidding on him if he insists on staying in."

Rachel groaned. "Why do you all think that's how this has to play out?"

"You know you don't want another woman bidding," Alexis laughed. "I take it your guy wants you to stake a claim on him, too?"

Throwing a glance over her shoulder, Rachel eyed her friend. "He's not my guy. I'm working on creating a countdown for the social media sites. Don't try to distract me with all this nonsense."

"I think hooking up with your friend several times in as many days isn't nonsense."

Ellie fell over once again, taking the stroller with her. Alexis eased down onto the floor and helped Ellie back up.

"I am not doing this," Rachel said, turning back to her screen. "But, if you'd like to discuss what happened in the barn with Daniel, I'm all ears."

Silence filled the room. Rachel bit the inside of her cheek to keep from laughing. Daniel's grandmother and Gus had been sworn enemies for years according to the chatter Rachel had heard. The two had once been so in love, but then they'd fallen apart and married other people. There was no way Rose or Gus would want to see their grandkids together.

If Rachel thought her personal life was a mess, she had nothing on Alexis.

"I know you're sneaking around." Rachel clicked on a different font, trying to make this conversation casual to get her friend to open up. "I also know why, so if you want to talk, I'm here."

"Nothing to talk about."

Rachel's hand stilled on the mouse. She didn't blame Alexis for not wanting to confide in her, but at the same time, she wished her friend would talk. She'd probably feel better if she had someone to spill her secrets to. Granted that person might be Daniel right now.

Ellie let out a whine. Rachel spun in her chair in time to see her daughter flop down onto her butt and rub her eyes.

"I guess it's naptime," she stated, pushing up from the desk chair. "Since we both know what's really going on, but we need these guys for the auction, let's just keep this to ourselves."

Alexis stared back at her and simply nodded, which was all the affirmation Rachel needed to know her friend was indeed keeping a dirty little secret. At this point in Rachel's life, she was the last person to judge someone's indiscretions.

Rachel scooped Ellie up and kissed her little neck, warranting a giggle from her sweet girl. Then Ellie rested her head on Rachel's shoulder and she realized there was nothing more precious or important than this right here in her arms.

"You're lucky," Alexis murmured with a sad smile. "I want a family one day."

Patting Ellie's back, Rachel focused on her friend. "You'll have one. Just make sure you find the right guy first."

"You make it sound like Billy wasn't the right guy."

Rachel swallowed the lump of guilt. She didn't want to speak ill of her late husband and she would never say a negative word to Ellie about her father.

"Billy was a great guy," Rachel said carefully. "I think we married too soon and confused lust for love, then expected that emotion to carry us through the rough patches."

Rachel wasn't ready to admit her fear of infidelity.

Alexis stepped closer and rested her hand on Rachel's arm. "Which is why you deserve this second chance. Bid on your man before someone else comes along and takes him from you."

There was no response Rachel could make at this point. Matt was hardly her man, and bidding on him wouldn't secure that spot in her life. Then again, she didn't want to bid on anyone else.

Rachel headed back to her room to lay Ellie down for her nap. Stifling a yawn, Rachel figured she might as well lie down, too. She didn't regret the lost sleep last night. In fact, she'd worried about Matt staying, but having him next to her had only made her realize she wanted him more.

Why had she let this happen? She'd warned herself going in that there was no room for emotions. Matt was the almighty ladies' man; there was no good ending to her getting this invested in their time together. Intimacy had clouded her judgment at first, but now she saw a clearer picture. Did she even risk her heart, her soul, by holding out hope that he'd love her back?

Could she even move on if he did?

The guilt had settled in long ago; at this point she had to remind herself she was young and it was okay to move on. But moving on with Matt? A man who was not in the market for a ready-made family? Maybe not the smartest choice she'd made. He'd never made any indication that he wanted a family life in Royal or that he wanted more than sex and friendship.

Rachel grabbed Ellie's favorite stuffed toy and silky blanket and laid her little girl down in her crib. The first few months of Ellie's life had been rough with trying to get her child to sleep. Between the grief over Billy and an insomniac baby, combined with her schooling, Rachel had nearly lost her mind.

Thankfully, she was on break and Ellie embraced the naps... for the most part.

After placing Ellie in her crib, Rachel tiptoed away and headed toward her own bed. She'd just lie here and stretch out for a bit. She had to meet with the new landscaper who was working at TCC for the auction. He had her list, but they hadn't spoken in person. She'd feel better if she went and discussed her plan.

Her cell vibrated in her pocket. Stifling a yawn, Rachel pulled it out and glanced at the screen. Her brother-in-law was calling. She couldn't keep dodging them.

With a quick glance to Ellie, Rachel eased out into the hallway and slid her finger across the screen.

"Hello, Mark."

"Rachel." He sounded relieved that she'd answered. "Glad I finally caught you. Is this a good time?"

Was there ever a good time when trying to dodge an uncomfortable conversation? She'd never felt a real connection to Mark and his wife, Kay. They were nice people; Rachel just didn't have anything in common with them.

She rubbed her forehead, feeling the start of a headache.

"I just laid Ellie down for a nap," she replied. "What's up?"

"When are you coming home?" he asked.

Home. Right now she didn't have one to call her own. If he meant Dallas, well, she wasn't going back there. No way was she going to stay with her in-laws again. It was well past time she find a place of her own. Not that she hadn't appreciated their help, but Royal felt more like home than Dallas.

"I'm actually helping with a charity auction here in Royal," she explained. "I'm not sure when I'll be back in Dallas."

Mark let out a sigh that slid through the line and wrapped her up in yet another layer of guilt. She hadn't lied, but she couldn't flat out tell him, either.

"We miss Ellie...and you."

Rachel didn't need the added compliment. She knew full well they all missed Ellie, and she wouldn't deprive them of seeing her. She would visit Dallas soon, but she wasn't moving back.

"I'll text you soon and we can all meet up for dinner. I start back to my classes next week and the auction is taking up much of my spare time. But...soon."

That sounded so lame. The struggle to do what was right for her daughter, Billy's family and herself was seriously real.

"We just want to help," he added. "Kay and I...we just want to help you."

"I know," Rachel conceded. "I appreciate it. Maybe you all could come to Royal for dinner one night."

"I'll see what we can do. I'll text you."

Rachel gripped her phone. "Sounds good. Bye, Mark."

She disconnected the call and leaned back against the wall next to her bedroom. Her headache had come on full force now.

Closing her eyes, Rachel willed for some sign to come...

something to give her clarity as to what the right answer was for her future.

Finishing her degree and finding a home of her own had to be her next steps. Her feelings for Matt couldn't override that; her guilt toward her in-laws couldn't interfere, either. At the end of the day, Ellie's needs and providing a stable life for her were all that mattered.

Suddenly, she wasn't so tired anymore. She peeked into the room, pleased when she saw Ellie was fast asleep. Rachel rushed to the office she'd been using and grabbed her laptop before returning to her room. She popped a few ibuprofen to help with her headache since she wanted to try to get some work done.

Over the next hour she polished up the multiple ads that would lead up to the auction. There was so much that went on behind the scenes: social media images to create, newspaper articles to write to draw interest beforehand, radio commercials to schedule and so many other things. This was exactly what she was meant to do. Her love of photography would only help her with her marketing career.

She couldn't wait to do this on a regular basis for an actual paycheck once her degree was in hand. Hopefully she could do some work from home and stay with Ellie. She hated the idea of finding a sitter, but she'd cross that bridge when she got to it.

The phone vibrated again in her hand, causing her to jump. Rachel's pulse skipped as a text from Matt lit up the screen.

Be at my penthouse at 7 for dinner. Bring Ellie.

She sighed. Her headache hadn't completely vanished and she still wasn't feeling that great. She settled onto the sofa in the sitting room of her bedroom. She didn't reply to Matt; he didn't expect one. He wanted her there and they both knew she'd go. Ignoring her need for him wouldn't make it go away.

Perhaps she should just rest while Ellie was still asleep. Perhaps when she woke she'd feel better and would be able to go to Matt's. Their time was limited and every day that passed brought them closer to being put back in the friend zone.

Fifteen

Matt ended the call and resisted the urge to throw his phone across his suite. He'd been arguing with Eric once again, only this time over the price. Matt knew what his 51 percent was worth and he wasn't taking a penny less. It wasn't like he had to sell for financial reasons. No, this move came strictly from an attempt to save his sanity and take the time to discover something that would make him feel whole.

The knock on his door had him jerking his attention toward the entrance. It was twenty minutes after seven, which also had put him in a bad mood because he'd convinced himself Rachel wasn't coming. She hadn't replied earlier and he hadn't spoken to her.

The concierge had set up quite the spread of food along the wall of the living area. Matt had literally ordered everything off the menu and even asked for specialty items for Ellie. He'd done a bit of research on babies to see what she could eat. He knew she only had three teeth, so he ordered extra cheesy mashed potatoes and some pureed fruit for her.

Matt raked a hand through his hair and pushed thoughts of

his business woes aside. Rachel was here and he wasn't going to let anything ruin his evening.

As soon as he opened the door, he found himself reaching for Ellie as he took in Rachel's state of disarray.

"What's wrong?" he demanded as he held Ellie against his chest and ushered Rachel inside.

Her hair was in a messy ponytail, her shirt was wrinkly and she hadn't a stitch of makeup. She was still stunningly beautiful, but definitely not herself.

What dragon did he need to slay for her? Because the thought of anything wrong with Rachel did not sit well with him.

"I'm not feeling well." She closed the door behind her and turned back to face him. "I fell asleep while she was down. I started working and the next thing I knew I was waking up, she was gone from her crib and my laptop was still in my lap. Alexis had taken Ellie out and I didn't hear a thing."

She was pushing herself too hard. Trying to do it all on her own, and Matt was done with this.

"Sit down," he demanded. "I'll get you some food."

"Don't fuss," she stated, but still made her way to the sofa and practically melted down onto it. "You're always trying to feed me."

"Because someone needs to take care of you."

Ellie smacked her little hand against the side of his face and rattled off some gibberish he was pretty sure wasn't real words.

"Has Ellie eaten dinner?"

"Gus said he gave her some pears and Alexis had the cook make some eggs earlier." Rachel laid her head against the back of the couch and let out a frustrated groan. "What kind of mother am I that I didn't even hear her when she woke up or someone came in and took her from the room?"

Matt turned from the array of food and crossed to her. Still holding on to Ellie, he eased down on the cushion beside Rachel.

"You're a mother who is trying to do too much and is going to make herself sick," he chided gently.

Ellie reached for her mom and Matt let her go, instantly realizing he missed the warm cuddles. When had he started craving holding a baby? He'd been so consumed with his yearnings for Rachel, this had crept up on him.

"I just needed a nap, that's all." Rachel smiled to Ellie and smoothed her blond curls off her forehead. "Since someone started walking, I'm constantly on the move."

"When do your online classes start back up?" he asked.

"Monday."

Matt rested his hand on her knee. "I'll hire you a live-in nanny."

Rachel jerked her gaze to his. "You'll do no such thing."

"Why the hell not? You need the help."

"Mae, the Slades' chef, has been helping so much, and I'm not letting you pay for my family."

Her family. She kept him at an arm's length—which was what he'd thought he wanted. So why, then, did it irk him so much right now?

"Billy would want me to help you."

Rachel grunted. "That was a ridiculously low blow."

Yeah, it had been. "You're my friend and I want to help. Don't make this more than it is."

"We're fine," she declared through gritted teeth. "Maybe I should've canceled. I'm tired and cranky."

And not going anywhere tonight.

"Which is all the more reason why you need to be here so I can pamper you."

She slid him a side-glance. "I'm not here for sex."

"I don't always think that's why you want to see me…though I'm flattered to know getting me naked is clearly on your mind."

Rachel rolled her eyes. "You're impossible."

She turned her attention back to Ellie and lifted her up before settling her back on her lap. "Uncle Matt is silly," she told her daughter.

The whole Uncle Matt reference seriously grated on his last nerve. He didn't want to be Ellie's faux uncle. He wanted…

Hell, he didn't know what he wanted.

In an attempt to pull himself together, Matt made up a plate for Rachel and a small one for Ellie.

"Come to the table," he told her.

Matt took Ellie and sat down with her resting on one of his thighs. "I have no clue if this is okay, but hopefully she'll like what I ordered."

Rachel glanced around at the spread. "I'd hate to see your bill when you check out."

Whatever his bill was would be worth it. He'd buy the damn hotel if he wanted just to make sure Rachel was comfortable and cared for. Anything to make her life easier.

"Talk to me about the auction," he said, spooning up a bite of potatoes.

Ellie put her hands right in the bite, then put her fingers in her mouth. Well, whatever. He'd discovered feeding a baby wasn't a neat and tidy process.

"We added a couple new faces. I'm supposed to shoot their pictures on Tuesday morning."

The growl of disapproval escaped him before he had a chance to stop himself.

Rachel smiled as she stabbed a piece of filet mignon. "Easy there, tiger. It won't end like *your* photo shoot did."

It sure as hell better not or he'd have a little one-on-one with those guys. Jealousy wasn't an emotion he'd ever been familiar with, and he sure as hell didn't want to experience it now. Rachel had made it clear they were back to friends as soon as the auction was over, so he knew he had no right to get all territorial.

"Gus is loving all of this and is constantly looking over the sheet of eligible bachelors," she laughed and shook her head, causing more golden strands to fall from her ponytail. "The two I added today piqued his interest and he's ready for Alexis to place her bid."

Matt gave Ellie a bite of mashed-up strawberries. "Does Alexis have her eye on one?"

"I'm pretty sure there's only one bachelor she's got her eye on, but she's keeping him a secret."

Matt raised his brows. "Kind of like us."

Rachel tipped her head. "Not exactly. Alexis has tried to brush me off when I broach the topic, but she has a thing for Daniel Clayton. They've been sneaking around."

"Why would they sneak? Just because of the auction?"

"The Slades and the Claytons make the Capulets and the Montagues look like playmates."

Interesting. No wonder Alexis had to sneak to see her guy. If Matt didn't have this damn title hanging over his head and hadn't been roped into starring as the headliner for the auction, he wouldn't have to sneak around with Rachel, either.

"Sounds like a mess," he said.

Ellie swatted at the spoon full of strawberries and it flung back onto his gray T-shirt.

"Oh, Matt, I'm so sorry." Rachel jumped from her seat and grabbed her napkin to dab at his shirt. "Let me get that."

"It's a shirt, Rachel. Relax."

There she went again trying to do even the simplest things for other people. She had a plate full of food still, and she looked like she was about to fall over.

"I've got this and Ellie," he informed her. "Your job is to eat. That's all."

Slowly, she sank back into her chair and dropped the napkin on the table. "Sorry."

"Stop apologizing." Damn it, he wished she'd see he was trying to help. "I've got this, really."

Rachel finished eating and Matt ignored the stained shirt and the fact it had soaked through to his chest. Once Ellie was done, he picked her up and grabbed the diaper bag.

"I assume she needs a bath?" he asked, shouldering the bag.

Rachel nodded. "I can do it when we get home."

"You're staying here tonight."

Those doe-like eyes widened. "I can't stay here."

Considering she looked like a soft breeze could blow her over, Matt didn't even consider this a fair fight.

"You're staying and I'll give Ellie a bath."

Rachel smoothed her stray hairs from her face and smiled. "You're joking, right? If you think dinner is a mess, you should see bath time. She loves splashing."

"It's water," he retorted. "I'll live."

Rachel eased her seat out and crossed her arms, leveling her gaze his way. "Don't do this, Matt. I can't…"

"Can't what? Let a friend help?"

"You know what I mean."

Matt shifted Ellie to his other side and couldn't deny his heart lurched when she put her head on his shoulder. How could he not fall for this sweet baby girl? She was innocent and precious and, with no effort on her part, had worked her way into his heart. Perhaps it was because she was his last connection to Billy or perhaps because she was a mirror image of her mother. Matt wasn't sure, but he knew for certain he wanted them both to stay here with him tonight.

"You can supervise," he told her. "Let's go."

Rachel got the water ready to the proper temperature and then started to remove Ellie's clothes. Rachel sank down next to the edge of the garden tub and sat Ellie in the water. Matt grabbed a cloth and a towel and sat next to Rachel.

Ellie patted her little hands on the water and giggled as she splashed herself in the face. Matt glanced for the soap and wondered if there was something special he needed to use.

"I have her soap in the diaper bag," Rachel stated, as if reading his mind.

She stood up and went to the vanity to her bag. Matt kept his hand on Ellie's back, not caring one bit that he was already getting soaked. Ellie's dimpled smile was infectious, and this familial moment was something he'd never thought he wanted.

Did he want it, though? Doing this one time was a far cry from being a permanent family man.

Damn it. He was getting too caught up in his thoughts and letting his heart guide him. He'd never let that happen. If he'd let his heart and hormones lead the way toward decision-making, he never would've become the successful businessman he was today…then again, he wasn't too happy with that job. At the end of the long, dragging days, he still felt lonely, empty. No matter how many mergers he secured, there was still the fact he came home to a quiet house.

Rachel came back with the soap, and after some more splashing and giggles, they finally got Ellie all washed up. Rachel grabbed a spare outfit from the bag and dressed her daughter while Matt cleaned up in the bathroom.

When he turned to face her, he realized her clothes had gotten soaked, as well. He didn't need that clingy fabric to remind him of how her waist dipped in and her hips flared. Those curves were made for a man's hands…his hands.

"Let me get her a bottle," Rachel said, pulling him from his thoughts. "She's going to be ready for bed."

"Why don't you take a relaxing shower or bath or whatever?" he suggested. "Get a bottle for me and I'll get her to sleep."

Rachel patted Ellie's back and smiled. "You're really determined to do this, aren't you?"

Matt reached for Ellie. "I'm determined to make sure you're safe and healthy, so if I have to feed you, bathe your child, make sure she gets to bed so you can rest, then that's what I'll do."

"We can't stay here," she argued, though there wasn't much heat to her voice. "Ellie still gets up at night to eat, and she'll wake you—"

Matt put his index finger over her mouth to silence her. She slid her tongue out, moistening her lips, but she brushed the pad of his fingertip. Heat coiled low and it was all he could do not to forget their responsibilities.

Her eyes widened, clearly when she realized what she'd done.

"I'll be fine," he growled. "Now, get that bottle and let me get her to bed."

Rachel finally nodded and Matt eased his hand away. By the time she came back with a bottle, Ellie had started fussing and was rubbing her eyes. The crib was still set up in the living area, so Matt dimmed the lights. He settled in the leather club chair and attempted to find a comfortable position to get into. Rachel stood in the distance and stared, worry etched on her face.

"Go on to bed, Rachel. I'll stay in here with her."

"I won't win this fight, will I?"

Matt smiled. "Good night, Rachel."

He stared back down at Ellie and wondered how the hell he'd gotten to this point. He never invited a woman to stay all night, and here he was about to spend his second night with Rachel because he couldn't bear to be away from her. He was getting her child to sleep like some fill-in dad. What the hell kind of poser was he? This wasn't what he'd meant to do. He never wanted to fill Billy's shoes.

Billy. His best friend and the man who had been cheating on his wife just before his death. The secret weighed heavy on Matt's mind. Rachel deserved to know, but on the other hand, why would he want to put her through more pain?

He didn't like lying by omission to her. He also didn't like the way his entire life was turning on its axis because he didn't even recognize himself anymore.

Most Eligible Bachelor in Texas was now playing house with a woman he shouldn't want, but couldn't seem to be without.

He was so screwed.

Sixteen

Rachel hadn't spent the night with any man other than Billy, but waking in Matt's bed didn't fill her with regret. If anything, she felt…complete. Having Matt take care of her when she felt bad, having him not mind looking after Ellie one bit only made Rachel fall for him even more.

She rolled over and checked her phone and was shocked to see it was well after nine. She'd missed a text from Billy's mother, but she'd answer her in a bit.

Rachel flung the covers back and rushed out to the living room. "I am so sorry—"

She stopped short when she spotted Matt reclined in the corner of the L-shaped sofa. He had pillows propped around him, Ellie sound asleep on his chest and his head tipped back against the cushions. He was completely out.

Well, if that didn't make her heart take another tumble, nothing would. She knew the friend side of Matt, the one that joked and was always there to lend a hand. Then she'd discovered the deliciously sexy side of him when he'd taken their relationship to a new level.

But seeing him hold her child, mimicking the role of a father, had her questioning just how deep she'd gotten with him. How could she ever reverse such strong feelings? Love was about as deep as it went, and there was no magical switch to just turn it off.

Rachel tiptoed toward them, but Matt stirred. He blinked a few times before focusing on her. A sleepy smile spread across his gorgeous face. This was the sexy side, the side she would never tire of seeing. She only wished they could take the day and spend it in his bed, forgetting the world and doubts and fears.

"She got up really early," he whispered. "I tried not to wake you, but I guess we fell back asleep."

"How early, and why didn't I hear her?"

Matt shifted, holding on to Ellie as he sat up a little more. "I was up working and it was around five."

Good grief. Here she'd slept like the dead and hadn't even noticed. That was the second time in as many days.

"Are you feeling better?" he asked softly.

Rachel nodded. "I can't believe I slept that long."

"You clearly needed it."

Ellie started squirming and Rachel stepped forward. "Let me take her."

Before she could reach her, Rachel's cell vibrated in her hand. She glanced down and frowned at the second message from Billy's mother.

"Everything okay?"

"Billy's family wants to come visit since I'm not getting back to Dallas fast enough," she sighed and sank down onto the couch next to Matt, taking Ellie from his chest. "I haven't told them I'm staying here permanently. They want to take Ellie so I can finish my degree. They've made it clear they can give her a good life."

Rachel kissed her baby on her head and nestled close. "I appreciate the sentiment, but there's no way in hell that's happening. Do they honestly think I'll give her up?"

"Have they seen her much since Billy's death?"

Rachel shrugged. "Some. They've just been hovering, and honestly, they're one of the main reasons I want to move. I can't handle being under their microscope. The calls, the texts—it's all day long."

Matt moved the pillows from between them and leaned in closer. His rumpled hair and the baby food on the shoulder of his T-shirt made him look like the opposite of the Most Eligible Bachelor in Texas. Yet he'd never looked hotter or more desirable. And she knew she was treading some very dangerous water here. Not only had she opened her heart to him, she'd let him in with her daughter, and that was an image Rachel would never be able to erase.

"Ellie is their only link to Billy," Matt said, resting his hand on her knee. "They just don't want to lose everything. Maybe you guys could come to some sort of visitation schedule that works for everyone."

"Mark and his wife asked me for full custody. Can you believe that?"

Matt shook his head. "Clearly that's a no, so sit down and talk with them. Tell them you'll be living here and see about letting them come to see Ellie. This doesn't have to be ugly, and it shouldn't be a fight. If you need, I have an excellent attorney I keep on retainer."

Rachel shook her head. "No. You're right. We can work through this. I'll call her in a bit."

When Ellie perked up and glanced around the room all bright eyed, Matt laughed. "At least she wakes up pleasant."

"She's usually a happy baby. I'd better call down and order some breakfast."

"I actually need to head over to the farmhouse and get a few things done," he told her as he came to his feet. "How about you meet me for lunch in town at the Royal Diner around one?"

Rachel smiled. "I'd love to. Are you sure you don't want me to order you something?"

He leaned down and kissed her. "I want you to stay as long as you like. In fact, why don't you stay with me while I'm in town? I want you in my bed, Rachel."

As much as she'd love to stay in his bed each night, she couldn't for so many reasons. Though that heated look he pinned her with had her questioning those reasons.

"If word got out that I was sleeping here with you, how well do you think that would go over at the auction?"

He stood straight up and cocked his head, smiling wide. Her toes curled and her belly tingled. "The auction where you'll bid on me and then take me home to have your wicked way with me?"

Rachel rolled her eyes and extended her leg to kick him slightly on his thigh. "Get out of here and take that ego with you."

But that's exactly what she wanted and he damn well knew it.

Holding on to her baby, Rachel eased to the corner of the sofa Matt had just vacated. She couldn't contain the smile and she wasn't even going to try. Maybe she would bid on him, but she had limited funds and probably wouldn't be able to compete with the other women of Royal and the surrounding area.

But what if she did bid and win? Then, when the auction was over, she'd tell him how she truly felt. If she had learned anything from Billy's death it was that tomorrow wasn't promised. Rachel never thought she'd feel such a strong pull toward another man, but everything she had inside her for Matt was completely different than her feelings for Billy.

And maybe she'd just have to let him in on her little secret.

Gus and Alexis had taken Ellie to the park for a picnic and to play. Rachel figured it was because there was a bit of tension swirling between the two Slades over the auction, but Rachel had her own issues to worry about.

She pulled up early to meet Matt at the diner. With a deep breath, she pulled out her phone and dialed her mother-in-law.

Matt was right...the sooner she discussed this situation, the better off everyone would be. It wasn't fair to deprive Ellie of her grandparents. They obviously loved her, and that was at least the mutual ground they'd need to build from.

The phone rang twice before Alma Kincaid answered. "Hello?"

"Alma? Um, it's me. Is this a good time?"

"Rachel," the woman practically squealed. "Of course, of course. How are you? How's our sweet Ellie-bug?"

Rachel gripped her cell and watched as a family of four went into the restaurant. "We're all doing great. I'm sorry I missed your calls. These past couple weeks have been busy. I'm working on a charity auction and I start back to class on Monday. My last semester before I earn my degree."

"That's wonderful," Alma praised. "You sound so swamped, though. Ellie is more than welcome to stay with me until your load lightens."

"That's one of the reasons I called to talk to you." *Please, please let this go smoothly.* "I know you guys miss Ellie and I'd like to see if we can come to some sort of agreement on a visitation schedule. My plan is to move to Royal...for good."

"For good?" Alma repeated. "Well, um, okay. I wasn't expecting that. But, I understand staying in Dallas might bring back some painful memories. Billy's death changed us all."

Wasn't that the truth?

"I'm just so thrilled you're going to let us see her," Alma went on. "I was so worried after he died that you'd shut us out. I tried to talk him out of going to that divorce lawyer and told him to work on your marriage. I mean, you were pregnant, and that certainly was not the time to end things."

Stunned, Rachel stared at the American flag flapping in the wind across the street at the courthouse. "Divorce lawyer?"

"I couldn't believe it myself," she added, oblivious to the bomb she'd just dropped. "But I love Ellie and I love you like my own, Rachel. I would love to come up with a visitation schedule. Whatever works best for you and Ellie. I'm willing to drive to Royal as often as I can."

Suddenly shaking, Rachel couldn't think. Billy had been ready to divorce her? She knew they'd been arguing, that they'd started growing apart, but that word had never been thrown around.

"Alma, I need to call you back. Will you be home this evening?"

"Of course, dear. It's so good to hear from you. Give Elliebug a kiss from Gran."

Rachel disconnected the call and rubbed her forehead. Pulling in one deep breath after another, she willed her breathing to slow.

The tap on her window had Rachel jerking in her seat. Matt stood outside her car with a smile on his face and opened her door.

When she slid out and looked up at him, his smile vanished. "What happened? Is it Ellie? Are you feeling bad again?"

She was feeling bad, almost nauseous, in fact. "I just got off the phone with Alma."

Matt's brows drew in. "Did she not agree to your idea? I can call my lawyer now—"

"No. We didn't even get to discuss the schedule. She was just glad I was letting Ellie be part of their life since Billy—uh—had already gone to a divorce attorney."

Matt eased back, his eyes showing no sign of shock. In fact, Rachel only saw one emotion, and that was acknowledgment.

"You knew?" she whispered hoarsely.

He slid a hand over the back of his neck and started to reach for her. "Listen—"

She slid from between him and the car to avoid his touch. "No. How dare you know and not tell me!"

Matt glanced around when she shouted, then took a step closer. "You don't want to do this here."

"I don't want to do it at all," she growled through gritted teeth. "You betrayed me."

Matt gripped her shoulders and came within a breath of her. Although she wanted nothing more than to shove him away, she didn't. Causing a scene wouldn't repair what had been done, wouldn't piece back together her shattered heart. She'd trusted him. Damn it, she'd fallen in love with him.

For the second time, she'd laid her heart on the line only to have it crushed and her trust betrayed.

"When did you want me to tell you?" he asked, lowering his voice. "I just found out the day he died. We were on the boat and he mentioned it, then I tried to talk to him. The accident happened so fast, then you were distraught from the loss. At what point should I have caused you more pain, Rachel?"

She closed her eyes, trying to force the truth away. Learning her most trusted friend had kept something so pivotal from her only exacerbated the pain he referred to.

When she focused back on him, Rachel's heart lurched. The way he held her, the way he looked at her all seemed so genuine and full of concern. But everything had been a lie.

"You knew this information and then you dodged me for a year," she accused. "I understand not telling me immediately, but did you ever think of reaching out to me after that? Is that why you really stayed away, because you wanted to keep your friend's secret? Did everyone know he didn't want me? Didn't want our baby?"

Damn, this hurt. The idea that she and Ellie were going to be tossed aside crushed her in ways she hadn't thought possible. And the fact that Matt knew and remained silent…well, she had no label to put on that crippling emotion.

"I never wanted you hurt," he ground out.

Rachel looked into his eyes, searching for answers she might never have. "Would you have ever told me?"

Matt's lips thinned as he remained silent. That told her all she needed to know.

"Let me go," she murmured. "I can't do this anymore."

"Rachel." His grip remained as he pulled her against his chest. "Let's go somewhere and talk. You have to know I never meant to hurt you."

"Yet you did."

He rested his forehead against hers. "Don't push me out. Let me explain."

"What else have you lied about?" she asked, her voice cracking, and she damned her emotions for not staying at bay until she was alone. "Did you actually want to be with me, or was this just because Billy—"

"None of this is because of Billy," he demanded. "I've wanted you for years, Rachel. You can't tell me you didn't feel it when I kissed you, touched you. Made love to you."

Rachel started to protest, but Matt's mouth covered hers. Their past kisses had been frenzied, intense, but this one could only be described as passionate and caring. He took his time as he framed her face with his hands. Despite everything, Rachel started to melt into him because she couldn't disconnect her heart from her hormones.

"Perfect."

They jerked apart at the unfamiliar voice. A young woman stood next to them with her phone, taking a photo.

"Mr. Galloway, can you comment on your relationship here?" the woman asked, whipping out a small notepad and pen. "Are you officially not the Most Eligible Bachelor in Texas anymore? And what about the charity auction? Rumor has it you're the star of the show."

Rachel backed away as Matt took a step toward the journalist.

"Delete that image now," he demanded. "And there will be no comment."

The lady's eyes widened as she slid her paper and pen back into her oversized purse, then she turned and ran. Matt cursed as he raked a hand through his hair. No doubt the woman was on her way to post the steamy picture on any and every social media site she could.

Dread racked through her. What had she been *thinking*? She couldn't kiss Matt on the sidewalk in broad daylight. He was the main attraction for the auction. Who else had seen the kiss?

None of this was going to work. She and Matt were nearing the end, and that reporter just solidified the fact. Rachel had a baby to look after; she had a career to get started and a new life to create. She needed to provide stability and a solid future for her and Ellie.

Matt's lie, even by omission, and now the fact she'd be all over social media in seconds…damn it, the forces pulling them apart were getting stronger.

Her mind scrambled in so many different directions. She couldn't stay here. That much she was certain of.

Rachel turned toward her car and opened the door.

"Wait," Matt commanded. "Don't go."

She threw a look over her shoulder. "We're done, Matt. And now I have to go do damage control to save you in this auction."

She settled behind the wheel and started to close the door.

"You can't run from us, Rachel," he called out.

One last time, she glanced up to him. "There is no us."

Seventeen

"The press conference is scheduled for tomorrow evening."

Rachel heard Gus's words, but she didn't look up. Since the debacle two days ago with Matt, social media had exploded. Between the media speculation about Texas's most famous bachelor being taken off the market and the biggest draw for the auction in question, Rachel figured the only way to combat this cluster was to hold a press conference. That way she could field questions and make a statement, focusing on the bachelors for the auction, including Matt, and putting to rest any claims that he was off the market.

He certainly wasn't hers—no matter how much she wished he was.

Rachel put another block on top of Ellie's and Ellie promptly kicked them down.

"Listen, darlin', I know you think your man betrayed your trust, but sometimes men do stupid things in the name of love."

Rachel jerked her attention toward where Gus had taken a seat in the leather recliner. "Alexis told you?"

"She gave the important details." He took off his Stetson

and propped it on his bent knee. "Don't be upset with her. She's worried about you and so am I. You're like family to us now."

Rachel couldn't suppress her smile. "You guys feel the same to me."

"As much as I wanted my granddaughter to bid on Matt, I have a feeling he's off the table."

Rachel shook her head and handed Ellie another block. "He's still on," she corrected. "Whatever we had, it's over."

"Because he didn't tell you your husband was going to leave you?" Gus blew out a sigh and eased forward in his chair. "If Matt cared about you even a little bit, he wouldn't want you hurt more than necessary."

Rachel didn't want to argue about this; she didn't want the voice of reason to enter in. Because as far as she was concerned, she had every right to be angry at Matt for keeping the truth from her. Especially after learning that he had no intention of ever telling her. Had his loyalties to her late husband been that strong? Had everyone known Billy was leaving but her?

"I'm sure your mind is racing," Gus went on. "But if you don't listen to anything I say, listen to this. Love doesn't always come around twice in a lifetime. Trust me on that. Very few are lucky enough to get another chance. If you feel anything for Matt, you need to tell him."

Rachel came to her feet and leaned down to pick Ellie up. "Gus, I've come to love you like my own grandfather, but right now I can't handle this. Matt isn't mine, and I'll be sure to emphasize that tomorrow at the press conference. Now, if you'll excuse me, Ellie needs a nap."

Rachel didn't want to sound rude, but she just needed to not talk about Matt or her feelings or anything to do with why she should forgive him. Billy had destroyed her by the hints of infidelity and then rejecting the pregnancy. Now she was going through betrayal all over again with Matt. She never expected him, of all people, to lie to her.

Rachel carried Ellie upstairs and took her time getting her

to sleep. She rocked her, sang to her, held her after her breathing had slowed and she was out. Rachel just wanted to hold on to the one person in her life she treasured more than any other.

Finally, Rachel laid Ellie into her crib and went over to the desk in the corner. She pulled up the screen on her laptop, ready to start looking for a home. It was time she pushed forward and made a life for herself and her daughter. Everything that happened before this moment didn't matter. She would finish her degree, find a house and make good on her promise to allow visitation with Billy's family.

But the second her computer came to life, she remembered she'd been working on a large spread with a photo of each bachelor. Her eyes instantly went to Matt. There was no competition as far as she was concerned. The image she'd used of him in the waterfall made him stand out and beg for attention…just like she'd intended.

Only her plan had backfired, and she had to stare at the photo knowing full well that only seconds after it was taken, her life had irrevocably changed. There would be no going back to friends, no matter how much she would miss him. Because, damn it, her heart hadn't gotten the memo that things were over. She still cared for him, still *loved* him. But how could she ever trust him again?

Rachel couldn't look away from the image. The longer she stared, the more mesmerized she became by that dark stare, those heavy lids, that white cotton shirt plastered in all the right areas.

But Matt wasn't just the sexiest man she'd ever known. He'd been her friend; he'd come to her defense in front of Billy more than once when her late husband had disrespected her. Matt had kept his needs to himself for a decade. Who the hell did that?

Were those the acts of a man in love? Had he loved her in that way? She didn't even know how to analyze all of this information without going absolutely insane.

Right now she had to push her emotions aside, no matter how

difficult the task might be. She had a speech to prepare and bachelors to introduce tomorrow during the press conference. Damage control was just part of marketing, and this whole situation sure as hell gave her much-needed experience...she just wished her heart hadn't been part of the experiment.

Matt pounded the hammer once more, driving the nail home. He came to his feet and surveyed the brand-new porch and roof he'd spent the better part of two days installing.

And no matter how much demolition or renovation he did of his grandfather's home, nothing had exorcised those demons from him.

Rachel still consumed every part of him. He missed the hell out of her. But it wasn't just Rachel; he missed sweet Ellie. The two females had slithered right into his heart and taken up so much real estate, he had no idea how he'd ever lived without them.

He did know one thing: he'd managed to sell off his 51 percent early this morning when Eric finally came up to Matt's asking price. The weight lifted somewhat, but still there was something missing.

The sale would take time to finalize, but Matt wasn't worried about it falling through. He'd make sure it happened so he was free to move on to...whatever the hell he wanted.

Who knew? Maybe he'd take up residence here in Royal and make this old homestead his farm.

Something akin to a blast erupted inside of him, and Matt's breath caught in his throat. He'd called off his contractor, stating he wanted to do the initial work himself. He wanted the grunt work, the outlet for his frustrations, and a way to get back to his roots when he'd bonded with his grandfather. He would have his guy come in and take over soon enough, but for now, this was his baby to nurture.

He'd brought Rachel here and she'd helped. The most precious times of his life were spent right here in Royal...both past and present.

How the hell had he not seen this before now?

Matt stared up the two-story home once again, now looking at it in a whole new light. He instantly saw the place transformed. He imagined Ellie on the steps playing with dolls and Rachel swinging on the porch with her belly swollen with his child. He saw love and he saw a family he never knew he wanted...but couldn't live without.

Matt checked the time on his cell and calculated. He had just enough of a span to put his plan into motion. There was no way in hell he was letting Rachel get away. He'd waited this long for her, and now that he realized his true feelings, the future he wanted with her, he couldn't let this opportunity pass him by.

She was his best friend, but he wanted more. He wanted everything, and Matt Galloway never stopped until he got what he wanted.

Eighteen

Rachel set her notes on the podium in the TCC clubhouse. She'd opted to use the back gardens as the area for the auction, and that was still being revamped. She wanted to keep the reveal of the changes a surprise. But she'd peeked in when she'd first arrived, and Austin Bradshaw was doing a fabulous job. She couldn't wait to see the end result.

As she glanced over her notes once more, she cursed her shaky hands. She just wanted to get this press conference over with so they could focus on what was important. The actual charity event. If they didn't bring in the projected goal, Rachel would never forgive herself. She only hoped she hadn't blown it with the whole kiss scene that had been plastered all over.

"All set?"

Alexis came up the aisle of chairs with a wide smile on her face. Her long hair spiraled down around her shoulders and she had on the prettiest floral dress with boots. If she didn't watch out, some man would make a bid for her.

"As ready as I can be," Rachel stated, stepping down from the stage. "It's almost go time. Is anyone out there?"

Alexis laughed. "Honey, this is the hottest thing in Royal and any surrounding town right now. There are hordes of people from several media outlets, plus some prominent citizens outside those doors."

"Well, that didn't help my nerves."

Alexis closed the distance between them and took Rachel's hands. "I figured you'd want to know what you were dealing with."

With a shaky breath, Rachel nodded. "You're right. I'd rather know what I'm facing."

Alexis gave a gentle squeeze. "You know, it's not too late to adjust those notes and have sixteen bachelors instead of seventeen."

Considering Matt hadn't contacted her since she drove away, she'd have to disagree. Not that she'd reached out to him, either. Apparently they were truly over and she'd just have to suffer through the auction in a few months and watch some lucky woman buy him up and whisk him away.

"Whatever we had, it's over." Maybe if she kept repeating those words out loud, and even in her mind, she'd start to believe them. "He hurt me and I just think we started off like Billy and I did. Maybe I mistook lust for love."

Liar, liar.

"You love Matt and he loves you." Alexis dropped her hands. "If you don't bid on that man, I'll bid on him myself."

Rachel smiled. "Well, that would make your grandfather happy."

Alexis tipped her head. "He would be a gift to you."

"Then save your money or bid on Daniel."

Alexis stiffened. "There's nothing going on there. I wish you'd quit bringing it up."

Rachel shrugged. "Then drop Matt and we'll call a truce."

After a long pause, Alexis nodded. "Fine. But you have nothing holding you back from taking what you so clearly want. You might never get a chance like this again."

Her friend turned and headed toward the doors leading into the clubhouse. Rachel closed her eyes and willed herself the strength to get through this press conference. She needed to sound convincing when she laid her claim that she and Matt were friends and the kiss was nothing.

Perhaps they wouldn't know she was lying to save her own ass.

Moments later the loud chatter enveloped her, and Rachel pasted a smile on her face as guests took their seats. This was the most pivotal moment before the auction because she would be quoted. And, to take the pressure off her and Matt and the scandal they'd created, she had visuals of the bachelors to hopefully get the media to focus on the auction and not the infamous kiss.

A kiss she was still feeling. Because no matter how much she tried to ignore her emotions, she couldn't get Matt out of her mind, and every moment she thought of him, her body heated.

Damn man had too much power over her. She fell in love with him easily; maybe she could fall out of love just as effortlessly?

If only flipping emotions on and off were a possibility, she could save herself more heartache.

Once everyone was seated, Rachel glanced toward the back of the patio area as Alexis closed the doors and gave her the nod to begin.

Gripping the edge of the podium, Rachel cleared her throat. "Good evening, ladies and gentlemen. I appreciate you all taking time to be here this evening. I have several points to address, but I promise to keep this short.

"There has been some chatter and misinformation spreading like wildfire," she went on. "I'd like to address that first." She took a deep, bracing breath, then continued. "Contrary to what you may have heard, Matt Galloway is still in the bachelor auction. We are thrilled he's contributing, and not only is he offering up his time for a fantasy date, he's also writing a check matching the winning bid for him."

The crowd murmured and a few clapped, just as she'd hoped. So far, so good.

"The picture of Matt and I kissing was harmless," she added with a fake smile as she lied through her teeth, but she pushed on. "We have been friends since college and he'd invited me for lunch to catch up."

After I'd spent the night in his bed.

"The timing was unfortunate and we do hope this will erase any doubt about him being in the auction. That kiss was meaningless and—"

"Nothing about that kiss was meaningless."

The crowd gasped in unison as they turned toward the back of the patio. Rachel shifted her focus as well and spotted Matt striding down the aisle. His dark suit screamed power and she wished she had her camera to capture that intense look on his face...a look all for her.

Her heart thudded even faster. What the hell was he doing here, and why was he sabotaging her press conference?

He stepped up to the stage and stood right next to her, reaching for the mic and angling it toward him.

"What Ms. Kincaid meant to say was there will now only be sixteen bachelors in the auction because I am removing myself."

"What the hell are you doing?" she whispered through gritted teeth.

Completely serious, he shot her a glance. "Saving us."

All at once, reporters shouted questions and came up out of their seats. Rachel glanced at the hyper crowd and in the very back stood her best friend with a wide smile on her face.

"I will take questions, but one at a time, please," Matt requested with so much dignity and authority, she wanted to smack him for...well this. How could she do damage control and hate him for lying when he was literally standing up for her?

"How long have you and Ms. Kincaid been seeing each other?" one reporter shouted.

Behind the podium, he reached for her hand. That was solely for her benefit, she knew, because nobody could see his actions.

Her heart tumbled.

"Like she said, we've been friends for years. We recently reconnected when I came to Royal for a getaway."

"Are you two getting married? Will you both live here?"

Matt laughed and the low, sensual tone sent shivers of arousal through her. He was making things nearly impossible for her when she just wanted to be angry. Why couldn't he let her be?

"Well, you're jumping the gun," he replied. "I have every intention of asking Rachel to marry me, but I'd hoped to get her alone."

The crowd erupted in cheers and Rachel froze. "You what?" she croaked out.

Matt turned toward her, ignoring the loud crowd. "I want to marry you, Rachel. I want to raise Ellie with you. I want to stay in Royal with you."

He threw those statements out like he was serious. He looked at her like she was the most precious thing in the world. The way he held her hands and waited for her to say something... was he serious?

"Matt—"

"Give me another chance, Rachel. I'll still make a donation to the charity—just name the amount. I love you, and I don't see a future without you in it. Without our family. I want to have more children with you and I hope you'll help me with the farmhouse, because I think it's the perfect place for us."

Well, now he'd gone and done it. Rachel's eyes swelled with tears and she glanced down to their joined hands. "I love you, too," she whispered. "But how can I trust you?"

She realized the room had gone silent. No doubt every reporter had their phones out trying to record this moment, but Rachel couldn't worry about them or what they might or might not put out to the masses.

"I'm terrified," he admitted, resting his forehead against

hers. "I've never done love before, but I want to do it with you. There's nobody else, Rachel. You're it. You can trust me with your heart, because I'm trusting you with mine."

The tears slid down and she could do nothing to stop them at his bold, heart-flipping statement.

"I've never known you to be afraid of anything," she laughed. "What about Dallas?"

He tipped her chin up so she looked directly at him. "Nothing matters but you saying yes."

"What exactly are you asking me for?"

That signature heart-stopping, toe-curling smile spread across his face. "Everything."

She slid a glance to the crowd only to find each and every person had scooted closer to the stage. Rachel laughed as she turned back to Matt.

"I need to finish the press conference."

Matt's eyes studied her, but then he took a step back. Rachel turned back to the podium, glanced down to her useless notes and flung them in the air.

"Bachelor Seventeen is officially off the auction block," she declared.

The hoots and shouts were deafening and Rachel squealed when Matt wrapped his arms around her and kissed the side of her neck as he spun her around.

"I knew you'd end up with me." He smoothed her hair back from her face. "I hate to say I told you so, but…"

Rachel wrapped her arms around him and smacked his lips with a kiss. "I don't mind. You're mine, Matt Galloway. My very own bachelor."

He kissed her back, pouring promises and love into each touch.

"As you can see, we've lost another bachelor."

Rachel laughed against Matt's mouth at Alexis's statement to the crowd.

"I assure you all, we will have plenty of available men to

choose from," Alexis went on, her voice echoing into the mic. "Rachel prepared a wonderful presentation, but she and Matt will be slipping out, and I'll be taking over and answering any questions."

Matt wrapped his arm around Rachel's waist and ushered her down the steps. They attempted to wade through the aisle, but kept getting high fives and hugs and smiles from each guest. Rachel wasn't sure how she'd gone from explaining why Matt was the greatest bachelor for the auction to removing him and agreeing to be his wife in the span of ten minutes.

That pretty much summed up their courtship, though, didn't it? He'd swept back into her life, dredging up emotions she never even knew she had and then forced her to see this second chance she'd been given at a lifetime of happiness.

Of course, to her this had been fast, but to him, he'd had feelings for a decade.

Once they reached the inside of the TCC clubhouse, Matt pulled her down the hallway toward the offices.

"Where are we going?" she asked.

"I have something for you."

Intrigued, she followed him into the office at the end of the hall. Matt closed the door and went to the desk.

"I brought this with me because I didn't want to wait." He pulled something from the drawer and turned back to her. "I'm sorry I hurt you, after Billy's death and again the other day. That was never my intention. Hell, Rachel, I'd do anything for you and Ellie."

The fact he always included Ellie warmed her heart. The small box he held in his hand had her heart catching in her throat.

"I didn't want to do this out there," he admitted, closing the space between them. "But I have this ring that belonged to my grandmother. I've had it since my grandfather gave it to me just before his death. He made me promise I would only give it to someone I loved."

Matt opened the blue velvet box and revealed a bright ruby with smaller diamonds flanking each side. Rachel gasped, her hand to her mouth as she tried to control her emotions.

"I know it's not the biggest or the flashiest," he went on. "I'll buy you anything you want. Hell, you wanted an island. I'll get you one of those, too."

Rachel shook her head, causing even more tears to spill down her cheeks. "No. I want this ring and I want your island."

Having something from his past made her feel even more special.

Matt pulled the ring from the box and slid the band onto her finger. "It fits," he said, relief flooding his tone.

"Of course it does." She admired the vibrant red stone. "We fit."

Matt circled his arms around her waist and tugged her against him. "Let's go get Ellie and head back to my penthouse."

"Were you serious about staying in Royal at the farm?"

Matt framed her face and placed a soft kiss on her lips. "If that's okay with you. We can escape to Galloway Cove any time you need a break, but I want you to finish that degree. Who knows, maybe we can start up a company together. What do you think?"

Rachel smiled. "I think we'd be a hell of a team."

* * * * *

Million Dollar Baby

Janice Maynard

USA TODAY bestselling author **Janice Maynard** loved books and writing even as a child. After multiple rejections, she finally sold her first manuscript! Since then, she has written fifty-plus books and novellas. Janice lives in Tennessee with her husband, Charles. They love hiking, traveling and family time. You can connect with Janice at www.janicemaynard.com, www.Twitter.com/janicemaynard, www.Facebook.com/janicemaynardreaderpage, www.Facebook.com/janicesmaynard and www.Instagram.com/janicemaynard.

Books by Janice Maynard

The Kavanaghs of Silver Glen

A Not-So-Innocent Seduction
Baby for Keeps
Christmas in the Billionaire's Bed
Twins on the Way
Second Chance with the Billionaire
How to Sleep with the Boss
For Baby's Sake

Highland Heroes

His Heir, Her Secret
On Temporary Terms

Visit her Author Profile page at
millsandboon.com.au,
or janicemaynard.com, for more titles.

Dear Reader,

My husband and I met in high school and married between our sophomore and junior years in college. (FYI: we graduated together *and* on time—go us!) I barely remember *not* loving Charlie, so my firsthand knowledge of "dating" as a twentysomething adult is nonexistent.

When I am writing a book, I have to put myself in the shoes of many different characters whose life experiences are different from mine. In the case of Austin and Brooke, who meet in a Texas bar, it was really a leap of faith for me to imagine that scenario.

Not only that, but I had to empathize with what it would be like to grow up in a town where everybody knows your business (and knows your parents).

I had such fun writing this book. Brooke became very special to me as she struggled to have the life she wanted. And my heart ached for Austin, who felt things so deeply and yet was a loner in many ways.

Thanks for loving books!

Janice Maynard

One

A dimly lit bar filled with rowdy patrons was an uncomfortable place to be on a Thursday night near the witching hour... if you were a woman without a date and too shy to make eye contact with anyone. The music was loud, masking Brooke's unease.

She was lonely and so very tired of being the forgotten Goodman child. She'd spent her entire life toeing some invisible line, and what had it gotten her? Neither of her parents respected her. Her two older brothers were out conquering the world. And where was Brooke? Stuck at home with Mom and Dad in Royal, Texas. Held hostage by their expectations and her own eager-to-please personality. The whole situation sucked.

She nursed her virgin strawberry daiquiri and stared at the tiny seeds nestling in the ice. Impulsive decisions were more her style than drunken peccadilloes. Brooke had seen too many of her friends almost ruin their lives with a single alcohol-fueled mistake. She might be crazy, but she was clearheaded.

Suddenly, she realized that the band had vacated the stage. The remaining plaintive music—courtesy of the lone guitar player—suited Brooke's mood. She didn't even mind the peanut-strewn floor and the smell of stale beer. At the same moment, she saw a man sitting alone at the bar, three empty stools on either side of him. Something about his broad shoulders made the breath catch in her throat. She had seen him walk in earlier. Instantaneous attraction might be a quirk of pheromones, but yearning had curled in the pit of her stomach even then. Sadly, the dance floor had been too crowded, and she had lost sight of him before she could work up the courage to introduce herself.

Now, here he was. All the scene needed was a shaft of light from heaven to tell her *this* was the man. *This* was her moment. She wanted him.

Butterflies fluttered through her. *Oh, God.* Was she really going to do it? Was she really going to pick up a stranger?

There was little question in her mind that he was her type. Even seated, she could tell that he was tall. His frame was leanly muscled and lanky, his posture relaxed. His dark blond hair—what she could see of it beneath the Stetson—was rumpled enough to be interesting and had a slight curl that gave him an approachable charm. Unfortunately, she couldn't gauge the color of his eyes from this distance.

Before she could change her mind, she lurched to her feet, frosty glass in hand, and made her way across the room. Not a single person stopped her. Not a single person joined the solitary man at the bar.

Surely it was a sign.

Taking a deep breath, she set her drink and her tiny clutch purse on the polished mahogany counter and hopped up on the leather-covered stool. No need to panic. It was only a conversation so far. That's all.

Now that she was close to him, she felt a little dizzy.

She gnawed her bottom lip and summoned a smile. "Hello, Cowboy. Mind if I join you?"

* * *

Austin glanced sideways and felt a kick of disappointment. The little blonde was a beauty, but she was far too young for him. Her gray eyes held an innocence he had lost years ago.

He shot her a terse smile. "Sorry, ma'am. I was about to leave."

Her face fell. "Oh, don't go. I thought we could chat."

He lifted an eyebrow. "Chat?"

Mortification stained her cheeks crimson. "Well, you know…"

"I *don't* know," he said. "That's the point. This could be a sorority prank, or maybe you're a not-quite-legal girl trying to lose her virginity. You look about sixteen, and I'm not keen to end up in jail tonight."

She scowled at him. "That's insulting."

"Not at all. You reek of innocence. It's a compliment, believe me. Unfortunately, I'm not the guy you're looking for."

"Maybe I want one who doesn't end sentences with prepositions."

The bite in her voice made him grin. "Are you insinuating that I'm uneducated?"

"Don't change the subject. For your information, I'm twenty-six. Plenty old enough to know my own mind." She took a deep breath. "I'm in the mood for romance."

"I think you mean sex."

He drawled the five words slowly, for nothing more than the pleasure of watching all that beautiful creamy skin turn a darker shade of dusky pink. "Sex?" The word came out as a tiny high-pitched syllable. Huge, smoky, thickly lashed eyes stared up at him.

This time he hid the grin. Poor kid was petrified.

He couldn't deny that he was tempted. She was genuine and sweet and disarmingly beautiful…in a healthy, girl-next-door kind of way. Her pale blond hair was caught up in a careless ponytail, and her royal-blue silk shirt and skinny jeans were nothing pretentious. Even her ballerina flats were unexceptional. She was the kind of woman who probably looked exactly this good when she rolled out of bed in the morning.

That thought took him down a road he needed to avoid. His sex hardened, making his pants uncomfortable. He held out his hand, attempting to normalize the situation. "I'm Au—"

She slapped her hand over his mouth, interrupting his polite introduction. "No," she said, sounding desperate and anxious all at the same time. "I'll call you Cowboy. You can call me Mandy."

He took her wrist and moved her hand away. "Not your real name?"

"No."

"Ah. Aliases. Intriguing."

"You're making fun of me." Her face fell.

"Maybe a little." He smiled to let her know he was teasing.

Without warning, their flirtatious repartee was rudely curtailed. A tall, statuesque redhead took the bar stool at his right shoulder and curled an arm around his waist. "Buy me another beer, will you? Sorry I was gone so long. Who the hell thinks it's a good idea to build a ladies' room with only a single stall?"

Austin groaned inwardly. *Damn.* He'd actually forgotten about Audra for a moment. "Um…"

Poor *Mandy* went dead white and looked as if she were going to throw up. "Excuse me," she said, with all the politeness of a guest at high tea with the queen. "It was a pleasure to meet you, but I have to go now."

Thank God Audra was a quick study. She sized up the situation in a glance. Her eyes widened. "Oh, crap. I'm sorry. Don't go. I'm his sister. Honest."

Mandy hesitated.

Austin nodded. "It's true. Underneath that bottled red hair is a blonde just like me."

Audra stood up and grimaced. "Forget the beer, little brother. I'll grab a cab. See you at the house later."

Then his five-years-older sister went completely off script. She stepped around him and took both of Mandy's hands in hers. "Here's the thing, ma'am. I know it's sometimes scary to meet men these days. Getting hit on in a bar can be dangerous."

"*She* was hitting on *me*," Austin muttered.

Both women ignored him.

Audra continued. "My brother is a good, decent man. He doesn't have any diseases, and he doesn't assault women. You don't have to be afraid of him."

"Audra!" His head threatened to explode from embarrassment.

Mandy barely glanced at him. "I see."

Audra nodded. "He doesn't live here. He's in town visiting me, and we came out tonight to...well..."

For once, his outrageous sister looked abashed.

Mandy gave him a puzzled look. "To what?"

Dear Lord. He gritted his teeth. If he didn't tell her, Audra would. "Today is the anniversary of my wife's death. She's been gone for six years. I finally took my wedding ring off, thanks to my sister's badgering. That's it. That's all."

Tears welled in Mandy's eyes. She blinked them back, but one rolled down her cheek. "I had no idea. I am so sorry."

Audra patted her shoulder. "It was a long time ago. He's fine."

Austin got to his feet and grabbed his sister's arm none too gently despite her glowing character testimonial. "You're leaving. Now."

He glanced back at Mandy. "Don't move."

On the way to the door, Audra smirked at him. "I won't wait up for you. Have fun tonight."

"You are such a brat."

Outside on the sidewalk, he hugged her. "I won't discuss my love life with you. A man has boundaries."

Audra kissed his cheek. "Understood. I just want you to be happy, that's all."

"I am happy," he said.

"Liar."

"I'm happier than I was."

"Go back in there before she gets cold feet."

"I love you, sis."

"I love you, too."

He watched his only sibling get into a cab, and then he looked through the window into the bar where not one but two men had taken advantage of his absence to move in on Mandy.

No way. No way in hell. The little blonde was his. At least for tonight.

Brooke breathed a sigh of relief when her cowboy returned and dispersed the crowd that had gathered around her. Apparently if the hour was late enough and the man drunk enough, even the most vehement no didn't register.

When it was just the two of them again, the cowboy gave her a slow, intimate smile that curled her toes. "May I buy you another drink?"

"No, thanks. I wasn't drinking. Not really. Alcohol clouds a person's judgment. I wanted to be clearheaded tonight."

"I see." He cocked his head and studied her. "Do you live here in Joplin?"

"Nope."

"So we're both just passing through?"

"It would seem that way."

A small grin teased the corners of his mouth. The man had a great mouth. Really great. She could imagine kissing that mouth all night long.

Finally, he shook his head, bemusement in his baffled gaze. "I know what *I'm* doing here, *Mandy*, but I'm still not clear about why you showed up at this bar tonight."

"Does it matter?" She hadn't expected a man to quiz her. The fact that her cowboy was slowing things down rattled her.

He nodded. "It does to me."

"Maybe I'm horny."

He snorted out a laugh and tried to turn it into a cough...unsuccessfully. Then he rubbed two fingers in the center of his forehead and sighed. "I'm not asking for your life story. But I'd like to know why me and why tonight. Is this a rebound thing? Are you trying to teach someone a lesson? Am I even warm?"

"Ninety-nine men out of a hundred would already have me in bed right now."

"Sorry to disappoint you."

The look in his eyes made her feel like a naughty schoolgirl. And not in a good way. She drained the last of her melted daiquiri and wrinkled her nose. "My life is boring. I'm having some family issues. For once I wanted to do something wild and exciting and totally out of character. Plus, you're really hot."

"So you *don't* frequent bars as a rule?"

"You know I don't," she grumbled, "or I wouldn't be so bad at it."

He flicked the end of her ponytail. "I never said you were bad at it."

Some deep note in his voice caught her stomach and sent it into a free fall of excitement and anticipation. "So are we good now?" she asked.

The cowboy stared at her. He stared at her for so long that her nipples pebbled and her thighs clenched. "What makes you believe that you and I will be wild and exciting? What if you chose wrong?"

She gaped. Words escaped her.

He closed her mouth with a finger below her chin. "It would seem prudent to take me out for a test drive ahead of time... don't you think?"

Before she could do more than inhale a sharp, startled breath, he slid one big hand beneath her ponytail, cupped the base of her neck and pulled her toward him just far enough for their mouths to meet comfortably.

Actually, *comfortable* was a misnomer for what happened next. Fireworks shot toward the ceiling in all directions. Angel choirs sang. A million dizzying pinwheels shot through her veins and rocketed into her pelvis.

The man was kissing her. Nothing more. So why was the earth shaking beneath her feet?

He tasted of whiskey and temptation. If she'd had any remaining reservations about her plan, they vanished in the heat of his lips on hers. It was possible she whimpered. She definitely leaned in and wordlessly begged for more.

Somewhere in the distance catcalls and whoops and hollers signaled an appreciative audience. But Brooke barely noticed. Her hands settled on the cowboy's shoulders. "Take off your hat," she begged.

"I only take off the hat in bed," he said, the words rough with lust and determination.

"Oh."

His smile was more of a grimace. "It's not too late for you to walk away. In fact, it's never too late. You started this little fantasy, but you can say no whenever you want."

She looked up at him, feeling the oddest combination of confidence and stomach-curling uncertainty. "I don't want to say no."

"Do you have a hotel room?"

"Not yet."

"Any preference?"

"Not somewhere fancy." Translation—nowhere that the staff might know her parents.

His terse nod seemed to indicate agreement. "Let's go, then." He tossed money on the bar for the tab and took her elbow as they walked out.

Outside, they paused on the sidewalk. It was August, and the air was pleasant at this hour. He pointed at a late-model pickup truck. "Would you like me to drive?"

Brooke shook her head. Who knew that the mechanics of a one-night stand were so tricky? "My things are in my car. I'll meet you there. How about the Sherwood Hotel? Two streets over?"

"I know it."

"I'm sorry," she said, feeling brutally young and stupid.

"For what?"

"I'm sorry you lost your wife."

He cursed beneath his breath, rolled his shoulders and stared up at the moon, his profile starkly masculine. "You told me we weren't going to use our real names," he said. "That was *your* rule. Well, mine is no rehashing the past. This is sex, Mandy. Wild and exciting and temporary—if that's not what you want, walk away."

His entire body vibrated with tension. She honestly couldn't tell if he was angry or sexually frustrated or both.

In that moment, she realized that her reasons for coming to Joplin no longer existed. She wasn't here to flirt or to pick up a stranger or to have an anonymous tryst to prove to herself that she wasn't boring.

Right here, right now…with her limbs shaking and her mouth dry and her nerves shot…the only thing she wanted was to undress this cowboy and to have him return the favor. Because this man, this beautiful, hauntingly complicated man, tugged at her heartstrings. She wanted to know him in every way there was to know a lover.

She only had one night. It would have to be enough.

Daringly, she reached out and put a hand on his arm. She could feel his taut, warm muscles through the soft cotton fabric of his shirt. "I don't want to walk away, Cowboy. I'll meet you at the hotel. Don't make me wait."

TWO

Austin Bradshaw couldn't be entirely sure he wasn't dreaming. This night was like nothing he had ever experienced. He glanced in his rearview mirror to make sure Mandy's little navy Honda was still behind him. He chuckled to himself, because he had a hunch the car was a rental. His mystery woman struck him as the kind of person who would attend to the details of a plan with great care.

The desk clerk at the midrange hotel was neither curious nor particularly friendly. He swiped Austin's credit card, handed over two keys and immediately returned his focus to whatever show he was watching on his laptop.

When Austin went back outside, he found Mandy leaning against the side of his pickup, an overnight case in her hand. She shifted from one foot to the other. "All set?"

He stared at her. "Are you sure you want to do this?"

"Quit asking me that," she huffed. "I'm here, aren't I?"

Releasing a slow, steady breath, he took the bag out of her death grip and set it on the ground. Then he cupped her head in his hands, tilted her face up to his and crushed his mouth over hers. He'd been in a state of arousal now for the better part of two hours. The faint scent of her perfume and the taste of her lips were imprinted on his brain.

He wanted her. Naked. Hungry. Begging. The more he thought about the night to come, the more he unraveled. At the rate they were going, there wasn't going to be much of the night left.

Reluctantly, he let her go. "Hurry," he said.

The hotel was three stories tall with indoor corridors and modern decor. At this point, Austin could have taken her up against the wall in the stairwell, but he resisted.

They rode the elevator to the top floor. Their room was at the end on the corner. His hand shook so badly it took him three tries to get the key in the door. He expected Mandy to give him grief about it, but she never said a word.

When they were finally inside, he closed the door carefully in deference to their fellow guests and leaned against it.

Mandy frowned. "Where's your bag?"

"I don't have one."

"Why not?"

"That's not really how a one-night stand works, honey."

She looked mortified. "Why didn't you tell me?"

"I thought you'd be more comfortable if you had your bag. Women like to have their little bits and pieces with them."

Mandy wrapped her arms around her waist and scanned the room like she was casing it for fire exits.

"What's wrong?" he asked, reminding himself that patience was a virtue.

Her bottom lip trembled. "I just realized something. If tonight is your first time to have sex in six years, I can't go through with this. That's too much pressure for me. Honestly."

He burst out laughing, and then laughed even harder at the look of indignation on her face. "Not to worry," he said, wiping his cheeks and trying to get himself under control. His companion clearly didn't see the humor in the situation. "I've had sex. Occasionally. And besides, if what you said were true, we'd never have made it out of the parking lot back at the bar. So no pressure, okay? Just you and me and all that wild excitement you wanted."

Some of the tension drained from her body. "Oh. Well, that's good. I guess."

"Come here, honey." He held out his hand.

She came to him willingly. But her gaze didn't quite meet his, and her cheeks were flushed.

He unbuttoned the top button of her shirt. "Your skin is like cream. Beautiful and smooth." Brushing the tops of her breasts with his fingertips, he smiled inwardly when she sighed.

"You're still wearing your hat," she said.

"And we're still not in bed."

"Close enough." She reached up and took off his Stetson. After tossing it on the nearest chair, she massaged his head with both hands. "You shouldn't cover up your hair. Women would kill for this color."

He could tell she was more comfortable with him now. That was a very good thing, because he didn't want a timid partner in bed. "Feel free to take off anything else that catches your fancy."

"Very funny." She toyed with his belt buckle. "Why aren't you calling me Mandy?"

"Because you don't look like a Mandy. It's not your real name. So I'll stick with *honey*. Unless you want to fess up and tell me the truth. It's not like I'm going to stalk you."

"I know that." The snippy response was the tiniest bit sulky. And her bottom lip stuck out. It was so damned cute, he wanted to suck on it.

Gently, he pulled her shirt loose from the waistband of her jeans and slid his hands underneath. Her skin was warm and soft. So soft. He wanted to make this night good for her.

He unhooked her bra. It still bothered him that he didn't know why she was here…not really. But his brain was losing the battle with the driving urge to give her what she wanted. What *he* wanted.

When he slipped her shirt from her shoulders and took her bra right along with it, she didn't protest. The sight of her standing there, all white creamy skin and big gray eyes and rosy pink nipples, stole his breath and tightened his gut. "God, you're gorgeous," he said huskily, breathing it like a prayer.

He hadn't lied to her. There had been a handful of women in six years. But those had been *real* one-night stands. Women whose names and faces he barely remembered. Divorcées. Widows hurting like he was. The sex had slaked a momentary physical need, but afterward, his grief had been just as deep, just as raw.

In a way, it had been easier *not* to have sex, because that way he didn't have to be reminded of all he had lost.

He scooped her up in his arms and carried her to the bed. Something about tonight felt different. Maybe because his mystery woman was ridiculously charming and vulnerable and maybe even a little bit naive. She brought out his protective instincts and tapped into raw emotions inside him that he would have sworn were dead and buried.

With her he felt the need to be tender.

"Hang on, honey." Hitching her higher on his chest, he grabbed for the comforter with one hand and dragged it and the sheet halfway down the bed. Then he dropped the big-eyed blonde on the mattress and tried not to pounce on her. Instead, he came down beside her and propped his head on his hand.

Lazily, he traced a fingertip from her collarbone, down between her breasts, over her concave belly to her tiny cute navel. "Tell me what you're thinking, sweet lady. I swear I don't bite."

Her body was so rigid it was giving *him* a headache.

She gnawed her lower lip. "I forgot about protection."

"Not to worry. We're good for two rounds." He reached in his back pocket and extracted a duo of condom packets. "I had these in the truck."

"Oh. That's nice."

"Tell me your name," he coaxed. He bent over her and kissed his way from her navel up along her rib cage, pausing just at the slope of her breast and waiting until her breathing ratcheted up a notch and a shudder worked its way through her body.

"You're not playing fair…" She gazed up at him from underneath sultry lashes.

Did she have any idea what that look did to a man? He flicked his tongue across her nipple…barely a graze. "I play to win, honey. You wanted wild and exciting? That usually means breaking the rules."

He was breathing hard, barely holding it together. Playing this game was fun, more fun than he'd had in a hell of a long time. But he wasn't sure how much longer he could last. Already he wanted her so badly he was shaking.

"Brooke," she whispered. "My name is Brooke."

The trust on her face made him ashamed. She was doing something out of character. He knew it. And he was prepared to help her in her quest for a night of reckless passion. What kind of man did that make him?

He swallowed hard. "Brooke. I like it. With an *e* or no *e*?"

She smiled. "Does it matter?"

"It does to me." And it did. When this was over and they went their separate ways, he wanted to remember her exactly like this. He wanted to know everything there was to know.

She caressed his chin, feeling the stubble. He'd shaved at six that morning. "With an *e*, Cowboy. Now it's your turn."

He didn't pretend to misunderstand. "Austin," he groaned. "My name is Austin." Moving his lips across her breast, he kissed his way up hills and down valleys and back again until Brooke panted and whimpered and begged. That was the sign he had been waiting for.

He rolled to his feet and ripped at his shirt, dragging it over his head in one frustrated motion. Then he toed off his boots and shucked out of his jeans and boxers. When he was buck-ass naked, he stood beside the bed and tried to catch his breath. It was embarrassing to be so winded when he hadn't even started yet.

Brooke came up on her knees and stared. "Are you normal?"

He blinked. "Excuse me?"

She waved a hand. "Your, um…you know. It seems kind of big."

A slither of unease sent ice water through his veins. "You wouldn't lie to me about that virgin thing. Would you?"

She straightened her shoulders, her eyes flashing. "I am *not* a liar."

"So you've definitely had sex."

"Of course."

"How many times?"

"That's none of your business." She unbuttoned her jeans and shimmied them down her thighs.

His mouth went dry. "I was gonna do that."

She gave him a look. "You were taking too long. I'm not sure I picked the right man. Are you positive you know what you're doing?"

He didn't know whether to laugh or howl with frustration. "God, you're a piece of work."

"You promised me wild and exciting. I'm still wearing panties."

He grabbed her around the waist and tumbled them both to the bed, rolling so they landed with Brooke on top. She was easily eight inches shorter than he was and forty pounds lighter. She pretended to struggle. He pretended to let her. When they were both breathless, he kissed her hard.

She melted into him, purring his name with soft, erotic yearning that made every cell in his body ache.

He rubbed her back. "I'm glad you walked into my life tonight, Brooke with no last name." Her ponytail had come loose. Pale, sunshiny hair tumbled around them, soft and silky. It smelled like lilacs and innocence and happy summer afternoons.

She nibbled his chin. "Me, too. I nearly chickened out, but then I saw you sitting there, and I felt something."

"Something?" He palmed her bottom. It was a perfect bottom. Plump and pert and exactly the right size for a man's hands.

"A zing, I guess. Animal attraction." She shifted her weight and nearly injured him. He was so hard his balls ached. The condom was in arm's reach. All he had to do was grab it. But he didn't want this to be over. He didn't want the night to end.

Without warning, Brooke rolled off him, settled onto her side, and took his sex in her hand. "I like the way you look, Cowboy." She stroked him slowly, her gaze focused on the task at hand.

The feel of her cool slender fingers on his taut flesh skated the line between pleasure and pain. He gritted his teeth and tried not to come. "I told you my name," he groaned.

She rested her cheek on his shoulder and continued her torture. "Yes, you did." She gripped him tightly. "Austin." She whispered it low and sweet.

Sweat broke out on his brow. This woman was killing him slowly...

Brooke was hot and dizzy and elated. For an idea that had begun so badly, this was turning out to be a night to remember. Austin was everything she could have asked for in a lover. Demanding and yet tender. Tough and masculine, but still considerate of her insecurities.

He grabbed her wrist and moved it away from his erection. "Enough," he croaked.

Before she could protest, he reached for the condom, rolled it on and dragged her panties down her legs. Then he was on top of her and in her and she forgot how to breathe.

He was heavy and wildly aroused. Thankfully, she was equally excited. Despite his impressive stats, her body accepted him easily. It had been a long time for her, but he didn't have to know that. She canted her hips, tried to relax and concentrated on the incredible sensation of fullness as her body became one with his.

Something about the moment dampened her eyes and tightened her throat. Maybe it was the thought of all he had lost. Maybe it was a breathless yearning to have a man like this for her own one day. Whatever it was, it made her weepy and left her feeling raw and vulnerable. As if it were impossible to hide from him.

He came quickly, with a muttered apology, his chest heaving. Brooke tried to squelch her disappointment. After a quick trip to the bathroom to dispose of the condom, he returned. In their hurry, they had left the lamp on. Now, he flipped the switch, plunging the room into darkness. Only an automatic night-light in the bathroom dispersed some of the gloom as their eyes adjusted.

Austin smoothed the hair from her face. "I'm sorry about that, honey. You had me pretty wound up, and it's been a little while for me."

"It's fine."

His grin was a flash of white. "It's *not* fine. But it will be. Spread your legs, darlin'. Let me show you the fireworks."

She moved her ankles apart obediently, but inside, she grimaced. This had never been her strong suit. It was too personal, too intimate. The only man who had ever gotten this far with her had been really bad at it.

Fortunately, Austin wasn't privy to her negative thoughts. He cradled her head in his arm and touched her with confidence, the confidence of a man who knew how to pleasure a woman and liked doing it. "Close your eyes," he crooned. "Relax, Brooke."

It was only when he said those two words that she realized her fingers were clenched in the sheets and her shoulders were rigid. "Sorry," she muttered. "You don't have to do this."

Austin frowned. "I need to touch you. Your body is beautiful and soft and so damn sexy. I want to hear you scream my name."

"Arrogant cowboy…"

He entered her with two fingers and used his thumb to stroke the spot where she ached the most. The keening cry that escaped her throat was embarrassing. But soon, embarrassment was the furthest thing from her mind.

Austin decimated her. He whispered naughty things and caressed her with sure steady touches until her own responses shocked her and her body became a stranger. Just as her spine arched off the bed, she did indeed scream his name. Moments later, he moved on top of her and entered her a second time.

The orgasm was incredible. On a scale of one to ten, it was some imaginary number that only scientists from outer space could decipher.

This time, Austin was just getting started as she tumbled down the far side of the hill. He laughed roughly and shoved her up the peak again, thrusting harder and faster and holding her tightly until they both found the pinnacle at almost the same moment and lost themselves in the fiery pleasure.

Brooke was boneless, elated and utterly spent. Never again would she settle for the kind of relationship that was boring and mundane. This wonderful cowboy had given her that.

They lay together in a tangle of arms and legs as their bodies cooled and their heartbeats slowed.

At last, Austin shifted so she wasn't bearing his full weight. "You okay?" he asked, sounding sleepy and sated and maybe a little bit smug.

She nuzzled her head against his warm, hard shoulder. "Oh, yeah. Better than okay." Tomorrow morning, she was going to get online and give this hotel five stars across the board.

He groaned and rolled away. "Don't move. I'm coming back."

She heard the water run in the bathroom. Then silence. Then a low curse.

"What's wrong?" she said, raising her voice in alarm.

He stumbled back into bed, his skin chilled. "The condom broke." His voice was flat. She couldn't read him at all.

"Oh."

"I'm sorry."

"It's okay. I'm on the pill. For other reasons. And besides, it's the wrong time of the month." She was due to start her period any day, actually.

"I'm healthy, Brooke. Nothing to worry about there."

"Then we're in the clear."

He yawned and pulled her into his arms, spooning her from behind. "Let me sleep for an hour, and we can go again."

"You're out of condoms."

He kissed the nape of her neck. "We'll improvise."

Brooke lay perfectly still and felt the exact moment when Austin crashed hard. His breathing deepened. The arm that encircled her became heavy.

She knew the time had come for her to go home, but she couldn't leave him. Not yet. This night had turned into something she hadn't anticipated, something she hadn't really wanted.

Here was a man who had known pain and loss. Even if they lived in the same town, he wouldn't want a woman like her. She couldn't even stand up to her parents. She had her own battles to fight. And she would have to do it without this sweet, gruff cowboy.

She inhaled his scent. Tried to memorize it. The way his body held hers seemed fated somehow. But that was a lie. He was a man she had picked up in a bar. A man with demons, like any other man.

Carefully, with her chest tight and her hands shaking, she extracted herself from his arms one heartbeat at a time. It wasn't easy. Fortunately, Austin slept like the dead. Once she was out of the bed, the rest went smoothly.

She visited the bathroom. She dressed quietly. She took her bag and her purse and slipped out into the hall.

On the other side of the door, she started to shake. Leaving her one-night stand cowboy was the hardest thing she had ever had to do.

The drive from Joplin to Royal in the middle of the night

seemed surreal. Punching in the alarm code and sneaking into the house was almost anticlimactic. She was too tired to shower. Instead, she tumbled into bed and fell asleep instantly.

Three

Two months later

Austin parked his truck across the street from the Texas Cattleman's Club, got out and stretched. It had been three years... maybe four...since he had last been in Royal, Texas. Not much had changed. An F4 tornado a while back had destroyed a few homes and businesses and damaged others, but the town had rebuilt.

The club itself was a historic structure over a hundred years old. The rambling single-story building with its dark stone-and-wood exterior and tall slate roof was an icon in the area. Ordinarily, Austin wouldn't be the kind of guy to darken the doors, but he was meeting Gus Slade here at 10:00 a.m.

Austin had plenty of money in the bank...likely more than he would ever need. But he didn't have the blue-blooded ranching pedigree that men like Gus respected. Still, Gus had invited him here to do a job, and Austin had agreed.

Audra was right. He'd been drifting since Jenny died. It was time to get his business back on track. He'd rambled all over a five-county area in recent years doing odd jobs to pay the bills. The truth was, he was a damned good architect and had been wasting his skills.

Even this job with Gus was a throwaway. But it could open the doors to something more significant, so he had jumped at the chance.

He took his time crossing the street. No need to look too eager. Already, he had made concessions. Instead of his usual jeans and flannel shirt, he had worn neatly pressed khakis, a spotless white dress shirt with the sleeves rolled up and his best pair of boots. Cowboys came in all shapes and sizes in Texas. Austin was shooting for ambitious professional for today's meeting.

It was who he had been once upon a time. Until Jenny got sick…

Shoving away the unhappy memories, he ran a hand through his hair, flipped his phone to silent mode and strode through the imposing front doors. A smiling receptionist directed him to one of the private meeting rooms partway down the hall.

Augustus "Gus" Slade was already there, deep in conversation with two other men. When Austin appeared, Gus's two companions said their goodbyes and exited.

Gus held out his hand. "There you are, boy. Right on the money. Thanks for coming. It's been a long time."

"It's good to see you, sir. Thanks for offering me the job."

Gus was an imposing figure of a man. He was tall and solidly built with a full head of snow-white hair. Piercing eyes that were blue like the Texas sky reflected a keen intelligence.

By Austin's calculations, the man was probably sixty-eight or sixty-nine. He could have passed for a decade younger were it not for the leatherlike quality of his skin. He'd spent decades working in the sun long before warnings about skin cancer were the norm.

At a time in life when many men his age began to think

about traveling or playing golf or simply taking things easy, Gus still worked his cattle ranch, the Lone Wolf, and wielded his influence in Royal. He had plenty of the latter to go around and had even served a few terms as TCC president. Though the burly rancher loved his family and was well respected by the community at large, most people knew he could be fierce when crossed or angered.

Austin had no plans to do either.

At Gus's urging, Austin settled into one of a pair of wing-backed chairs situated in front of a large fireplace. The weather in Royal was notably mercurial. Yesterday, it had been in the fifties and raining. Today, the temperature was pushing seventy, and the skies were sunny, so no fire.

Gus took the second chair with a grimace and rubbed his knee. "Got kicked by a damned bull. Should have known better."

Austin nodded and smiled. "I worked cattle during the summers when I was in college. It was a great job, but I went to bed sore many a night." He hesitated half a breath and plunged on. "So tell me about this job you want me to do."

When he had been in Royal before, Gus had wanted him to design and build an addition onto his home. Austin had still been paying for Jenny's medical bills, and he had needed the money. So he had worked his ass off for six months...or maybe it was seven.

He'd been proud of the job, and Gus had been pleased.

The older man twisted his mouth into a slight grimace. "I may have brought you here under false pretenses. It's not like last time. This will be a one-and-done project. But as I mentioned on the phone, I think being here at the club for a few weeks will give you the chance to meet some folks in Royal who are movers and shakers. These are the kind of men and women who have contacts. They know people and can make things happen to push work your way."

Austin wasn't sure how he felt about that. On the one hand, it made sense to rebuild his career. It had stalled out when he made the choice to stay home with Jenny during what turned out to be the last months of her life. It was a choice he had never regretted.

Even in the depths of his grief, when he had drifted from town to town and job to job, his skill set and work ethic had made it possible for him to command significant compensation for his quality work.

Did he really want to go back to a more structured way of life?

He honestly didn't know.

And because he didn't, he equivocated. "I appreciate that, sir. But how about you tell me the details of this particular project?"

"The club is hoping to do more with the outside space than we have in the past. Professional landscapers are in the process of developing a site plan for the area around the gardens and the pool. What I want from you is a permanent outdoor venue that will serve as the stage for the charity auction and can later be used for weddings, etc. The audience, or the guests, will be out front…under a circus tent if the weather demands it."

"So open air, but covered."

"You got it. Plus, we want the stage to have at least two or three rooms behind the scenes with bathrooms and changing areas…you get the idea."

"And what is this auction exactly?"

Gus chuckled. "It's a mouthful…the Great Royal Bachelor Auction." He sobered. "To benefit the Pancreatic Cancer Foundation. That's what my Sarah died of, you know. My granddaughter Alexis is on the foundation board. I'd like for you to meet her. Your wife has been gone a long time. It's not good for a man to be alone."

"I mean no disrespect, sir, but you don't seem to be taking your own advice. And beyond that, I have no interest at all in a relationship, though I'm sure your granddaughter is delightful."

Gus scowled at him. "Maybe you shouldn't be so quick to

turn her down. A lot of men would jump at the chance to have my blessing."

Austin smiled. "If Alexis is anything like her grandfather, I'm guessing she doesn't appreciate you meddling in her affairs."

"That's true enough," Gus said. "She seems determined to fritter away her time with a man who is all wrong for her."

They had strayed off topic again, which made Austin realize that Gus was inordinately interested in matchmaking. He sighed. "I'll need a budget. And the exact specs of the area where I'm allowed to build."

"Money's no object," the older man said. "We want top-of-the-line all the way. And make sure to include some kind of outdoor heating units, concealed if possible. You know how it is in Texas. We might wear shorts on Christmas Day, and it can snow eight hours later."

"What's my timetable?" Austin asked.

"The auction is the last Saturday in November."

Austin tried to conceal his shock. "Cutting it a little close, aren't you?"

Gus nodded. "I know. It will be tight. But the club's custodial staff has been given instructions to help you in any way possible, and we've also allotted extra funds to hire part-time carpenters to rough in the framing and anything else you need. I have faith in you, boy."

"Thank you, sir. I won't let you down."

"Call me Gus. I insist."

After that, they made their way outside so Austin could see exactly what he had to work with. Despite his reservations about the quick turnaround, excitement bubbled up in his chest. This was always one of his favorite phases of a project—looking at a bare plot of ground and imagining the possibilities.

The gardens were soggy, but Austin could see that someone had already begun placing markers and lining off planting areas.

Gus pointed. "Over there is where the stage will be."

Austin nodded. "I can work with that."

In the distance, he could see the pool, now closed for the season. The new structure would tie in with the gardens and the rear of the original building to create a peaceful, idyllic setting for entertaining.

To their left, a small figure in stained overalls stood three feet off the ground on a stepladder painting a colorful mural on an outer wall of the club. Gus waved a hand. "Let's go say hello," he said.

It was only a matter of fifteen yards. Twenty at the most. They were close enough for Austin to recognize the pale, silky ponytail when it hit him.

The woman turned around as Gus hailed her. The paintbrush in her hand clattered to the ground. Her face turned white. She clutched the top of the ladder.

Austin sucked in a shocked breath. It was *her*. Brooke. His mystery lover.

Only a clueless fool would have missed the tension, and Gus was no fool. He frowned. "Do you two know each other?"

Austin waited. Ladies first. Brooke stared at him, her eyes curiously blank. "Not at all," she said politely. "How do you do? I'm Brooke Goodman."

What the hell? Austin had no choice but to follow her lead. Or else call her a liar. He stuck out his hand. "Austin Bradshaw. Nice to meet you."

The air crackled with electricity. Brooke didn't take his hand. She held up both of hers, palms out, to show they were paint streaked. "You'll have to excuse me. I don't want to get you dirty." She shifted her attention to Gus. "If you two don't mind, I'm trying to get this section finished quickly. They tell me another band of showers is going to move in tonight, so the paint needs to dry."

And just like that, she turned her back and shut him out.

Four

Brooke felt so ill she was afraid she might pass out right there on the ladder. She stood perfectly still and pretended to paint the same four-inch square of wall until she heard a door open and shut. Out of the corner of her eye she saw the two men disappear inside the building.

What was Austin doing in Royal? Had he come to find her? Surely not. He'd been with Gus Slade. If she put two and two together, maybe Austin was the architect Gus had hired to build the fancy stage and outdoor annex. How did Gus even know Austin?

Who could she ask? Alexis? Then again, did she really want to draw attention to the fact that she was interested in Austin? She wasn't. Not at all.

Liar.

What made the situation even worse was the expression on Austin's face when he saw her. He'd been equal parts flabbergasted and horrified. Not the look a woman wanted to see from a man she'd spent the night with.

And see what he'd done to her, damn it…now he had *her* ending sentences with prepositions.

When the coast was clear, she wiped her brush and gathered her supplies. Ordinarily, she went inside the club to a utility sink and cleaned up before going home. Today, she couldn't take that chance.

For the rest of the afternoon and all night long, she fretted. She'd spent the last eight weeks trying to forget about her one-night-stand cowboy. Now he had appeared in Royal, completely out of the blue, and looking about ten times as gorgeous and sexy as she remembered. If he really was the new architect, she was going to be forced to see him repeatedly.

Her body thought that was a darned good idea. Heat sizzled through her veins. But her brain was smarter and more sensible. This was a bad development. Really bad.

The following morning, when the sun came up on another beautiful October day, she wanted to pull the covers over her head and not have to *think*. Still, the memories came rushing back. An intimate hotel room. A rugged cowboy. Two naked bodies. What was she going to do? With yummy Austin in town, there would be hell to pay if her secret came out.

More than ever, she needed to get her own place to live. With the money Alexis was paying her for the murals, there would soon be enough in her modest bank account for first and last month's rent on a decent apartment. In three and a half years, she would receive her inheritance from her grandmother and thus be able to start her after-school art program. Everybody took dance lessons and played sports—Brooke wanted to build a small studio where dreamy kids like she had been could dabble in clay and paint to their heart's content.

All she had to do in the meantime was find a permanent job, any job, that would give her financial independence from her parents. That task was tough in a town where the Goodmans pulled strings right and left. Brooke had been unofficially blacklisted time and again.

Her parents' behind-the-scenes manipulations were humiliating and infuriating. And all because they wanted her to be the kind of high-powered entrepreneurs they were.

It was never going to happen. Brooke liked who she was. It wasn't that she lacked ambition. She simply saw a different path for herself.

Fortunately, her parents were both early risers and left for the office at the crack of dawn. Brooke was able to enjoy her toast and coffee in peace. Her stomach rebelled at the thought of food this morning, probably because she was so upset about the prospect of seeing Austin again.

What was she supposed to say to him?

Could she simply avoid him altogether?

She was small. Maybe she could hide.

When she couldn't put it off any longer, she drove into town. Her parents' Pine Valley mansion had been her childhood home. She'd left it only to go to college and grad school. Now it had become a prison. Her whole family was seriously broken in her estimation. Her brother Jared's poor fiancée had been forced to run away from her own wedding to escape.

Brooke was still trying to find a way out. It wasn't as easy as it sounded. But she was at least working on a plan.

When she arrived at the club, she parked one street over and gathered up the canvas totes that contained her supplies. At least she knew what Austin's truck looked like. So far, she didn't see it anywhere around. Maybe he was at his hotel doing whatever architects did on their laptops before they started a new job.

Hopefully she could get her murals done before he showed up again. Didn't a project like this require site prep? Surely an architect wasn't involved in that phase.

Her heart slugged in her chest. This was exactly why she had gone to another town for her secret fling. She hadn't wanted to face any ramifications of her indiscretion afterward.

Remembering that night was both mortifying and deeply arousing. What thoughts had gone through his head when he woke up and found her missing? She had second-guessed that decision a thousand times.

In the end, though, it had been the only choice. She and Austin had been strangers passing in the night. Joplin wasn't home for either of them. It had been the perfect anonymous scenario.

Except now it wasn't.

To access the gardens, it was first necessary to go through the club. She greeted the receptionist and made her way down the corridor hung with hunting trophies and artifacts. Both of her parents had been members here for years. The building was familiar.

What wasn't so familiar was the sensation of apprehension and excitement. She told herself she didn't want to see Austin Bradshaw again. But the lie wasn't very believable, even in her head.

It was almost anticlimactic to arrive in the gardens and find herself completely alone. The landscaping crew came and went at odd hours. This morning, no one was around to disturb Brooke's concentration. Up until now, she had enjoyed the time to focus on her creations, to dream and to let her imagination run wild. Today, the solitude felt disconcerting.

Doggedly, she uncapped her paints and planned the section she would work on next. It was a large-scale, multilevel task. Instead of two long gray stucco walls at right angles to one another, Alexis had charged Brooke with creating a whimsical extension of the gardens. When spring came and the flowers bloomed, there would be no delineation between the actual gardens and Brooke's fantasy world.

The work challenged her creativity and her vision. Not only did she have to paint on a very large canvas, but she had to think in bold, thematic strokes. It was the most ambitious project she had ever tackled, and she was honored that Alexis trusted her to handle the makeover.

When the stage was built, the new landscaping was complete and Brooke's paintings were finished, the outdoor area would be spectacular. It felt good to be part of something that would provide enjoyment to so many people.

She selected the appropriate brush and tucked it behind her ear. Soon she would need a taller ladder, but for now, she was going to finish the portion she had abandoned yesterday. It was a border of daisies and baby rabbits that repeated along one edge of her mural.

Grabbing the metal frame that held four small paint pots, she climbed up three steps and cocked her head. White first. Then the yellow centers.

"Are you avoiding me, Brooke?"

The voice startled her so badly she flung paint all over herself and a huge section of blank wall and the grass below. "Austin," she cried.

He took her by the waist, lifted her and set her on the ground. "So you *do* know who I am." He smirked. "Yesterday, I wasn't so sure."

She scowled at him, trying not to notice the way sunlight picked out strands of gold in his hair without his hat. "What was I supposed to do? I couldn't tell Gus how we met."

Austin's lips quirked in the kind of superior male smile that made her want to smack him. "Most people would have come up with a polite lie."

"I'm a terrible liar," she said.

"I'll have to remember that. It might come in handy."

The intimate light in his warm brown eyes and the way he looked at her as if he were remembering every nanosecond of their night together made heat curl in her sex. "Why are you here, Austin?"

"I have a job to do. Why are *you* here, Brooke Goodman?"

"I live in Royal. And I have a job to do as well. So that makes this terribly awkward."

"Not at all." He eyed her mural. "This is your work? It's fabulous. You're very talented."

His praise warmed her. Other than Alexis, few people knew

what she was capable of doing—at least, few people in Royal. "Thank you," she said. "I still have a long way to go."

"Which means I'll get to watch as I build the stage."

Her heart stuttered. He didn't mean anything by that statement...did he? "Austin, I—"

He held up his hand. "You don't have to say a word. I can see it on your face. You're afraid I'll spill your secret. But I won't, Brooke, I swear. You had your reasons for what happened in Joplin, and so did I." He cleared his throat, then went on. "The truth is, as much as I like you, we need to leave the past in the past. I'm done with relationships, trust me. And in a town like this, you clearly can't do anything without the whole world knowing your business."

He was saying all the right things. Exactly what she needed to hear.

So why did she have a knot in her stomach?

"I should get started," she said.

"For the record, I was damned disappointed when I woke up and you were gone."

"You were?" She searched his face.

He nodded slowly. "Yes."

"It was an amazing night for me, but I didn't have much basis for comparison."

He chuckled. "Your instincts were spot-on. If I were in the market for a girlfriend and you were five years older, we might give it a go."

Her temper flared. "Do you have any idea how arrogant you sound? I'm getting very tired of everybody in my life thinking they know what's best for me."

"Define *everybody*."

Brooke looked over his shoulder and grimaced. "Here comes one now."

Margaret Goodman was dressed impeccably from head to toe. Though she was well into her fifties, she could easily pass for a much younger woman. Her blond hair, sprinkled with only the slightest gray, received the attention of an expensive stylist every three weeks, and she had both a personal trainer and a dietitian on her payroll.

Brooke's mother was ambitious, driven and ice-cold. She was also—at the moment—clearly furious. A tiny splotch of red on each cheekbone betrayed her agitation.

"What are you doing here, Mama?" Brooke stepped forward, away from the cowboy architect, hoping to defuse the situation and at the same time possibly avoid any interaction between her mother and Austin.

Her mother lifted her chin. "Are you trying to spite me on purpose? Do you have any idea how humiliating it is to know that my only daughter is grubbing around in the gardens of the Texas Cattleman's Club like a common laborer?"

Brooke straightened her backbone. "Alexis Slade hired me to do a job. That's what I'm doing."

"Don't be naive and ridiculous. This isn't a job." Her mother flung a hand toward the partially painted wall in a dramatic gesture. "A child could do this. You're avoiding your potential, Brooke. Your father and I won't have it. It was bad enough that you changed your major in college without telling us. We paid for you to get a serious education, not a worthless art degree. Goodmans are businesspeople, Brooke. We *make* money, we don't squander it. When will you realize that playing with paint isn't a valid life choice?"

Her mother was shouting now, her disdain and reproach both vicious and hurtful.

Brooke had heard it all before, but with Austin as a witness, it was even more upsetting. Her eyes stung. "This *is* a real job, Mama. I'm proud of the work I'm doing. And for the record, I'm planning on moving out of the house, so you and Daddy might as well get used to the idea."

"Don't you speak to me in that tone."

"You don't listen any other way. I'm twenty-six years old. The boys moved out when they were twenty-one."

"Don't bring your brothers into this. They were both far more mature than you at this age. Neither of them gave us any grief."

Brooke shook her head, incredulous. Her brothers were sycophants and weasels who coasted by on their family connections and their willingness to suck up to Mommy and Daddy. "I won't discuss this with you right now. You're embarrassing me."

For the first time, Margaret looked at Austin. "Who is this?" she demanded, her nose twitching as if sniffing out an impostor in her blue-blooded world.

Before Brooke could stop him, Austin stepped forward, hand outstretched. "I'm Austin Bradshaw, ma'am…the architect Gus Slade hired to build the stage addition for the bachelor auction. I'm pleased to meet you."

His sun-kissed good looks and blinding smile caught Margaret midtirade. Her mouth opened and shut. "Um…"

Brooke sensed trouble brewing. She took her mother's arm and tried to steer her toward the building. "You don't want to get paint on your clothes, Mama, and I really need to get back to work. We'll discuss this tonight."

Margaret bristled. "I'm not finished talking to you, young lady. Put this mess away and come home."

"I won't," Brooke said. She felt ill, but she couldn't let her dislike of confrontation or the fact that they had an audience allow her mother to steamroll her. "I've made a commitment, and I intend to honor it."

Margaret scowled. When Brooke's mother was on a rant, people scattered. She could be terrifying. "I demand that you come with me this instant."

Brooke swallowed hard as bile rose in her throat. She wasn't wearing a hat, so the sun beat down on her head. Little yellow spots danced in front of her eyes, and her knees wobbled.

This was a nightmare.

But then, to her complete and utter shock, Austin intervened. He literally inserted himself between Brooke and her mother, shielding Brooke with his body. "You're out of line, Mrs. Goodman. Your daughter is a grown woman. She's a gifted artist, and she's being paid to use that talent for the good of the community. I won't have you bullying her."

"Who the hell are you to talk to me that way?" Margaret shrieked. "I'll have you fired on the spot. Wait until Gus Slade hears about this. You'll never work in this town again."

The whole thing might have been funny if it wasn't so miserably tragic. Brooke's mother was used to getting her way with threats and intimidation. Her face was ugly beneath her makeup.

Austin simply ignored her bluster. "I'd like you to leave now," he said politely. "Brooke and I both have work to do for the club, and you are delaying our progress."

Margaret raised her fist...she actually raised her fist.

Austin stared at her.

To Brooke's amazement, her mother backed down. She dropped her arm, turned on her heel and simply walked away.

"Oh my God, you've done it now." Brooke felt her legs crumpling.

Austin whirled and caught her around the waist, supporting her as she went down. She didn't faint, but she sat down hard on the grass and put her head on her knees. "She's going to make your life a living hell."

"Sounds like you know something about that." He crouched beside her and stroked her back, his presence a quiet, steady comfort after the ugly scene.

"I appreciate your standing up for me, but you shouldn't have done it. She doesn't make idle threats. She'll try to get you fired."

"I've dealt with bullies before. But I confess that I've never had to deal with it in my own home. I'm sorry, Brooke."

She wiped her eyes and sniffled, too upset to be embarrassed anymore. "I've applied for six different jobs here in Royal since I finished school, and in every instance I got some flimsy excuse about why I wasn't qualified. The first couple of times I wrote it off to the fact that I was straight out of college and grad school and had no experience, but then I got turned down for a waitressing gig at a place where one of my friends worked. I knew she had put in a good word for me." She released a quavering breath. "So I couldn't understand what I had done wrong...how I had interviewed so poorly that they didn't want me."

"Did you ever find out what happened?" he prodded gently.

"Yes. I couldn't let it go, so I screwed up my courage and went back to the restaurant and talked to the manager. He admitted that my mother had called him and threatened him."

"Son of a bitch."

Austin's vehement shock summed up Brooke's reaction in a nutshell. "Yep. Who does that to their own kid?"

"What exactly is it that she wants you to do?"

"Daddy would be happy if I went to law school and joined him in his firm. Mama is Maverick County royalty. Her family owns one of the richest ranches in Texas. I'm supposed to play the part of the wealthy socialite. Wear the right clothes. Hang out with the right people. Marry the right man."

He grimaced. "Sounds wretched."

"You have no idea. And my mother is relentless. I have an inheritance coming to me from my grandmother's estate when I turn thirty. All that's necessary for me to get my money sooner is to be married or to have my parents' permission. But my mother has convinced my father not to let that happen." She lifted her chin. "So I've decided I'll do whatever it takes to get out from under their roof. This job is the first step toward my liberation. Alexis isn't afraid of my mother. This is real employment with a real paycheck."

"But it won't last long, surely."

"No. The garden part will only take a few weeks. After that, Alexis wants me to do the walls in the childcare center. I'm saving every penny so I can rent an apartment."

He put the back of his hand to her cheek and gazed down at her in concern. "You don't look good, honey. Maybe you should go home."

Brooke struggled to her feet. "Absolutely not. I won't let Alexis down."

He sighed. "When do you quit for the day?"

"Around four."

"How about afterward we grab some food and take a picnic out in the country...find a quiet place where we can talk?"

"What if someone sees us and asks questions?"

His grin was remarkably carefree for a man who had recently tangled with the Goodman matriarch. "Let's live dangerously."

Five

Gus peered through the French doors and frowned when he spotted Brooke Goodman getting chummy with Austin Bradshaw. He'd have to nip that in the bud. Austin was on his radar as the perfect match for Alexis, even if neither of them knew it yet.

Impulsively, he strode out to the parking lot and climbed into his truck. There was one person who shared his goals, one woman who would understand his frustration. He drove out to Rose Clayton's Silver C Ranch feeling more than a little regret for all the years of bitterness and recrimination that lay between him and Rose. She had hurt him badly when he was a young man. Betrayed him. Broken his heart.

Still, five decades was a long time to carry a grudge.

The only reason they were speaking now was because they were both determined to keep their grandchildren from *hooking up*. Wasn't that what the kids called it these days?

Hell would freeze over before Gus Slade would let his beloved granddaughter Alexis marry a Clayton.

Rose answered the door almost immediately after his knock. She had aged well, her frame slim and regal. Chin-length brown hair showed only a touch of gray at the temples. Her gaze was wary. "Gus. Won't you come in?"

He followed her back to the kitchen. "I found a good prospect for Alexis," he said.

Rose waved him to a chair and poured him a cup of coffee. "Do tell."

"His name is Austin Bradshaw. Architect. Widower. Did some work for me a few years back...a handsome lad."

"And what does Alexis think?"

Rose's knowing smile irritated him. "She doesn't know my plans for the two of them yet, but she will. I need some time, that's all. As long as you keep Daniel occupied, we'll be fine."

"You can rest easy on that score. I'm sure there will be any number of eligible women bidding on him at the bachelor auction."

Gus drained his cup and leaned his chair back on two legs. "Did Daniel actually agree to the auction thing? It doesn't sound like his cup of tea."

Rose's face fell. "Well, I had to coax him. I did point out that he and Tessa Noble would make a lovely couple, if she bids on him."

"I agree. Makes perfect sense."

"Unfortunately, Daniel gets quite frustrated with me when I try to give him advice about his love life. He has come very close to telling me to stay out of his business. Imagine that. His own grandmother."

Gus snorted. "The world would run a lot more smoothly if young people did what their elders told them to."

Rose went white, her expression agitated. "You don't know what you're talking about, old man."

Her demeanor shocked him. "What did I say, Rose?" The change in her was dramatic. He felt guilty and didn't know why.

"I'd like you to leave now. Please."

Her startling about-face stunned him. He thought they had worked through some of their issues. After all, she had wronged *him*, not the other way around. Was she implying somehow that she had been manipulated by her father? Gus had worked for Jedediah Clayton. To a sixteen-year-old kid, the ranch owner had been both vengeful and terrifying. Yet that hadn't stopped Gus from falling in love with the boss's daughter.

Gus had finally made the decision to leave the Clayton ranch. He'd spent four years on the rodeo circuit, saving every dime. Then he'd returned to Royal, bought a small parcel of land and gone back to claim the woman he loved.

His world had come crashing down when he discovered his childhood sweetheart had married another man. Even worse was Rose's crushing rejection of the love they had once shared. The long-ago heartache was still vivid to him.

He had married her best friend.

But now he was confused.

"Go," she cried, tears gleaming in her eyes.

He caught her hands in his and held them tightly, even when she tried to yank away. "Did your father do something to you, Rosie?" His heart sank.

Her lower lip trembled. Suddenly, she looked every one of her sixty-seven years. "None of you cared," she whispered. "I was a prisoner, and you and Sarah never saw through my facade."

"I don't understand." His chest hurt. He couldn't breathe.

"He threatened me. My mother was desperately ill. He was going to let her die if I married you, refuse to pay for her treatments. So I had no choice. I had to pretend. I had to choose my mother's life over my happiness. I had to marry another man."

"My God."

Rose stared at him, her eyes filled with something close to hatred and loathing. Or maybe it was simply grief. "Go, Augustus. We'll continue our plan to keep Daniel and Alexis apart. But please don't come to my house again."

Somehow Brooke managed to work on her mural hour after hour without passing out or giving up, but it wasn't easy. The episode with her mother had upset her deeply. She felt wretched. Even now, her legs trembled and her stomach roiled. Her life was a damned soap opera. Why couldn't her family be normal and boring?

She paused in the middle of the day to eat the peanut butter sandwich she had packed for her lunch. The club had a perfectly wonderful restaurant, but dining there would have meant changing out of her paint-stained clothes, and Brooke simply didn't have it in her today. So she sat on the ground with her back to the wall and ate her sandwich in the shade.

She half hoped Austin would show up to keep her company. But clearly, he was very busy with the new project. She saw him at a distance a time or two. That was all.

On the one hand, it was good that he didn't hover. She would have hated that. She was a grown woman. Still, she'd be lying if she didn't say she was looking forward to their picnic.

By the time she finished a section at three thirty and cleaned her brushes, she was wiped out. Today's temperature had been ten degrees above normal for mid-October. It was no wonder she was dragging. And she had forgotten to wear sunscreen. So she would probably have a pink nose by the end of the day.

She stashed her supplies in her car, changed out of her work clothes into a cute top and jeans, and went in search of Austin. Her palms were damp and her heart beat faster than normal. The last time the two of them had spent any amount of time together, they'd been naked.

Despite that anomaly, they really were little more than strangers. Perhaps if she treated this picnic as a first date, she could pretend that she hadn't propositioned him in a bar and made wild, passionate love to the handsome cowboy.

That was probably impossible, given the fact that she trembled every time he got close to her.

She rounded a corner in the gardens and ran straight into the man who occupied her tumultuous thoughts.

He steadied her with two big hands on her shoulders. "Slow down, honey. I was just coming to find you."

She wiggled free, trying not to let him see how his touch burned right through her. "Here I am. Shall we swing by the corner market and pick up a few supplies for our picnic?"

Austin took her elbow and steered her back inside the club, down the corridor and out the front door. "I've already got it covered," he said. "I called the diner and had them make us a basket of fried chicken and everything to go with it."

Brooke raised an eyebrow. "I'm impressed." The Royal Diner was one of her favorite places for good old-fashioned comfort food. "I hope you asked for some of Amanda Battle's buttermilk pie."

Austin grinned. "I wasn't sure what kind of dessert you preferred, so I had them include four different slices."

"I like a man with a plan."

They were flirting. It was easy and fun. Something inside her relaxed for the first time all day.

Of course, it made sense to take Austin's truck. It was the nicer, bigger, newer vehicle. He stepped into the diner to pick up their order, and then they were on their way. It was a perfect fall afternoon. The sky was the color of a Texas bluebonnet, and the clouds were soft white cotton balls drifting across the sky.

Brooke was content to let Austin choose their route until it occurred to her that he didn't live in Royal. "Do you even know where you're going?" she asked.

"More or less. I did a big job for Gus some years ago. It's been a little while, but this part of the county has stayed the same."

They drove for miles. The radio was on but the volume was turned down, so the music barely intruded. Brooke sighed deeply. She hadn't realized how tightly she was wound.

Austin shot her a sideways glance. "Has your mother always been like that?"

"Oh, yeah."

He reached across the small space separating them and put a

hand on her arm. Briefly. Just a touch of warm, masculine fingers. But the simple gesture made her nerves hum with pleasure.

"Tell me why you came to Joplin that night," he asked softly.

"It was a stupid thing to do," she muttered.

"You don't hear me complaining."

The sexy teasing made her cheeks hot. "I was furious at my parents and furious at myself. Some people might have gotten stinking drunk, but that's not my style."

"So you decided to seduce a stranger."

"I didn't seduce you...did I?"

He parked the truck beneath a lone cottonwood tree and put the gear shift in Park. Half turning in his seat, he propped a big, muscular arm on the steering wheel and faced her. He chuckled, scratching his chin and shaking his head. "I don't know what else you would call it. I came in with my sister and left with you."

"Oh." When you put it like that, it made Brooke sound like the kind of woman who could command a man's interest with a crook of her finger. That was certainly never an image she'd had of herself. She kind of liked it. "Well," she said, "the thing is, I was upset and angry, and I let myself get carried away."

"Had something happened at home? Was that it? After what I witnessed today, I can only imagine."

"You're very perceptive. It's a long story. Are you sure you want to hear it?"

He leaned over without warning and kissed her. It was a friendly kiss. Gentle. Casual. Thrilling. His lips were warm and firm. "I've got all night."

She blinked at him. He sat back in his seat as if nothing out of the ordinary had happened. Her toes curled in her shoes. "Well, okay, then." It was difficult to gather her thoughts when what she really wanted to do was unbutton his shirt and see if that broad, strong chest was as wonderfully sculpted and kissable as she remembered.

"Brooke?"

Apparently she had lapsed into a sex-starved, befuddled stupor. "Sorry. I'll start with Grammy, my dad's mother. She died when I was seventeen, but she and I were soul mates. It was Grammy who first introduced me to art. In fact, when I was twelve, she took me with her to Paris, and we toured the Louvre. I remember walking through the galleries in a daze. It was the most extraordinary experience. The light the artists had captured on canvas...and all the colors. The sculptures. Something clicked for me. It was as if—for the first time in my life—I was where I was supposed to be."

"She must have been a very special lady."

"She was. I was crushed when she died, utterly heartbroken. But I made several decisions over the next few years. First, that I wanted to become an artist. And secondly, that I wanted to take part of my inheritance and tour the great art museums of Europe in Grammy's honor."

"And was there more?"

She smiled, for the moment actually believing it might happen. "Yes. Yes, there was...there *is*. I want to open an art studio in Royal that caters to children and youth. Families pay for piano lessons and ballet lessons and soccer and football all the time. Yet there are tons of children like me who need a creative outlet, but their parents don't know what to do for them."

"I think that's a phenomenal idea."

"I did, too. I even went to the bank and filled out the paperwork for a small business loan to get things started. My inheritance would serve as collateral, but I was hoping my parents would see the sense in letting me have part of the money now as an investment in my future."

"I'm guessing they didn't share your vision."

She shook her head and swallowed against the sudden dryness in her throat. "I might have swayed my father...eventually. But my mother was outraged, and he does whatever she tells him to. That ugly scene went down the day I showed up in Joplin."

"Ah. So you were trying to punish them?"

"No. It wasn't that. I was just so very tired of them controlling my life. I'm sure you think I'm exaggerating or overreacting, but I'm not. Did you know that my brother was engaged to be married recently? His poor fiancée, Shelby, ran away from the church, and then my parents tried to blackmail her into coming back by freezing all her assets and hunting her down like an animal."

"Good Lord."

"I know! It's Machiavellian."

"Come on, darlin'," Austin said. "We need to take your mind off your troubles. Let's get some fresh air."

Brooke climbed out of the truck and stretched. Actually, she had to jump down. Being vertically challenged meant that half of the vehicles in Royal were too big for her to get in and out of comfortably.

The thing about an impromptu picnic was that a person couldn't be too picky. Instead of an antique quilt smelling of laundry detergent and sunshine, Austin grabbed a faded horse blanket from the back.

"I think this is fairly clean," he said.

They spread the wool blanket beneath the tree and anchored one corner with the wicker basket. The diner had recently begun offering these romantic carryout meals for a small deposit.

Austin handed her one container at a time. "Here you go. See what we've got." Brooke's stomach rumbled as the wonderful smells wafted up from the basket.

The meal was perfect, but no more so than the late-afternoon sunshine and the ruggedly handsome man at her side. She fantasized about what it would be like to kiss him again. Really kiss him.

Austin ate in silence. His profile was unequivocally masculine. Lounging on one elbow, he personified the Texas cowboy, right down to the Stetson.

"Will you tell me about your wife?" Brooke asked.

* * *

Austin winced inwardly. He'd been expecting this question. Under the circumstances, it was a reasonable request, and nothing about Brooke's tentative query reflected anything but concern.

The diner was famous for its fresh-squeezed lemonade. It was served in retro-looking thermoses that kept the liquid ice-cold. Austin drained the last of his and set it aside. Wiping his hands on his jeans, he sat up and rested his forearms on his knees. "Jenny was the best. You would have liked her. She had a big heart, but she had a temper to match. When we were younger, we fought like cats and dogs." He laughed softly, staring into the past. "But the making up was always fun."

"Where did you meet?"

"College. Pretty ordinary love story. I always knew I was going to be an architect. Jenny was in education. She taught high school Spanish until she got sick."

"When was that?"

"We'd been married almost five years and were living in Dallas. She had a cold one winter that never seemed to go away. We didn't think anything about it. But it got worse, and by the time I made her go to the doctor, the news was bad. Stage-four lung cancer. She'd never smoked a day in her life. None of her family had. It was a rare cancer. Just one of those things."

"I'm so sorry, Austin."

He shook his head, even now feeling the tentacles of dread and fear left over from that time. "We went through two years of hell. The only saving grace was that we hadn't started a family. Jenny was so glad about that. She didn't want to leave a child behind without a mother."

"But what about you?" Brooke said, her gray eyes filled with an ache that was all for him. "Wouldn't a baby have been a comfort to you?"

He stared at her. No one had ever asked him that. Not Jenny. Not Audra. No one. Sometimes—way back then—the thought had crossed his mind. The idea of holding a baby girl who looked like Jenny—teaching her to fish when she was a little kid—had rooted deep inside him, but then the chemo started and fertility was a moot point.

"It wouldn't have worked out," he said gruffly. "What did I know about babies?"

"I suppose…"

"In the end, Jenny was ready to go, and I was ready to let her go. There are some things no one should have to endure. She fought until there was no reason to fight anymore." He swallowed convulsively. "When it was over, I didn't feel much of anything for a few days. Nothing seemed real. Not the funeral. Nothing. I didn't even have our house to go back to."

"What happened to your home?" she asked quietly.

"When Jenny's disease had progressed to the point that I couldn't work and care for her, we sold everything and moved to Joplin. Audra and I cobbled together a schedule for looking after Jenny and filled in the gaps with temp nurses and hospice toward the end."

"You and your sister are close."

"She saved my life," he said simply. "I don't know what I would have done without her. I had no rudder, no reason to get out of bed in the mornings. Audra forced me into the world even when I didn't want to go. Eventually, I started picking up work here and there. I didn't mind traveling."

"But what about your career in Dallas?"

"It had been too long. I didn't want to go back there. But Joplin was where Jenny died, so I didn't want to live there, either."

"Then you've bounced around?"

He nodded slowly. "For six years. Pathetic, isn't it?"

Brooke scooted closer and laid her head on his shoulder. "No. I can't imagine loving someone that much and losing them."

He wrapped an arm around her waist and inhaled the scent of her hair. Today it smelled like strawberries. Arousal curled in his gut, but it simmered on low, overlaid with a feeling of peace. It had taken him a long time, but he had survived the depths of despair. He would never allow himself to be that vulnerable again.

"Brooke?" he said quietly.

"Yes?"

"I know you're feeling sorry for me right now, and I don't want to take advantage of your good nature."

She pulled back and looked up at him. Her hair tumbled around her shoulders, pale gold and soft as silk. A wary gray gaze searched his face. "I don't understand."

"I want you." He laid it out bluntly. There didn't need to be any misunderstandings between them. If she was interested in a sexual liaison with him, he was definitely on board, but he wouldn't be accused of wrapping things up in romantic words that might be misconstrued.

Brooke frowned. "I heard you say very clearly that you weren't interested in a relationship."

He rubbed his thumb across her lower lip, tugging on it ever so slightly. "Men and women have sex all the time without relationships. I like you. We have chemistry in bed. If you're interested, I'm available."

Six

Brooke stepped outside her body for a moment. At least that's how it seemed in that split second. The scene was worthy of the finest cinema. A remote setting. Romantic accoutrements. Handsome cowboy. Erotic proposition.

This was the part where the heroine was supposed to melt into the hero's arms, and if it were a family-friendly film, the screen would fade to black. The trouble with that scenario was that Brooke didn't see herself as heroine material in this picture.

You had the leading man who was most likely still in love with his dead wife. A second woman who was far too young for him—case in point, she was having trouble extracting herself from under her parents' oppressive influence. And a red-hot, clandestine one-night stand that had catapulted an unlikely couple way too far in one direction and not nearly far enough in another.

Brooke knew the size and shape of the mole on Austin's right butt cheek, but she had no idea if he put mayo on his roast beef sandwiches.

That was a problem.

She tasted his thumb with the tip of her tongue, her heart racing. How bad could it be if she had naughty daytime sex with this man? He needed her, and that was a powerful aphrodisiac.

Putting a hand on his denim-clad thigh, she leaned in and kissed him. "I could get on board with that idea."

A shudder ripped its way through Austin's body. She felt it. And she heard his ragged breathing. "Are you sure? What changed your mind?"

She reached up and knocked his Stetson off his head. "I'm sure. I can't resist you, Cowboy. I don't even want to try."

They were parked beside a wet weather stream. The land was flat for miles in either direction. No one was going to sneak up on them.

Austin eased her onto her back. "I need to tell you something."

Alarm skittered through her veins. "What is it?

He leaned over her, his big frame blocking out the sun. "I haven't slept with any other women since you. I was serious when I said I'm not looking for a relationship. But I didn't want you to think you were one in a long line."

"Thank you for telling me that."

She couldn't decide if his little speech made her feel better or worse, but soon, she forgot to worry about it. Austin dispatched her clothes with impressive speed and prowess. The air was cool on her belly and thighs. When she complained, he only laughed.

He sheathed himself, came down between her legs and thrust slowly. Oh, man. She was in deep trouble.

Austin Bradshaw was the real deal. He kissed her and stroked her and moved inside her as if she were his last chance at happiness and maybe the world was even coming to an end. That was heady stuff for a woman whose only real boyfriend had lasted barely six months...during senior year in college.

She wrapped her legs around his back. Her fingers flexed

on his warm shoulders. He had shed his shirt and his pants, but he was still wearing socks. For some odd reason, that struck her as wildly sexy.

Sex had never seemed all that special to her. Oh, sure, she thought about it sometimes. When she was lonely or bored or reading a hot book. But her life was full and busy, and the only experience she'd had up until two months ago had convinced her that the movie version of sex was not realistic.

As it turned out, that was true.

Sex with Austin Bradshaw was way *better* than the movies.

He nibbled the side of her neck right below her ear. "Am I squashing you, honey? This isn't exactly a soft mattress at the Ritz."

She tried to catch her breath, but the words still came out on a moan. "No. I'm good. I think there may be a small rock under my right hip bone, but my leg went numb a few minutes ago, so no worries."

"You should have said something." He rolled to his back, taking Brooke with him.

"Oh, gosh." Now she was on top. Exposed. Bare-assed naked. In the daytime. Well, the sun was *trying* to go down, but there was still plenty of light if anyone was looking.

This was far different from dimly lit motel sex in the middle of the night. Austin noticed, too. He suckled each of her breasts in turn, murmuring his pleasure and sending liquid heat from there to every other bit of her. "I love your body, Brooke. Do you know how beautiful you are?"

How was a woman supposed to answer that? Brooke wasn't a slug. She worked out and she was healthy. But beautiful? She had always wanted to be taller and more confident and to have a less pointy chin. "I'm glad you think so," she said diplomatically.

He bit a sensitive nipple, making her yelp. "If we're going to have sex with each other on a regular basis, you have to promise me you'll love your body." He ran his hands over her bottom, pulling her a little closer against him, filling her incrementally more.

"Yes, sir," she said, kissing his nose and his eyebrows and his beautiful, gold-tipped eyelashes.

He thrust upward. "We'll be exclusive," he groaned. "No one else while we're together. Understood?"

Was he insane? What woman was going to fool around when she had Austin Bradshaw in her bed? Nevertheless, Brooke nodded. A plan began forming in her head, but it was hard to focus on anything sensible when her body was like hot wax.

He gripped her hips tightly and moved her against him. Need flared, hot and urgent and breathless. She was burning up from the inside out, even though parts of her were definitely cold.

It was dusk now. The stars were coming out one by one. Or maybe she was the starry-eyed dreamer. How had she gotten so lucky? Like a rare comet, men of Austin's caliber came around once in a long time. She wouldn't be greedy. She wouldn't ask for more than he had to give.

He kissed her roughly, his lips warm, his breath feathering the hair at her temple where it fell across his face. "I don't want to send you home tonight, Brooke. But I'm staying in one of Gus's bunkhouses. We're gonna have to figure something out."

She nodded again, the speech centers in her brain misfiring. "Working on it," she stuttered. His fingers slid deep into her hair, tipping her head so he could nip her earlobe. He sucked on the tiny gold stud. "You make me want things, honey."

"Like what?" She was breathless, yearning.

"If I tell you, you might run away."

"I won't, I swear."

She ran her hands over his arms. Despite the plummeting temperatures, his skin was hot. His muscles were impressive for a man who called himself an architect. Clearly he did more than wield a pencil all day.

He was barely moving now, his body rigid. His chest heaved. "Damn it."

"What's wrong?" She probably should be alarmed, but she was concentrating too hard on the finish line to care.

"I only have one condom," he growled.

The pique in his voice struck her as funny. "We'll improvise later," she said, laughing softly. "Make me come, Cowboy. Send me over the edge."

Austin Bradshaw was clearly a man who liked a challenge. With a groan, he rolled her beneath him again and pistoned his hips, driving into her over and over until they both went up in a flare of heat. Brooke unraveled first, clutching Austin because he was the only steady point in a spiraling universe.

She was barely aware of his muffled shout and the way he shuddered against her as he came.

It took a long time for reality to intrude. Gradually, her breathing settled into something approaching normal. Her heartbeat dropped below a hundred.

Austin grunted and shifted to one side, dragging her against him. "Damn, girl, you're freezing."

"I don't care," she mumbled, burrowing into his rib cage. The man smelled amazing.

He yawned and lifted his arm to stare at his watch. "It's late."

"Yeah." Apparently, neither of them cared, because they didn't move for the longest time.

Eons later, he stirred. "Is there any food left?"

The man must be starving after burning all those calories. "Probably." Her heart began to race. She had reached a pivotal moment in her life, and she didn't want to screw it up. "Austin?"

"Hmm?"

"I want to ask you a question, but you have to promise me you'll think about it, and you won't freak out."

He chuckled. "I'm feeling pretty mellow at the moment. Ask me anything, honey."

"Will you marry me?"

Austin rolled to his feet and reached for his clothes, panic slugging in his chest. "We need to get in the truck. I think you have hypothermia."

"I'm serious," Brooke said, her voice steady and determined.

"Get dressed before you freeze to death." That was the thing about October. It could be really warm on a nice afternoon, but when the sun went down and the skies were clear, it got cold fast.

They found all their clothing. Between them, they repacked the picnic basket. "We can snack in the truck," Brooke said.

He folded up the blanket and tossed it in the back. They climbed into the cab. The picnic hamper was between them. Austin found a lone chicken leg and munched on it. He wasn't about to say a word at the moment. Not after that bomb she had just tossed at him.

Brooke finished off a bag of potato chips and stared out through the windshield into the inky darkness. "I was serious," she said at last.

"Why?" He could barely force the word from his throat. He'd done the marriage thing, and it had nearly destroyed him.

She reached up and turned on the small reading light that cast a dim glow over the intimate space. With the doors closed and the body heat from two adults, they were plenty warm now.

Brooke looked tired. She had smudges of exhaustion beneath her eyes and her cheekbones were hollow, as if she had lost some weight. "I'm not in love with you, Austin, and I don't plan to be. You can rest easy on that score. But I could use your help. You told me yourself that you've been bouncing from town to town since your wife died. Royal is as good a place as any to put down temporary roots."

"And why would I do that?"

"To help me get my inheritance. You met my mother today. You saw what she's like. You actually made her back down, Austin. You were the alpha dog, and she respected that. Marry me. Not for long. Six months. Maybe twelve. By then I'll have my inheritance and I can have my art studio up and running."

"What's in it for me?" It was a rude, terrible question, but he was trying to shock her into seeing how outrageous her plan was.

She smiled at him, a surprisingly sweet, guileless smile given the topic of conversation. "Regular sex. Home-cooked meals. Companionship if you want it. But most of all, the knowledge that you're doing the right thing. You're making a difference in my life."

Well, hell. When she put it like that... He cleared his throat, alarmed by how appealing it was to contemplate having Brooke Goodman in his bed every night. "Your parents will go ballistic," he pointed out. "I'm nobody on their radar. To be honest, I'll be seen as a fortune hunter by the whole town. That's not a role I'm keen to play."

She nodded slowly. "I understand that. But my parents have no say in the matter when it comes to marriage. I'm well past the age of consent, and my grandmother's will is very clear. The money is mine if I'm married. As for the other...if it would make you feel better, we could sign a prenup, and I could spread the word that you insisted on having one because you're such a Boy Scout."

"You seem to have thought of everything."

"Not really. The idea only began percolating this morning when I saw how you handled my mother."

"I can't *make* her hand over your inheritance."

"Exactly. That's why I began thinking about a temporary marriage." She reached out and stroked his arm. "You're a good man, Austin Bradshaw. Life has knocked you down once. I won't give you any grief, I swear. We'll make our agreement, and when the time is up, you'll walk away free and clear, no regrets. You have my word."

He looked down at her slender fingers pressed against the fabric of his shirt. Her touch burned, as if it were on his bare skin. Already, he could see the flaw in this plan. Brooke Goodman tempted him more than any woman had since Jenny died. He didn't want to *need* anybody else. He didn't want to crave that human connection. Being alone had been comfortable and safe.

"I'll think about it," he said gruffly. "But don't get your hopes up."

Seven

Austin avoided Brooke for an entire week. He was ashamed to admit it, even to himself, but it was true.

He saw her, of course. Across the courtyard garden. They were both working at the same outdoor location. But he kept his distance. Because he didn't know how the hell he was going to respond to her proposal.

With each hour and day that passed, he wanted more and more to say yes to her wild and crazy idea. That was insane enough to stop him in his tracks.

Fortunately, Gus's job kept Austin legitimately busy. Getting the stage ready in time for the upcoming auction required long hours and plenty of focus. Thanks to having an inside track, the plans were approved by the zoning board immediately. Austin had ordered the materials on the spot, and they had already begun arriving pallet by pallet. Soon, the first saws would start humming.

Gus had hired a foreman, but Austin was the boss. He liked the hands-on aspect of the project, and he was a bit of a control freak. It was his design, his baby. In the end, any problems would fall to him. He intended to make sure everything was perfect.

It amused him to realize that a number of the club members had taken to dropping by during the week to gauge the progress on the new stage addition. At first he thought it was to check up on him. Later, he realized that most of them, the men in particular, were simply interested.

One of the younger guys, Ryan Bateman, turned out to be very friendly. He even wrangled Austin into joining a pickup basketball game one evening. After that, when Austin was still avoiding Brooke later in the week, Ryan issued a lunch invitation.

"Let's eat in the club dining room," the other man said. "My treat. I think I know someone who could throw some work your way. You'll like him a lot."

"I don't know that I'm planning on staying in Royal," Austin said, wondering if Brooke had put Ryan up to this. Ryan was a club member, of course. Austin was not.

"At least come for the free food," Ryan chuckled. "What could it hurt?"

Austin glanced down ruefully at his dusty work clothes. "I'm not exactly dressed for the club dining room."

Ryan shook his head. "No worries. The old-school days with the rigid dress code are long gone—well, at least during lunchtime."

The other man looked pretty scruffy as well, to be honest. He had a day's growth of beard, and his green eyes twinkled beneath shaggy brown hair. His broad shoulders stretched the seams of a plain navy Henley shirt.

"A decent meal sounds good," Austin said, giving in gracefully. "Let me wash up, and I'll meet you inside."

At the end of the building where he was working, there was an outdoor faucet. He shoved his shirtsleeves to his elbows and threw water on his face and arms. Using a spare T-shirt to dry off, he tucked his white button-up shirt into his ancient khakis and scraped his hands through his hair. Rich people didn't spook him. They had their problems, same as anybody else.

Up until now, he'd been swinging by the convenience mart at the end of town each morning and picking up a prepackaged sandwich for his lunch so he didn't waste time on a midday meal. But he had to admit, he was looking forward to something more substantial.

Ryan was leaning against a wall in the hallway waiting on him. The two men made their way into the dining room where a uniformed maître d' seated them at a table overlooking the gardens. Except for a variety of chrysanthemums and a few evergreens, the area was dull and brown. Presumably the landscapers would bring in some temporary plants and foliage for the auction, ones that could be whisked away for the winter.

Just as they got settled, another club member joined them. If Ryan and Austin were on the scruffy side, this guy was a young George Clooney who had just stepped off his yacht. He was easily six foot three. Black hair. Blue eyes. A ripple of feminine interest circled the dining room.

Ryan grinned broadly. "Austin, meet Matt Galloway. Matt, Austin Bradshaw. Austin is new in town. He's the architect Gus hired to do the stage addition out in the gardens."

Matt shook Austin's hand. "It's a pleasure. I like what you've done so far out there."

"Thank you," Austin said. "Are you a cattle rancher like Ryan here?"

Ryan snorted. "Not hardly. Galloway is an oil tycoon. And did I mention that he's newly engaged?"

Despite his sophisticated appearance, Matt's sheepish smile reflected genuine happiness. "I am, indeed."

Austin smiled. "Congratulations."

Ryan summoned the waiter. "A bottle of champagne, please. We need to toast the groom-to-be."

While they placed their lunch orders and waited for the

drinks to be poured, Ryan pushed his agenda. "Austin, Matt's going to be needing a house. Tell him, Matt."

Matt nodded. "My fiancée and I do want to build. We have ideas, but neither of us has the skill set to get our vision on paper, so to speak. I was hoping you might be the person to help us."

Austin frowned slightly. "The stage addition is hardly a true showcase of my work. You do realize that, right?"

"Of course." Matt grinned. "But Ryan here is a pretty damn good judge of character, and if he likes you, that's good enough for me. Rachel and I want someone we feel comfortable with, someone who can guide us without taking over."

"I don't even know if I'm planning on sticking around," Austin admitted, feeling the sand eroding beneath his feet.

Ryan jumped in. "Where's home?"

"Dallas originally. And I've spent time in Joplin."

Matt paused as the waiter delivered their appetizers. "Are you footloose and fancy-free like Bateman here?"

Austin hesitated. He never knew quite how to answer this question. "I was married," he said simply. "But my wife died some years back. Cancer. I've moved around since then."

Ryan sobered. "Sorry, man. I didn't know."

Matt stared at him. "I'm sorry, too. But I have to tell you, Royal is a great place to live. Maybe it's time to put down a few roots."

"It's possible." Austin flashed back suddenly to a vision of Brooke's naked body and her unexpected proposal.

"Take your time," Matt said. "I'm not in a huge rush. When the auction is done, maybe you could have dinner with Rachel and me and we could kick around a few ideas. No pressure."

Austin nodded slowly. "That's doable. Thank you for the offer, and I'll be in touch."

The conversation moved away from personal topics after that. Austin realized that he had missed the camaraderie with other guys since he had given up his formal career. He had bounced from job to job, keeping to himself and walling off his emotions. Perhaps it was time to let the past go...

Still, it was a hell of a jump from moving on to being stupid enough to put his heart on the line again. Losing Jenny had ripped him in two and nearly made him give up on life. For several years, he had done little more than go through the motions.

He was not the same man he had been before Jenny died.

With an effort, he dragged his attention back to the present. Ryan and Matt seemed to enjoy poking at each other. While they dived into a heated argument about the upcoming World Series, Austin gazed through the large plate-glass window nearby, looking for Brooke. She had finished one entire section of her mural this week. Unicorns and fairies danced with odd little creatures that must be trolls or something like that.

He loved seeing Brooke's art. It gave him an insight into her fascinating brain. Suddenly, there was movement at the far end of the wall on the other side of the garden.

There she was. Her small aluminum stepladder caught the sun for a moment and cast a blinding reflection. He squinted. What the hell? She was working all the way up under the eaves. Surely the club had an extension ladder. Brooke wasn't tall enough to reach that section...was she?

He couldn't really tell from the angle where he was sitting. Austin stood up abruptly, an odd premonition of danger making him jumpy. All three men had finished their meals. Ryan had already signed his name and put the lunches on his account. "I should get back out there," he said. "Thanks for lunch, guys. I'm sure I'll see you around." He shot out of the dining room so fast he was probably being rude, but he couldn't get over the sight of Brooke stretching up on her tiptoes six feet off the ground.

He strode down the hall and through the terrace doors. At first he didn't see her at all. But then he spotted her. After doing his damnedest to ignore her for an entire week, suddenly he felt compelled to hunt her down.

"What do you think you're doing?" he called out, irritation in every syllable.

She looked over her shoulder at him, one eyebrow raised. "Painting a mural." With one dismissive wrinkle of her cute little nose, she returned to her task.

"Don't you think you need a taller ladder?"

"Don't you think you need to mind your own business?"

He counted to ten. "I'm looking out for your well-being."

"That's odd. I could have sworn you've been avoiding me. Why the sudden change?"

The tops of his ears got hot. "I've been busy."

"Uh-huh."

Pale denim overalls cupped her ass in an extremely distracting fashion. Her silky, straight blond hair was caught up in its usual ponytail, but today a streak of blue paint decorated the tips, as if she had brushed up against something.

"I like what you've done so far."

"Super."

"Are you mad at me?"

"I'm not *happy*."

He grinned, feeling better than he had all week. "I've missed you," he said softly.

Brooke turned around on the ladder. It wasn't an easy task. She rested her brush on the open container of paint and stared at him. "I thought you were done with me."

Beneath the flat statement lay a world of hurt. His heart turned over in his chest. "Don't be ridiculous."

She lifted one shoulder and let it fall. "I let you do wicked things to my naked body. And that's the last I saw or heard from you. How would you read that situation?"

"I was thinking about stuff," he protested.

"You mean the marriage proposal?"

He looked around to see if anyone was listening. "Keep your voice down, for God's sake. Of course that's what I mean. You can't throw something like that at a man and expect an answer right off the bat."

"Ah." She looked at him as if he were a slightly dim student. "It doesn't matter anyway," she said. "I've changed my mind. You're off the hook."

"What the hell." He bristled. "I thought I was your best shot?"

She shrugged. "I read the situation wrong. I'm working on a backup plan."

"I didn't even give you an answer."

"My offer had an expiration date," she said, giving him a sweet smile that was patently false. "No need to worry. Your bachelorhood is safe from me."

"You really are pissed, aren't you?"

"I'm nothing, Mr. Bradshaw. You and I are nothing. Now go away and let me work."

With her on the ladder and him on the ground, the conversation was literally not on equal footing. He ground his teeth in frustration. One quick glance at his watch told him now was not the time to push the confrontation to a satisfactory conclusion. "We're not done with this topic," he said firmly. He had people waiting on him. Otherwise, he would have yanked her off that ladder and indulged in a good old-fashioned shouting match. The woman was driving him crazy.

She turned and looked down her nose at him. "It's *my* topic, Austin. You're merely an incidental."

When Austin strode away, his face like a thundercloud, Brooke tasted shame, but only for a moment. She was not a vindictive person. If anything, she leaned too far in the direction of being a people pleaser. But in this case, self-preservation was paramount.

Already her eyes stung with tears and her stomach felt queasy. She was letting herself get in too deep with Austin Bradshaw. Too intimate. Too fast. Too everything.

It was a good thing he hadn't accepted her stupid, impulsive proposal. His heart was ironclad, safely in the care of his dead wife. But Brooke was vulnerable. She liked Austin. A lot. Given enough time, she might fall in love with him. And therein lay the recipe for disaster.

Suddenly, she needed to put some space between them. Even knowing that he was at the far side of the club grounds wasn't enough. She felt wounded and raw. After capping her paint tin and wiping her brush, she climbed down the ladder and headed inside.

Her next project would be painting murals on the inner and outer walls of the club's day-care center. She kept a notepad and pencil in her back pocket. Maybe now was a good time to take a few measurements and begin sketching out ideas for the traditional nursery rhyme motifs she planned to use.

She had already received permission and a visitor's badge to enter the day care itself. Since two classrooms were outside playing, it turned out to be a perfect time for her to eye the walls and brainstorm a bit.

The creative process calmed her. Gradually, she began to feel better. Everything was fine. It was a good thing that he hadn't accepted her proposal. She wouldn't see Austin socially again. It was better that way.

He was clearly on board with the idea of having recreational sex, but Brooke had never been that kind of woman.

Tons of people were. It wasn't that she was a prude. Despite what she'd agreed to the other day in the heat of the moment, though, she simply didn't have the personality to throw herself into a relationship that was strictly physical. She didn't know how to separate emotional responses from physical ones.

Perhaps she was too needy. A lifetime in a family that thought she wasn't good enough had given her some issues. Maybe instead of having hot, no-strings sex, she should find a good shrink.

Was it so wrong to want to be loved without reservation?

When Austin talked about his late wife, she could hear that

deep, abiding love in his voice. Even though the end had been horrible, Austin had experienced the kind of relationship Brooke wanted.

Unfortunately, he wasn't keen to get involved again. Which meant that Brooke would be foolish to let herself fall for him. The best thing for her to do was concentrate on her current job and also to keep the bigger picture in focus. Somehow, some way, she was going to make her dreams come true.

She finished up her notes. Realizing she couldn't put off her outside project any longer, she headed for the door, only to run into James Harris, the current president of the TCC. "Hi, James," she said. The two of them were friends and moved in the same social circles, but she hadn't seen him in some time.

"Hey, Brooke." The tall, African American man gave her a smile that was strained at best. Clinging to his leg was a cute toddler about a year and a half, give or take.

"I was so sorry to hear about your brother and his wife." They had been killed in a terrible car accident and had left James custody of their infant son. "That must have been a dreadful time for you."

James exhaled. Lines of exhaustion marked his handsome face. "You could say that. Little Teddy here is a bit of a terror. And to be honest, I don't think I would have agreed to be president of the club if I had known what was coming. I'm barely keeping my head above water. Nannies are coming and going at the speed of light."

Brooke crouched and smiled at the boy. His golden-brown eyes were solemn. She didn't try to touch him but instead spoke in a soft, steady voice, aiming her remarks toward the child's uncle. "You'd be a terror, too, if your world had been turned upside down...don't you think?"

James nodded slowly. "That's true. I know you're right. The poor kid is stuck with me, though, and I know squat about how to care for him. I don't suppose you'd be interested in a job?"

The hopeful light in his eyes, mixed with desperation, made

Brooke grin. She stood and squeezed his arm lightly. "Thanks, but no, thanks. I probably know less than you do about kids. Things will get better. They always do."

"I hope so. At least he likes coming here to the day-care center. I kept him at home this morning so he could have a good nap, but I think getting out of the house is good for him. He's incredibly smart."

"See," Brooke said, grinning. "You're already talking like a proud parent."

"But he *is* smart," James insisted.

"I believe you." She brushed Teddy's soft cheek with a fingertip. "Have fun in there, little one. Maybe you'll see me with my paintbrush soon."

James scooped up his nephew and held him close. "I just want to do right by him. What if I screw this up?"

For a moment, she glimpsed his fear. "You won't," she said firmly. "This isn't what you expected from life, James, but we all make adjustments along the way. Deep down, you know that. I have confidence in you. So did your brother, or he never would have left Teddy in your keeping."

James nodded tersely, as if embarrassed that he had let down his guard even for a moment. "Thanks, Brooke."

She gave him a quick hug. "I've got to get back to my murals. Don't give up. It's always darkest before the dawn and all that."

His grin flashed. "Maybe I'll get you to paint that on one of my stables."

"Don't laugh," she said. "I might just do it."

Eight

Austin stood in the shadows, unobserved, and watched as Brooke said her goodbyes to the man and the boy and headed back outside. He couldn't quite identify the feelings in his chest. None of them were ones he wanted to claim. Was Brooke seriously already moving on in her quest to find a convenient husband?

The wealthy horse breeder was a far more logical match for Brooke than Austin, even on a temporary basis. Gus had introduced Austin to James several days ago and had filled Austin's ear about the current TCC president. James Harris was charismatic, intelligent and a darling of Royal's social scene. To be honest, the guy needed a woman in his life. He had inherited a kid.

Brooke needed a husband. It all made a dreadful kind of sense.

Watching the two of them as they chatted casually told Austin that Brooke was comfortable with the other man. Was she thinking about proposing to James now that Austin had turned her down?

To be fair, Austin hadn't said no. He hadn't said anything at all. He'd been too damned shocked.

He was torn…completely torn. The smart thing to do would be to stay as far away from Brooke as possible until the job was done and he could hit the road again. He was used to being a wanderer now. It was the man he had become.

Even so, something inside him couldn't let Brooke go. Her innocence drew him like a gentle flame. Innocence was more than virginity. Brooke had an outlook on life that Austin had lost. Despite her parents' inability to see her worth, Brooke had not become bitter.

He went back to work, but his brain was a million miles away. Somehow, he had to mend the rift he had caused. Before he did that, he had to decide how to respond to Brooke's shocking request.

He possessed the power to make her life better. She had told him so. Having met her mother, Austin believed that statement to be true.

The only real question was—could he serve as Brooke's pretend husband and still barricade his heart?

Daniel Clayton pulled up at his grandmother's house and cut the engine, leaning back in his seat with a sigh. He loved Rose Clayton and owed his grandmother everything good in his life, but things were getting way too complicated.

After swallowing a couple of headache tablets with a swig of bottled water, he wiped his mouth and got out. The Silver C Ranch was home…always would be. Still, no one had ever told him how the older generation could muck things up.

Knowing he couldn't ignore the summons any longer, he strode up to the porch and rang the bell.

His grandmother answered immediately, looking as if she had just spent several hours at a spa. "Hello, sweetheart. Come on in. I made a pie, and I have coffee brewing." Though she was sixty-seven, she didn't look her age. Her soft voice did little to disguise her iron will. He had both adored her and feared her since he was a child.

They made their way to the warm, inviting kitchen and sat down. While Rose poured the coffee and served the warm apple pastry, Daniel studied his grandmother, wondering why he couldn't just say no to her and be done with it.

He didn't have long to wait. Rose sat down beside him, pinned him with a pointed stare and ignored her dessert. "You haven't had much to say about the upcoming bachelor auction."

"No, ma'am. To be entirely honest, I was hoping I could convince you to get someone to take my place. I really don't want to do it. At all."

"I've told all of my friends that you've agreed to participate."

She said it slyly, using guilt as a sharp weapon. Daring him to protest.

He set down his fork, no longer hungry. "It's not my thing, Grandmother. I know I said yes, but I've changed my mind."

"The money will benefit the Pancreatic Cancer Foundation, a very worthy cause."

"Then I'll write a check."

"Our family has to be front and center. The Slades are integral parts of this event, and we will be as well."

"So it's a competition."

"Nonsense. I am a long-standing member of the Texas Cattleman's Club and a well-known citizen of Royal. Of *course* I volunteered my dear bachelor grandson for the auction. It was the least I could do. Surely you want to support me in this. And don't forget, I was hoping sweet Tessa Noble might bid on you. That would be a lovely outcome."

Daniel's headache increased despite the medication. He rubbed the center of his forehead. "Please don't try to play Cupid, Grandmother. That never ends well for anyone. Besides, I'm pretty sure Tessa is interested in her best friend, Ryan."

"Ryan Bateman?" Her eyebrows rose.

"Yes. But don't go spreading that around."

"Of course not." His grandmother seemed disappointed.

"I really don't want to do this bachelor thing," he said, trying desperately for one last chance to escape the inevitable.

Her eyes flashed. "Is it because *you're* interested in someone, Daniel?"

His stomach clenched. No matter how he answered, he was in trouble. And besides, what did it matter now? His love life was toast.

With a big show of glancing at his watch, he stood up and drained his coffee cup. He had barely touched the dessert. "If I can't change your mind, then yes…of course you can count on me."

His grandmother beamed. "You're a wonderful grandson. This will be fun. You'll see."

Brooke painted one last daisy petal and stood back to examine her work. She was proud of what she had accomplished… very proud. So why did the memory of her mother's harsh criticism still sting?

As she was gathering her things in preparation for heading home, she saw a familiar figure striding toward her across the open space that would soon be planted with lush garden foliage. Her heart beat faster. Austin.

Unfortunately, he didn't look too happy. He stopped six feet away and jammed his hands in his pockets. "We need to talk," he declared.

Her heart plunged to her feet. "No," she said. "We really don't. It's okay, Austin. I shouldn't have asked you. It wasn't fair. I'd like to pretend it never happened."

He gave her a lopsided grin. "All of it?"

Her knees went weak. How could he do that to her so easily? Three sexy words and suddenly she was back in his arms, breathless and dizzy and insane with wanting him.

She swallowed. "Be serious."

He inched closer. "You don't look good, Brooke."

"Gee, thanks."

"I'm serious. You're pale and a little green around the gills. Do you feel okay?"

She definitely did *not* feel okay. She was queasy and light-headed. She had been for several days now. But that was nothing, right? "I'm fine," she insisted.

Now he eliminated the last of the buffer between them and took her in his arms. "I'm sorry, Brooke."

His gentle apology broke down her defenses. Her throat tightened with tears. "Someone might be watching from the windows," she choked out.

"I don't really give a damn. Relax, sweetheart. You're so tense it's giving *me* a headache."

She started to shake. A terrible notion had occurred to her this afternoon—a dreadful prospect she had been refusing to acknowledge for the past two weeks. Though it was the last thing she wanted to do, she made herself pull away from his comforting embrace. "I need to go home now. Goodbye, Austin."

He scowled. "You're in no shape to drive. I'll take you."

Hysteria threatened. She had to get away from him. Her stomach heaved and sweat beaded her forehead. "I'll take it easy...roll the windows down. It's not far." Tiny yellow spots began to dance in front of her eyes. "Excuse me," she said, feeling her knees wobble and her hands turn to ice.

With a moan of mortification and misery, she darted into the narrow space where an air-conditioning unit loomed and proceeded to vomit until there was nothing left but dry heaves.

When her knees buckled, strong arms came around her from behind and eased her to the ground. "I've got you, Brooke. It's going to be okay."

They sat there on the dead grass for what seemed like an eternity. Only the ugly industrial metal protected them from prying eyes. Brooke leaned against Austin's shoulder and stared at an ant who was oblivious to their presence.

He stroked her hair, for once completely silent.

At last, a huge sigh lifted his chest, and he exhaled. "Brooke?"

"Y-yes?"

"Are you pregnant?"

The shaking got worse. "I don't know. Maybe."

Austin cursed beneath his breath and then felt like scum when Brooke went whiter still. He wanted to scoop her up in his arms and carry her to a safe, comfortable place where they could talk, but they were trapped. The three exits at the rear of the property were delivery bays that would be locked by now. The only way out was to march through the French doors, into the club and out the front entrance.

He stroked Brooke's arms, concerned by how cool her skin felt to the touch. "Do you feel like you're going to be sick again?"

She shook her head. "No. I don't think so."

"Can you walk if I keep my arm around you? I can't have you fainting on me."

"I won't faint."

"All we have to do is make it out to my truck. We can we leave your paints here, can't we?"

"I suppose."

He stood and pulled her with him, waiting to see if she really was steady. Brushing her hair back from her face, he bent to look into her eyes. "One step at a time, honey. Look at me and tell me you're okay."

Brooke sniffed. "I'm swell," she muttered. "But don't be nice to me or I'm going to cry all over your beautiful blue shirt."

"Duly noted."

"Get me out of here. Please." Her skin was translucent. Her bottom lip trembled ever so slightly.

Austin wrapped an arm around her waist and said a quick prayer that no one would stop them. He sensed that Brooke was close to the breaking point.

Fortunately, the clock was on their side. They were too early to run into the dinner crowd, and most of the daytime regulars were gone already. Austin whisked his companion inside, down the hall and into the reception area. Other than a few quick greetings and a wave, no one stopped them.

In moments, they were outside on the street. Austin steered her toward his vehicle. When she didn't balk, his anxiety grew. "I think we need some expert advice, Brooke. Do you have a doctor here in Royal?"

Her eyes rounded. "Are you kidding me? I can't walk into some clinic and tell them I might be pregnant. My parents would know before I got back home."

"You're not a child. And besides, there are privacy laws."

"That's cute. Clearly you don't know my mother."

"Then I have a suggestion to make."

Brooke climbed into the passenger seat and covered her face with her hands. "Oh…" The strangled moan made him wince.

"What if we drive over to Joplin? My sister is a nurse. We can talk this over with her."

Brooke wiped her face with the back of her hand, her big-eyed gaze chagrined. "What's to talk about? Either I am, or I'm not."

He kept his voice gentle. "You can't even say the *P* word out loud. Do you want *me* asking the questions, or would you feel more comfortable with another woman?"

"You think I'm an idiot, don't you?"

"No," he said carefully. "But from what you've told me, you haven't been sexually active recently, and I think this thing took you by surprise. I know the condom broke, but you told me you were on birth control."

Her face turned red. "The morning I left the hotel I was so flustered I forgot to take my pill. I didn't realize it until a few days later when I got to the end of the pack and had one left over."

He frowned. "And your period?"

"It started eventually… Well, there was…" She bowed her head. "This is so embarrassing."

"You're saying you had some bleeding."

She nodded, her expression mortified. "Yes."

He drummed his fingers on the steering wheel. "Stay here for a minute. Try to relax. Let me call my sister. I won't mention your name, but I'll ask a few questions."

Without waiting for Brooke to answer, he hopped out of the truck and dialed Audra's number. The conversation that followed was not one a man liked having with his sister, but it was necessary. The longer Audra talked, the more his stomach sank. At last, he got back in the truck.

Brooke was curled in a ball, her head resting on her knees.

He touched her shoulder. "Look at me, honey."

She sat up, her expression wary, and exhaled. "Well, what did she say?"

He shrugged. "According to Audra, you can get pregnant on any day of the month, even if you only miss one pill. It's far less likely, of course, but it happens."

"And the bleeding?"

"It could be spotting from hormonal fluctuations during implantation and not a real period. The only way to know for sure is to take a test."

A single tear rolled down her cheek.

Austin felt helplessness and anger engulf him in equal measures. *This* was exactly why he didn't let himself get involved with sweet young things who didn't know the score. Brooke was vulnerable. She'd been under her parents' intimidating influence for far too long.

To her credit, she'd been doing everything she could to strike out on her own. But the gap between her and Austin was still too great. He was worlds ahead of her in life experience. He knew what it was like to love and to suffer and to lose everything. He wouldn't allow that to happen to him again. Ever.

No matter how much Brooke tugged at his heartstrings, he had no place for her in his life. In his bed, maybe. But only for a season.

So what now?

"I'm sorry," she said, the words dull. "I take full responsibility. This has nothing to do with you."

"Don't be stupid." His temper flared out of nowhere. "Of course it does. I could have said no at the bar. I should have. But I wanted you." He touched her cheek, stroking it lightly. His heart turned over in his chest when she tilted her head and nuzzled her face in his palm like a kitten seeking warmth. He pulled her across the bench seat and into his arms. "Don't be scared, Brooke. We'll figure this out." He paused, afraid to ask the next question but knowing he wouldn't be able to move forward without the answer. "Did you propose to me because you thought you might be pregnant?"

She stiffened in his embrace and jerked backward. Her indignation was too genuine to be feigned. "Of course not. I need my inheritance. That's all."

"Okay. Don't get your feathers ruffled."

She bit her lip. "Oh, hell, Austin. I don't know. Maybe I did. I've been feeling weird for the past week. But I've ignored all the signs. It seemed too impossible to be true. I didn't want it to be true."

They sat there in silence for what seemed like forever. Outside, the sky turned gold then navy then completely dark. Brooke's stomach rumbled audibly.

"Here's what we're going to do," Austin said, trying to sound more confident than he felt. "There's a truck stop halfway between Royal and Joplin. We can get a meal there. It will be reasonably private, and if we're lucky, the convenience mart will have a pregnancy test. How does that sound?"

"Like a bad after-school movie."

He chuckled. The fact that she could find a snippet of humor in their situation gave him hope. "That's my girl. Where's your purse?"

"In my car. One street over and around the corner."

Once they had retrieved what she needed, they set out. Austin tuned the radio to an easy listening station, pulled onto the highway and drove just over the speed limit. His stomach was jittery with nerves.

Brooke was quiet—too quiet. Guilt swamped him, though he had done nothing wrong, not really. Other than not resisting temptation, perhaps.

The truck stop was hopping on this particular night. That was a good thing. Brooke and Austin were able to blend into the crowd. The hostess seated them at a booth with faux leather seats and handed them plastic-coated menus that were only slightly sticky.

Brooke studied hers dubiously.

He cocked his head. "What's wrong?"

"I'm starving, but I'm afraid to eat."

"Start with a few small bites. We've got all night. Or will your parents be expecting you home?"

"No. I told them I was spending the evening with a friend. They don't really care what I do on a small scale. It's the big picture they want to control."

After the waitress took their order, Austin reached across the table and gripped Brooke's hand. "I won't leave you to face this alone," he said carefully. "I need you to know that."

Her eyes shone with tears again. "Thank you."

"Do you want me to go buy the test now and get it over with, or would you rather wait until after dinner?"

She seemed stricken by his question. "Let's eat first. Then maybe we could book a room? Even if we only use it for a couple of hours?" She winced. "OMG. That sounds sleazy, doesn't it?"

The look on her face made him laugh. "I think it's a fine idea. In the meantime, let's talk about your inheritance and what you hope to do with it. I really want to know."

Brooke sat up straighter, and some of the strain left her face. "Well, I told you about starting the art school."

He nodded. "Yes. Do you have a business plan?"

"Actually, I do," she said proudly. "I even have my eye on a small piece of property near the center of town. It's zoned for commercial and residential both, but the woman who owns the land is partial to small-business owners. She and I have talked in confidence, and she really wants me to have it. The only missing piece is capital."

"Which marrying me will provide."

"Exactly."

"Even without a possible pregnancy, I'm surprised you're not more worried about your parents' reactions to me being your fiancé," he said quietly. "I'm not exactly upper-crust. Audra and I have done well for ourselves, but our mom cleaned houses for a living, and our dad was a plumber."

"They're both gone? But you're so young."

"Mom and Dad were never able to have kids. They adopted Audra and me when they were forty-nine. We lost them both within six months of each other last year. Pneumonia."

"I'm so sorry." Her empathy was almost palpable. "That must have been devastating, especially for you. Did it bring back bad memories of losing your wife?"

Nine

As soon as the words left her mouth, Brooke wanted to snatch them back. The flash of bleak remembrance she saw in Austin's eyes crushed her. It was as if the grief was fresh and new. Did he carry it always like a millstone around his neck, or did it come and go only when insensitive friends, like her, for instance, brought it up out of the blue?

Fortunately, the waitress arrived with their meals, and the moment passed.

Brooke, though she was leery of getting sick again, couldn't resist the sight and smell of the comfort food. She was starving and, thankfully, was able to eat without consequences. Austin cleared his plate as well.

The truck stop was as close to a good ole Texas honky-tonk as a place could get. The atmosphere was rowdy and warm and filled with laughter and the scents of cold beer and warm sweat.

It was not the kind of spot Brooke frequented, but tonight, it was perfect. As long as she didn't move from this booth, she was insulated from the consequences of her actions.

Unfortunately, though, the clock continued to move. The

check was paid. The evening waned. Though Austin had said little during the meal, his gaze had stayed on her constantly. In his eyes she saw concern and more. Certainly a flash of sexual awareness. They were both thinking about the escapade that had brought them to this moment.

She bit her lip. "Have you heard of Schrödinger's cat?"

Austin sighed. "Here we go."

"What?" she said, indignant.

"Everyone who's ever watched a certain TV sitcom has heard of Schrödinger's cat. You're saying that as long as we sit in this booth and never leave, you're both pregnant and *not* pregnant. Have I got that?"

"Works for me," she said, stirring the melting ice in her Coke moodily.

"You're not a coward, Brooke Goodman. Knowledge is power. One step at a time. I can quote you clichés till the cows come home. Let's go buy that test and see what we're facing."

"It might be negative," she said, desperately clinging to one last shred of hope.

"It might be…"

His impassive expression told her nothing.

The minimart, unlike the truck stop, was *not* crowded. Brooke, her face hot with embarrassment, snatched two boxes—different brands—off the shelf, plunked down her credit card and hastily signed the receipt. Fortunately for her, the employee manning the counter was more interested in his video game than he was in her purchases.

Soon after, Austin secured two keys to room twenty-four, the last unit on the far right end. They parked in front of their home away from home. He unlocked the door and waited for Brooke to enter.

Could have been better. Could have been worse.

The decor was late '80s, but everything appeared to be clean.

She stood, irresolute, in the middle of the floor.

Austin locked the door, took her in his arms and kissed her forehead. "Get it over with. I'll be right here."

The list of humiliating things she had experienced today was growing. Now she had to add peeing on a stick with a tall, handsome cowboy just on the other side of the door. Fortunately, directions for pregnancy tests were straightforward. She read them, did what had to be done and waited.

After the first result, she ripped open the second box. Pee and repeat.

There was no mistaking the perfect match.

She didn't feel like throwing up. She didn't feel anything at all.

Austin knocked on the door. "You okay in there, honey?"

"Yes," she croaked. "Give me just a minute." She dried them, hoping to erase the evidence. Still the same. Taking a deep breath, she opened the bathroom door and leaned against the frame, feeling breathless and dizzy and incredulous. "Well," she said, "I'm pregnant."

Austin went white under his tan. Which was really pretty funny, because it wasn't exactly a huge surprise. Apparently, like her, he had been hoping against hope that her barfing had been a fluke.

He swallowed visibly. "I see."

"Say something," she begged. Why couldn't this be like the commercials where the woman showed the man the stick and they both danced around the room?

"What do you want me to say?" His gaze was stoic, his stance guarded.

"I keep feeling the need to apologize," she whispered. The tears started then in earnest. They rolled down her cheeks and onto her shirt. Austin didn't want a wife, not even a temporary one. And he surely didn't want a child. This man had been badly hurt. All he wanted was his freedom.

Though she didn't make a sound, her distress galvanized him. He closed the space between them and scooped her up in his arms, carrying her to the bed. He sat down and held her on his lap. "Things happen, Brooke. This situation isn't your fault. It isn't mine."

Time passed. Maybe five minutes, maybe an entire day. So many thoughts and feelings rushed through her body. Having Austin hold her like this was both comforting and at the same time wildly arousing. Her body tensed in heated reaction. In his arms, she felt as if she could handle any obstacle in her path. But at the same time, he made her want things that were dangerous to her peace of mind.

Beneath her, his sex hardened. The fact that Austin Bradshaw was now unmistakably *excited* made her want to strip him and take him without a single thought for the future.

Instead, she scooted off his lap and stood, scrubbing her face with her hands, trying not to compound her mistakes. One thing she knew for sure. "I know I have…options, but I want this baby. Maybe *want* is the wrong word. I'm responsible for this baby. I'm the one who walked into a bar to do something foolish. Now I'm pregnant. So I'll deal with the consequences."

"A baby will change everything about your life," Austin said. His dark gaze was watchful. "It will be a hell of a long time before you can take that months-long trip to Europe to visit art galleries and study the grand masters."

The enormity of the truth in his words squeezed her stomach. "Yes. But that was a selfish bucket list item and one that can wait indefinitely."

"I'll provide for the child financially. You don't have to worry about money."

She winced. "I appreciate the sentiment, but with my inheritance, that won't be necessary. I'm assuming this pregnancy will tip the balance in my favor. My parents are not fond of babies. They won't want me in the house, so I think they'll have no choice but to turn over what is legally mine."

"Having met your mother, I think you're being naive. If I had to guess, I'd say they'll use your child as a bargaining chip to control you. Your situation hasn't gotten better, Brooke. It's gotten worse."

She gaped at him, studying the grim certainty on his face and processing the truth of his words. "I hadn't thought of it that way."

He stood as well, jamming his hands in his pockets and pacing. "We'll get through this…"

"We?" she asked faintly, feeling as if she were an actor in a very bad play.

He shot her a hard glance, his face carved in planes and angles that suggested strong emotion tightly under wraps. "*We.*" His forceful tone brooked no argument. "We're a family now, Brooke…whether we want to be or not. Our only choice is how to handle the way forward. You asked me to marry you. Now I'm saying yes."

"This isn't your problem," she insisted. "It's *my* baby."

He stopped in front of her, their breath mingling, he was so close. At last, the rigid posture of his big frame relaxed, and a small smile tilted those masculine lips that knew how to turn a woman inside out. "Sorry, honey. It doesn't work that way. There were two of us in that bed."

"But you don't want to be here," she cried. "You're only planning to stay in Royal for a couple of months at the most."

He slid his hands into her hair and cupped her neck, tilting her head, finding her lips with his. "So I'll change my plans," he said, kissing her lazily. "Some women sail through pregnancy. But a lot of them don't. You need someone to care for you and support you. Right now, that someone is going to be me."

Kissing Austin was never what she expected. He could take her from gentle bliss to shuddering need in a heartbeat. Tonight, he gave her something in between. He held her and made her believe, even if for only a moment, that everything was going to turn out okay.

She rested her cheek against his chest, feeling and hearing the steady *ka-thud* of his heartbeat. "I can't ask you to do that."

Even if the prospect of having Austin in her corner made her soul sing.

"You don't really have a choice." When he chuckled, the sound reverberated beneath her ear. He was so big and hard and warm. Nothing in her life had ever felt so good, so perfect.

But the perfection was a mirage. Her heart screamed at her to proceed with caution. Austin was being kind. Honorable. He was the sort of man who did the right thing regardless of the cost.

That didn't mean he wouldn't inadvertently break her heart.

She pulled away, needing physical distance to be strong. "I'll talk to my parents tomorrow. If they agree to give me the inheritance, the baby and I can have a home of our own. You don't even have to be involved."

Austin shook his head, his smile self-mocking. "I'm involved up to my neck, Brooke. And I'm not going anywhere for the moment."

For the moment... Those three words were ominous but truthful. She'd do well to plaster them on her heart, so she didn't get any foolish ideas. Suddenly, her knees felt weak. She staggered two steps toward the bed and sat down hard.

His gaze sharpened. "What's wrong?"

"Nothing. Not really. Just a little light-headed. It will pass."

He crossed his arms over his chest. "Do you want to stay here until morning? I can buy what we need at the convenience mart."

From his expression, she hadn't a clue what *he* wanted to do. Probably run far and fast in the opposite direction.

The prospect of spending the night with Austin, even in this unappealing motel room, was almost impossible to resist. It was easy to imagine making love to him all night long and waking up naked in his arms. Her breath caught.

Austin's gaze narrowed. "Are you sure you're okay? You're all flushed."

"I'm fine."

If she were going to be a mother, she had to start making mature decisions. "We can't stay here," she said slowly. "I need to be at the club tomorrow to work on the murals. And before that, I'll have to face my parents at breakfast and tell them the news."

"Don't you want to give yourself time to get used to the idea first? You've had a shock, Brooke."

"I can't have this hanging over my head. I believe in ripping off the Band-Aid."

"Fair enough." He nodded slowly. "And you won't be alone. I plan on being there beside you when you break the news."

"Oh my gosh, no," she squeaked, already imagining the fireworks. "That's a terrible idea. I'm not going to tell them about you."

"Don't be ridiculous. We've already established that I can handle your mother. Besides, the truth will get out sooner or later. This isn't going to be our guilty secret."

Though she was skeptical, she nodded. "If you insist. But don't say I didn't warn you."

Austin took Brooke home. Dropping her off at her parents' house was more difficult than he had expected. Already he felt possessive. Even if he kept himself emotionally divested, Brooke was the mother of his child. That meant something.

The following morning, he dragged himself out of bed, wondering if she had slept any more than he had. A shower did little to offset the effects of insomnia. He shaved and dressed carefully, not wanting to give the Goodmans any overt opportunity to look down their noses at him. Not for his sake, but for Brooke's.

Austin had already seen firsthand how her mother treated her. It didn't take a genius to deduce that a man like Austin would not be on their list of suitable husbands for their daughter.

Brooke had insisted that she be the one to do all the talking, because she knew how to handle her mother and father. Austin had reluctantly agreed.

When he showed up at the imposing Goodman residence, the house looked even more opulent than it had the night before. As an architect, Austin knew plenty about price points and quality building materials. The Goodmans had spared no expense in building their Pine Valley mansion. He wondered if Brooke had lived here her entire life.

He rang the bell. A uniformed maid answered the summons and escorted him through the house. A full hot breakfast was in the process of being laid out on a mahogany sideboard. Sunlight flooded the room through French-paned windows. The dining table was set with china, crystal and antique silver that sparkled and gleamed.

Brooke greeted him with a smile, though he could see the strain beneath the surface. The elder Goodmans were cool but polite in their welcomes. Once everyone was seated, the grilling commenced.

Simon Goodman eyed Austin with more than a hint of suspicion. "My wife tells me you're doing a temporary job for Gus Slade."

No mistaking the emphasis on *temporary*.

"Yes, sir. Or for the Cattleman's Club, to be more exact. I'm overseeing the outdoor addition to the facilities."

"And you have the suitable credentials?"

Austin swallowed his ire. "An advanced degree in architecture and a number of years' experience at a firm in Dallas."

"But you're no longer with that firm?"

"Daddy!"

Brooke's indignant interruption had no discernable effect on the interrogation. For some inexplicable reason, Margaret Goodman was oddly silent. Austin sighed inwardly. "When my wife became very ill, I worked until she needed constant care, and then I quit my job. Since she passed away six years ago, I've chosen to be a bit of a nomad."

"I can't believe this." Brooke stood up so abruptly, her chair wobbled. She glared at her father. "You're embarrassing me.

And you're being horribly rude. Austin is my friend. He doesn't deserve the Spanish Inquisition."

Brooke's mother waved a hand. "Sit down and eat, Brooke. You aren't fooling anyone. Your father is well within his rights to ask as many questions as he sees fit. That's why you've brought Austin here, isn't it? To convince us that you've fallen madly in love with a handyman? And that we're supposed to throw you a lavish wedding and hand over your inheritance?"

The silence that fell was deafening. Scrambled eggs congealed on four plates. Though every bit of the breakfast was spectacularly prepared and worthy of a five-star restaurant, Austin suspected that most of the food would end up in the trash. *He* had certainly lost his appetite. And poor Brooke looked much as she had yesterday when she had gotten sick behind the club.

Every instinct he possessed told him to take charge of the situation, but he had promised to let Brooke do the talking, so he held his tongue. It wasn't easy.

She sat down slowly. Her face was the color of the skim milk Mrs. Goodman was adding to her coffee from a tiny silver pitcher. Brooke cleared her throat. "I was going to broach the subject more gently than Daddy did, but yes, Austin and I are going to get married. We haven't talked about a ceremony yet. I don't even know if I want a big wedding. I'm telling you because you're my parents, not because I expect you to pay for anything."

Poor Brooke looked frazzled. Austin swallowed a bite of biscuit that threatened to stick in his throat. "I am perfectly capable of paying for our wedding. All Brooke needs from you is your blessing and your support. She loves her family and wants to include you."

Austin infused his words with steel. Though it might have gone over Brooke's head given her current physical discomfort, it was clear from Margaret and Simon's expressions that they heard his ultimatum. They could treat Brooke well, or they could lose her...their choice.

Unfortunately, Brooke's mother refused to go down without a fight. "Please understand, Mr. Bradshaw. It's a parent's obligation to protect his or her child from fortune hunters."

The blatant insult was almost humorous. How could sweet, openhearted Brooke have come from such a dreadful woman?

Fortunately, Austin had always relished a good battle. "In that vein, I'm sure you'll understand it's *my* job to make Brooke happy. And by God, that's what I intend to do."

Simon's face turned an ugly shade of puce. "You don't know who you're dealing with, Bradshaw."

"I know that you've blackballed your daughter. That you've made her a prisoner in her own home. That you've deliberately sabotaged her search for meaningful employment. That you've refused to acknowledge she's an adult and one who deserves respect and autonomy."

Margaret slammed her fist on the table. "Get out," she hissed, her gaze shooting fire at him as if she could incinerate him on the spot.

Austin looked across the table at Brooke. He smiled at her, trying to telegraph his unending support and compassion. "Do you want me to go, honey?"

Brooke stood up, seeming to wobble the tiniest bit. She dabbed her lips with a snowy damask napkin and rounded the table to put a hand on his shoulder. "Yes. But not yet. I'll leave with you in a moment."

He heard her take a quavering breath. Now he knew what was coming. Her tension was palpable. Quickly, he got to his feet and put an arm around her waist. Not speaking, just offering his silent support.

Brooke stared at her mother, then her father. She cleared her throat. Her eyes glistened with tears. Austin wanted to curse. This should be a joyful moment. He hated that it was playing out like a melodrama with Brooke's parents as the wicked villains.

"Here's the thing," she said quietly. "Austin and I are getting married. Very soon. After that, I will petition the court for my inheritance. You know it's mine. For you to interfere would be criminal, mean-spirited and petty."

Her fathered puffed out his chest. He glared. "You'll squander every penny in six months. Don't think you can come crawling back for more."

Austin's arm tightened around Brooke. He could literally *feel* the blow of her father's cruel words. "I won't come back home, Daddy," she said. "At least not to stay. I'm a grown woman."

Margaret shoved back from the table and approached Brooke, using her physical presence as a threat, just as she had in the club gardens. Her smile was cold and merciless. "You're a child. This man doesn't love you. He's using you. All I've ever wanted is what's best for you, baby. Let's put this awful business behind us. Start over. Turn back the clock."

Brooke's spine straightened a millimeter. She slid her hand into Austin's and gripped it so hard her fingernails dug into his skin. "I can't turn back the clock, Mama. I'm pregnant."

Ten

Margaret's infuriated shriek reverberated in the confines of the room. For one terrible moment, Austin thought she was going to strike her own daughter. He thrust Brooke behind him and confronted her mother. "Tread carefully, Mrs. Goodman. There are some bridges you don't want to burn. I think it's best if we continue this conversation at another time."

Without giving anyone a chance to protest, he grabbed Brooke's hand and hurried her out of the room and away from the house. After he hustled her down the front walk to where his truck was parked, he cursed beneath his breath when she leaned against the hood of the vehicle and covered her face with her hands. A pregnant woman needed sustenance. Between morning sickness and emotional trauma, Brooke had barely swallowed a bite as far as he could tell.

He tucked her into the passenger seat and ran around to the other side. Once the engine started, he sighed. Taking her hand in his once again, he lifted it and kissed her fingers. "I am so very sorry, sweetheart."

Brooke shrugged, her gaze trained somewhere beyond the windshield. "It's nothing new. Not really."

"I have a proposition for you," he said, wanting desperately to erase her sorrow.

"Isn't that what got us into this mess?" she said wryly.

Something inside him eased. If she could joke about it, even now, all was not lost. "You can't stay there anymore, Brooke. It's not healthy for you or the baby. Gus has been hosting me in the bunkhouse out at the ranch, but frankly, that's getting old. I've taken a look at some new rental condos on the east side of town. They're really nice. What if we go right now and sign a twelve-month lease?"

Her eyes rounded. "*Live together?*"

"You already proposed to me. This seems like a logical step."

Her face turned pink. "I'm sorry I've complicated your life."

"Stop it," he said. "And relax. Stress isn't good for a woman who's expecting. If nothing else, my job is to pamper you and make sure you have a healthy pregnancy. We enjoy each other's company. What do you say?"

Half an hour later, Brooke took slow, shallow breaths and tried to convince herself she wasn't going to barf. After escaping the uncomfortable breakfast with her parents, she and Austin had used the drive-through at a fast food restaurant and picked up sausage biscuits and coffee.

They sat in the parking lot and ate the yummy food, barely speaking. Even so, the silence was comfortable. Austin didn't *crowd* her. Most men in this situation would be demanding an answer.

He finished his meal and crumpled up the paper wrapper. "How's your stomach?"

She held out her hand and dipped it left and right. "So-so."

"I can't read your mind, honey. What are you thinking?"

"Honestly?" She grimaced. "As soon as you and I look at condos together, the gossip will be all over town."

"Doesn't change anything, does it?"

"I can't afford to rent a condo. I don't have any money, Austin," she said bluntly. "And even if we were to get married today, the process to claim my inheritance would take longer than you think to work its way through the court system."

"Forget about that," he said, his voice quiet but firm. "I've lived very frugally for six years. I've got money in the bank. Plenty for you and me and the baby."

She felt her face heat. "I've tried so hard to be independent. This feels like a step backward."

"Not at all. This is *us* making a home for our baby. If you don't leave that house, your parents will only find more ways to make your life miserable and to try and control you."

"I want to be clear about our expectations," Brooke said slowly. "Are you suggesting cohabitation or marriage or both?"

His expression shuttered suddenly, every nuance of his real feelings erased. That sculpted masculine jaw turned to granite. "This would be a practical marriage partnership between two consenting adults. I was considering your proposal even before we found out you were pregnant. Now, it makes sense all the way around. Once the baby comes and you're back on your feet physically, emotionally and financially, we'll reassess the situation."

"You mean divorce."

He winced visibly. "That's what you suggested earlier, yes. But even if we separate, I'll always be part of your life on some level. Because of the child."

So clinical. So sensible. Why did his blunt, rational speech take all the color and sunshine out of the day?

"What will you do when the project at the club is finished?"

"Matt Galloway has talked to me about building a house for him. That would take the better part of a year. After that, I don't know. I suppose I may want to stay in Royal because of the baby. I can't imagine not seeing my son or daughter on a regular basis."

And what about me? She wanted him to tell her how hard it would be to walk away from *her.*

Swallowing all her nausea and her misgivings and the pained understanding that Austin was offering so much less than forever, Brooke summoned a smile. "Okay, Cowboy. Let's go look at these condos. Window-shopping doesn't cost a thing."

An hour later, she ran her hand along the windowsill of a cheery, sun-filled room overlooking a koi pond and a weeping willow. The backyard was small but adequate. And it was fenced in. Perfect for a toddler to stagger across the grass chasing a ball or laughing as soap bubbles popped.

This particular condo, the fourth one they had looked at, had three bedrooms—plenty of space for a loner, a new baby and a woman whose life was in chaos. The complex was brandnew, the paint smell still lingering in the air. The rentals were designed primarily for oil company executives who came to Royal for several months at a time and wanted all the comforts of home.

The agent had stepped outside to give them privacy.

Austin put a hand on her arm. "You like it, don't you? I can see it on your face."

She shot him a wry glance over her shoulder. "What's not to like? But these places have to be far too expensive." The units were over three thousand square feet each. They weren't the type of starter homes young newlyweds sought out. Each condo Brooke and Austin had toured was outfitted with high-end everything, from the luxurious marble bathrooms and the fancy kitchens to the spacious family rooms wired for every possible entertainment convenience.

"I told you. Money is not a problem."

Panic fluttered in her chest. "I'll pay you back. Half of everything. As soon as I have my inheritance."

He frowned. "That's not necessary.

"Those are my terms."

Even to her own ears she sounded petulant and ungrateful.

But she was scrambling for steady ground, needing something to hold on to, some way to pretend she was in control.

"So we'll get married?" He stood there staring at her with his hands in his pockets and a cocky attitude that said *take me or leave me*.

"You don't have to do this, Austin."

"You promised me home-cooked meals and hot sex."

He was teasing. She knew that. But suddenly, she couldn't make light of their situation. Tears clogged her throat. Creating a home with a baby on the way should be something a man and a woman did that was almost sacred. Brooke and Austin were making a mockery of marriage and family. "I need to visit the restroom," she muttered. "Will you see how long we can wait to give them an answer?"

She locked herself in the nearest bathroom, sat on the closed commode lid and cried. Not long. Three minutes, max. But it was enough to make her eyes puffy. Afterward, she splashed water on her face and tried to repair the damage with her compact.

In the mirror over the sink, she looked haggard and scared. Poor Austin hadn't signed on for all this drama. She used a tissue to wipe away a smudge of mascara and dried her hands on her pants.

Then—because she quite literally had no other choice—she unlocked the door and went in search of her cowboy.

Austin and the rental agent, an attractive woman in her early forties, were chatting comfortably when Brooke emerged onto the front porch. The other woman gave her a searching look. "Everything okay? I have bottled water in my car."

Brooke nodded. "I'm fine."

Austin curled an arm around Brooke's waist, drawing her close. She leaned into his warmth and strength unashamedly. He smelled good, though his nearness made her knees wobble. She couldn't seem to stop wanting him despite everything that had happened.

The agent eyed them both with a practiced smile. "I was telling Mr. Bradshaw that there are three other couples on the books to see this unit today, two this afternoon and one tonight. As you probably know, decent rental property is hard to come by in Royal. This new development is very popular, and this particular condo was only finished two days ago. This one is outfitted as a model, though you certainly don't have to take the furniture if it's not your taste. If you're interested, though, I wouldn't wait too long."

Austin tightened his arm around Brooke. "Give us a few minutes, would you?"

The woman walked down the steps and out to her car.

"Well," he said. "What do you think?"

Brooke wriggled free, needing a clear head. She couldn't get *that* standing so close to the man who made her breathe faster. He rattled her. "You know it's perfect. Of course, it's perfect. But that's not really the point. Aren't we rushing into this?"

He lifted an eyebrow. "You're already pregnant. The clock is ticking. You're the one who asked for marriage. I'm happy for the both of us to move in here either way. I'm already imagining all the ways we can use that big Jacuzzi tub."

So could she. The intensity of her need for him made her shiver.

She licked her lips. "I don't think pregnant women are supposed to use hot tubs."

"Then we'll improvise in the shower."

The heat in his gaze threatened to melt her on the spot.

"How can you be so cavalier about the situation?" she cried. There was absolutely nothing she could do about the panic in her voice. The fact that Austin was cool and unruffled told her his emotional involvement was nil. It was Brooke who was unraveling bit by bit.

Austin shook his head slowly. "Take it easy. I didn't mean to pressure you. But it made me so damn mad to see your parents play the bully. Sit, honey. Breathe."

He summoned the agent with a crook of his finger. Brooke sank onto the porch swing, half numb, half scared.

Austin gave the woman a blinding smile. "I'll take it," he said.

The agent faltered. "You?" She glanced at Brooke. "But I thought…"

"The contract will be in my name only," Austin said cheerfully. "Just mine. I asked Ms. Goodman to come along and give me advice. She likes all those flopping and flipping shows, don't you, sweetheart?"

Brooke nodded. Austin was giving her a way out. Was she being a coward? Maybe so. But his gesture touched her deeply, because it told her he understood her fears.

While Austin wrote a check for first and last month's rent and signed a dozen pages of an official-looking contract, Brooke moved the swing lazily, pushing her foot against the crisply painted boards of the porch. Halloween was only a few days away. This house would need a smiling jack-o'-lantern.

Was she going to live here? For real? Or was this some kind of bizarre fantasy?

She tried to imagine it. Coming home each night to Austin Bradshaw. Sharing his bed.

Every scenario that played in her head was more delicious and tempting than the last. Under this roof, she and Austin would be *alone*. She could indulge her lust for his magnificent body over and over and over again. Intimate candlelit dinners for two. Watching movies on the couch and pausing the action on the screen when they couldn't resist touching each other. Lazy Saturday morning sex when neither of them had responsibilities. It would be one long, sizzling affair.

She blinked and came back to reality with a mental thud.

In one blinding instant, she saw the impossibility of her situation. She *did* need Austin. Marrying him would free up her inheritance and thus finance her dreams of owning an art studio in Royal…of training and inspiring the next generation of artists and dreamers.

Marrying him would make her child legitimate in the eyes of the law, an outdated concept no doubt, but one that was nevertheless appealing. Marrying Austin would give her the freedom to finally be her own person.

But at what cost? Living with him would end up breaking her heart.

She watched him as he talked and laughed with the rental agent. He was making a concerted effort to charm the woman, to keep her from spending too much time wondering why Brooke was not signing on the dotted line, as well. Hoping, perhaps, to deflect the inevitable gossip.

Everything about this man was dangerous. From the very first moment Brooke saw him in that crowded bar in Joplin, something about him had spoken to her deepest needs. She was already half in love with him. The only remedy was to stay far, far away.

Instead, she was about to do the exact opposite.

With a sigh, she pulled out her phone and tried to distract herself with emails while she waited for Austin to finish up. At last, the formalities were done. The agent locked up the property and drove away.

Austin sat down beside Brooke and stretched his long arms along the back of the swing. Yawning hugely, he dropped his head back and sighed. "She's going to meet me here at 8:00 a.m. on Monday to pick up the keys. I'll pack my stuff at Gus's this weekend, so I can move in after work that afternoon."

"And me?"

He curled one hand around her shoulder and caressed her bare arm below the sleeve of her top. His fingers were warm against her chilled skin, eliciting delicious shivers. She'd left her jacket in the car, so she snuggled closer, welcoming his body heat.

"Well," he said slowly. "I suppose that's up to you. I hate the thought of you going back to that house."

"It's my home, Austin. They're not going to poison my soup or lock me in my room."

"Don't be too sure. I wouldn't put anything past your mother." He shuddered theatrically. "She scares me."

His nonsense lightened the mood. "Do you really think we can make this work?"

"I do. We're reasonable adults with busy schedules, so we won't be together 24/7. We both have plenty of work ahead of us at the club, not to mention the fact that we have to get ready for a baby. And when it comes to that, by the way, I can be involved as much or as little as you want me to…"

"Okay." She was feeling weepy again. Lost and unsure of herself. Not an auspicious start to a *convenient* relationship. She swallowed. "Are you still willing to marry me?"

His gaze remained fixed out on the street where two delivery trucks were wrangling about parking privileges. "Yes." The word was low but firm.

"Not a church wedding," she said. "Something small. And very simple."

"The courthouse?"

"Yes." Sadness curled in her stomach. If she were marrying the love of her life, even a courthouse wedding would be romantic. However, under these circumstances, it seemed sad and a bit tawdry.

"I have one requirement."

She stiffened. "Oh?"

He shifted finally, half turning so he could see her face. "I want you to buy a special dress. It's doesn't have to be a traditional gown. But something to mark the day as an occasion. Will you do that for me?"

He leaned forward and brushed her cheek with his thumb. Suddenly, her heart thudded so loudly in her chest she was sure he could hear the ragged thumps. "Yes," she croaked. "I'll go tomorrow."

"Brooke?" He leaned in as he said her name, his lips brushing hers once...twice. "I care about you. I'll never do anything to hurt you, I swear. And I will protect you and this baby with my life."

It was as solemn and sacred a vow as any she had ever heard. Even without the word *love*, it would have to be enough. Austin had already made that other vow on another day with another woman. Brooke would have to be satisfied with these very special promises he had given to her as the father of her baby.

She kissed him softly. "Yes," she said. "I will marry you, and I will live with you. For this one year. And I will do everything in my power to make sure that you don't regret your decision. Thank you, Austin." Curling her arms around his neck, she let herself go, gave herself permission to lower her defenses and simply enjoy the moment.

He wrapped her in his arms tenderly, as if she were breakable...as if all the passion between them had to be kept in check, muted, held at bay to keep from crushing her. Paradoxically, his gentleness made the moment all the more arousing. Their heartbeats, their longing clashed, and like an almost palpable force, the wanting grew and multiplied.

Emboldened, she slid a hand beneath his shirt and caressed the hard, warm planes of his back.

They were outside. In public. Only the confines of the porch gave them any privacy at all.

Austin groaned.

"What?" she whispered, pressing into him, needing him so badly she shook with it.

"I should have written her a check for three more days and taken the keys right now."

Brooke pulled back and stared at him. "That was an *option*?"

His sheepish smile softened the moment, though not the intensity of her desire for him. On the other side of the door lay at least two brand-new, fully serviceable beds. "I wasn't thinking too clearly. It's not every day a man buys a house for his wife and child."

"Rents," she corrected, reminding herself of the tenuous nature of their agreement.

"Whatever." He glanced at his watch and muttered a curse. His disgruntled expression was almost amusing.

"I take it we're through here?"

He stood and stretched. "I have to meet someone at the club. It's important. Or I wouldn't leave you."

The odd choice of words gave her pause. "I have to go, too. I want to finish up the last outdoor mural so I can start on the day-care walls next week. The weather is supposed to turn dreary."

Austin tugged her to her feet. He rested his forehead on hers. "Will you be here with me Monday night?"

Her heart beat faster. Moving out of her parents' house would be no picnic. "Yes," she said clearly. "You can count on it."

Eleven

They wasted no time in heading for the Texas Cattleman's Club. Austin found a prime parking spot, gave Brooke a quick kiss and ran off for his appointment. She stopped by her own car—still parked where it had been overnight—grabbed a couple of items she needed out of the trunk and went inside to change into her work clothes, engulfed in a haze of giddy anticipation and cautious optimism.

The sun was shining, and the temps were balmy. It was a perfect day to paint, though she missed Austin already. In the distance, she could see the stage addition taking shape. It was going to be a push, but Austin swore he would have everything ready in time for the auction. Already, the landscapers were putting down sod and laying out string and markers for the plants, both temporary and permanent, that would turn the gardens into a fall foliage paradise.

The whole thing was exciting. Not that Brooke would attend the auction itself. At least she didn't think so. She certainly wasn't going to bid on a bachelor. She would, however, make an extremely modest donation to the charity, despite her financial woes. This event was important to Alexis, and Brooke wanted to support her friend in every way she could.

Because she was so close to finishing the entire outdoor project, she opted for peanut butter crackers at lunch. To appease her conscience, she resolved to have a healthy dinner when she got home.

The day flew by. She was in the zone. Anytime her heart was in the midst of a painting, it was as if the brush moved on its own. At four o'clock, she was limp with exhaustion but filled with elation. Two huge outdoor walls now burst with life and color.

As she cleaned up her supplies and packed everything away, she kept an eye out for Austin, but he was nowhere to be found. She told herself not to be silly. Going home to face her parents was something she could do on her own. She didn't need a man to help with that.

In the end, the expected confrontation never materialized. She had completely forgotten that her mother had a huge real estate conference in Las Vegas. Her father had gone along to play golf. Brooke glanced at the calendar in the pantry. They had flown out at 3:00 p.m. Wouldn't be back until Monday night.

She stood in the empty kitchen with an odd feeling in the pit of her stomach. Instead of facing an unpleasant weekend of arguments and emotional upheaval, all she had to do was pack her things and say goodbye to her childhood home. This time when she walked out, it would be for good.

There were sweet memories in the huge house. Not everything had been a struggle. But unfortunately, the lovelier moments of her childhood had been somewhat obliterated by events in recent years.

The cook had left two different casseroles in the fridge. Brooke picked the one with carrots and other veggies. She needed to eat well. Unfortunately, the smell of the food heating in the microwave made her stomach heave. She rushed outside and leaned against the house, breathing in the night air. No one had ever told her that morning sickness could last all day.

On a whim, she sent a text to Alexis...

Are you busy? Want to come over? I haven't seen you in ages...

Alexis's response was almost immediate.

Sounds great. Are your parents home?

Brooke grinned. Alexis was no more a fan of Simon and Margaret Goodman than Austin was. She typed a single-word reply and threw in a few happy-face emojis for good measure...

NO! ☺☺☺

Alexis replied quickly.

See you soon.

While Brooke cleaned up the kitchen and waited for her friend, she debated how much of the truth to share. She could trust Alexis with her secrets. She had no doubts about that. But she didn't want to feel disloyal to Austin. The confusion was a dilemma she hadn't expected.

Alexis arrived barely half an hour later. After the two women hugged, Brooke led the way into the comfy den. "You want something to drink?" she asked. "A glass of wine, maybe?"

The other woman plopped down on the sofa with a sigh. "What are you having?"

Brooke felt her cheeks get hot. "Just water. Trying to be healthier. You know."

"Yeah. Probably a good idea. This whole bachelor auction may turn me into a raving alcoholic before it's over anyway."

Brooke curled up in an adjoining chair. "How are things going?"

Alexis shrugged. "I suppose you could say we're on schedule. Still, I'm putting out new fires every day. I can't imagine why there are people who *want* to do event planning for a living."

Brooke laughed, but she sympathized with her friend's frustration. Gus Slade, Alexis's grandfather, had insisted his granddaughter be in charge of the bachelor auction. No one ever said no to Gus, least of all his beleaguered family members.

Alexis was similar in height and build to Brooke, though Alexis was a bit taller, and her eyes were blue, not gray. The two women had been friends since childhood. Alexis was the same age as Brooke, but unlike Brooke, Alexis had been sent away to school at a young age and had developed a sophistication and confidence Brooke wondered if she herself would ever match.

Brooke studied the lines of exhaustion on her friend's face. "Sounds like you need a break. Have you seen Daniel lately?"

"No," Alexis said sharply. "Daniel and I are history. End of story."

"Sorry for bringing him up," Brooke muttered.

"No, I'm sorry," Alexis said quickly. Her guilty smile was apologetic. "But let's talk about you."

"Okay." Brooke paused, struggling for words. There really was no way to dance around the subject. "I'm pregnant."

Alexis's jaw dropped. She sat up straight and stared. "You're joking."

"No." Brooke shook her head.

"But who?" Her friend was understandably bewildered.

"Austin Bradshaw. The architect your grandfather hired to design and oversee the new club addition."

"I've run into him. Briefly." Alexis frowned. "He only arrived two weeks ago. Maybe not even that long."

"We met in Joplin just before Labor Day. It was never supposed to be anything more than a..." The words stuck in her throat.

"A one-night stand?" Alexis winced.

"Yes. The pregnancy was an accident."

"Are you okay, Brookie?"

The childhood nickname suddenly made Brooke want to bawl, but at the same time, it was comforting in an odd way. This woman had known her forever. They had been through a lot.

"I've been sick. It's not fun, I'll tell you that. But I've decided I want the baby. I really do. Before we found out about the pregnancy, I was trying to talk Austin into a temporary marriage, so I could get my inheritance." Alexis knew all about the money from Brooke's grandmother and how her parents were refusing to let her open an art school.

"Do you think you can trust this man? He's practically a stranger. I don't like the idea of him having a shot at all those millions."

Brooke frowned. Alexis's concern made perfect sense, but she felt the need to defend her husband-to-be. "Austin is a decent, wonderful person. I have no worries on that score at all. In fact, he was the one who insisted on a prenup. He doesn't want people thinking he's a fortune hunter."

"Maybe he's just saying that to win your trust."

"He's not like that. He's a widower who loved his wife."

Alexis snorted. "And widowers can't be villains?"

"He's not a villain. He's a great guy."

"But he knocked you up, so there's that."

"It was an accident," Brooke said. "Neither of us did anything wrong. It just happened."

"Are you in love with him?" Alexis asked.

"No. We hardly know each other."

"Then why are you blushing?"

"I *could* love him, I think," Brooke said. "But he's still hung up on his dead wife." She released a heavy sigh. "They were college sweethearts. I can't compete with that. Besides, Austin has told me flat out that he's not interested in a relationship."

"Was that before or after you found out about the baby?"

Brooke gaped, trying to remember. "It doesn't matter. We've been very careful to talk about everything as *short-term*. I'll admit that the baby complicates things."

"I've got a bad feeling about this, Brooke. I understand why you need to get married. But this can't be a paper commitment only…not with the baby. You and Austin are going to be inextricably involved, indefinitely. Life will be messy. Particularly if you fall in love with him."

Having all her doubts spoken aloud was sobering. "I hear what you're saying… I do. But I have to make the best of a difficult situation. Austin has offered to support me until the inheritance comes through the courts. He's renting a house for the three of us."

Alexis arched a brow. "He's being awfully accommodating for a guy who buried his heart with his dead wife."

"Don't be like that."

"Like what?" Alexis's cynical smile was disturbing.

"I want the fairy-tale romance," Brooke cried. "Don't you think I do? When you and Daniel tried to run away as teenagers and then everything went south, I ached for you. And then all these years later you reconnected. Of *course* I want a love like that. But not everyone gets that chance. I have to make do with what I have."

Alexis stood and prowled, her expression tight. "You can forget about Daniel and me. Nothing has changed even though we're back in the same town. Ours was no grand love affair, believe me. All the reasons we couldn't make it work as teenagers are still there." She thumped her fist on the mantel. "I told you I don't want to talk about Daniel." She wiped her face, though Brooke hadn't realized until then that Alexis had been crying. "When is the wedding?" she asked.

Brooke pulled her knees to her chest. "I don't know," she said glumly. "We'll go the courthouse, I suppose. In Joplin, maybe. Not here."

"Do you want me to be there with you?"

Brooke nodded, her throat tight. "I'd like that."

"Okay, then." Alexis sighed, visibly shaking off her mood. "What can I do to help tonight?"

"Well," Brooke said, "I have two large suitcases and four boxes upstairs ready to be packed. I wouldn't mind a hand with that."

"Only two suitcases?"

"None of my clothes are going to fit…remember? I'll get the other stuff later. When my parents have had a chance to get used to the idea of me being gone."

"And being pregnant. And being married."

"You're not making me feel better."

"Sorry." On the way up to Brooke's room, Alexis ran her hand along the banister. "I wonder how many nights I spent in this house over the years."

"Who knows? But it was certainly a lot. I think my parents liked having you here, because you were a Slade and thus a good influence on me."

"Not after I tried to run off with the help and got banished for my indiscretions." The bitterness in her voice was impossible to miss.

Brooke paused on the top step and turned, looking down at Alexis. "I'm really sorry. This stupid town puts far too much emphasis on social standing. My mother actually called Austin a *handyman*. As if that was the worst insult she could come up with at the moment."

They walked down the hall and into Brooke's childhood bedroom. The toys and school trophies had long since been packed away. The room had been professionally redecorated and painted. But Disney posters still hung inside her walk-in closet. At one time, Brooke had considered becoming a graphic artist. She loved color and design.

Alexis flopped down on the bed and stretched her arms over

her head. "I feel like I should throw you a party. After all this time, you're finally escaping your parents' clutches."

"I love my mom and dad."

"I know you do, darlin', and that's why I love *you*. Despite the way they've treated you, you won't turn your back on them. Not everyone is as forgiving as you are."

Brooke gave her friend a pointed look. "Don't make me out to be a saint. I'm not inviting them to the wedding. In fact, I'm not even telling them when it is. My mother would probably call in a mock bomb threat to the courthouse."

"Or she'd have your father fake a heart attack."

They dissolved into laughter, and the conversation moved onto lighter topics. In an hour, the packing was done.

Alexis studied the partially denuded bedroom. "Do you want to come to my place tonight? I hate to think of you staying here all by yourself."

"I appreciate the offer. But honestly, I need some time to think. To make sure I'm doing the right thing."

"It sounds like you've already made up your mind."

There was no criticism in Alexis's statement...only quiet concern.

Brooke shrugged. "I guess I have. I like Austin. He's willing to help me get my inheritance. He's interested in supporting his child, and he wants to play a role in the baby's future."

"What about you, Brooke? What do you want?"

"I'm not entirely sure. But I'll figure it out soon. I'm running out of time."

Austin drove to Joplin on Saturday. He didn't have to. There sure as hell was plenty going on at the club that needed his attention. But he had learned—when Jenny was ill—there was more to life than work.

His sister was thrilled to see him. A pot of his favorite chili bubbled on the stove, and she had gone the extra mile to make chocolate chip cookies. He shrugged out of his light jacket and hung it on the hook by the back door. "Hey, sis. Smells great in here."

Audra hugged him. "It's a sad day when I have to bribe you to get a visit."

Not for the world would he ever tell her this house held too many painful memories. Jenny had died in the bedroom just down the hall. Six years had passed. The raw grief had healed. Still, the house was not comfortable to him. Perhaps it never would be.

They had lunch together, talking, laughing, catching up. Audra was almost six years older than he was. In many ways she had been a second mother to him. She had been married briefly when he was in high school. But apparently the guy was a jackass, because the relationship ended after eighteen months. Audra never spoke of it, and she never dated seriously since.

Come to think of it, she and Austin had a lot in common. Too much pain in their pasts. Too little inclination to try again.

He knew that sooner or later she would grill him because of the phone call he had made to her the day he discovered Brooke was pregnant. She waited until he was on his second cup of coffee and his third cookie.

"So," she said, leaning her chair back on two legs and looking at him over the rim of her pink earthenware mug with the huge daisy painted on the side. "You want to tell me what's going on?"

He sighed inwardly. "Brooke's pregnant."

"The cute blonde from the bar?"

"Yep."

"Did she set you up?" Audra's suspicious frown had *mother hen* written all over it.

"Stand down, sis. This was entirely an accident. I won't go into details, but the kid is mine."

"What now?"

He told her about Brooke's inheritance and her dream of opening an art school and her crazy-ass parents. "I've rented a condo as of Monday. And I've offered to marry Brooke so she can get her money. Temporarily only."

Audra scowled. "You are so full of crap."

"Hey…" He held up his hands. "Why the attitude? I'm the good guy in this scenario."

"Are you planning on sleeping with her?"

"The condo has three bedrooms."

"That's not an answer and you know it. Tread carefully, Austin."

His neck got hot. "I don't follow."

She leaned forward and rested her elbows on the table. "I love you, little brother. But you're not the same man you were before Jenny got sick. When you were younger, you were the life of the party, always joking and laughing. After she died, you changed. I miss that old Austin. Honestly, though, I doubt if he's ever coming back."

His stomach curled. Nothing she had said was news to him. "What's your point?"

"Don't hurt this girl."

"I don't plan to hurt anyone."

"But that's the problem, kiddo. You think everything can stay light and easy. But you're not able to see this from a young woman's perspective, especially the one I remember from the bar. She still had stars in her eyes, Austin. I'll bet when she looks at you, her heart races and she starts imagining a future where the two of you grow old together."

"That's where you're wrong," he said defensively. "I've been very clear about that. I told her I don't want another relationship."

Audra's visible skepticism underscored his own doubts. But what could he do? The course was set. He and Brooke were getting married.

Twelve

While Austin was busy with his own agenda Saturday morning, Brooke sat in her car in front of Natalie Valentine's bridal shop and tried to think of a cover story that wouldn't sound too unbelievable. Her phone said it was 9:57. The store opened at ten.

After Alexis left last night, Brooke had spent an hour wandering from room to room of her family home, wondering if she was jumping from the proverbial frying pan into the fire. How could she marry a man she barely knew?

On the other hand, how could she not?

She had eventually slept from midnight until seven and then spent an hour in the bathroom that morning retching miserably. This pregnancy thing was taking a toll on her body already. Her weight was down five pounds.

When she saw the hanging placard in the glass doorway flip from *Closed* to *Open*, she climbed out of the car and marched inside.

Natalie greeted her with a smile. "Hi, Brooke. You're out early. Can I help you find a dress for the auction? I assume that's why you're here. I've sold ten gowns in the last week already. If my business is any indicator, the charity bachelor gig is going to be a huge success."

"I'll just browse for a bit if that's okay," Brooke said, avoiding the question.

"Of course. Make yourself at home. There's coffee in the next room if you get thirsty."

When Natalie moved to greet another customer, Brooke breathed a sigh of relief. She wasn't prepared to explain why she needed a dress. The traditional wedding gowns in the back half of the salon beckoned with their satin and lace and bridal splendor, but she wouldn't let her wistful imagination go there. Reality was her currency. She had plans to make and a future to plot out.

She tried on six dresses before she found one that didn't make her feel self-conscious. The winning number was an ivory silk affair, strapless, nipped in at the waist, ending just below the knee. It was sophisticated, elegant and bridal enough for an informal courthouse wedding.

With the dress draped over her arm, she bumped open the fitting room door with her hip and nearly ran into Tessa Noble. The curvy African American woman with the sweet smile greeted Brooke warmly. "Hey, Brooke. I haven't seen you in forever. Are you shopping for a charity auction dress...like me?"

Brooke hugged the other woman. "*You're* going? Tripp, too?" Tessa's brother was as popular as his sister, though Tripp was an extrovert, and Tessa definitely preferred staying out of the limelight.

Tessa chuckled. "Would you believe that Ryan Bateman has talked Tripp into being one of the bachelors?"

"Oh, wow. Your brother is a hunk. The bidding will go wild."

Tessa rolled her eyes. "Yeah. That's what I think. He'll eat it up. But it's all for a good cause."

"So what kind of dress do you want? I bet you would look amazing in hot pink. Or scarlet maybe. Even emerald green."

Tessa chewed her bottom lip. "Oh, I don't know, Brooke. I was thinking something a little less flashy."

"I can understand that. But every woman deserves to look her best. Do you mind if I hang around and see what you try on?" She sensed that Tessa might need a gentle push in the right direction.

"Of course not. Is that what you're going to wear?"

Brooke felt her face get hot. "Maybe. I have a couple of other occasions coming up during the holidays, so I wanted to be prepared. Here," she said, pulling two outfits off the rack when she saw what size Tessa was eyeing. "Humor me." The red or the fuchsia—either choice would be sensational.

Tessa seemed dubious. "I'd prefer something with a little less wattage. This one might work." She held out an unexceptional gown that was perfectly plain.

Brooke wrinkled her nose. "Basic black is acceptable for a formal occasion, of course, but you have a majestic figure, Tessa. Play to your strengths. Don't hide in the shadows."

"I'm not hiding," Tessa insisted. "I love my body. Or at least as much as any woman does." She grinned. "But that doesn't mean I want everyone gawking at it."

"Isn't there something in between? Then again, my life isn't exactly going according to plan lately, so who am I to hand out advice?" Brooke admitted the truth ruefully.

Natalie had apparently been watching the good-natured standoff. She joined them and gave Tessa a reassuring smile. "You're not the first woman to be nervous about stepping out of your comfort zone. Here's an idea. Take all three possibilities home overnight, plus another one or two if you like. Try them on in the comfort of your own bedroom with your own shoes and jewelry. Keep the tags attached, of course. I think—under those circumstances—you'll end up with exactly the right outfit for the occasion."

While Tessa took her time selecting from a wide array of choices, Brooke said her goodbyes and followed Natalie back to the cash register to pay for her purchases. Natalie took Brooke's credit card, then slid the dress into a clear garment bag. "This one is lovely. You can dress it up or down so many ways. And if it's a cooler evening, some kind of golden, gauzy shawl would be pretty."

Brooke nodded. "Yes." She was almost tongue-tied. It had never been her intention to hide her pregnancy forever. But now it seemed difficult to dump the news on people without divulging far more than she wanted to about her personal life.

By the time she made it back to her car and spread the dress bag out in the trunk, she was starving. She still had two stops to make, but they would have to wait. Instead, she drove the short distance to the diner and grabbed chicken noodle soup and a chicken pita sandwich to go.

It wasn't the easiest meal to eat in the car, but she didn't want to run into anyone she knew. How was she going to explain Austin to the world? How was she going to explain her pregnancy? The deeper she got into the chaotic whirl of events she herself had set in motion with one crazy night in Joplin, the more out of control she felt.

Babies were amazing and wonderful. She truly believed that. But this little one was turning Brooke's world upside down and backward in a big way.

She parked beside the courthouse and ate her lunch slowly, huddling in her navy wool sweater and wishing she had dressed more warmly for the day. The weather, as predicted, had taken a nasty turn. The skies were dull and gray. The temperature had dropped at least fifteen degrees. A steady, driving rain stripped any remaining leaves from the trees. Fall, her favorite season, would soon turn to winter.

Royal's winters were mild, for the most part. Still, it was a good thing she had finished the outdoor murals. She couldn't risk getting sick. Not with so much at stake.

What was Austin doing right now? Was he at the club? Working on the new addition? It pained her that she had no idea.

When she couldn't put it off any longer, she got out and locked the car. The wind made her umbrella virtually useless. The lawyer her parents used occupied an office in the annex across the street from the courthouse. Brooke had an appointment.

The dour older gentleman took her back to his overly formal suite right on time. He didn't seem happy to see her, particularly after a tense fifteen-minute conversation. "So you see," Brooke said, "I'll need the prenup right away. And I'll need your assurance that what we've discussed doesn't leave this room. I know my mother tries to twist people to her way of thinking, but you are obligated to keep my confidence. Right? I've told her I'm getting married. I just haven't said when."

The lawyer blustered a bit, pretending to be insulted, but Brooke knew there was a better than even chance he would dial her mother's cell number as soon as Brooke walked out of the room.

The man scowled. "Your parents are looking out for your best interests, Miss Goodman."

"It's *Ms.*," she said. "I'm twenty-six years old. Plenty old enough to know my own mind. I'll bring you the marriage license as soon as I have it. And then?"

He shrugged. "I'll file the paperwork. Barring any kind of hiccups, the transfer of your grandmother's assets should be fairly straightforward."

"What kind of hiccups?" Brooke asked, mildly alarmed.

"Merely a figure of speech."

She left the office soon after. This time the queasiness in her stomach had nothing to do with her pregnancy. Surely her parents wouldn't try to contest her grandmother's will. It was ironclad. Wasn't it?

Unfortunately, the meeting with the lawyer directly preceded her first visit with the ob-gyn who would be caring for Brooke during her pregnancy and birth. The woman frowned when she saw Brooke's blood pressure. "Have you had issues with your BP in the past, Ms. Goodman?"

Brooke flushed. "No, ma'am. I had kind of an upsetting afternoon. That's all. I'll be fine."

The appointment lasted almost an hour. Brooke was poked and prodded and examined from head to toe. Except for the blood pressure thing, she was in perfect health. The doctor gave her a stern lecture about stress and demonstrated a few relaxation techniques. At the very last, Brooke received the piece of information she had been waiting for.

The doctor smiled. "Since you seem to know the exact date you conceived, it makes things easier. I've marked your due date as May 14. Congratulations, Ms. Goodman. I'll see you in another month."

Brooke took her paperwork, handed over the copay and walked out of the office on unsteady legs. Deep down, perhaps she had been hoping that the whole pregnancy thing was a mistake. Except for the nausea and occasional light-headedness, she still didn't *feel* pregnant.

But now, there was no doubt.

She stopped at the pharmacy to pick up her new vitamins—tablets the size of horse pills—and then she drove by the piece of property she hoped to buy soon. The empty lot sat forlorn. Brooke leaned her arms on the steering wheel and stared through the rain-spattered windshield.

Her art center would be the kind of place where she could bring her infant to work. Being her own boss would be the best of both worlds. She could be a parent and still create her dream of a thriving studio for children and young teens to pursue their artistic endeavors.

She wished she had brought Austin here. He needed to see what he was helping her accomplish. And besides, she missed him. Her body yearned for his in a way that was physical and real and impossible to ignore. Already, her life seemed empty when he wasn't around.

That thought should have alarmed her, but she was too tired to wrestle with the ramifications of falling for the handsome cowboy. She would try to protect her heart. It was all she could do.

When she returned home, it was as if her wistful thoughts had conjured a man out of thin air. Austin was sitting on the front porch when she walked up the path. Her parents had given the house staff the weekend off, not out of any sense of altruism but because they didn't want to pay hourly employees when they were out of town.

Hence, there had been no one to answer the door.

Austin unfolded his lean, lanky body and stretched. "I was beginning to think you weren't coming back."

"I live here," she pointed out calmly, trying not to let him see that her palms were sweaty and her heart was beating far too fast.

He grinned. "Not for long." He dropped a kiss on her forehead. "I have a surprise for you. Will you come with me? No questions asked?"

She hadn't been looking forward to an evening all alone. "Yes. Do I need to change?"

"Nope." He steered her back down the walk in the direction she had come moments before. Her wedding dress was still in the trunk of her car, so she used her keys to beep the lock. It would be fine for the moment. Before she could climb into the cab of the truck, Austin put his hands at her waist, lifted her and set her gently on the seat.

She wanted to make a joke about how strong he was and that he was her prince charming, but she stopped herself. This wasn't an ordinary flirtation. They weren't an ordinary couple.

Once they began driving, it didn't take long for her to realize that Austin was taking her to their new condo. When he parked at the curb, she shot him a teasing glance. "Breaking and entering? Not really my style."

Austin reached in his pocket and dangled a set of keys in front of her face. "I sweet-talked the rental agent into the giving me the keys early. She made me swear we wouldn't move in until Monday. Insurance regulations, you know. But tonight, it's all ours."

On the top step sat a jaunty pumpkin. His jack-o'-lantern face had been carved into a perpetual glare.

Brooke laughed softly. "You did this?"

Austin nodded. "Yes."

"I love it." Warmth seeped into her soul. That and the re-assurance that she wasn't being entirely foolish. All her doubts settled for the moment, lost in the excitement of being with Austin. "Did you mention dinner? I seem to be perpetually hungry these days."

"Follow me." He unlocked the front door with a flourish. In the living room, he had somehow managed to procure a roman-tic meal, complete with candles and strawberries and a crystal vase filled with daisies. "You've had a lot of stress lately, dar-lin'. I thought we both deserved a break."

She looked up at him through damp eyes. "A lovely idea. Thank you, Austin."

He cocked his head, a slight frown appearing between his eyebrows. "Something's wrong."

Brooke sat down on the floor and leaned back against the sofa, stretching out her legs. "Not really. Just a lot of *adulting* today."

"Like what?" he asked, joining her.

"Well, the lawyer's office, for one."

His gaze sharpened. "The prenup?"

"Yes."

"Good."

"And I got a dress for our wedding."

"Excellent."

"And I also had my first visit with my ob-gyn."

His lips twitched. "I'm impressed."

"No, you're not," she said slowly. "You're making fun of me."

"I'm not, I swear. You're a list maker, aren't you?"

"To the bone. Is that a bad thing?"

He leaned over and kissed the side of her neck, sending shivers down her spine. "I like a woman who can focus."

She moaned when he pulled her close and found her mouth with his. His lips were warm and firm and masculine. Arching her neck, she leaned into him and, for a few exciting moments, let herself indulge in the magic that was Austin.

But when the kiss threatened to burn out of control, she pulled back, still hesitant, still unsure of the big picture, no matter how much she craved his touch.

She cleared her throat. "Will I seem needy if I say I missed you today?"

"I missed you, too, Brooke." His smile was lopsided, almost rueful. "In fact, I should have taken you with me, I think."

"Taken me where?"

He hesitated briefly before responding. "I went to see my sister, Audra."

"The tall redhead?"

"The one and only."

"Was it a friendly, low-key visit, or an I'm-about-to-get-married announcement?" she asked.

He scraped his hands through his hair. "The second one. Audra thinks I'm making a big mistake."

"Oh." Brooke's stomach curled into a tight knot of hurt and embarrassment. "She's probably right."

"Audra didn't have all the facts. I filled her in. And of course, the baby was the tipping point."

"Oh, goody. She's probably out right now getting my sister-in-law-of-the-year T-shirt."

"You're getting cranky," he said. "Eat a taco."

Austin must have had help with this picnic, because the food was still warm. Even so, her stomach revolted. She took one bite and set the plate aside. "Alexis thinks we're making a big mistake, too."

"Alexis Slade? Gus's granddaughter?"

"I told you she's my friend. She gave me the mural job, remember?"

He nodded. "I do. What's her beef with me?"

"It's not you," Brooke said. She rested her chin on her knees. "She thinks I'll let my gratitude for what you're doing cause me to confuse sexual attraction with love."

He went still, his entire body frozen for a full three seconds. At last he sighed, almost silently. "But you told her we've been very clear about our expectations...right?"

"I told her."

"Then what's the problem?"

The problem was that Austin Bradshaw was a gorgeous, sexy, intensely masculine man who also happened to be a decent, hardworking, kind human being. A platonic relationship might have worked if Brooke had thought of him as a brother. But from the first moment she'd set eyes on him in that bar in Joplin, she had wanted him. Badly.

Wanting was a short step to needing. And needing segued into loving with no trouble at all.

She managed a smile. "We don't have a problem. I think everything is going exactly according to plan."

Thirteen

In hindsight, Austin had to admit that preparing a romantic indoor picnic for a woman might be sending mixed signals. All he had wanted to do was reassure Brooke about moving in with him. To let her know that leaving her parents' house was the right thing to do.

But now she seemed skittish around him, especially after that kiss.

Making Brooke smile and laugh was rapidly becoming an obsession. The way her gray eyes lit up when she was happy. The excitement in her voice when she told him about her plans. Even her shy anticipation about having a baby she had never meant to conceive at all.

Perhaps he was the one in danger.

He filled his plate in hopes that Brooke would follow suit. She had been so very sick these last few days, she was losing weight already. Her petite frame didn't have pounds to spare. Right now, her cheekbones were far too pronounced—her collarbone, too.

She carried an air of exhaustion, though he had a hunch her

fatigue was as much emotional as it was physical. Hearing and seeing what her parents had put her through in recent months made him angry on her behalf.

Out of the corner of his eye, he saw her take a bite of the savory shredded-pork taco. Soon, she finished the entire thing, including most of the brown rice alongside it.

"Another one?" he asked.

Brooke eyed the platter longingly. "I don't know. I don't want to push it. The food is amazing, though. Where did you get it?"

"One of my carpenters is from Mexico. He and his family just opened a new restaurant on the south side of town. I told him what I was doing tonight, and he helped me get everything together."

"Give that man a raise." She put a hand on her stomach and grimaced. "I'll wait fifteen minutes, and if everything stays down, I'm going to have a second." She wiped a dollop of sour cream from the edge of her mouth, eyeing him with an expression he couldn't decipher. "I've been thinking," she said slowly.

"About what?" He dunked a chip in cheese sauce and ate it.

"Marriage. My art studio. Us."

His gut tightened. "I thought we settled all that."

"Well, when the two most important people in our lives wave red flags, it *should* make us think twice."

"Our business is our business, Brooke. Neither of them understand where we stand on this."

"At least hear me out. You don't want to be married again. And you don't want to have a child. I can't do anything about that second part, but I did think of a way we could skip walking down the aisle."

He stood up and folded his arms across his chest. "Oh?"

"The terms of Grammy's will state that I get the money when I marry or on my thirtieth birthday. I'll hit that mark three years and two months from now. Instead of marrying me, you *could* simply cosign the loan for my art studio with me. Then my parents wouldn't try to contest the will or stop the wedding.

You wouldn't be legally tied to a woman who isn't Jenny. And I wouldn't have to feel guilty for ruining your life."

Austin stared at her, feeling shifting sand beneath his feet. Everything she said made sense. Yet he hated every word. "Come here, woman." He reached down, grabbed her hand and drew her to her feet. He put his hands on her face, cupping her cheeks in his palms. "No one," he said firmly, "makes me do something I don't want to do. I'm not marrying you because I *have* to. I don't feel trapped. You're not taking advantage of my good nature."

Her eyes widened. "I'm not?"

He dragged her against him, letting her feel the full extent of his arousal. His erection throbbed between them, pressing into her soft belly, telegraphing his intent. "This marriage is convenient for me, too," he drawled. "I want you in my bed every night. I want you in a million different ways. I want to take you over and over again and make you cry out my name until neither of us can remember to breathe. You're a fire in my blood."

He paused, his chest heaving. The words had poured out of him like hot lava, churning to the surface without warning.

Brooke stared at him, eyes wide, lips parted. He put a hand on her flat belly. "This baby is *ours*," he said softly. "Yours and mine. I never had that with Jenny. So that makes you pretty damned rare and unique. I don't have it in me to love again. I won't lie about that. But I'll be good to you, Brooke. Can't that be enough?"

Her lower lip wobbled. "I suppose." Dampness sheened her eyes. He could fall into those deep gray pools and never come up for air. For six long years he had wandered in a wasteland of despair and pain. Every part of his soul was awakening now. The rebirth hurt in a different kind of way, which was why he had put safeguards in place.

This thing with Brooke was special, but he wouldn't let it drag him under.

He scooped her into his arms and walked toward the master bedroom. The house had been staged for showing. Only a bedspread covered the mattress. Austin didn't care. It had been too long since he'd been intimate with Brooke and felt her soft body strain against his.

Brooke was silent. For once, he couldn't tell what she was thinking. He laid her down and lowered himself beside her, settling onto his right hip and propping his head on his hand. "I didn't ask," he said slowly, suddenly unsure of the situation. "I want to make love to you. Is that okay?"

She chewed her lip. "Have sex, you mean?"

"Don't do that."

"Do what?"

"Pick at words. You know what I mean."

She laughed softly, though he was convinced he saw doubts in her eyes. "I do know what you mean," she said. "And yes. I want to have sex."

He winced inwardly at her insistence on the more clinical phrase. Was she trying to make a point, or was the *L* word as much a problem for her as it was for him?

Shaking off the worrisome thoughts, he unbuttoned her designer jeans and placed a hand flat on her belly. "This is the first time we've done this knowing that you're..." The word stuck in his throat. With some consternation, it occurred to him that he had *never* made love to a woman who was growing another human.

Brooke grinned. "Pregnant? Is that the word you're looking for? All the parts still work the same. The doctor said I have no restrictions in that area. And the good news is... I can't get pregnant *again*."

"Very funny."

He leaned over and kissed her taut stomach. "You have a cute navel, Ms. Goodman. I can't wait to see it grow."

"I'll have to finish the day-care murals soon before I get too fat to climb up a ladder."

"Not fat," he muttered, reaching underneath her to unfasten her bra. "Rounded. Voluptuous. Gorgeous."

Brooke giggled until he took one nipple in his mouth and suckled it. Her tiny cry of pleasure sank claws of hunger into his gut. She tasted like temptation and sin, a heady cocktail.

"Tell me you want this."

"I already did."

"Beg me…"

The gruff demand showed Brooke a side of her cowboy she had never experienced before tonight. He wasn't above torturing her. The rough slide of his tongue across her sensitive flesh was exquisite.

She cradled his head in her hands, sliding her fingers into his silky hair and pulling him closer. "Please," she whispered. "Please, please, please make love to me, Austin."

"I thought you'd never ask."

He undressed her slowly. The house was warm. Even so, the erotic pace covered her body in gooseflesh. Austin's hooded gaze and flushed cheekbones signaled a man on the edge.

In the silence, his ragged breathing was unsteady. Brooke, on the other hand, wasn't sure she was breathing at all.

She hadn't expected this time with Austin to be any different. But the baby was changing things already. This tiny life growing inside her had seemed like an ephemeral idea…a hard-to-believe notion.

Here…now, though, the child was almost tangible. She and Austin had created something magical. Was it her imagination, or was the tenderness in his gaze more pronounced tonight? Despite the unmistakable hunger in his touch, he had reined in his need. He was handling her like spun glass.

Unbuttoning his shirt was the next logical step. It was easier now to touch him, easier than it had been the first time, or even the second. She was beginning to know what he liked, what brushes of her fingertips made him groan.

He had undressed her down to her bikini underwear. She straddled him and leaned forward to stroke the planes of his chest. His skin was hot. The place where his heart thudded beneath her fingertips beckoned. She kissed him there, lingering to absorb his strength, his wildly beating life force.

"I won't regret this," she whispered. "I won't regret *you*." She hoped it was a vow she could keep.

Austin lifted her aside and rolled to his feet...just long enough to strip off his remaining clothes. He was magnificent in his nudity. Not even the scar on his left thigh from a childhood injury could detract from his power and virile beauty.

He came back to her, scooted her up in the bed and settled between her thighs. "I can't wait," he growled. He took her in one forceful thrust, stealing her breath. The connection was electric, the moment cataclysmic.

For a panicked instant, Brooke saw the folly of her plan. Doggedly, she shoved the painful vision aside. She had Austin in this moment. Nothing could ruin that.

The condo faded away. Not even the smell of fresh paint nor the faint sounds of laughter and traffic on the street outside could impinge on her consciousness. Nothing existed but the feel of Austin's big, warm body loving hers.

Emotion rose in her chest, hectic and sweet. She wanted to call out his name, to tell him how much he gave her, how much she wanted still.

But she bit her tongue. She kept silent. She would not offer what he did not want or need.

Perhaps pregnancy made her body more receptive, more attuned to the give and take between them. She felt as if she had climbed inside his skin...as though the air in his lungs was hers and the beat of her heart was his.

They moved together slowly, all urgency gone. It was as if they had been lovers for a hundred years. Because despite the differences that kept them apart, she knew him. *Intimately.* And in that moment, she fell all the way into the deep. She loved Austin Bradshaw.

The knowledge was neither sweet nor comforting. It was a raw, jagged blade that ripped at her serenity, severing her hope for the future.

Her arms tightened around his neck. "Don't stop," she groaned. "Please don't stop." She concentrated on the physical bliss, shoving aside all else that would have to be dealt with later.

This was Austin, her Austin. And she loved him.

Her climax was explosive and deeply satisfying. Austin groaned and found his release. Seconds later, he reached for a corner of the bedspread and pulled it over their naked bodies. Rolling onto his back, he tucked her against his right side. In moments, she heard the gentle sound of his breathing as he slid into sleep.

Presumably he had been up early for the drive to Joplin. Chances were, he had gone by the club to check on his big project before arranging this surprise. The man worked hard.

His left hand rested flat on his chest. She lifted it and played with his fingers, twining hers with his. Then she saw something that somehow she had never noticed before—perhaps because it was the kind of thing a person could only see if they were staring closely.

On the third finger of Austin's left hand, there was a white indentation where his wedding ring had resided. The sight shocked her. She rubbed the shallow groove. Austin never moved. His hand was lax in hers, trusting.

Pain like she had never known strangled her. She swallowed a moan. The night she had met him was the first time he had been without that ring. She had coaxed him into bed that night. Or maybe he had coaxed her. The lines were fuzzy. If they were to marry this week, would he be expecting a wedding band from Brooke?

She couldn't do it. She couldn't replace a man's devotion to the love of his life with an empty symbol of a convenient union.

Stricken and confused, she climbed out of bed and dressed. Ironically, despite her emotional upheaval, her stomach now cooperated and announced its displeasure by growling loudly.

The sparsely outfitted kitchen did have a microwave. She fixed a plate of leftover food, nuked it and sat at the table.

Austin found her minutes later. He had dressed, but his shirt was still unbuttoned, giving her glimpses of his hard chest. He yawned and dropped a kiss on top of her head. "Sorry. I've had a few late nights recently. This project is one snag after the other."

She murmured something noncommittal.

He grabbed seconds for himself as well and joined her. "You okay, honey?"

"Yes." It was a humongous lie, but under the circumstances, perhaps the Almighty would forgive her.

Austin wiped his mouth. "I don't see any point in postponing our wedding. Does Wednesday work for you? I thought I'd tell my crew I have personal business that day. I happen to know that Audra is free. Do you think Alexis can join us?"

Brooke's throat was so tight it was difficult to speak. "I'll ask her. But I'm sure her schedule is flexible."

He frowned, staring off into space. "I know there will be gossip. Can't be helped. People will wonder why we're not taking a honeymoon. We'll simply say that the club-addition project is under a tight deadline so we're waiting until after Thanksgiving."

"That makes sense."

"What about your parents? I don't want you to have regrets, Brooke."

Too late for that. Hysteria bubbled in her throat. "The old me would have invited them. Even knowing what I know, I would have invited them because it's the proper thing to do. But they don't want to come, and even worse, they would almost definitely give us grief."

"Your brothers?"

She shook her head. "They won't have any interest in this, believe me. Alexis is all I need."

"Okay, then." He reached across the table and took her hand. "What kind of flowers do you like? I want you to have a bouquet." His gaze was open, warm...nothing at all to suggest that this wedding ceremony—modest though it was to be—might bring back memories of another, happier day.

"That's not necessary."

He squeezed her fingers, his smile teasing and intimate. "You'll be my bride, Brooke. Despite the circumstances, that's a fact. If you don't tell me, I'll get something atrociously gaudy, like purple carnations."

She laughed in spite of herself. "Oh, heck, no. Make it white roses." She paused. "And maybe white heather." Once upon a time she had researched flower meanings for an art project in college. White heather symbolized protection and a promise that wishes do come true. If any of that nonsense were real, she needed all the good karma and mojo she could summon.

"I'll do my best," he said.

They gathered up the remains of the dinner. Darkness had fallen.

"We should go," Brooke muttered. "I have a few more things to pack." She didn't really want to leave, but the longer she stayed, the more she felt the pull of that bed and this man and those impossible dreams.

"How 'bout I come with you now and load up the boxes you already have finished?"

"You wouldn't rather do that tomorrow?"

"No. I plan to spend most of the day at the club. Since I'm missing work Wednesday, I want to get a jump on this week's schedule. Things are moving fast now."

They *were* moving fast...too fast. "That makes sense," she said.

"And what about you?"

"Me? Um..."

He grinned. "Sorry. Didn't know it was a hard question."

"Alexis and I usually go to early mass and then have brunch. But she's not available this Sunday. I thought I'd finish the last of my packing and then maybe call my parents. I won't be there when they get home Monday night. Might as well break the news to them now."

"That won't be pleasant." He sobered, his jaw tightening.

"No. But it has to be done."

He pulled her into his arms and held her close. "They should be proud of you, Brooke. I'm sorry your mom and dad haven't been there to support you. I wish things were different."

The painful irony of his statement mocked her. *I wish things were different.* So did she. A million times over. No matter how much she told herself she was making the best of a difficult situation, she couldn't escape the gut-clenching certainty that she was making the biggest mistake of her life.

Fourteen

Sunday felt like the equivalent of a condemned man's last meal. Tomorrow Brooke would move into a new home with Austin. Wednesday she would legally become his wife.

These last peaceful hours in her childhood house constituted one final chance to make a run for it…to change the course of her destiny. Had it not been for a broken condom and a forgotten birth-control pill, perhaps she would have done just that. Maybe she would have found other businesspeople in Royal besides Alexis who were willing to stand up to Margaret Goodman and give Brooke a job. Maybe Brooke could have then found a roommate and a simple, inexpensive apartment.

Maybe she could have been free.

Her dream of an art studio would have been majorly postponed, but that was the case with a lot of people's dreams. And then some just never came true.

Now she faced the prospect of being trapped in a loveless marriage with the one man she wanted more than life itself. Her body craved his lovemaking. She yearned for his smiles, his teasing touch. But she was very much afraid that she had no future with Austin. How could she compete with the memory of his dead wife?

She slept fitfully and woke up sick. The routine was becoming familiar to her now—lukewarm tea and plain crackers after she emptied her stomach. The doctor had told her the nausea might subside in another few weeks as she entered her second trimester. Then again, it might not.

Eventually, her energy returned, at least enough to finish cleaning out the last of her bedroom closets and bathroom drawers. Though the housekeeper would return tomorrow, Brooke did all the vacuuming anyway. By two o'clock, her presence in the Goodman mansion was virtually erased. All that remained were her toiletries and one small overnight case.

Because Austin had loaded her boxes and large suitcases into his truck last night, tomorrow morning would be almost anti-climactic. All she would have to do on her way to work would be to walk out and shut the door.

She was putting the vacuum away in the utility closet off the kitchen when she heard a commotion in the garage. Her heart jumped. The alarm beeped, signaling that someone had shut it off.

Moments later Brooke's parents walked into the kitchen.

She gaped at them, glanced at the calendar and frowned. "I thought you weren't coming back until tomorrow." Her stomach clenched. That last awful meal with her parents and Austin had been a dreadful experience. She didn't want a repeat. The one saving grace was that her mother's temper usually burned hot and quick, and then she moved on to her next victim.

Either that or her parents were biding their time, preparing for their next military offensive. Brooke would be on her guard, just in case.

Margaret Goodman waved a hand and dumped her purse and tote on the island, her expression harried. "Your father wasn't feeling well. We managed to book an earlier flight. I'm going to call Henrietta immediately and have her come fix dinner."

Brooke winced inwardly. Her mother was essentially helpless in the domestic arena. "I don't mind cooking for you, Mama. Something simple, anyway. Baked chicken? A nice salad?"

Her father's face brightened, but her mother was already shaking her head. "I pay for the privilege of having my staff on call. It's not like I'm dragging her out of bed at midnight. Henrietta won't mind at all."

Maybe she would and maybe she wouldn't. It was a moot point. When Margaret Goodman delivered an edict, everyone jumped.

Despite what Brooke had told Austin about making a phone call to her parents today, she changed her mind. She had been preparing herself mentally to come over at dinnertime tomorrow before going to the condo. She had concluded that the conversation was one she needed to have face-to-face. Now fate, or her father's indigestion, had offered a much quicker and easier solution.

But it also meant delaying the inevitable for several hours, a nerve-inducing span of time in which she rehearsed her speech a dozen times. She had to wait for her mother to take a shower and change out of her *nasty* travel clothes. The Goodmans always flew first-class, so it was hard to imagine how much nastiness there could be on Margaret's powder-blue Chanel pantsuit. Still...

And her father had to catch up on sporting events he had missed while he was gone. He holed up in his man cave immediately.

Brooke was left to hide out in her room with her laptop researching baby furniture online. It was a delightful pastime. Even so, it wasn't enough of a distraction to calm her nerves.

Too bad she couldn't be over at the new condo handing out candy to trick-or-treaters. That would be fun. The Goodman home was in a gated community where the houses were spread far apart. No little ghosts and goblins would be ringing the doorbell here tonight.

The minutes on the clock crept by. Henrietta arrived. Brooke saw the cook's car out her window. Soon afterward, appetizing smells began wafting upstairs. Dinner was almost invariably served at six thirty. Margaret's doctor had told her that eating too late would make her gain weight.

At last, the three Goodmans sat down together in the formal dining room, and the first course was served. Brooke would have far preferred eating at the cozy kitchen table in the breakfast nook. Her mother, however, believed in keeping up appearances. Brooke's father didn't have a dog in the fight, but he had given up caring about such things years ago.

Because Brooke was uncomfortable talking about very personal subjects in front of staff, she waited until dessert was served. Fresh apple tarts with cream. The timing meant Henrietta would be in the kitchen for at least the next half hour cleaning up the dishes.

Brooke took a deep breath. "Mom, Dad... I wanted to let you know that I'm moving out tomorrow."

Her father never lifted his head. He continued to eat his dessert as if afraid someone was going to snatch it away from him. Since it was definitely not on his approved diet, perhaps that was a valid fear.

Margaret, however, swallowed a bite, took a sip of wine and sat back in her chair. "Where on earth would you go, Brooke? You haven't a dollar to your name."

"And whose fault is that, Mama? You've deliberately sabotaged every attempt I've made to be independent."

Her mother didn't deny the charge. "Perhaps I'm afraid of the empty-nest syndrome."

Brooke rolled her eyes. "Oh, please."

Her mother lifted a shoulder. "I'm told that's a *thing*."

"Not for you. You're too busy conquering the world. And that's not bad," Brooke said quickly. "You've always set a good example for me as a woman who can do anything she sets her mind to..."

"I sense your compliment is wrapped around a piece of rotting fish."

Margaret Goodman had always been a drama queen, a larger-than-life figure. She ruled her world by the sheer force of her personality—along with fear and intimidation.

"The compliment is sincere, Mother. But I'm telling you it's time for me to find my own way in the world."

"With this *handyman*?"

"Austin is a highly trained architect. He's brilliant, in fact."

"He hasn't held down a job in over six years. Your father and I had him investigated."

Brooke swallowed her anger with difficulty. "He nursed his dying wife. He told you that."

Her father looked up. "People say a lot of things, Brooke. Don't be naive. We won't apologize for being concerned."

Margaret nodded. "Besides, the wife has been gone a long time."

"My God, Mama. Have some compassion. He loved her. I think he still does."

For once, a tinge of genuine concern flickered in her mother's expression. "Then why, in God's name, Brooke, are you so hell-bent on throwing in your lot with this cowboy? He'll break your heart. Tell her, Simon."

Brooke's father grimaced. "Your mother may sometimes be prone to overstating the facts, but in this instance, I happen to agree with her. The man got you pregnant, Brooke, fully aware that you're an heiress. It looks bad, baby. And I know you. You've got romance in your soul. You want the happily-ever-after. But this architect isn't it. Give it time, Brooke. Someone else will come along."

The fact that they weren't yelling was actually worse. To have her parents speak to her as an adult was such an anomaly she felt as if the universe had tilted. "I appreciate everything you both have done for me. And even now, I appreciate the fact that you want me to be happy. I do. But I have to stand on my own feet. I'm going to be a mother."

"You could put the baby up for adoption," Margaret said. "Privately. In Dallas. This will change your whole life, Brooke."

"Yes, Mama. You're right. I didn't want to get pregnant. I didn't plan to have a baby so soon. Still, that's where I am. Despite the circumstances, I do want this child. He or she will be the next in a new line of Goodmans. Doesn't that excite you even a little bit?"

Both of her parents stared at her. Her father's expression was conflicted. With Brooke gone, there would be no one around to deflect Margaret's crazy train.

Brooke's mother's seemed to age suddenly. "I've never seen you like this, Brooke. So calm. So grown-up."

"Well, Mom, it had to happen sometime. I don't want to fight with either of you. I love you. But I have new priorities now. If you can respect those, I think we'll all be happier."

Her father grimaced. "It's not too late to break things off with the Bradshaw man. If this art studio business is so important to you, I can fund that, whether or not your mother agrees."

"Simon!" Margaret's outrage turned her face crimson.

He gave his wife a truculent stare. "Well, I can." He shrugged sheepishly, coming around to hug Brooke before releasing her and pouring himself another scotch. "I've let your mother take the reins, but I won't stand by and see you heartbroken by a bad relationship. You're my baby girl."

Brooke was completely caught off guard. "Thank you, Daddy. That means the world to me. I'll keep your offer in mind."

Margaret Goodman stared at her daughter. "I hope you won't do anything to tarnish our standing in the community."

Brooke flinched. The chilly words were their own condemnation. "I understand your concern, Mother. I'll do my best."

Monday morning, Brooke didn't see either of her parents when she came downstairs. While she had been in her bathroom miserably ill, Margaret and Simon Goodman had left for work.

The much-dreaded confrontation was over. Brooke had faced her two-headed nemesis and won. Or so it seemed.

Shouldn't there be some kind of trophy for what happened last night? When an adult child navigated the chilly waters of independence, surely there needed to be some permanent marker. The feeling of anticlimax as she said goodbye to her childhood home and climbed into her car was disheartening.

She had been counting on an exciting day at the club to boost her spirits. Fortunately, that was an understatement. While she was outdoors taking one last critical look at her garden murals, a crew showed up from a regional magazine to do a story about the bachelor auction and all the renovations.

The reporter interviewed Brooke. The photographer took dozens of shots. Alexis was escorting the duo.

While the two professionals conferred, Brooke pulled Alexis aside. "Any chance you're free to be my maid of honor on Wednesday morning?"

She'd been hoping Alexis would squeal with excitement. Unfortunately, nothing had changed. Her friend wrinkled her nose. "You realize I can't say no to you, Brookie. But I have strong reservations."

"Duly noted."

"What time?"

"I don't know. We'll probably leave for Joplin first thing. Austin and I will talk tonight."

"So you're really moving in with him?"

"I am."

Alexis gnawed her lower lip. "I wish I could talk you out of this. But I'm hardly in a position to hand out romantic advice. Just promise me you'll be careful."

"What does that even mean? The man is only trying to do right by me and his child. He's not some wacko ax murderer."

"I'm not worried about your physical safety. I'm afraid he'll break your heart."

I'm afraid he'll break your heart.

Alexis's words reverberated in Brooke's head for the remainder of the day. Perhaps because they echoed Brooke's worst fears.

Could she keep her emotional distance? Was that even possible?

Austin met her on the front steps of the club just after five. They had texted back and forth during the afternoon, and his mood was upbeat.

When she stepped outside, he gave her a big grin. "I skipped lunch. What if I take you to dinner at La Maison? To celebrate?"

What exactly were they celebrating? She was afraid to ask.

Instead, she looked down at her black pants and cream sweater. "I'm not really dressed for that place." La Maison was one of Royal's premier dining establishments.

Austin waved a dismissive hand. "It's Monday night. Nobody will care."

Again, they left her car behind. The restaurant was in the opposite direction from the condo, so they could pick up the vehicle later.

Once they were seated at a table for two beside the window, Brooke felt herself relax. "This was a great idea," she said. "I didn't realize how stressful it was going to be to talk to my parents. They didn't go ballistic, but it wasn't easy."

Austin poured her a glass of sparkling water from the crystal carafe the waiter had left on their table. "You should be proud of yourself."

"I am," she said, sipping her water slowly and gazing absently at their fellow diners. It was true. Despite her current circumstances, she felt in control of her life. It was a heady feeling.

They stuck to innocuous topics during dinner. Austin had changed out of his work gear into a sport coat and dark slacks. His white shirt and blue tie showed off his tan.

The man was too handsome for his own good.

Despite her best efforts, Brooke couldn't keep herself from repeatedly sneaking a peek at that tiny, telltale white line on the third finger of Austin's left hand. She noticed it every time he reached for the bread basket or picked up the saltshaker.

"I should tell you something," she said, the words threatening to stick in her throat.

Austin stilled, perhaps alerted by the note of gravity in her voice. "Oh?"

"My father stood up to my mother. It was remarkable, really. He said he would fund my art studio despite her wishes."

"What are you telling me, Brooke?"

Now she felt like a bug on the end of a pin. Austin's piercing gaze dissected her and found her wanting. "Just that my dreams are within reach with or without a marriage license."

That was a lie. A whopper, really. Her dreams were no longer limited to an empty, weed-choked lot in downtown Royal. Now they included a cowboy architect with a big smile and a closed-off heart.

The man in question picked up a silver iced teaspoon and rolled it between his long fingers. The repetitive motion mesmerized her.

"I thought we had a deal, Brooke. You've bought a dress. I've ordered flowers. The appointment with the judge is on the books."

She reached across the table and took the spoon out of his hand. Then she linked his fingers with hers, feeling his warm, comforting grasp ground her...give her courage. "I know what we said. But I want you to know there's an escape clause. You can bail right now. Free and clear."

Part of her wanted him to take the bait. So that she would no longer be clinging to this terrible, fruitless yearning to lay claim to this man's heart and soul.

Austin squeezed her fingers. His smile was both sweet and mockingly erotic. "I know what I want, Brooke. You're the only one dithering."

And there it was. The challenge.

She took a deep breath. "Okay, then. If you're sure. I asked Alexis about Wednesday morning. She's free."

"Good."

He reached into his pocket and extracted a slim white envelope. "This is for you, Brooke."

She took it from him gingerly. "What is it?"

"Open it, honey. You'll see."

Inside was a gift certificate to a baby store in Dallas. The certificate had a lot of zeroes at the end. "Austin," she said softly. "This is too much."

"Get everything you need for the nursery. Everything. You can wait until we know if it's a boy or a girl, or you can go with a unisex theme and start shopping now. I want you to have plenty of time to get the baby's room ready. If you'd like to paint, I can handle that on the weekends."

"I don't know what to say."

He rubbed the back of her hand with his thumb, sending tingles down her spine. "Tell me you're happy, Brooke."

That was a heck of an order. Why did he have to ask for so much?

"I'm happy," she whispered, her throat tight. "Of course I'm happy."

It was clear from his face that her words were not entirely convincing.

Even so, he smiled. "Ready to get settled into our new digs?"

"Oh, yes. I forgot we'll have to make up beds."

"Nope. I had a service come in today. They've outfitted the entire house with the basics, so we'll be all set until we have time to pick out our own things. And they've stocked the fridge and cabinets with staples and perishable items."

"Looks like you've thought of everything."

"I tried," he said. "We'll see how well I did."

Fifteen

Austin kept waiting for the other shoe to drop. Brooke seemed matter-of-fact about their new living arrangements, but he couldn't be sure what she was thinking. The woman had learned to hide her emotions and feelings from him. He didn't like the change. Not one bit.

On a more positive note, she was less frazzled now. Clearly she had come to terms with her pregnancy. He could almost see the mental switch that had flipped inside her. Deciding to embrace motherhood wholeheartedly was a huge step.

At the condo, she flitted from room to room, examining every nook and cranny, though she had seen it all twice before. He gave her space. She was nervous. Understandably so.

For his part, Austin was glad not to be living in the bunkhouse at the Lone Wolf anymore. He had appreciated Gus's hospitality, but it was time to put down more permanent roots, at least for the short term. The irony of that equivocation didn't escape him.

As the hour grew later, Brooke got quieter. It occurred to

him that she was on edge about the sleeping arrangements. That was easy enough to fix. He didn't want her coming to him out of any sense of obligation.

When they passed in the hall for the fifth or sixth time, he put out a hand and caught her by the wrist. Her bones felt small and fragile in his grasp. "Relax, honey. You have your own room."

She chewed her lower lip, making no pretense of misunderstanding. "I know. But I thought we agreed this would be a real marriage."

Her anxiety caught him off guard. And though he would be loath to admit such a thing, it hurt. "I'm not buying a wife," he said, the words sharper than he had intended.

She flinched. "I didn't mean it like that."

"Look," he said. He stopped, scraped his fingers through his hair and pressed the heel of his hand to his forehead. He sighed. "I need to go to Dallas tomorrow. Just for the day. Why don't you come with me?"

"No," she said quickly. "There's lots to do here." She grimaced. "Do you have to go?"

He shrugged. "Jenny's father died this past weekend. They've asked me to say a word at the funeral. I don't want to. Not really. But I couldn't think of a polite way to say no."

"I'm so sorry." Brooke's expression was stricken. "We should postpone the wedding. You'll be expected to stay longer than one day, surely."

"Brooke…"

She stood there staring at him. "What?"

"This isn't because of Jenny. It's not, I swear. I'm not doing this for her. But her mom…well, she…"

"She loves you," Brooke said, her voice flat.

"Yes. I know it's been a long time. It shouldn't matter."

"People are entitled to their feelings, Austin. I understand that. You should be honored."

"I wanted this to be a special week for you and me."

She wrapped her arms around her waist. "I'm not a child. Things happen. Please don't worry about me. Do what you have to do."

Austin went to bed alone that night. He lay in the darkness on an unfamiliar mattress with his hands linked behind his head and tried not to think about Brooke sleeping just a few feet down the hall.

His sex hardened as he imagined her soft body tucked up against his. The scent of her hair was familiar to him now. The curve of her bottom. The way her breasts warmed in his palms.

In less than forty-eight hours, she would be his wife. At one time, that notion would have scared him. Now he was confident he could handle it. Brooke knew the score. She understood what he could give and what he couldn't.

Despite his very real aversion to opening himself up to an intimate relationship, this was going to be a good thing.

He was looking forward to fatherhood. Brooke was going to be an amazing mom, even though she was understandably scared. Hell, so was he. What did he know about raising a kid? But it was something he wanted, something he had always wanted.

Jenny's death had been the death of that dream, too.

In the silence of the darkened room, he could hear himself breathing. Soon, Brooke would be here beside him. He couldn't deny the rush of pleasure and anticipation in his gut at that thought.

Brooke was awakening feelings in him that he'd been sure he would never experience again. Affection. Warmth. The need to protect.

To say that he was conflicted was like saying Texas was a big state. He was looking forward to his new future. But at the same time, he was skittish.

He didn't want to hurt Brooke. But his heart wasn't up for grabs. Period.

* * *

Though it pissed him off, Brooke managed to avoid him the following morning. He was forced to head for the airport without seeing her at all. Leaving town with things rocky between them made him uneasy.

They were supposed to be getting married tomorrow, so why was that prospect seeming less and less likely?

The funeral was difficult and sad. Seeing Jenny's mother even more so. He had dreaded coming, because he thought it would cause him to relive every minute of Jenny's funeral. In the end, that didn't happen. Not really.

His grief was different now. It would always be a part of his past, but it was no longer a searing pain that controlled his days.

The realization brought first dumb shock, then quiet gratitude.

At last the funeral and the accompanying social niceties were over. Traffic on the way back to the airport made him miss his flight. He cooled his heels for an hour and a half and finally caught a later flight. After a hot, crowded hop to Royal, he landed and retrieved his truck for the drive to his new home.

The condo was dark when he arrived. It was after eleven. It made sense that Brooke would be asleep.

Disappointment flooded his stomach as he unlocked the front door and let himself in quietly. He stood in the foyer and listened. Not a sound broke the silence.

With a sigh, he carried his bag to his bedroom and tossed it on the chair beside the bed. After a long, hot shower, he felt marginally more human.

His lonely bed held no attraction at all. Wearing nothing but a pair of clean boxers, he tiptoed down the hall and stopped at Brooke's door. It was not closed completely. He eased it open and stood in the doorway until his eyes grew accustomed to the semidark. Her body was a small lump under the covers. A dim night-light cast illumination from the bathroom.

This entire day he had been driven by a need to return home.

Here. To this house. A place where he had slept only one night so far and that could not—by any conceivable standard—possibly be considered home already.

What had drawn him back from Dallas was more than drywall and shingles and wooden studs. The invisible homing beacon was wrapped up in a petite woman with a big heart and an endless capacity for hope.

Guilt flooded him without warning, leaving sickness in its wake. He was about to marry her tomorrow for no other reason than because she drove the cold away. And he needed that. He needed her.

But it wasn't love. It couldn't be. Never again.

He couldn't even pretend to himself that he was her savior. Brooke's father had offered to finance her studio dream. Brooke didn't need Austin at all anymore. The best he could offer was giving the baby his name.

He must have inadvertently made a sound. The lump beneath the covers moved. Brooke sat up in bed, scrubbing her face like a child. "Austin? Sorry. I was waiting up for you. I must have dozed off."

Her hair was loose around her shoulders. The scent of her shampoo reached him where he stood. She was wearing an ivory camisole that clung to her small breasts.

"I didn't mean to wake you."

"It's okay. How was the funeral?"

He shrugged, one hand clenched on the door frame to keep himself in check. "It was fine. Saw a lot of old friends."

"And your mother-in-law?"

"She'll be okay, I think. Her sister is going to move in with her. She's a widow, too."

The silence built for a few seconds.

Then Brooke held out a hand. "You must be exhausted. And cold. Come get in bed with me."

He stumbled toward the promise of salvation, knowing full

well that he was a selfish bastard who would take and take and give nothing in return.

Brooke lifted the covers and squeaked when he climbed in. "Your feet are like ice," she said.

"Sorry." He spooned her from behind, dragging her close and wrapping his arms around her so tightly she protested. His world was spinning. Brooke was his anchor. He rested his cheek on the smooth plane of her back. "Go to sleep, honey. It's after midnight."

"But you're…"

He had an erection. Pike hard. Impossible to hide.

"Doesn't matter," he said.

For hours he drifted in and out of sleep. It was as if he was afraid to let down his guard. He'd been half convinced she would bolt when he was out of town. Until he had his ring on her finger, he couldn't be sure this peace would last.

Exhaustion finally claimed him. When he next awoke in the faint gray light of dawn, Brooke had scooted on top of him and joined their bodies. She kissed him lazily, nipping his bottom lip and sucking it until he groaned aloud.

He was too aroused for gentleness. He gripped her ass and pulled her into him. Feeling her from this angle was sensory overload. He shoved up her camisole and toyed with her raspberry nipples.

Brooke's head fell back. She cried out. He felt the ripple of inner muscles caressing his hard length as she found her release.

Groaning and cursing, he rolled them in a tumble of covers. Lifting her leg onto his shoulder, he went deeper still, thrusting all the way to the mouth of her womb, claiming her, marking her, saying with his body what the words would never offer. She was his.

They slept again.

The next time they surfaced, pale sunshine spilled into the room.

Brooke stirred drowsily, yawning and stretching like a little cat. She burrowed her face into his side. "Don't wanna get up," she mumbled.

He tightened an arm around her and kissed the top of her head, feeling a bone-deep contentment inexplicably overlaid with dread. "It's your wedding day, sweetheart."

She opened one eyelid. "Don't you mean *our* wedding day?"

His face heated. "Yes. Of course." Pressure built in his chest. He wanted to *do* something, *say* something.

But he couldn't.

Instead, he nuzzled her cheek with his and climbed out from under the covers. It was an asinine thing to do. Any man with an ounce of testosterone would have stayed right there and claimed what was his.

But a chasm had opened at his feet. Terrifying. Endlessly deep.

He'd been down that canyon once before.

"How long before you'll be ready to leave?" he asked, feigning cheerfulness.

Brooke rolled to her back, her expression hard to read, though she seemed more resigned than delighted about her upcoming nuptials. "Half an hour, I guess."

"Sounds good."

He shaved and dressed with little recollection of his jerky, automatic movements. Putting on his newest suit with a crisp white shirt and a royal blue tie made him marginally calmer.

He'd worn a tux when he married Jenny. This was not the same at all.

The florist delivered Brooke's bouquet right on time. Austin signed for it and tipped the guy.

In the meantime, he texted back and forth with Audra. She was meeting them in Joplin. At her insistence, she had procured a small cake for afterward at her house.

Austin was completely unprepared when Brooke walked out of the bedroom. The sight of her as a bride, even a less than formal one, slammed into his chest like a gunshot. And was equally painful.

Her blond hair was caught up on top of her head in one of those fancy knots women manage, with little wisps artfully framing her flushed cheeks. Subtle makeup emphasized smoky gray eyes. Soft lips covered in pale raspberry gloss made him want to snatch her up before any other man caught a glimpse of her delicate beauty.

The dress she had chosen was perfection. Her shoulders were bare. Ivory silk flattered her delicate curves. The skirt was narrow with a hint of swish. Her legs, those legs that could twine around his back and take him to heaven, looked a million miles long. Ivory pumps to match her dress had three-inch stiletto heels that gave her more height than usual.

He tried to swallow the boulder in his throat. "You look breathtaking."

Her smile was more cautious than radiant. "At least the dress still fits. I suppose that's the upside of being sick every morning."

"Is it awful? Even now?"

She lifted one pale, perfect shoulder. "I think we may be getting past the worst of it. We'll see."

"Good."

He hated the stilted conversation, hated the distance she had set between them.

He knew why the awkward wall was there. Brooke was protecting herself. Austin had insisted on a sterile, emotionless union, so his bride was doing her best not to *care*.

His own jacked-up psyche had created this mess.

Brooke reached for her clutch purse. "We should go. Alexis will be waiting."

Alexis had offered to meet them in Joplin, but Brooke had insisted her friend travel with them. Austin wasn't an idiot. His bride didn't want an intimate car ride with him.

Outside on the front porch, they both huddled into their coats.

If the weather was any harbinger of marital luck, they were doomed. November had come in with steel-gray skies and chilling rain.

Austin struggled to lock the front door. The new key wanted to stick. "Damn it," he said, after it got stuck a third time and he had to take it out and try again.

Brooke hopped from one foot to the other. "I'm going to wait in the truck. I'm freezing."

"Wait," he said. "You'll ruin your dress. Let me hold the umbrella."

At the last moment, the dead bolt finally clunked as it was supposed to. He dropped the keys in his jacket pocket and reached for the large black umbrella. But Brooke had already taken it and stepped off the porch.

In slow motion, her shoe hit the top step—the newly painted top step that was slick as glass in the pouring rain. Her flimsy heels wobbled, giving no purchase as all. As he watched in horror, unable to reach her, she fell down seven stairs, striking her shoulder and her head and finally crumpling onto the sidewalk.

His entire body was paralyzed. A roaring in his head made it almost impossible to think. To breathe.

He was at her side in seconds, calling 9-1-1. Feeling like a fool because he couldn't remember his new address.

"Brooke. Brooke, sweetheart."

Her eyes were closed. A large, ugly bruise already bloomed on her right cheekbone. Blood seeped from a gash just above it. He wanted to scoop her up and hold her, but he was terrified to risk further injuries.

He knew the first-aid drill. Brooke might have damaged her spine during the fall. To lift her limp body could do irreparable harm.

Shrugging out of his coat, he draped it over her, covering as much of her small, broken body as he could. He left her only long enough to retrieve the damned umbrella. Then he opened it and crouched beside her, keeping the rain at bay as best he could.

With one hand, he stroked her face, held her wrist, felt her pulse. "Hang on, Brooke. Help is on the way. You're going to be fine." Though it seemed her heart beat strongly, what did he know?

Royal's emergency services were top-notch. Austin knew they must have arrived in mere minutes. But the delay seemed like an eternity.

When at last they pulled up with a cacophony of sirens and a barrage of flashing lights, he should have felt relief. Instead, he was numb. The fear had overtaken him…had frozen every cell in his body.

Forced to step back, he watched, agonized, as they eased Brooke onto a board and strapped her down. Started an IV. Wrapped her in a blanket.

"She's pregnant," he blurted out suddenly. "She's pregnant."

One of the female EMTs gave him a sympathetic smile. "We'll take good care of her, sir. You can meet us at the hospital. Okay?"

He nodded. Hospital. Right. Not a courthouse. Not today.

He should call Audra. And Alexis.

The idea of making meaningful conversation was beyond him.

Instead, he took Brooke's phone from her purse and found Alexis's info. Adding Audra's number to the text, he sent word to both of them.

Brooke fell. We're at the hospital. I don't know about the baby.

His own cell phone rang immediately. He didn't answer. He couldn't speak. He was so cold and so scared and so damned helpless.

He couldn't lose someone again. He couldn't.

In retrospect, he shouldn't have driven himself to the hospital. There was no time to waste, though, so he did it anyway.

The emergency room waiting area was crowded. After struggling to find a parking space, he was then forced to cool his heels for several minutes before it was finally his turn at the counter.

"They brought my fiancée in by ambulance," he said. "Brooke Goodman?"

The woman consulted her computer. "The triage nurses are with her now. As soon as they get her in a cubicle, I can send you back."

"Can you tell me anything?"

The middle-aged woman, harried, impersonal, glanced at him a second time, and whatever she saw on his face must have cut through her professional reserve, because her expression softened. "I'm sorry. I can't give out any information like that. But it won't be long. Please take a seat, and I'll call you."

Sixteen

Brooke stirred, tried to breathe and groaned as a sharp pain lanced through her chest. A feminine voice broke through the fog. "Easy, Brookie. Not so fast. I'll hold a straw to your mouth. Open your lips."

It was simpler to cooperate than to protest. A trickle of cool liquid soothed her parched throat.

Why was she here? What happened to her?

Moments later, she sank back into sleep.

Her dreams were not pleasant. In them, she struggled. She cried out. And always, the pain.

Gradually, the fog receded. But the pain did not. Breathing was agony. "Alexis?" Her voice sounded thin and reedy.

"I'm here, baby. What do you need?"

"More water, please."

Swallowing didn't hurt. As long as she stayed perfectly still.

Unfortunately, that wasn't going to be an option for much longer. An overly cheerful nurse came in and unhooked an IV. "Gotta get this young lady up and moving around before pneumonia sets in. I'll be back shortly."

Brooke put an arm over her face. "Damn, that hurts."

Alexis pulled a chair closer to the bed. "You have two cracked ribs. And a broken wrist. The wrist required surgery. But everything is going to heal nicely. Those ribs will give you hell, though. Nothing they can do about that."

Gradually, snippets began to return. Her wedding day. The rainy morning. A slow-motion tumble off the porch. She remembered hearing Austin's panicked shout. Her own scream. And then multiple jolts of pain before she blacked out.

"The baby?" she croaked, suddenly terrified. "What about the baby?"

Alexis stroked her hand. "The doctor says the baby is fine. There was a bit of bleeding initially. They were concerned you might lose the pregnancy, but that has settled down. Your poor body took the brunt of the damage. They can't give you the best pain meds, though, because of the pregnancy. That's why you're hurting."

"Ah…"

Brooke turned her head slowly and scanned the room. As far as she could tell, she was in one of the very luxurious private suites at Royal Memorial Hospital.

Alexis hovered. "Can I get you anything?"

"What day is it?"

"Thursday afternoon. They'll bring you dinner shortly. You didn't get to eat yesterday because of the surgery. Then today when you woke up, the morning sickness kicked in. They're concerned about your weight."

"Where's Austin?" She couldn't hold back the words any longer.

Alexis blanched. "Well, um…"

The door opened and a familiar redhead walked into the room. She smiled gently at Brooke. "We've met. I'm Audra."

"Austin's sister."

"Yes."

"Where is he?"

The other two women looked at each other and back at Brooke. Alexis swallowed. "We're not exactly sure, honey. He took off."

Brook tried to sit up in the bed, alarmed. "What do you mean?" Pain forced her back down.

Audra took over the narrative. "Austin was here with you when Alexis and I arrived. He stayed through the surgery, until the doctor assured all of us you were safe and out of the woods. And then he…"

"Then he left." Alexis had a militant look in her eyes. "No one knows where he is. I'm sorry, Brooke."

Before Brooke could process that extraordinary information, the officious nurse was back. With the help of Audra and Alexis, the uniformed professional hustled Brooke out of bed and into a robe before making her stand and take a stroll down the corridor and back.

At first the pain was enough to make Brooke's forehead bead with sweat. Gradually, it subsided to a dull ache. Her legs moved slowly, as if she had been bedridden for a week and not a mere thirty-six hours.

Finally, the ordeal was over and she was allowed to return to her bed.

She fell asleep almost instantly.

When she awoke, Brooke instinctively looked for Austin, but her heart cried out in disbelief. He was nowhere in sight. Only Audra was in the room.

Austin's sister was as gentle as Alexis and even more comfortable with the routine. Brooke remembered that she had been—or still was—a nurse. "Thank you for helping me," Brooke said. She didn't know the protocol for dealing with Austin's sister.

All she could think about was Austin admitting that Audra had said marrying Brooke was a bad idea.

Great. Just great.

The dinner trays were delivered. As darkness fell outside the window, Brooke made herself eat.

Audra didn't say much.

When Brooke had finished half a baked chicken breast and some mashed potatoes, Audra sighed. "My brother isn't answering his cell phone. But while you were sleeping, this was delivered by hand to the front desk."

It was a plain white envelope with the word *Brooke* scribbled on the front. Though Brooke had never actually seen Austin's handwriting, the bold masculine scrawl was somehow familiar.

Her hands shook as she opened it.

Dear Brooke,

I've moved my things out of the condo for the moment. I want you to be comfortable there. And I'm trying to clear my head. If you need anything at all, Audra has access to my accounts. I'll be in touch soon.

AB

Brooke handed the single sheet of paper to Austin's sister. "I don't really know what this means." Horrible feelings assaulted her. Hurt. Abandonment. A deep sense of betrayal.

Audra glanced at the terse note and winced. "Nor do I. But he was a mess yesterday. Don't give up on him, Brooke. Please. I love my brother, and I want him to be happy."

Brooke's throat hurt. Some aspects about this interlude were going to take far longer to heal than a broken wrist. "The songwriters and poets tell us we each have one great love in our lives."

"That's bull crap. Austin loved Jenny. Of course he did. But I've seen a change in him since he met you. I have to believe that means something."

"Wishing doesn't make it so." The facts were damning.

Both Austin and Brooke had struggled with mixed emotions about marrying for the baby's sake. Austin had been willing to help Brooke secure her inheritance, but once her father relented, that excuse was no longer valid.

In the end, the wedding hadn't happened. Now, it likely never would. Even though she knew it was probably for the best, the crushing weight in her chest made it hard to breathe.

The following morning Brooke convinced Alexis to take her home—to the condo, though Brooke's friend was not at all happy about it. "Come to my house, damn it," Alexis said. "We have a million servants. You'll recover in the lap of luxury. I don't want you spending time alone."

Actually, time alone sounded heavenly. Brooke needed to be on her own to lick her wounds and regroup. "I'll be fine," she insisted. "The doctor said I don't have any special restrictions. They gave me plastic to wrap around the cast when I shower, and the ribs themselves will be self-limiting. I have to move slowly or pay the price."

"You are *so* stubborn."

Brooke grinned. "Pot. Kettle." She slipped her arms into the loose cardigan Alexis had brought to the hospital. That, along with a solid T-shirt and knit stretchy pants were destined to be Brooke's wardrobe for the near future.

At the moment, she and Alexis were waiting on the nurse to bring the discharge forms.

Audra had driven back to Joplin late last night.

Austin had been spotted on the job site at the club this morning, but that was the only information Brooke had been able to pry out of her closemouthed friend.

Brooke picked at a loose thread on her sweater. "Where's my wedding dress? Is it ruined?"

Alexis grimaced. "I won't lie. It was a mess. Blood. Mud. A rip or two. But my dry cleaner is a miracle worker. I took it to him yesterday and promised him a pair of tickets to the charity gala if he could work his magic."

"You didn't have to do that."

"For you, Brookie, anything." Alexis paced the confines of the small room. "You won't be able to work at the club for a few weeks, but not to worry. I'll pay you anyway. You know... sick leave."

"Don't be absurd. I'm on contract. Sick leave wasn't part of our agreement."

Alexis bristled, her eyes flashing. At times like this, Brooke could see the resemblance to her grandfather. "It's *my* budget and *my* event. I can do as I please."

Brooke blinked back tears. She was dispirited and exhausted and barely hanging on to hope for the future. In spite of everything, she missed Austin's steady, comforting presence, his support. And she missed *him*. He was like a drug her body craved without ceasing.

To have Alexis in her corner meant everything. "Thank you. At least it was my left hand. I can still work on pencil sketches for the day-care murals. So I won't fall completely behind."

"Well, there you go."

Soon, the paperwork was complete, and they were on their way.

The most logical route from the hospital to the condo would have taken them directly past the Cattleman's Club. Instead, Alexis drove three blocks out of the way.

Brooke pretended not to notice.

When they reached the street where Austin had leased a home for himself and his child and his temporary wife, Brooke struggled with a great wave of sadness. She had tried so hard to do the right things in her life.

Yet lately, everything she touched seemed to turn to ashes.

The attached garage at the back of the house made it possible for Brooke to enter the condo by negotiating only two steps. If she and Austin had gone out this way on Wednesday, the accident never would have happened. She would be his wife by now.

A shiver snaked its way down her spine, though the day was warm. In true Royal fashion, the cold snap had moved on.

Now November was showing her balmy side. Who knew how long it would last? And who knew if Brooke would ever again share Austin's bed?

Alexis helped her inside and went back to unload Brooke's few personal possessions from the car. In the meantime, Brooke stood in the doorway of Austin's bedroom and surveyed the emptiness. He hadn't been kidding. Every trace of his presence had been erased from the condo.

Was he avoiding *her*? Or a ghost who wouldn't let go?

Alexis made a pass through the kitchen, muttering to herself. "You have the basics," she said. "But I'll send over meals, at least for a few days. The doctor says you're to do nothing but rest and get light exercise."

"Yes, ma'am." Brooke smiled. "I would hug you, but I don't think I can."

Alexis smirked. "I'll take a rain check. Seriously, Brookie. Promise me you'll text any time, night or day. I won't sleep a wink worrying about you."

"I swear. I'll be a model patient."

"Okay. I've got to get to the club. I'll send over lunch, and I'll check on you midafternoon."

The day dragged by. Brooke had never been much of a TV fan. She wasn't in the mood for a movie, either.

Instead, she listened to music, talked to the baby, worked on her sketches and pondered her immediate life choices. The past three months had changed her. She was done letting other people control her fate. She and her child were a unit. A family. It was up to Brooke to create a home and a future for her son or daughter.

Saturday ambled along as slowly as the day before. Some tiny part of her hoped to see Austin, but it was a futile wish. He had missed a day of work for his father-in-law's funeral and another day of work for the almost wedding and the hospital kerfuffle. He would need today to catch up, especially in light of the glorious weather.

By the time Sunday rolled around, Brooke was feeling much better physically. The jagged fissure in her heart was another matter. Every time she walked past Austin's door, the empty room mocked her.

For all her brave notions of independence, she hadn't quite figured out her next step when it came to housing. Should she stay? Should she go? Would Austin ever want to come back to the condo?

With every hour that passed, more questions arose.

Around three in the afternoon, the sunshine was so bright and so beautiful, she couldn't resist any longer. Grabbing a blanket from the closet, she made her way to the small, private backyard, spread her cover on the ground and stretched out on her back.

Getting down was harder than she'd anticipated. Her damaged ribs protested vociferously. But once she was settled, she closed her eyes and sighed. She had slathered her face and arms with sunscreen, so she had no qualms about soaking up the warm rays.

With her hands tucked behind her head and her legs crossed at the ankles, she concentrated on relaxing her entire body, muscle by muscle. Peace came slowly but surely.

No one had ever died from a broken heart.

Loving Austin was a gift. A bright, wonderful gift. As much as it hurt to contemplate letting him go, knowing him had brought her immeasurable joy.

Still, knowing that didn't stop the flood of aching regret and the stab of agony over everything she had lost.

When she awoke, the angle of the sun told her she had slept for a long time. It was no wonder. Her body was still playing catch-up.

Instead of rolling to her feet—a move that would most certainly involve a sharp jolt of pain—she stayed very still and amused herself by cataloging the myriad sounds in her new neighborhood.

Despite the calendar, someone nearby was mowing their lawn. Dogs, more than one, barked. Staking a claim. Marking territory.

Childish laughter was harder to catch in the distance, but it was there.

As she wrinkled her brow and concentrated on the odd plinking sound nearby, a shadow fell across her body.

She shielded her eyes. "Alexis?" No one else had a key.

No one but Austin.

He crouched beside her. "No. It's me."

If she tried to sit up, it would hurt. He would try to help, and he would touch her, and she would fall apart.

So she didn't move. "What are you doing here?"

"I live here," he said.

"Do you? I wasn't sure."

"You're angry," he said.

"No. Not angry. Confused maybe. And sad." She shielded her eyes. The sun was low on the horizon. "What time is it?"

"Almost five."

"No wonder I'm hungry."

She tried to speak matter-of-factly, but her heart was racing. No matter his reasons for coming, this conversation was going to be tough.

Austin sat down on his butt, propped up one knee and slung an arm over it. "Aren't you cold?"

"I wasn't earlier. I guess it's cooling off now."

"Can I help you up?"

She shook her head. "I can do it myself. Please don't touch me."

He flinched. Perhaps the words had come out too harshly. That wasn't her problem. She was in self-preservation mode.

Taking a deep breath, she rolled to her side, scrambled to her knees and cursed as pain grabbed her middle and squeezed. Then at last, she was on her feet. "We should go inside," she said. "It's going to get dark."

Without waiting to see if he would follow her, she clung to the stair rail and hobbled up the steps one at a time, as if she were an old lady.

Inside the house, she made her way to the den. One of the recliners had become her nest of choice. It was relatively easy to get in and out of, and once she was settled, it didn't put pressure on her ribs.

She stood behind the chair, using it as a shield. "Is this going to take long?"

"Stop doing that," he said, the words laced with irritation.

"Doing what?"

"Acting weird."

Her eyebrows shot to her hairline. "*I'm* acting weird? Give me a break, Austin. I'm not the one who disappeared into thin air."

She tried to study him dispassionately, as a stranger would. His face was haggard, as if he had aged ten years in a handful of days. He looked thinner. Paler. There was an air of suffering about him.

He was wearing an ancient leather aviator's jacket and jeans. The soft, long-sleeved Henley shirt underneath was a caramel color that complemented his dark brown eyes.

Everything about him was intensely masculine. The casual clothes, slightly unkempt blond hair and ruggedly handsome stance made him the poster boy for *lone wolf*. Brooke got the message loud and clear.

She was trembling inside, but she dared not let it show. Not for anything in the world would she let him think his desertion had crippled her. She could stand on her own.

She *would* stand on her own. She had no other choice.

Seventeen

Austin wasn't sure what he had been expecting, but it wasn't this. Brooke looked at him as if they were strangers. She didn't appear to be angry. If anything, all of her usual animation had been erased.

He was accustomed to her laughter and her quick wit and her zest for life. This woman was a shadow.

"How are you feeling?" he asked gruffly. It had infuriated him to find out that Brooke was alone…that neither Alexis nor Audra was by her side.

"I'm fine," Brooke said. "Sore, of course, but that will pass. This little cast isn't too much of a bother since it's on my left wrist. I won't have to wear it very long."

"And the baby?"

"One hundred percent perfect."

"Good."

His chest ached. His throat hurt. His head throbbed.

Brooke was so beautiful, he wanted to grab her up and hold her until the terrible ice inside him melted. But the fear was greater than the wanting.

She bit her bottom lip, a sure sign she was nervous or upset or both. "Where do we go from here, Austin?"

He hadn't expected the blunt question.

"Stay as long as you like," he muttered.

"So you're going to support the baby and me out of the goodness of your heart?"

The snippy sarcasm raked his raw mood. "I'm trying to be the good guy in this situation."

"News flash. You failed."

He reared back, affronted. "What do you want from me, damn it?"

"An explanation would be nice. I never tried to trap you into anything, Austin. I'm not sure why you felt the need to hide out."

"It's complicated."

"Try me." Brooke glared at him, her gray gaze stormy. Her cheekbones were too pronounced. Her turquoise knit top and cream sweater swallowed her small, delicate frame. Even though she wore thin black leggings, there was no visible sign of a baby bump yet.

"Do we have any coffee?" he asked.

Brooke frowned. "That's all you're going to say?"

He put a hand to the top of his head, where a jackhammer burrowed into his skull. "Let me have some caffeine," he pleaded. "And I'll make us a couple of sandwiches. After that, I'll answer all your questions."

It was a magnanimous offer and one he might later regret. But he needed sustenance.

He followed Brooke to the kitchen, careful to keep his distance. Despite her injured ribs, she moved gracefully, putting coffee on to brew, getting out cups and saucers, directing him to what he needed for cobbling together thick roast beef sandwiches with slices of freshly cut Swiss cheese.

At last, they sat down at the table together.

He fell on the sandwich with a groan of appreciation.

Brooke ate hers with more finesse, though she eyed him with a frown. "When was the last time you had a real meal?"

"I don't know," he said. "Breakfast with you Wednesday morning, maybe? I've had a few packs of peanut butter crackers along the way. It's been busy at the club. Haven't felt much like eating."

Without another word she stood and fixed him a second sandwich.

Three cups of coffee later, he felt marginally more human.

When the plates were empty, there was nothing left but the silence.

He stood and paced again.

Brooke remained seated. He had already noticed that standing and sitting aggravated her ribs. It was a wonder she hadn't punctured a lung when she fell.

Dizziness assailed him, and he sat down hard. The image of Brooke tumbling down those damn stairs was one he couldn't shake. It haunted his dreams.

Her expression softened, as if she could see his inner turmoil. "Talk to me, Austin."

He dropped his head in his hands and groaned. "I lied to you from the beginning," he said.

She blinked at him. "I don't understand."

"You made the assumption that I was still in love with Jenny. That fiction suited my purposes, so I let you believe it. Even though I knew the lie caused you pain. So there. Now you know what kind of man I am."

Brooke's bottom lip trembled. "The day I met you was the first time you had taken off your wedding ring."

"That much was true. But I continued wearing the ring as long as I did because it kept women like you from getting ideas."

"Oh."

"I loved Jenny. Of course I did. But that wasn't why I wore my wedding ring for six long years. I wasn't still wallowing in my grief or clinging to her memory, not by that point. All I wanted was to be left alone. The ring was a useful deterrent."

He laid out the facts baldly, painting himself in the worst possible light. Brooke needed to know the whole truth.

"But you had taken it off that night when I met you."

He nodded. "Audra wouldn't let up. She said I was turning into a soulless jackass, and she insisted I return to the land of the living."

"I see."

"I *knew* you thought I was still in love with Jenny, Brooke. And I let you believe it. Aren't you going to ask me why?"

Her eyes were huge, her face pale. "Why, Austin?"

He scraped his hands through his hair. "Because you scared me more than anything that had happened to me in forever. You gave me a glimpse of light and warmth and happiness, and I wanted it. God, Brooke, I wanted it."

"But…"

"I was terrified," he said simply. "I don't know if I can make you understand. I don't know if anyone can understand unless they go through it. Watching a loved one die like Jenny died is worse than being sick yourself. She waded through hell. The truth is, I would literally have cut off one of my limbs, Brooke, to have spared her even a day of the agony. But I couldn't. She had to walk that road alone, and the best I could do was walk beside her."

"Walking beside someone is a lot. It's *everything*."

"It didn't seem that way. I've never felt so helpless in my life. So when I met you with your sunshiny spirit and your sweet smile and your utter joy for life, I wanted to let you into my heart and into my soul, but I was too damned scared."

"Scared of what?" she asked softly.

"Scared to care. I never want to feel that pain again."

Her heart sank. "But then I got pregnant and you had to come up with plan B."

"Exactly. Even then, I hedged my bets. I told myself I could sleep with you and provide for the baby, but that was my line in the sand."

"Then why marry me?"

He jumped to his feet, pacing again. Restless. Overwhelmed with a million conflicting emotions. "I don't know."

Brooke stood up slowly, wincing. "I think you do know, Austin." Her smile was wistful. As if her endless fount of hope had dried up.

"I wanted our child to be legitimate," he said.

"No one cares about that kind of thing anymore."

"They do in Royal."

"Maybe. But that's not why you agreed to my proposal, is it?"

"It was one reason." The other reason was harder to admit. Almost impossible, in fact.

He shoved his hands in his pockets to keep from reaching for her. "Are you sure the baby is okay?"

"Yes. Quit changing the subject." Brooke leaned back against the fridge, gingerly shifting her weight from one foot to the other. "Tell me how it felt when you saw me fall."

He gaped at her. *No!* Reliving that moment made him light-headed. "I was worried," he said. "It all happened so fast. I was afraid you were seriously injured. That you might never wake up. That you could have a miscarriage."

Big gray eyes stared at him, eyes that seemed to see deep inside to every screwed-up corner of his psyche. "Did you blame yourself, Austin?"

He started to shake. Ah. There it was. The truth. Again, he saw her tumbling down those damn stairs. He should have been close, holding her arm. "You didn't wait for me," he croaked.

"Exactly. And Jenny was a grown woman who could have made an appointment and gone to the doctor for her cough long before she actually did." She released a shuddering breath. "I'm sorry I scared you. Truly, I am. But you're not in control of the world, Austin. You never were."

"You were unconscious," he said, reliving that horrific moment four days ago when he had lost his shit completely. "It was raining and you were wearing that beautiful silky wedding dress, and all I could do was crouch over you and pray you didn't lose the baby."

"Losing the baby would have solved your problem."

Fury rose in him, choked him, sickened him. "By God, don't you say that. Don't you *dare* say that!"

She wrapped her arms around her slender waist, fearless and unflinchingly brave in the face of his wrath.

"Why not, Austin? It's true."

The chasm was there at his feet again. No matter how much he backpedaled, he couldn't escape it. Brooke kept pushing him and pushing him. As though she thought he was brave enough to jump across. He wasn't brave. He was blind with fear.

She held out her hand, her smile tremulous. "Tell me why you were so upset when I fell. Tell me why you weren't at the hospital when I woke up. Tell me why you rented this beautiful condo for us and then moved out so I'm forced to sleep here all alone at night. Tell me, Austin. Why?"

He couldn't say it. If he did, fate would smack him down again...would bring him to his knees and punish him for daring to believe he might find happiness one more time in his life.

But he owed Brooke something for what he had put her through. She at least deserved the truth. Even if Austin had not turned out to be the man she thought he was.

Before he could speak, Brooke came to him and laid her head on his shoulder. She slid her arms around his waist. "You've given me so much, Austin. I wanted to break free of my parents' influence and stand on my own two feet. You helped me get there. I'll always be grateful to you for supporting me."

"*You* did that," he said. "You're brave and determined and so strong." He held her tightly, but with infinite gentleness. Her warmth broke through the last of his painful walls. "I love you, Brooke Goodman," he whispered. "Body and soul. Jenny was my first love, the love of my youth. You're my forever love, the mother of my child, the woman who will, please God, grow old with me."

"I love you, too, stupid cowboy. Don't ever leave me again."

Her voice broke on the last word, and she cried. The tears were cathartic for both of them. They clung to each other—forever, it seemed.

At last, Brooke pulled back and looked up at him, her eyelashes damp and spiky, her eyes red rimmed. "I'm not jealous of Jenny. I'm really not. I'm glad she had you when it mattered most."

Austin shook his head slowly, rescuing one last teardrop with his fingertip. "You are an extraordinary woman. But hear this, my sweet. I'm going to spend the next fifty years making up for the fact that your family hasn't appreciated you. I'm going to shower you with love and affection, and it's entirely possible that I may spoil you rotten."

A tiny grin tipped the corners of Brooke's mouth. "Is that a threat or a promise?"

He sighed deeply, feeling contentment roll through him like a golden river. "Either works. How do you feel about an after-Christmas wedding? With all the trimmings. I'm not a fan of the way we were headed the first time."

Brooke pouted. "I don't want to wait that long to be your wife."

"I'm open to debate, but we're staring down the gun at this auction thing. I have promises to keep. More importantly, I've decided you and I are going to take a grand honeymoon. Like in the old days, when couples went to Europe for a month. I want to take you to all those art galleries before the baby comes. How does that sound?"

She beamed up at him. "I think it sounds amazing. But I'd still be willing to do a quickie courthouse ceremony."

"Nope. We're going the whole nine yards. An engagement ring, for starters. And a bridal gown that will be the envy of every woman in Royal. Empire waisted, of course," he said with a grin.

"I love it." Brooke tried to dance around the kitchen and had to stop and grab the counter when her ribs protested.

"Plus," he said, "I'd like for my bride to be able to take a deep breath without being in pain."

"Details, details." Brooke waved a dismissive hand, but she was pale beneath her excitement-flushed cheeks.

"Then it's settled." He took her in his arms and kissed her slowly, long and deep. Lust filtered through his body, overlaid with gratitude and tenderness. Brooke's lips clung to his, her ragged breaths matching his own.

He wanted her so badly, he trembled.

But her injury made his hunger for her problematic. He released her and brushed a strand of hair from her forehead. "I can't sweep you off your feet right now, can I?"

"Not unless you want me to pass out."

"Duly noted. How do you feel about really, really careful sex?"

"I thought you'd never ask."

Brooke climbed up onto the mattress and watched Austin undress. She would suffer a dozen broken ribs if this were the payoff. Hearing Austin say he loved her made up for endless days of heartache.

He ditched the last of his clothing and joined her. Brooke had done her own restrained striptease moments earlier, because Austin was afraid of hurting her.

Now here they were. Both of them bruised and broken in different ways.

She ran a hand down his warm, hair-dusted thigh. "Did I ever tell you that my grandmother was a twin?"

Austin raised one eyebrow as he coaxed her nipples into tightly furled buds with his thumbs. "You might have forgotten to mention that."

"How do you feel about multiple babies?"

He nibbled the side of her neck. His big body was a furnace. "I like making them. A lot. And though I prefer them to arrive one at a time, I'll keep an open mind."

He scooted lower in the bed and kissed her still-flat tummy. "You're going to be the most beautiful pregnant woman in Royal."

"You might be a tad prejudiced."

"Maybe." He kissed the inside of her thigh.

Her breath hitched. "When you finish Matt Galloway's house, will you design one for us? I thought we could start looking for land in the meantime. And don't get all prissy about my inheritance. We can split the price fifty-fifty if it makes you feel better."

His grin was brilliant. Carefree. It made her heart swell with happiness and pride. "I could live with that." He eased her onto her side and scooted in behind her, joining their bodies with one gentle push. "Is this hurting you?"

She gasped as he shifted and his firm length hit a sensitive spot in her sex. "Yes, Cowboy. But only in the best possible way."

He kissed the nape of her neck, his breath warm. "I adore you, Brooke."

Pleasure rolled through her body in a shimmering wave. "You're mine, Austin. Now and forever. Don't you forget it."

Then, with a gentle, thorough loving, he took them home...

* * * * *

Keep reading for an excerpt of
Colton's Secret Service
by Marie Ferrarella.
Find it in the
The Coltons: Family First Volume One anthology,
out now!

Chapter 1

His neck was really beginning to ache.

It amazed him how these last ten years, after steadily climbing up the ladder, from cop to detective to Secret Service agent, Nick Sheffield found himself right back where he started: doing grunt work. There was no other accurate way to describe it: remaining stationary, hour after hour, waiting for a perpetrator to finally show up—provided he did show up, which was never a sure thing.

But, at least for now, Nick had no other recourse, no other trail to pursue. This lonely ranch was where the evidence had led him.

He'd always hated surveillance work. Ever since he'd been a young kid, patience had never been in his nature. He was much happier being active. *Doing* something instead of just standing as still as a statue, feeling his five o'clock shadow grow.

However, in this particular instance, it was unavoidably necessary. He had no other way to capture his quarry.

Nick supposed he should consider this a triumph. After all, less than twenty-four hours ago, he still hadn't a clue where all those threatening letters and emails aimed at the man whose life he was to safeguard, Senator Joe Colton, came from. These days, it seemed like every crazy malcontent and his dog had access to a computer and the Internet, which made tracking down the right crazy malcontent one hell of a challenge. One that fortunately, he was more than up to—with a healthy dose of help from the reformed computer hacker, Steve Hennessey, who now worked for his security staff.

Technically, it was the Senator's staff, but he ran it. Hand-picked the people and ran the staff like a well-oiled, efficient machine ever since he'd been assigned to the Senator. He liked to think that he was doing his bit to help the Senator get elected to the highest post of the land.

There was no doubt in his mind that unless something unforeseen or drastic happened, the Senator would go on to become the next President of the United States. In his opinion, and he'd been around more than a little in his thirty years on earth, there was no other man even half as qualified to assume the position of President as Senator Joe Colton.

He didn't just work for the Senator, he admired the man, admired what he stood for and what he hoped to accomplish once elected. In the last few months, he'd seen Senator Colton up close and under less-than-favorable conditions. In his opinion, they just did not come any more genuine—or charismatic—than the Senator.

Nick doubted very much if he would have spent the last eight hours standing behind a slightly open barn door, watching the front of an unoccupied, ramshackle ranch house for anyone else.

Damn it, where the hell was this creep? Was he going to show at all?

He didn't want to have to do this for another hour, much less entertain the prospect of doing it for another day.

Nick's temper was getting frayed. It was late and humid, and the mosquitoes kept trying to make a meal out of him. He waved another one away from his neck even as he felt sweat sliding down his spine, making the shirt beneath his black jacket stick to his skin. Talk about discomfort.

Nick blew out a frustrated breath.

Why couldn't this crazy be located in one of the major cities, living in a high-rise apartment? Why did it have to be someone who lived the life of a hermit? The IP address that Steve had miraculously tracked down had brought him to a town that barely made the map. A blip of a town named Esperanza, Texas.

Esperanza. Now there was a misnomer. His Spanish wasn't all that good, but he knew that *esperanza* was the Spanish word for "hope" and in this particular case, Nick had no doubt that the hope associated with the town was reserved for those who managed to escape from it. If it wasn't for the fact that Esperanza was a sub-suburb of San Antonio, Nick doubted that he and his GPS system would have been able to even locate it.

And this person he was after didn't even reside within the so-called city limits. He lived in an old, all-but-falling-down ranch house that stood five miles from the nearest neighbor, and was even farther away than five miles from the town.

Hell, Nick thought impatiently, this character could be cooking up bombs and nobody would ever be the wiser—until the explosion came.

Nobody but him, Nick thought. But that was his job, tracking down the crazies and keeping them away from the best man he'd met in a long, long time.

"You're sure?" the Senator had asked him when he'd walked into his office with the news yesterday that his hacker had finally managed to isolate where the emails originated. He'd quickly given him the exact location.

For the most part, Nick didn't even bother telling the Senator about the nuisance calls, emails and letters that had found their way into the campaign headquarters. Anyone in public office, or even the public eye, was a target for someone seeking to vent his or her discontent. It came with the territory.

But this was different. These emails and letters smacked of someone dangerous. Someone seeking to "take you out" as one of the last ranting communications had threatened.

Nick had learned a long time ago to take seriously anything that remotely resembled a threat. The risk was too great not to.

He'd just informed the Senator that the sender was someone living in or around Esperanza, Texas, and that he intended to confront the man face-to-face. It was against the law to threaten a presidential candidate.

"That it's coming from there?" Nick asked, then went ahead as if he'd received a positive response. "I wouldn't be coming to you with this if I wasn't sure," he told the Senator simply.

Between them, on the desk, was a thick pile of papers that Nick had emptied out of a manila folder. Letters that had arrived in the last few weeks, all from the same source. All progressively angrier in nature. It couldn't be ignored any longer, even if he were so inclined.

"We've tracked him down," Nick repeated. "And, unless you have something specific that only I can take care of here, I'd like to go down to this little two-bit hick place and make sure that this nut-job doesn't decide to follow through with any of his threats." He had no qualms about leaving the Senator. He was the head of the Secret Service detail, but by no means was he the only one assigned to the popular Senator. Hathaway and Davis were more than up to watching over the man until he got back.

"These are all from him?" Nick nodded in response to the Senator's question. "Sure has spent a lot of time venting," Joe commented. He picked up a sheet of paper only to have Nick stop him before he was able to begin to read it.

"No need to read any of it, Senator." Nick wanted to spare the man the ugliness on some of the pages. "It's pretty awful."

Joe didn't believe in isolating himself, but he saw no reason to immerse himself in distasteful lies and name-calling, either. He let the letter remain in Nick's hand. "Then why did you bring it to me?"

In Nick's opinion, the volume of mail spoke for itself. No sane person invested this much time and effort in sending vicious missives, and the future actions of an insane person couldn't be safely gauged. It would take very little to push a person like this to where he would become dangerous.

"To let you see that the man could be a threat and that I'd like the chance to stop him before he becomes one," Nick stated simply.

In the short time they had been together, Joe had learned to both like and rely on the head of his Secret service detail. Nick Sheffield had impressed him as a hard-working, honorable man whose interest was in getting the job done, not in gathering attention or praise for his actions. He more than trusted the man's instincts.

Joe liked the fact that Nick always looked him in the eye when he spoke. "When would you leave?" he asked.

"Tonight." Nick saw a glint of surprise in the Senator's eyes. "I should be back in a couple of days—a week at most," he promised, although he was hoping that it wouldn't take that long. He intended to locate the sender, take him into custody and bring him back. The federal authorities could take it from there.

Joe nodded. There had been mutual respect between the two men almost from the very first day. Their personalities complemented one another. Joe trusted Nick not only with his life, but, more importantly, the lives of his family who meant more to him than anything else in the world, including the bid for the presidency.

"All right," the Senator agreed. "Go if you really think it's necessary."

There was no hesitation on Nick's part. "I do."

"That's good enough for me," the Senator replied. And then he smiled that smile that had a way of cutting across party affiliations and verbose rhetoric, burrowing into the heart of the recipient. "Just get back as soon as you can, Nick. I feel a whole lot better knowing that you're on the job."

Nick knew the man was not just giving voice to empty words, that praise from the Senator was always heartfelt and genuine. While exceedingly charming, with a manner that drew people to him, the Senator was not one to toss around words without thought or feeling behind them, like so many other politicians.

"I'll be back before you know it," Nick had promised, taking his leave. At the time, he sincerely meant what he said.

Georgeann Grady, Georgie to everyone who knew her, struggled mightily to keep her eyes open. For the last twenty minutes, she'd debated pulling over to the side of the road in order to catch a few well-deserved winks before falling asleep at the wheel. But she was only five miles away from home. Five miles away from sleeping in her own bed and after months of being on the road, sleeping in her own bed sounded awfully good to her.

She told herself to keep driving.

Digging her nails into the palms of the hands that were wrapped around the steering wheel of her truck, Georgie tried to shake off the effects of sleepiness by tossing her head. It sent the single thick, red braid back over her shoulder. Squaring them, she glanced into the rearview mirror to check on her pint-sized passenger.

Big, wide green eyes looked right back at her.

Georgie suppressed a sigh. She might have known that Emmie wasn't asleep, even if her nonstop chatter had finally run its course. Ceasing about ten minutes ago.

"Why aren't you asleep?" she asked her precocious, almost-five-year-old daughter.

"Too excited," Emmie told her solemnly in a voice that could have easily belonged to someone at least twice her age.

Emmie sounded almost happier to be getting back home than she was. Sometimes, Georgie thought, it was almost as if their roles were reversed and Emmie was the mother while she was the daughter. There was little more than eighteen years between them. They could have just as easily been sisters instead of mother and daughter.

And, as far as daughters went, she couldn't have asked for a better one. Raising Emmie had been a dream, despite the unorthodox life they led. A good deal of Emmie's life had been spent on the road, as a rodeo brat. It was out of necessity so that Georgie could earn money by competing in various rodeo events—just as her mother and her grandfather had before her.

At all times, her eye was on the prize. The final prize. Not winning some title that would be forgotten by the time the dust settled, but amassing as much money as she could so that she and her daughter could finally settle down and live a normal life.

She owed it to Emmie.

Her mother, Mary Lynn Grady, had quit the life, walking away with nothing more than medals and trophies, as she took up the reins of motherhood. But she intended to be far more prepared than that. It took money to make dreams come true.

Emmie was coming of age. She'd be turning five next week and five meant kindergarten, which in turn meant stability. That translated into living in a home that wasn't on wheels, nestled in a place around people who loved her. That had been the plan for the last four-something years and Georgie was determined to make it a reality.

Every cent that hadn't been used for clothing and feeding them, or for entrance fees, had faithfully been banked back in Esperanza. By her tally, at this point, thanks to her most recent winning streak, the account was exceedingly healthy now. There was finally more than enough for them to settle down and for her to figure out her next move: finding a career that didn't involve performing tricks on a horse that was galloping at breakneck speed.

Any other career would seem tame in comparison, but right now, tame was looking awfully good. The accident that she'd had a few months ago could have been disastrous. It made her very aware that she, like so many other rodeo competitors, was living on borrowed time. She wanted to get out before time ran out on her—and now, she could.

Independence had a wonderful feel about it, she thought.

Emmie's unbridled excitement about coming home just underscored her decision. There'd be no pulling over to the side of the road for her. Not when they were almost home.

Leaning forward, Georgie turned up the music. Tobey Keith's newest song filled the inside of the cab. Behind her, in an enthusiastic, clear voice, Emmie began to sing along. With a laugh, Georgie joined in.

In the overall scheme of things, eight hours was nothing, but when those hours peeled away, second by second, moment by moment, it felt as if the time was endless.

He wanted to get back to the action, not feel as if his limbs were slowly slipping into paralysis. But he didn't even dare get back to the car he'd hidden behind the barn. He might miss his quarry coming home. The man *had* to come home sometime. The emails had been coming fairly regularly, one or more almost every day now. Because there hadn't been anything yesterday, the man was overdue.

Nick took out a candy bar he'd absently shoved into his pocket last night. It was just before leaving Prosperino, California, the Senator's home base, to catch the red-eye flight to San Antonio. After checking in with his team to see if there were any further developments—there hadn't been—he'd rented a car and then driven to this god-forsaken piece of property.

He'd found the front door unlocked and had let himself in, but while there were some signs here and there that the ranch house was lived in, the place had been empty.

So he'd set up surveillance. And here he'd been for the last interminable eight hours, fifteen minutes and God only knew how many seconds, waiting.

It would be nice, he thought irritably, if this character actually showed up soon so he could wrap this all up and go back to civilization before he started growing roots where he stood.

How the hell did people live in places like this? he wondered. If the moon hadn't been full tonight, he wouldn't even be able to *see* the house from here, much less the front door. Most likely, he'd probably have to crouch somewhere around the perimeter of the building as he laid in wait.

He supposed that things could always be worse.

Stripping the wrapper off a large-sized concoction of chocolate, peanuts and caramel, Nick had just taken his first bite of the candy bar when he heard it. A rumbling engine noise.

Nick froze, listening.

It was definitely a car. From the sound of it, not a small one. Or a particularly new one for that matter.

Damn, but it was noisy enough to wake the dead, he thought. Whoever it was certainly wasn't trying for stealth, but then, the driver had no reason to expect anyone to be around for his entrance.

Because he was pretty close to starving before he remembered the candy bar, Nick took one more large bite, then shoved the remainder into his pocket.

All his senses were instantly on high alert.

He strained his eyes, trying to make out the approaching vehicle from his very limited vantage point. He didn't dare open the door any wider, at least, not at this point. He couldn't take a chance on the driver seeing the movement.

It suddenly occurred to him that if the driver decided to park his truck behind the barn, he was going to be out of luck. That was where he'd left his sedan.

Nick mentally crossed his fingers as he held his breath.

The next moment, he exhaled. Well, at least one thing was going right, he silently congratulated himself. The vehicle, an old, battered truck, came into view and was apparently going to park in front of the ranch house.

A minute later, he saw why the truck's progress was so slow. The truck was towing an equally ancient trailer.

As he squinted for a better view, Nick tried to make out the driver, but there was no way he could see into the cab. He couldn't tell if the man was young or old. The vague shadow he saw told him that the driver appeared to be slight and even that might have just been a trick of the moonlight.

Nick straightened his back, his ache miraculously gone. At least the ordeal was almost over, he told himself.

The truck finally came to a creaking stop before the ranch house, but not before emitting a cacophony. It almost sounded as if it exhaled. Straining his eyes, Nick still heard rather than saw the driver getting out of the truck's cab.

Now or never, Nick thought.

"Stop right there," he shouted, bursting out of the barn. He held up his wallet, opened to his ID. As if anyone could make out what was there, he thought ironically. To cover all bases, he identified himself loudly. "I'm with the Secret Service."

In response, the driver turned and bolted back toward the truck.

"Oh, no, you don't," Nick shouted.

A star on his high school track team, Nick took off, cutting the distance between them down to nothing in less than a heartbeat. The next moment, he tackled the driver, bringing him down.

"Get the hell off me!" the driver shouted.

Nick remembered thinking that the truck driver had a hell of a feminine voice just before he felt the back of his head explode, ushering in a curtain of darkness.

Subscribe and fall in love with a Mills & Boon series today!

You'll be among the first to read stories delivered to your door monthly and enjoy great savings.

WE
SIMPLY
LOVE
ROMANCE

MILLS & BOON

JOIN US

Sign up to our newsletter to stay up to date with...

- Exclusive member discount codes
- Competitions
- New release book information
- All the latest news on your favourite authors

Plus...
get $10 off your first order.
What's not to love?

Sign up at **millsandboon.com.au/newsletter**